More praise for *Willing Spirits*

"*Willing Spirits* is like a string of pearls—one familiar, fragile moment linked to another and another to form the rope of women's lives twined together. Beautifully written, full of wit and wisdom and heart—read this one with your mother, your daughter, or your best friend."
—Jodi Picoult

"Women are still from Venus and men from Mars in Schieber's strong debut, a paean to the healing power and enduring strength of female friendship."
—*Publishers Weekly*

"What a warm, oh-so-human account of love and women's friendship! These are women I know, and I'm recommending the book to all my female friends and students."
—Rosemary Daniell, author of *Sleeping with Soldiers*

The
Sinner's Guide to *Confession*

Phyllis Schieber

BERKLEY BOOKS, NEW YORK

THE BERKLEY PUBLISHING GROUP
Published by the Penguin Group
Penguin Group (USA) Inc.
375 Hudson Street, New York, New York 10014, USA
Penguin Group (Canada), 90 Eglinton Avenue East, Suite 700, Toronto, Ontario M4P 2Y3, Canada
(a division of Pearson Penguin Canada Inc.)
Penguin Books Ltd., 80 Strand, London WC2R 0RL, England
Penguin Group Ireland, 25 St. Stephen's Green, Dublin 2, Ireland (a division of Penguin Books Ltd.)
Penguin Group (Australia), 250 Camberwell Road, Camberwell, Victoria 3124, Australia
(a division of Pearson Australia Group Pty. Ltd.)
Penguin Books India Pvt. Ltd., 11 Community Centre, Panchsheel Park, New Delhi—110 017, India
Penguin Group (NZ), 67 Apollo Drive, Rosedale, North Shore 0632, New Zealand
(a division of Pearson New Zealand Ltd.)
Penguin Books (South Africa) (Pty.) Ltd., 24 Sturdee Avenue, Rosebank, Johannesburg 2196, South Africa

Penguin Books Ltd., Registered Offices: 80 Strand, London WC2R 0RL, England

This book is an original publication of The Berkley Publishing Group.

This is a work of fiction. Names, characters, places, and incidents either are the product of the author's imagination or are used fictitiously, and any resemblance to actual persons, living or dead, business establishments, events, or locales is entirely coincidental. The publisher does not have any control over and does not assume any responsibility for author or third-party websites or their content.

PRINTING HISTORY
Berkley trade paperback edition / July 2008

Library of Congress Cataloging-in-Publication Data

Schieber, Phyllis.
    The sinner's guide to confession / Phyllis Schieber.—Berkley trade paperback ed.
      p. cm.
    ISBN 978-0-425-22153-2
    1. Female friendship—Fiction. 2. Middle-aged women—Fiction.   I. Title.

PS3569.C48515S56 2008
813'.54—dc22   2007050594

PRINTED IN THE UNITED STATES OF AMERICA

10 9 8 7 6 5 4 3 2 1

For everyone who asked . . .
especially Shelly.

Acknowledgments

I have been blessed with a formidable cheering section. Harvey Klinger, my loyal, oh-so-smart, funny agent prodded me when necessary and never gave up on me. For all of this, I am truly grateful. My editor at Berkley, Jackie Cantor, gave me consistently wise counsel and unflagging support, as well as genuine friendship. I could not have worked with a more approachable editor. Much appreciation also to Leslie Gelbman and everyone at Berkley.

As I was writing this novel, I depended on the honesty, insights, and encouragement of Claudia Hall, Maryann Johnson, Kathy Levitt, and Candy Schulman. They read for me devotedly, chapter after chapter, and were always free with their praise and blunt with their concerns. Melissa Parish deserves many thanks for her web mistress skills, as well as for her constancy in our most unusual friendship. There were others, however, whose spiritual and creative energy were ever present and profoundly felt. I am indebted to Marlene Schieber Kazir, Claire Kotchmar, Phyllis Nobile, Jacob Rubinstein, and Tamar Rubinstein. I continue to feel the influence of my late father, Kurt Schieber, and the love of my mother, Henia. Of course, the generous heart and steadfast presence of my husband, Howard Yager, has made my life easier. I thank him for that and for our Isaac, who inspires me with his joyfulness and makes me laugh each and every day.

One

THE woman behind the cosmetics counter was so young that looking at her was like looking at an eclipse of the sun. Kaye had an urge to shield her eyes, to pull out her dark glasses, perhaps even to improvise some sort of viewing contraption with one of the signature cardboard boxes that were stacked flat behind the counter. She might still remember how to build the eclipse box that everyone had fashioned from instructions printed in the newspaper when she was a little girl. Now Kaye could have a designer eclipse box. But the beautiful young woman was already impatient with Kaye (the young woman did not like stragglers at her counter) and without even the slightest hint of a smile said, "May I help you?"

Kaye peered at her name tag. *Tammy.* Her parents must have predicted that their daughter would be a Tammy. Her jet-black hair was pulled tightly back into a simple ponytail, leaving nowhere else to look but her deep-set blue eyes and her pouty lips that made Kaye believe the same shade of pink that Tammy wore could change a woman's life forever.

"May I help you?"

Tammy was humorless. Kaye saw that immediately and so there was no point in telling Tammy, *Of course, you can help me. I want to look like you, or at least like myself at your age. I want my braid of silky auburn hair and my luminous skin. I want my full breasts that stayed high on my chest. I want to be seen again.*

Instead, Kaye said, "I need a lipstick."

"Color?"

"Sure."

Poor Tammy. She was easily confused, and when she said, "Excuse me," Kaye was impressed with her obvious disdain.

"Can *you* suggest a color?" Kaye said.

Tammy took a step back and pursed those pouty lips and moved her head from side to side, assessing Kaye's features and complexion before confidently choosing something from a startling display of lipsticks. She wiped off the tester with a tissue and handed the tube to Kaye.

"Try this," Tammy said.

The color was actually perfect. When Kaye hesitated just slightly, Tammy smiled for the first time, like a mother urging her child to take just one more bite. Then she adjusted the mirror on the counter and said, "Go ahead," in a voice so tender it nearly brought Kaye to tears. Ever so gingerly, Kaye applied a light coat of lipstick and turned to Tammy for approval.

"Hmm," Tammy said. "I like it a lot. It's definitely your color. Do you ever use a lip pencil?"

Kaye shook her head, ashamed. Tammy clucked her tongue against the roof of her mouth, clearly disappointed, and chose a lip pencil a slightly darker shade of the lipstick Kaye was wearing. Tammy said, "May I?" Without waiting for approval, she applied the pencil. Kaye envied her presumptuousness and stood absolutely still, humbled by Tammy's skill and eager for more magic.

"You should really apply the pencil first," Tammy said.

Her face was so close to Kaye's that she could feel her breath on her skin. The scent of something musky and expensive hovered between them, inviting, seductive.

"Just outline your lips with the pencil," Tammy said. "I like to apply the lipstick to my top lip only and then rub my lips together. Like this." She demonstrated. "It creates a more even look. I would even like to see a thin coat of lip gloss as a final touch."

"Lip gloss?"

Tammy nodded firmly, and chose yet another item from the display. Kaye allowed it because it meant Tammy would apply it, and Kaye hoped the closeness of the young woman would have some sort of miraculous effect.

"Lip gloss gives your lips a nice wet look," Tammy said.

"I want that?" Kaye said.

"Oh, definitely." She stepped back to take in the whole effect. "Look." She turned the mirror toward Kaye. "It is *so* the right color for you. It looks great with your skin and your gray hair. You have such a natural look, but you still shouldn't leave the house without lipstick and mascara. Gray is great, but it can be a little drab. Do you have mascara? No? Black. Definitely. It'll bring out your eyes. And I wouldn't say no to a little liquid foundation and some sheer powder. You need to even out your skin tone just a bit."

Kaye studied her reflection in the mirror. Yesterday's haircut had been a really bad idea, and the true motivation for this trip to the cosmetics counter. She must have hoped that if she cut off all her hair, she would be young again. She would go home to find Ruby in her cradle, and Charlie with his peanut butter breath eager to divulge absolutely everything about his day, punctuated only by kisses and unsolicited promises of his eternal love. Sadly, none of that happened. She was still herself. Her children were grown. She was still married to George and in love with Frank. At least now, staring back at her, Kaye saw a fifty-two-year-old, overweight gray-haired woman with lipstick and mascara. By the time Tammy was finished with Kaye, she had a bill for more than a week's worth of groceries and a promise that "your man won't recognize you." Kaye blushed and said thanks—not because she believed it was true, but because she didn't know which man in her life Tammy meant.

*   *   *

BARBARA, Kaye's oldest and funniest friend, however, did not believe in sympathy, either giving it or receiving it. When Kaye tried to explain what had prompted her impulse to cut off all her hair, Barbara dismissed the plea for nostalgia with a biting parallel to Yoko Ono, whose antiwar passions (according to Barbara) had simply resulted in just another really, really bad haircut.

"The war's over, Yoko, and from the looks of that haircut, you lost," Barbara said.

Kaye laughed and ruefully ran a hand over her head, feeling the bump left over from a childhood collision with a brick wall.

"Do I look worse than Yoko did?" Kaye said.

"Worse?" Barbara shook her head. "That would be impossible."

They were sitting on the terrace of Barbara's apartment. Although she had moved in well over a year ago, there were still boxes waiting to be unpacked. She was a recent widow. If two years could be counted as recent. Barbara felt that if a bride could be considered a bride for one year, then she should only have to be referred to as a widow for the same period of time.

Her husband, Roger, had died without warning. He simply went to work one morning and never came home. "It's like those stories you always hear," Kaye's George had said. Barbara loved George, but she always found him mildly irritating and rather enjoyed toying with him. "And," she had been unable to resist asking, "Which stories are those, George?" She paused, although she knew no answer would be forthcoming. "The stories about the men who go to work and never come home?" At least George knew better than to take the bait.

Soon after Roger's death, Barbara sold the house and moved into an apartment. She thought briefly about moving into the city, but she wanted to stay in the community where people recognized her in the market and in the post office, and where the shopkeepers knew her by name and said how sorry they were about Roger and asked about her children. How were they coping? How was she getting along now? From her new bedroom window, she could even see her old house. It was weird at first to see strangers going in and out of her front door, which, of course, was not her front door anymore. Once or twice in the beginning, she had caught a glimpse of abandoned bikes and a lone pink plastic scooter. Once or twice, she could have sworn she saw her own kids in the yard. One morning, and she had even confided this to Kaye, there was no doubt that Daphne was sitting on the front steps in a rare moment of stillness, watching Michael do somersaults while Justine, already in leg braces, leaned against the oak for support. It was a perfect picture, three beautiful children, enjoying a fall morning. But Barbara's life was already flawed, even then, even before it was considered trendy to have a secret existence.

Barbara told Kaye that the oddest thing about these wistful mirages was that they never included Roger.

"Shouldn't he be somewhere . . . *anywhere*?" Barbara said. "I can't even dredge him up in a hallucination."

Kaye reached over and touched her arm.

"You can't dictate the cast in a hallucination," Kaye said.

They owed their friendship to their sons. The boys had found each other in nursery school, encouraging the women to inch toward each other the way women do, using their children's play dates as a way to forge their own friendship.

"What about in a dream?" Barbara said. "Can I choose my own cast in a dream?"

"I think the ghosts are too close from here," Kaye said. She shivered slightly, still unused to the sensations resulting from an exposed neck. "Much too close."

Barbara arched her right eyebrow, a knack that Kaye had always envied, and reached into her sweater pocket for a fake cigarette. It was cooler than usual for late September. She rolled the plastic cigarette between her thumb and forefinger, shook her head sadly, and then took a whiff of the substitute.

"Don't worry, sweetie. They're friendly ghosts, and I like them." She looked at the plastic cigarette, ran it under her nose, and inhaled. "It smells like plastic."

"It *is* plastic," Kaye said.

"Is nothing real anymore?" Barbara drew hard on the cigarette and looked glum. "It's depressing."

"Betrayal is real," Kaye suggested.

Now they were talking about their friend Ellen, whose husband Bill had only recently left her for the twentysomething law clerk in his firm. Her name was Daisy, but Barbara had immediately named the girl Dixie and then amended that almost as quickly with Lose Dixie (a derivative of Winn-Dixie, the popular supermarket chain down South). There was no particular prototype for Barbara's penchant for renaming people she wanted to bequeath infamy upon. She merely believed that those who took on new identities should also be renamed, if only for the sake of clarity. Once Barbara heard that Bill (who had never wanted to be called anything other than Bill) now preferred to be called William, she dubbed him William Formerly Known as Bill.

"Lose Dixie should be ashamed of herself," Barbara said. "Along with William Formerly Known as Bill."

"Maybe they are. Who knows?" Kaye sighed deeply. "What do

you suppose they talk about? William Formerly Known as Bill is going to be sixty this year. Remember when he thought he was too old for Ellen? It's unbelievable. I'm so disappointed. I really thought he loved Ellen."

"He did," Barbara said. "But now he loves Lose Dixie." She took another long, pointless drag and shook her head with self-pity. "I guess they talk about him. We'll never know the whole story, not if it's up to our Ellen. That's for certain."

It was Barbara who had brought Ellen into their little circle soon after hiring her to redecorate her office and her bedroom. At the time, Ellen had been fiercely single and determinedly independent. Barbara had found Ellen's warmth disarming even though it was curious how little of herself she was willing to reveal. Barbara had described Ellen to Kaye as a "name, rank, and serial number type," but Kaye had been equally enamored of the somewhat younger yet so serious woman. No matter how much Barbara and Kaye poked and prodded, Ellen remained firmly resolute, fielding their questions with practiced deftness. Her past was clearly none of their business. She became a devoted auntie to their children, providing a strong influence and a consistently loving presence. Nevertheless, there was always a line that all of them knew not to cross. Ellen had marked that line from the onset and remained firm. She seemed to soften quite a bit after she met Bill, and so he was a welcomed addition to their group. Ellen seemed less guarded, and Kaye and Barbara hoped he had become the confidant she so needed. Together they waited for her to conceive, knowing that as much as Ellen loved their children, a child of her own would complete her happiness.

"Poor Ellen," Barbara continued. "She so wanted a baby. We know that for sure. It's so unfair."

"What a bastard," Kaye said. "And now he's going to have one with that girl. How can he do that to Ellen?"

"Why not? He's already done the unthinkable. Let's face it," Barbara said. "Husbands die. Husbands cheat. And husbands forget how to love. That's just the way it is."

"Maybe wives forget how to love."

"I'm sure they do."

"Do you think that's what happened to me?"

Barbara bit down hard on her plastic cigarette and squinted. "Ah, so this is really about you?" she said.

"You can be such a bitch sometimes, Barb," Kaye said.

"Yes. Sadly, that's true," Barbara agreed.

Kaye fussed with the buttons on her sweater, turning them and pulling at loose threads and even unbuttoning and then buttoning several of them. No two buttons were alike. It was a simple cardigan, but she loved its softness and its color. Garnet. So beautiful. When she was younger, she only wore black and gray and beige. But now she craved color, reaching for deep golds and blues and greens before she even checked an item for its size or the designer. She bought things she did not need just to have the pleasure of opening a drawer or looking into her closet and seeing it awash with color. The sweater she was wearing now had been a rummage sale purchase. Its buttons had been missing, but the garnet had called to her, insistent. Along with the sweater she had searched through the bins marked *Odds and Ends* and fortuitously found and purchased a Ziploc bag filled with mismatched buttons: a reindeer that must have been a leftover from a Christmas sweater, a shoe, a rhinestone button, a heart, a plain black circle, and a gingham-covered oval. She sewed them onto the garnet sweater, proud of her discoveries and her cleverness. When George came home and saw the sweater with its motley arrangement of buttons, he said, "Can you do that?" She took the sweater off and put it away, forgetting all about it until she had reclaimed it in a recent bout of wardrobe purging.

"Do you really think it's me, Barb?"

Barbara leaned all the way over, wrapped her arms tightly around Kaye, and kissed her head.

"You have a surprisingly little head," Barbara said. "And, no, I don't think it's you. I think you know how to love."

Kaye pulled away gently from Barbara and straightened up. "What would I do without you? Without my children?" She shook her head again. "Poor Ellen. She must be so lonely sometimes."

"I'm lonely sometimes too. Aren't you?"

"Yes, I guess so." In truth, she had been feeling much less of that indefinable loneliness since she met Frank. "But it's different for Ellen."

"She'll be all right," Barbara said.

"Maybe I should leave George."

"You're *always* leaving George." Barbara sighed and then caught Kaye's hurt expression just as it took shape and quickly added, "Sorry. I'm really sorry. That was *really* bitchy."

"No, you're right. It must be tiresome to hear me complain about the same stuff over and over and never do anything about it."

"I had to wait for Roger to die."

Kaye laughed. "Well, that was convenient."

Barbara shivered. It was really cold now that the sun was gone.

"Let's go in," she said. "I'm freezing. I'll make some espresso." She stood and turned to look down at Kaye. "You know I didn't want Roger to die. He was hard to live with. But I didn't want him to die."

"I know that, Barb."

Barbara nodded and smiled, tight-lipped, the way people do when otherwise they might cry. She winked at Kaye and held out a hand to help her up.

"Let's go inside," Barbara said.

Kaye squeezed the offered hand and said, "Are you doing all right? Financially, I mean."

Tilting her head slightly and pulling Kaye up at the same time, Barbara asked, "Where did that come from? Are you asking me for a loan, or offering me one?"

"Well, if I needed money, would you have it to give?"

"Clever answer."

"Well? And be serious."

"I'm fine, Kaye. But thank you for your concern."

"Even after all those debts Roger left?"

They had never really talked about Roger's business or the people he did business with because there was nothing to really say. Barbara knew that Kaye knew, and that Ellen and Kaye talked about Roger's questionable business connections and the feast-or-famine situation that defined their week-to-week economic status. But even after Roger's death, neither Kaye nor Ellen broached the subject with Barbara. Until now, and even now, Kaye's question was thinly veiled behind genuine concern.

"Yes, even after all those debts." Barbara smiled. "I do have a career, you know."

"Don't get huffy," Kaye said. "I don't know how well romance writing pays."

Barbara held the screen door open for Kaye. "It pays. Don't worry."

Kaye looked at her watch. "Let's get going. We'll be late. Ellen always blames me when we're late even if it's usually your fault."

Barbara locked the door and checked it again. She had never checked the doors before, nor the windows or the stove. But everything was different now.

*   *   *

"I HAVEN'T had sex since Roger died," Barbara said.

"I know," Kaye said. "Put that in one of your novels."

Barbara's romance novels could not be considered great literature, but she had a considerable following. Her friends found her work trivial, but they were proud of her success. Barbara was not offended by their criticism, especially since they didn't know everything about her career. Over the top of her menu, Barbara gave Kaye a pointed look but said nothing.

"Two years?" Ellen said. "That's a long time."

"It's not *that* long," Barbara said. "Most people go longer than that with a husband who isn't dead."

Kaye laughed, took a roll from the basket, slathered it with butter, and then sprinkled it with salt.

"I hate unsalted butter, she said, taking a big bite. "I wonder how much fatter I could get."

"You've been fatter than this," Ellen said.

Barbara snorted, sputtering her Bloody Mary all over the table. Kaye put the roll down and looked at Ellen, who said, "What? I didn't mean it badly."

"Ellen," Kaye said, "there's no good way to tell someone that she has been fatter than she is now. Do you understand that?"

"Stop it," Ellen said. "I think you're beautiful. And I love your hair short."

"But she's never seen your head look smaller than it looks now," Barbara said. "Isn't that right, Ellen?"

Ellen opened her mouth to contradict her, but Kaye interrupted, saying, "Be quiet. Both of you. I don't care what either of you thinks of my hair or my voluptuous body."

"We should go see that Gauguin exhibition next weekend," Ellen said. "I heard it was grand."

"I hate Gauguin," Barbara said.

"Since when?" Kaye said.

The waitress brought their food, and they waited for her to leave before resuming their conversation.

Barbara poked at her salmon and then immediately forked one of the roasted potatoes.

"I should have told them not to bring the potatoes," she said. "Damn, they're good."

"I like food better than I like men," Kaye said.

"That's why I said I hate Gauguin," Barbara said.

"He was a great artist," Ellen said, almost reverentially. "Those colors."

Barbara leaned over to her and said, "He left his wife and kids to starve while he went off to Tahiti to paint and frolic with the little native girls. Wouldn't you hate him if he were my husband? I hate William Formerly Known as Bill, and he can't even paint."

Ellen's cup stopped midway to her lips, but she hurriedly regained her composure and continued as though nothing had happened.

"Oops," Barbara said. "Sorry."

"I think this fish is fried—not baked," Ellen said. "Do you think it's fried or baked?"

"Ellen," Barbara said, looking to Kaye for help. "I'm really sorry."

"I really don't want to talk about this," Ellen said.

"C'mon, Ellen," Barbara said. "You have to admit, Bill turned out to be a real disappointment."

"To you or to me?" Ellen said. "And when did you bestow that new identity on Bill?"

"Do you like it?" Barbara said. "I think it so suits him."

"Please," Ellen said. Her chin was already quivering. "I know you never approved of Bill, but the truth is that I still love him. There. I said it. I won't let you influence me into hating him. I may hate Daisy, but I don't hate Bill. And truthfully, Barbara, sometimes I find your little game of attaching new names to people a little silly and a little presumptuous."

"Actually, it's not Daisy anymore," Kaye said between mouthfuls of buttered roll. "It's Lose Dixie."

"Well, thanks," Barbara said. "That was extremely helpful. Did you learn that in therapy school?"

"What can I say?" Kaye said, smiling sweetly.

Ellen shook her head, but she laughed. She had to admit that Barbara had found extremely suitable new names for both players in the timeless drama that had so caught her by surprise.

"No wonder we have trouble holding on to our men," Ellen said.

"Mine died," Barbara said.

"I just sometimes wish mine would," Kaye said.

"Can I change the subject?" Ellen said. She continued on without waiting for an answer. "I saw the oddest thing on the crosstown bus yesterday. I can't get it out of my mind."

"You took a bus?" Barbara said. "That's odd."

"I couldn't get a cab," Ellen conceded. "Sometimes I have to mingle with regular folk. It keeps me humble."

"See?" Barbara said. "I know my girl."

"What did you see on the bus?" Kaye said.

Barbara took a plastic cigarette from her purse and clamped down on it, offering a newly wrapped duplicate to Kaye, who waved it away and rummaged through the breadbasket for another roll.

"I saw a woman with a beard," Ellen said. "A real beard, not just whiskers. She was beautifully dressed in a brown cashmere coat and a lovely silk scarf around her neck, and she was reading the *Wall Street Journal* as though it were perfectly normal to be a woman with a beard."

"Are you sure it wasn't a cross-dresser you saw on the crosstown bus?" Barbara said.

"I'm sure. She was definitely a woman. I saw her hands. They were a woman's hands. I'm certain. And she had a diamond wedding band. I even missed my stop because I was so engrossed. And she was so pleasant. She smiled at people and seemed entirely oblivious to the stares and the whispers."

"She must be used to it," Kaye said.

"Can anyone ever get used to something like that?" Ellen wondered more to herself than to either of them. "I mean it was so shocking, and then it wasn't shocking at all."

Barbara blew imaginary smoke in her direction. "Is there a point to this story?"

Ellen ignored her and turned her attention to Kaye.

"How did she manage it, I wonder?" Ellen said. "This rather attractive thirtysomething woman with a black beard sat on the bus as though there were nothing unusual about her appearance."

"It's hard to keep a full beard secret." Barbara said. "Even if she tried to hide it, she would always know the truth."

"So you think the beard is her truth?" Ellen said.

"Or," Kaye said, "the beard is a diversion. Maybe she has an even bigger secret that she doesn't want anyone to know about. Maybe we all have our versions of a beard, a way to deflect attention from our real secrets, from our real selves."

"Well," Ellen said, "I think we never really know everything about anyone."

They looked from one to the other rather quickly as if each knew the conversation was no longer about the bearded woman on the crosstown bus. A casual observer—even one who knew nothing about the women—would have noticed a sudden discomfort among these typically guileless friends. It was, in fact, so palpable that Ellen almost asked the others if they too felt the otherworldly presence of something indefinable as it slithered across their bare skin, raising gooseflesh where there had been smoothness before. Instead, Ellen said nothing. She had said too much already. And she was not as brave as the woman with the beard. For the rest of the evening, no one mentioned the bearded woman who rode the crosstown bus and seemed so brazenly defiant. Little did they know what it had taken for the woman with the beard to accept her truth, and then to live it.

Two

FROM time to time, strange men came to the house to speak to Roger. At least, that was what he told Barbara as he shut the door to the bedroom behind him. "We just need to talk," he said. "It won't take long." Then he smiled and said, "Everything will be all right." And that was when Barbara knew there was trouble. His smile turned the corners of his mouth up, but his eyes remained vacant and distant. Exactly the way she would have described their relationship as he became more involved in his business and more secretive about the nature of his work. Their children were still very young then, and Barbara was too tired all the time to question Roger when he came home late or took phone calls in the middle of the night. She had married him straight out of high school, but it seemed as though she hardly knew him. It had been exciting to date a college man. Her mother warned her it would come to no good. But Barbara thought she was in love. She thought she would die if she lost him. It seemed to her then that she was alive only when his hands and lips were on her. If he said everything would be all right, then everything would be all right. She was much too young then to challenge his wisdom and by the time she found out she was pregnant, it was too late to do much more than call him, wailing into the phone: "But you said you loved me. You promised me that everything would be all right." And because Roger was a decent fellow who fancied the idea of Barbara in his bed on a regular basis, he married her under the apocalyptical weeping willow in her parents' backyard.

When she evoked that memory, it horrified her more than the truth about why those men came over from time to time. She could no longer pretend ignorance about anything. All her dreams had been forgotten because she had been foolish enough to believe that Roger would deliver her from mediocrity. She was barely nineteen when Michael was born, but he inspired her. If he could tolerate her fumbling attempts at motherhood, she would have to be worthy of him.

Falling out of love was even more profound than falling in love. It was a pithy revelation for one so young and already a mother and a wife, but before Barbara could grasp that reality, she was a mother again. Daphne was born when Michael was only eighteen months old. She seemed even more astonished to be in the world than Barbara was to find herself the mother of two. Daphne came into the world backward. She had flipped herself around, managed to wind the umbilical cord around her neck, and then resisted all efforts to be turned in the right direction. Barbara was convinced it was only inexperience that made Daphne lose the battle.

"Who are they?" Barbara asked the first few times the strange men came. Then there was a long period when they stopped coming, and she did not have to ask anymore. But when they came back again, and she heard shouting from Roger's office and no response from Roger, Barbara knew something was terribly, terribly wrong. And then, at last, when everyone except Roger emerged, she swallowed her fear and stepped forward, meeting the bold smile of the taller man who she somehow guessed was the shouter. "Sorry," he said. "Things got a little heated. Hope we didn't wake the little ones." Barbara's first inclination was to cower and run. She was horrified that he even knew about her little ones. She felt threatened, especially when she realized this had been his intent. Silently, she followed them to the front door and closed it, turning both locks and then checking and double-checking each one. It took her a moment to catch her breath before she headed for Roger's office. His big leather chair faced the wall. "I really screwed up this time, Barb," he said without turning around. "Really, really badly this time." Barbara took in one long, deep breath and waited, staring at his broad back and hunched shoulders. "Turn around," she said. His ashen face made her realize her suspicions had been accurate all along.

Going Places had been her idea when they had to pick a name for the business, which rented and leased luxury cars for television and movies. Roger called this his main bread and butter. He also rented stretch limos and vintage cars, mostly for wedding parties and proms. Business was very good. Too good, maybe. Roger was a benevolent boss, and his employees were loyal to him; too loyal, maybe. Someone should have told Barbara that Roger was in over his head. At the very least, Jack, Roger's longtime partner and friend, should have given her a heads-up that the business was in jeopardy. Roger was a gambler. Football games, especially college football. And the ponies. Oh, how Roger had loved those ponies. "How much?" Barbara was finally able to ask. "A lot," he said. She wanted a number, but he refused to oblige. "What did those men want?" she persisted. He explained that in the absence of his ability to successfully repay his debts, they represented a corporation that had become silent partners in the business. "Silent partners?" she said, thinking of the shouting she had heard. "They didn't sound so silent to me." Roger put his face in his hands and wept. "I'm sorry, Barb," he said. "I'm so sorry." He kept one hand over his face and held out the other for her to take. She wondered how long he had kept his hand like that, suspended in midair, waiting to be brought into safety before realizing that no one was coming.

She stayed with him because . . . just because. The reasons were too ordinary and too embarrassing to admit. Not only did she stay, but she slept with him. And then she just found that she could not bear his touch anymore, and Roger was not okay with that at all. That was Barbara's cue to leave. And that was when she found out that she was pregnant again.

Justine was six weeks premature. It was immediately evident that something was wrong. Even after she was aspirated, she did not cry. Barbara was fond of telling Justine that she had been stubborn from the start, holding her breath, determined not to give in to anyone. It was a sweet story. But the truth was that at three months, Justine was diagnosed with cerebral palsy. Barbara assessed her situation. Three small children. Two toddlers and a newborn who needed considerably more care than the first two had ever required. Barbara was not going anywhere, not for a long while. Her children came first. Roger was a good father, but a lousy gambler. She had to do something to guarantee that she would be able to take care of her children if necessary.

Barbara was a pragmatist. She needed a way to make money without leaving her children. There was nothing she could do that would bring in enough money to justify competent child care, so it would have to be something she could do at home. As she nursed Justine, Barbara made a list of her talents. Her first talent would be illegal as a way to generate income, but her second and third talents—a good imagination and excellent writing skills—could be used in combination with the first to create stories that pleased women. Barbara had made a study of the books the women on the playground read. They were too exhausted for great literature; they wanted tales of lives that were out of their reach for now, for perhaps forever. The men had to be handsome and amorous, and the women had to be beautiful and glib. Romance. These women were starved for romance, and Barbara would rescue them. She would write romance stories. It was a long shot, of course. Still, she was diligent, carving out a few early morning hours in which she wrote daily. When she wasn't writing romance, she was reading it, fashioning her own tales on the same formula. Finally, after almost a year of rejections, she sold a story to a women's magazine. It didn't pay much, but it was enough to motivate her to write another one. After she had sold several stories, Barbara decided to write a romance novel. Something simple, something with a basic story line. Barbara was a good writer, and she already knew how to persevere. Her editor at the magazine suggested an agent, who was immediately interested. When Barbara received a call that her manuscript had been sold, she opened a separate bank account under her unmarried name. Barbara Shore. It was a good name for a romance writer. A post office box took care of all her correspondence from the magazines, and then from her agent and publisher. It was a steady income, and Roger was grudgingly impressed. Barbara would take care of herself and her children.

* * *

ALTHOUGH Roger's death was a shock to everyone, the men who came to mourn him may have been even more shocking. Men in flashy suits and dark glasses arrived in limos that Barbara recognized as part of Roger's fleet. She was really stunned when she realized the men now owned most of the fleet. Huge floral arrangements arrived and were set up around the casket. Mourners whispered among themselves about how loved Roger had been, and then pretended not to notice the arrangement in the shape of a horseshoe that was in such bad taste it made Barbara laugh.

"At least the ends are pointing up," she said. "It would be bad luck if the ends were pointing down."

Kaye and Ellen exchanged looks as they linked their arms through Barbara's and held on for dear life. When it was time to move into the chapel, Barbara kissed them and took her place with her children. Ellen had noted this with some envy even though Bill was still Bill then and had led her away, following behind Kaye and George. Nor did Ellen miss the way Ruby and Charlie cozied up to their parents, especially to their father, when it was time for the mourners to take their seats. Ruby slid her hand into George's and rubbed her cheek against his shoulder. He kissed the top of her head. Charlie placed a protective arm around Kaye's shoulder, and they formed a united front against death. They were a family. Disappointment had not yet initiated Kaye's infidelity. George and Kaye seemed inseparable. Their children appeared grateful to be part of a loving and intact family. Even with Bill leading her by the elbow, Ellen felt dolefully alone as he led her into the chapel where they took seats in the row behind Barbara and the children.

Each of Barbara and Roger's children had prepared something to say about Roger. Michael recalled how he had learned to ride a two-wheeler under his father's careful watch. "Dad held the back of the bike and didn't let go until I said it was safe to," Michael said. "I trusted him. I knew he wouldn't trick me." Between sobs, Daphne remembered how her father had always prepared Sunday breakfast for them, chocolate-chip banana waffles and hot choco-late with real whipped cream. He taught them old show tunes while they ate. They knew every song from *Oklahoma*, *My Fair Lady*, *The King and I*, *The Sound of Music*, and *Fiddler on the Roof*. Those were their best shows. "Belt it out!" Daphne said. "That's what Dad told us to do. So, I want to belt it out one last time. I love you, Daddy," she said.

Everyone was moved to tears, except Barbara. She smiled at Daphne when she came off the podium and whispered how well she had done and how lucky Roger had been to have a daughter like her. But Barbara did not cry. At least not until after Justine began to speak. She made her way to the front slowly, as always, dragging one leg behind and using her arm brace to negotiate the space. She looked so much like Roger: dark eyes, dark hair, strong nose and chin, lips that were almost too thin for the rest of the face, but still attractive. And tall. Justine was the tallest of her siblings. "A head-turner," Roger always said, laughing because she resembled him so.

Justine spoke quietly, as if she were telling the story to someone over coffee. But more than two hundred people had filled the chapel; many were standing, crammed into every inch of space. Justine spoke about the day she had come home from school crying because a group of kids had made fun of her, calling her retarded and mimicking her gait. She said that her father had listened while she recounted the details and had stroked her hair as she cried. At that point, Justine looked up and smiled. It was Roger's smile, full and mischievous. The smile he had before he began to make really bad decisions.

"Daddy had a plan," she said. "He said, now listen up. We're not going to take crap from those little fuckers. Next time one of them calls you a name, take your brace and hit him over the fucking head." The laughter in the chapel was deafening, and she paused, waiting for it to subside enough to be heard again. "Well, I was ready. The next day one of those little fuckers came after me again. I raised my brace up like this and flapped it like some crazed prehistoric bird, madly flapping its wing. That kid took off like a bat out of hell. But that wasn't even the best part. The best part was that when I turned around there was my dad, leaning against his car, just outside the school playground. He had been there the whole time. He clasped both hands over his head in victory, and then he got in his car and left." She paused again, swallowing hard before she could continue. "He taught me to be brave, and I am more grateful for that than for anything else. I will miss him."

She looked up and saw Barbara, tears streaming down her cheeks, hands clasped and raised up high over her head in victory. Justine stumbled, just slightly, and Barbara almost rushed forward to help. But she didn't. Roger would have insisted she remain in her seat. So, for this one last time, Barbara did as Roger would have wished.

*   *   *

ROGER'S affairs were in complete chaos. Or so Jack maintained. "Chaos," he kept repeating. "Almost impossible to imagine. An absolute disaster."

Barbara listened. She really wanted to ask if all this had actually transpired in the few weeks since Roger's death. Certainly, there had been some warning, some indication that intervention was necessary. But she knew Jack, knew he would insist that he had done everything he could to avoid this catastrophe. She knew how stubborn Roger could be, didn't she? There was no talking to him when he got an idea in his head. Barbara just listened, occasionally adding, "Uh-huh" or "I see." Jack was unlikely to benefit from Roger's death. No one would really, except for his silent partners. They were the reason for Jack's visit. "They want to buy us out," he said. "Us?" Barbara said. "You mean I have a choice?" Poor Jack. In spite of how angry she was, she really did feel sorry for him.

After a long and awkward pause, Jack cleared his throat and explained that in light of Roger's inveterate love of the ponies, the settlement was quite fair. "After all," he said, "Roger was in pretty deep to these guys." She blinked. "How deep?" she said. "Deep enough that you should settle," he said. "Well," she said, "I guess it wouldn't be the first time I ever settled." This time, Jack blinked. Then, he ventured that it was all for the best. "Even Roger's death?" she said. Ball busting. That's what Roger had called it. She was good at it too. Jack told her that when all this was over, he planned to sell the house, move away. Arizona, maybe. He did the whole nine yards about life being short and unpredictable, and all the while, Barbara wondered if he and Shirley still had sex. "So, should I set up the meeting with the attorneys?" he said. And she said, "Of course." They nodded at each other, and then Jack cleared his throat again. He wanted to be sure she was going to be all right. "In what sense do you mean that, Jack?" It might have been her fault because he seemed to take it as an opening. "I always thought Roger was a lucky guy to have you in his bed every night." If she were writing the scene, she would have dropped to her knees and taken his throbbing manhood in her mouth. But she was living this scene, and she said, "Are you trying to seduce me, Jack?" He was indignant, of course. How could she think such a thing? She was his best friend's wife. "Widow," Barbara said. "Your best friend's widow. You fucked him, and now you want to fuck me." Jack flushed, but he did not argue. He picked up his coat from the back of the chair and said, "I'm sorry about Roger. He was like a brother to me." Barbara waited for him to leave before she started to cry.

She never told anyone—not even Kaye or Ellen—about the business meeting with Jack. It was nobody's problem but hers. It was all up to her now. She had to clear up the mess Roger had left behind and take care of herself and their children. And she would. The day she left Jack's office, Barbara went home and got busy with a new story. A novella, perhaps. This time, the heroine, Eva, was not young. But she was smart. When Eva's husband Brian died very suddenly, and his business partner Ayden tried to seduce her in his office, she was not about to fall apart.

Ayden went over to the file cabinet and rummaged through the files, pretending to look for something. But Eva knew he was trying to inch his way closer. He had just delivered an impassioned speech about how her dear late husband had left her with a mess that would not be easy to resolve. This speech was delivered with a lot of head shaking and admonitions about how she should proceed.

"So," Eva said. "What are my options?"

"I was hoping we could work something out," he said. "You know, something that would be equitable, a good arrangement for both of us."

"I know what equitable means, Ayden." She crossed her long legs. She had purposely worn a skirt. Her legs were still very good, and she was prepared to do whatever was necessary to protect her share of the business. She uncrossed her legs, leaving enough space between her thighs to invite interest. "I have a really excellent vocabulary."

"I bet you do," he said. "You seem to have many assets. Do you know any dirty words?"

"I do," Eva said. She stood. "In fact, I know them all."

Ayden took several small steps toward her. As soon as he was close enough, she reached for him through the fine wool of his trousers. He was impressively hard. She applied just enough pressure to give him the wrong idea, and then she squeezed with enough force to eradicate his smug grin and cause him to yelp in pain.

"Fool," Eva whispered. "Fucking stupid fool. Do you know those words?"

It was not exactly the way Barbara would write the scene in her final draft, but it was cathartic. Later, Barbara would revise, allowing Eva to have her way with Ayden. Eva would mount him, riding him to just the point where he, squeezing her firm buttocks, would be crying out. And then, Eva, every woman's heroine, would lift herself from his throbbing erection and explain that she was no longer in the mood. Barbara opened her desk drawer and took out a new plastic cigarette. She peeled off the cellophane wrapper and crushed it into a ball, not unlike Eva's cautionary move, and continued to write with renewed purpose . . . stopping only occasionally to use the back of her hand to wipe away her tears.

It was not till after Roger's death that Barbara began to write erotica. She took a sobriquet. Delilah. Just one name. Like Cher. Delilah. Barbara kept her identity secret; she told no one, absolutely no one. At first she rationalized that secrecy was necessary to protect her career. After all, the women who bought her books would have been mortified to learn that their favorite romance novelist wrote erotica. The secrecy was never supposed to extend to Barbara's inner circle, but she kept putting off telling. She worried about how her children would react. The longer she waited to tell, the harder it was to find the right moment. And then she stopped looking. She wanted the stories all for herself. *Cock, pussy, clit, dick.* Eventually, her hands stopped shaking when she wrote. She sat up straight. *My, my, my Delilah,* she always thought as she wrote. *My, my, my.*

Three

SINCE the day she turned twelve, Ellen had not left the house without false eyelashes. What began as an act of rebellion turned into a trait that distinguished her in ways she could not have predicted. In the coastal Connecticut town where she grew up and later in rural Vermont where she attended college, people made assumptions about her based almost exclusively on those eyelashes. The eyelashes gave her confidence and, at twelve, confidence was in short supply even if prettiness was not. The eyelashes made her feel glamorous. Glamour. That was what Ellen was after. Her mother, ever critical, insisted that Ellen always looked as if she were on her way to a costume party. "Are you going as a tramp?" she asked. But Ellen thought the false lashes completed her. She batted them at herself in the mirror, standing sideways and then looking over her shoulder. The eyelashes never seemed anachronistic to her twelve-year-old self. Soon her life was divided into two periods: before the false eyelashes and after them. And "after" definitely seemed like a much better time.

The adult Ellen learned to read people by their reactions to her extravagant lashes; two full sets, professionally trimmed, were meant to be noticed. More than anything else, Ellen was intrigued by the assumption that she was stupid just because she wore false eyelashes. Even after she moved to New York and established a successful career as an interior designer, the eyelashes encouraged assumptions. The ultimate incongruity was that after Ellen began to wear false eyelashes, she could read contempt and disregard with ease. It was almost as if the eyelashes had honed all her other senses, giving her a keener understanding of human nature and all its foibles.

Certainly, Ellen drew her own conclusions based on casual observations or offhand comments. Early on, she knew that nothing was as it seemed to be, especially when it came to men. Her three older brothers had given her a basic introduction to the duplicitousness of their species. She watched the way her brothers treated girls, lying to them and taking advantage of them whenever possible. It made her ashamed, but it also taught her what to expect. Regrettably, knowing what to expect was not enough to save her from herself and her own poor judgment.

By the time she was seventeen, Ellen had decided never to marry. She simply believed marriage was not something she would be good at. She dated in college, usually more than one boy at a time. It was easier not to get involved that way. After she graduated, she allowed herself the occasional fling, mostly with married men whom she met on business, either at some horribly boring dinner or at some vast showroom she was prowling for the perfect corner table or area rug. Her work created odd opportunities for trysts. A doorman in a posh building, a tiler, a son home from college who had been coerced into waiting for her to drop off plans or fabric swatches. They were all easily seduced. She typically saw these men only once. If someone wanted more of her time, she deflected his interest by saying, "I had a dream about you." Dreams were always impressive. And while everyone loved to be the star of someone else's dream, good or bad, a dream suggested something deeper and more meaningful than most men were prepared to take on. Ellen always made sure that what happened in her dream was much more important and powerful than the mere telling of that event would have been. It was too plain, too ordinary to simply tell someone she was no longer interested. Men were afraid of women's dreams, and before long Ellen was happily alone again.

And then there was Bill Hennessy. She had not been looking for him. She was still not interested in marriage. Even a serious relationship was not on her agenda. And Bill seemed an unlikely candidate for any sort of encounter. He was a recent widower with a need to talk. He had lost his much-loved wife to cancer. His eyes grew misty when he described her suffering, especially in those last few weeks. The first two years were difficult, but the last year was grim. Well, it was time to move on. He said this with good cheer, but he was so sad. He wanted the apartment redone, hoping to escape the final dark months of her suffering. Ellen had been touched by his sweetness. Then, their eleven-year age difference had seemed very impressive. She might even have considered him wise. They spent hours together, poring over fabrics and paint charts. She suggested gray, off-white, and brown for the bedroom with some spots of a chalky blue here and there. He nodded agreeably to everything. Together they shopped for furniture and lunched in small out-of-the-way places that she had discovered over the years. During those lunches, Ellen learned that Bill had chosen law because his father and grandfather were lawyers. "It didn't seem as though I had much of a choice," he said. Had it been up to him, he would have taken his chances as an actor. He had starred in his high school and college productions. "My father said that criminal law was a good substitute for acting." Bill laughed ruefully. "I guess he was right, but I sort of miss the applause." She fell in love. Head over heels and helplessly in love. But Bill was always a gentleman, never once making an overture or hinting at anything between them.

It happened the day they went shopping for sheets and towels and comforters. He seemed a bit on edge, rejecting several of her suggestions. Ellen moved from stripes to solids and back to stripes before gently asking, "What did you have in mind?" Bill took her hand, the first time ever, and said, "Anything that complements your perfectly hued skin." What Bill did not know was that Ellen would have done it with him in the middle of the store if he had been willing. But she knew he was a little conservative, a tad stuffier than anyone she had been with before. Calmly, Ellen said, "Green is my color. And I prefer cotton to silk." Bill bought two sets of apple-green cotton sheets, a matching duvet cover, and more towels than he would ever be likely to need. In the cab, he kissed her, and she acted demure and innocent as if she had never had sex in a cab or in an elevator. She waited until they got back to his place, and then she helped him put the sheets on the bed and kissed him. This time it was not a lie when she told him that she had dreamed about him. She had, in every position imaginable. They did not leave the apartment for three days, canceling all their appointments and living on whatever they found in the cupboards and the fridge. Even takeout seemed too much of an effort, too much of an intrusion. Effortlessly, she told him the secret she had hoarded all her life. It was the secret that had taught her restraint; the secret that had made her suspicious of love. Bill wrapped his arms around her and listened. Bill had secrets of his own, and he shared them with such relief that Ellen cried with him as he confessed his transgressions and his sorrows. In those early times, he tolerated her endless stream of questions about matters that might seem obvious to others. And never, ever once did he say a word about her eyelashes even as he watched her peel them off at night and reapply them first thing in the morning. He seemed to anticipate her needs, bringing her a blanket before she shivered, a cup of tea before she asked, a back rub just as she was about to stretch. And when he finally asked about those silly lashes (that's what he called them, but lovingly) all he said was, "How have they changed your life, Miss Ellen?"

And that was why she could not believe he did not love her anymore.

*   *   *

ELLEN thought it was odd how the very traits Bill had extolled in her were the very first things he suddenly seemed to develop an aversion to once he no longer loved her. Ellen knew right away that Bill was cheating on her. The mysteries of marriage are so private and so inaccessible to outsiders. It took only a few words from Bill for Ellen to know everything without knowing anything. Of course, Ellen surmised, the woman had to be young. And she probably wore black, all black, all the time. And good pearls, pearls he had probably bought her to mark some insignificant anniversary, like the first time they spoke or the first time they had sex. She was certain to have a good education, perhaps even Ivy League, something that would justify the attraction. That is, something other than youth. Later, Bill would explain how well she could orchestrate a conversation and make strangers feel comfortable. Small cruelties like that would finalize their parting. She might even have a tiny, almost minuscule diamond stud in one nostril. Such subtleties could be titillating. False eyelashes were not out of the question, but if she wore them it was likely she had them applied at one of those new lash bars that were springing up everywhere. False eyelashes, it seemed, were suddenly the new must-have accessory. Mostly, however, she scorned most artifices. She barely wore any makeup at all. Ellen hated everything about her. Unfortunately, Ellen still loved Bill.

*   *   *

AS she readied herself one evening to attend a black-tie retirement dinner for an attorney from Bill's office, Ellen, lulled by the routines of preparation, did not immediately notice Bill, already in his tuxedo, impatiently pacing in the hallway of their apartment. Soon after they married, Ellen had given up her prewar two-bedroom with a view of Central Park for Bill's contemporary three-bedroom on the Upper East Side. She had been willing to compromise on everything, except infidelity. It was the only ultimatum she had given Bill before they married. He swore that he would never be unfaithful to her. Never. When Ellen had told this to Barbara and Kaye, they explained that *never* had a very different meaning for men than it did for women. "For a middle-aged man," Barbara said, "*never* means until a twentysomething takes an interest in him."

The night of the retirement dinner, Ellen was applying makeup, chatting on about a new client's proclivity for fifties kitsch, and putting the finishing touches on her lipstick when she looked up and saw Bill in the mirror. His expression was critical and in spite of whatever she might have already suspected, she was stunned. It was the first time she had seen a look of such disapproval directed at her by her husband, the love of her life.

"I'm almost ready," she said.

"It's going to be a very Republican crowd," Bill said.

"Isn't it always?"

"More so tonight than usual."

"And?"

She turned to look at him. Handsome as ever. Handsomer really.

"Maybe you could go a little lighter on the makeup tonight," Bill said.

No one, especially Bill, had ever accused her of wearing too much makeup. She knew exactly where this was going.

"Lighter? I'm not sure what you mean." She stared at him, keeping her expression even, her voice steady. "No lipstick?"

Bill cleared this throat. "No, lipstick is fine . . ."

"Then what is it, Bill? Are you afraid your colleagues will find me stupid?"

"Why would they find you stupid?"

He knew she knew. They were just doing the preliminary warmup now.

"Do you think I'm stupid?" she said.

"No, Ellen. I know how smart you are."

"Why do you suppose then that some people find me stupid, Bill?"

He took the bait. Not because he failed to see that it was the bait, but because he wanted to bring it out in the open. His infidelity. His treachery. His heartbreaking fickleness. And the fact that he did not love her anymore.

"Maybe it's because you haven't left the house without those silly false eyelashes since you were twelve," Bill said.

There was nothing loving in his words anymore. In her head, Ellen heard the explosion. She thought someone should invent a video game called End of a Marriage in which the husband and wife try to kill each other. They would never use weapons. No guns or knives. Something much more deadly. An arsenal of potential destruction. Words. Words and indifference and cruelty.

"Actually, darling, they're all the rage now. Imagine, after all these years, I'm finally in. I had these applied at a lash bar just this morning." Bill blanched at this revelation. "Surely you didn't think *hers* were real? The lashes, I mean, of course." She batted her lush lids at him. "Poor dear. You always were a sucker for a pretty girl."

Bill's stare was cool and implacable. He was long lost to her.

"We're late, Ellen," he said. "You know how much I hate to be late."

Yes, she did. She knew that and more. She put a tissue between her lips to even out the lipstick and checked the shine on her nose one last time. Ready. She was ready.

*   *   *

SOMEWHERE between the grilled shrimp appetizer and the cold berry soup (it was late August, and so hot outside that everyone's hair had frizzed just getting from the limos or cabs into the hotel lobby), Ellen realized she was the only woman at the table who had not been traded in for a younger version. Six corporate attorneys at one table, and the average age of their new wives was twenty-seven. Alan, the attorney to Ellen's left and Bill's golf buddy, had recently wed a loquacious brunette from Atlanta, Sherri, whose impressive cleavage screamed augmentation. Sherri, wearing a strapless black number, leaned over more than necessary and smiled much too sweetly at Ellen.

"Are you still working, Ellen? Or are you retired?"

Stillness enveloped the table. Ellen read the fear in Bill's eyes as he tacitly implored her to resist a crude response. Her gaze replied, *How can I?* She just dabbed at the corners of her mouth with her linen napkin. Next, she set it on her lap just as Allegra, the instructor, had advised. *Your napkin remains on your lap until after the meal. If you have to get up from the table during the meal, leave your napkin on your chair.* Worried about protocol at formal functions, Ellen, soon after she married Bill, had sought the help of an etiquette advisor who counseled corporate wives, new-money socialites, and people from the diplomatic corps. Kaye and Barbara had begged to attend one of these sessions with her, but Ellen had remained staunch. Absolutely, no way, never, ever. Barbara said she simply wanted to ask Allegra about the protocol for condom use. Was the woman supposed to put it on the man, or was he supposed to do it while she watched? Kaye thought it was a personal choice, but that without the advice of an expert, they would never know the true answer. Ellen dismissed their pleas as childish.

She went to each and every one of the classes, learning everything she believed would make her an asset to Bill and to his career. She took copious notes in class, observing the right way to wipe her mouth before drinking so that she would not leave food or lipstick on the rim of the glass. Allegra said that while you ate, it was best to imagine that you had books beneath your arms. This was likely to prevent you from flapping your arms around like a chicken. By the end of the six-week course, Ellen knew the difference between the European and American styles of eating, how to hold a red wineglass (never by the stem), what to do if she dropped a piece of silverware, and how to discreetly dislodge a piece of food caught between her front teeth. She had even been advised about how to appropriately answer tactless or antagonistic questions.

Allegra would have advised Ellen to respond to Sherri's inquiry by politely saying, "I'm flattered by your interest in my personal affairs." It would even have been acceptable to say, "I'm gainfully employed. And what do you do?" Allegra had been cautionary, warning them that making a fuss was even worse than having the accident. So when Ellen stood, knocking over her glass of red wine (causing all at the table to push back their seats so quickly that two more glasses toppled), she was no longer mindful of any protocol. She let her napkin fall to the floor. But her worst blunder of all was that she could not stop laughing. It just all seemed so ridiculous. The waiters and waitresses scurrying to clean the mess, the men helping their horrified trophy wives soak up wine stains from their designer gowns, and her own husband, tight lipped and ghostly pale (but with his napkin still in his lap), staring straight ahead while she threw her head back and laughed and laughed. Finally, Bill tapped her elbow, simultaneously pulling her back to her seat. Covering her mouth with her hand, she cleared her throat, trying to quell her laughter, and complied. Everyone avoided her gaze, which made her want to laugh again. Instead, she turned to Sherri and smiled.

"Sherri?" she said. "It is Sherri, isn't it?"

Everyone at the table froze.

"Yes," Sherri said. Her voice was timorous now, and her eyes pleaded with Ellen. "It's Sherri."

"Well," Ellen said. "I thank you for your interest. It was awfully rude of me to ignore your question."

"I'm the one who should be apologizing—"

"No. No. I insist on giving you an answer." She smiled again. "How old are you, dear? Twenty-seven? Twenty-eight?" Ellen didn't wait for an answer. There was really no need to wait. "No matter, I was just wondering. You seem even younger."

"Ellen . . . ," Bill said.

Without even looking at him, Ellen patted his shoulder, still the reassuring wife.

"I just want Sherri and all the other young ladies here tonight to know that all the women they have replaced were worthy people. They had children with these men, created families. They built histories with these men. Something none of you has yet acquired. You're all beautiful, young and beautiful. I'm certain that my Bill's girlfriend is also young and beautiful. And I'm certain you will take her into the fold and welcome her." She noticed that seven pairs of eyes, including Bill's, suddenly found the tablecloth very interesting. "Dear me, how awkward. I see. Well, don't feel sorry for me. I really come out ahead in this saga. Bill turned out to be such a stinker, but then all of you are such stinkers too." She patted Bill's shoulder again and reached for her purse. "Enjoy the rest of your meal."

It was the last time she would attend a dinner as Bill's wife.

*   *   *

SHE still cringed when she thought of that night. Calling every-one a stinker. She had never used that word in her life. *Stinker.* She shuddered and covered her face with her hands. "My mother used to call us all stinkers," she wailed. "I haven't even heard that word in over thirty years." Barbara had howled when she heard the story and said, "That was the best you could do?" And Kaye just kept saying, "You didn't, did you?" But Ellen had. She admitted it over and over. Ellen was a fairly stand-up sort of gal. Everyone said so. She would eventually make her peace with Bill's betrayal. What other choice was there? But she would never be able to accept that Bill was going to have a baby. William Formerly Known as Bill and Lose Dixie were going to have a baby. Thirty-five years between Dixie and William, and they were going to have a child together. Shaking her head, Ellen sipped her coffee and stared out at the East River from her bedroom window. Bill had scoffed at her wish to adopt a child when they were unable to conceive. He told her they were too old. Apparently, it was she who had been too old, not Bill. He was going to have his very own baby now. A baby. Just like the one she had been forced to give away.

*   *   *

IT was a girl baby. And even though everyone advised her not to, Ellen held her. They would not let her nurse her daughter, because it was only a matter of days before she would be whisked off to an eager family in some unknown location. Ellen signed countless forms, relinquishing all her rights and agreeing to a closed adop-tion. She was only sixteen, and her parents made it very clear that unless she complied, they would have nothing to do with her. Of course, that was incentive enough to refuse to go along with their wishes. But she was too young and too afraid to be brave. Ellen meekly acquiesced to everything. She could not risk what the cost would be for her baby daughter, who would surely have a better life if she was adopted (or so Ellen was smilingly told by everyone—the director of the maternity home, the nurses, the priests, the nuns, the social workers—all with the same fixed and reassuring smile that signaled sincerity to the terrified young girls who passed through their doors). Ellen named her baby Faith. It was a rather predictable choice, but for a sixteen-year-old it seemed romantic and full of promise, and it was their secret.

The baby's father was eighteen. Ellen had met him at a college party. They both drank too much and went too far. Poor little Faith was the product of a drunken one-night stand. Her father's name was Sam. He was nice enough. After all, he gave Faith her pointy little chin. He never even knew that Ellen was pregnant. She never saw him or spoke with him again after that night. It wasn't until after she missed her second period that she told her friend Celia. Ellen was afraid that she might be sick. She had been feeling ill in the morning, unable to hold down any food. When Celia told Ellen she was probably pregnant, Ellen was shocked. It had just been that one time, and she had been drunk. It was impossible. Celia knew someone who could help, but it would cost three hundred dollars. Ellen refused. She was afraid for her eternal soul. Their parish priest had been very clear about what happened to bad girls who had abortions. In truth, Ellen should have been more afraid of her mother. Alice was disgusted and said so. "You make me sick," she said. She slapped Ellen and called her a tramp. That hurt more than the slap. Her parents fabricated some story about a sick aunt who needed looking after, and so Ellen was sent away to a maternity home until after the baby was born. It was only upstate New York, but it was spring, and it was wonderful to be alone with her baby. Ellen pressed the tape recorder to her hard belly, offering Mozart and Brahms, as well as the Beatles and Bob Dylan. She read aloud verses from Shakespeare's sonnets, assuring herself that her baby would remember the sound of her mother's voice.

During the long walks she took each morning, Ellen told her baby about herself, hoping Faith would understand and forgive her mother's awful predicament. Although everyone was kind, no one could understand the depth of her sadness. They tried to reassure her that she was doing the right thing, giving her baby a chance for a good life. That made Ellen cringe each time. She could not wrap her mind around that phrase. *A good life.* Ellen was told to put it all behind her. She was assured that she would forget all about the baby. It would be as if it had never happened. Alice offered parting words that chilled Ellen to the core. "Unless you want everyone to know you're a whore," Alice said, "you will never tell anyone that you got yourself pregnant." After all, Alice said, no one wanted the cow if the milk was free.

After Faith was taken away, Ellen returned to her parents' home, where everyone pretended that she had never been pregnant. When her breasts became engorged, Ellen's mother gave her a breast pump and an instruction booklet, advising her to wrap her chest between expressing. But the ache of Ellen's breasts was nothing compared with the dull, persistent pain that accompanied every waking moment since she had said good-bye to Faith. Ellen had studied her daughter's tiny face, memorizing every detail, forcing herself to believe that the years would not change the miniature physiognomy of this tiny, perfect creature. At the final moment, Ellen kissed her full on the mouth, tasting the sweetness of her breath and blowing gently into her, wanting to give something of herself. That very same day, a Wednesday, Ellen went home. By Monday, she was back at school, wearing her old clothes and participating in the charade her parents had invented. She kept her promise not to talk about The Baby. (They never referred to her as Faith.) And Ellen never broke that promise until she met Bill. The tenderness of his response when she divulged her secret unleashed a lifetime of sadness. He clucked his tongue, just like a woman would, and kept repeating how sorry he was for her loss. *Loss.* The import of that statement made Ellen reel. In Bill's arms, she cried for her lost baby as if years had not passed.

Bill even offered to help find Faith. There were ways. It was done all the time now. The Internet had made everything possible. Even closed adoptions had been revoked in some states. But Ellen felt that she had to follow Faith's cue. She had never come in search of her birth mother, and Ellen felt compelled to respect her daughter's wishes. Bill thought it was nonsense. Perhaps Baby Faith, as he called her, did not even know she was adopted. It was a possibility, Ellen agreed. Maybe her adoptive parents had cautioned her against a search. There were any number of possibilities. Still, she would not take the lead in this search. Faith would come to her when she was ready.

The next cruelest blow was also the greatest irony. Ellen's yearning to be a mother again could not be met on any level. The infertility procedures were futile and humiliating. Bill had probably already been thinking that she had suddenly become too old for him and could, therefore, be cavalier about her desire to mother. He scoffed at her unsatisfied emotions and encouraged her to find other outlets for her maternal energies. He could afford such disregard for her feelings because while Ellen was engrossed with the Internet researching adoption alternatives, he was no longer interested in her. But he was not entirely indifferent to her anguish. Perhaps, he even suggested to Ellen, she might volunteer at the local hospital. They were always looking for people to hold crack babies. Yes, Ellen agreed, blinking back tears, holding crack babies was much better than having a child of her own. She could not imagine why she had not thought of it herself. And off Bill went, smug with self-satisfaction, while Ellen reassured herself he would come round eventually.

And now she was alone. Ellen did not mind being alone. The

humiliation of Bill's betrayal still smarted, but she refused to hate him. When she looked in the mirror, she was not saddened by the lines around her eyes or the slack in the skin on her neck. Bill used to tease her that being pretty was more important than anything else in her life. Bill had been wrong about that too, of course. Nothing had ever been as important to Ellen as finding Faith. Not then . . . and not now. Not *ever*.

Four

BECAUSE Kaye often used anecdotes as a way to communicate with George, she was mindful of tales with import. Therefore, when Kaye read about a young New York couple visiting with family in California who were forced to take the northern route back home after an ice storm shut down I-40, she was immediately intrigued. The story was really about how some people just knew how to make the best of a bad thing. When the young couple stopped at a gas station on I-80, the attendant suggested they take advantage of the detour and get married in Reno. Because Reno was better known for quickie divorces than for marriages made in heaven, the would-be groom picked a number between one and ten. If she guessed correctly, the wedding was on. She guessed it.

Within hours, she found a gown and a veil on the clearance rack of the local department store, opting to wear her hiking boots because they were so comfortable and no one would see them anyway. He bought a tuxedo, a shirt, and a purple cummerbund and matching bow tie. His black Converse sneakers would do just fine. Rings were easy to buy, as pawnshops were in abundance. She would carry red roses tied with a ribbon, and they bought a cake at the supermarket and had it inscribed with their names inside a red heart. They consummated their marriage at a roadside truck stop and spent their wedding night at a cheap motel.

What Kaye loved most about the story was that the new bride wore her wedding dress for the remainder of her five-day journey back to New York because she wanted to see the reactions of strangers. In Wyoming, a hunter asked to photograph the bride, so his wife would believe him that he had really seen a bride pumping gas; children clapped when she made snow angels; and a trucker congratulated them, promising them that marriage was filled with rewards. He said he should know, because he had been married for twenty years and had eight children.

Road trips, any trip for that matter, could be seen as a tired metaphor for marriage. Kaye was very much aware of that. However, it was the comment of a checker in a 7-Eleven in Nebraska who said that the bride was spreading happiness wherever she went simply because she was wearing her wedding gown that struck a chord with Kaye. It suddenly seemed so easy to make others happy that Kaye wondered why so few were ever good at it.

* * *

THE story about the bride seemed to completely throw George. From the outset, he was confused about the story's intent. As Kaye recounted the events of the new bride's journey from California to New York in her wedding dress, he sporadically interrupted, peppering her reading with a few *isn't that something*s and one or two *that must have been a sight*s. Encouraged by this response, Kaye said that she wished she had been driven by such exuberance after their wedding, eliciting an agreeable nod from George. But when she said she thought it would be grand to put on her wedding gown and set out on a similar adventure, George looked entirely baffled.

"Didn't you borrow your wedding gown from your cousin Paula?" he said.

She stared at him, watching him blink.

"I think you're missing the point," Kaye said.

"Why do you say that?" he said.

"Because it has nothing to do with the wedding gown, and you know it."

"How would I know that?"

Kaye was always the one with regrets. Regrets about everything. Instead of the fish, she wished she had ordered chicken. The salad instead of the soup. The dress that looked perfect in the store suddenly looked too tight when she tried it on at home. And the chair for her living room that had to be special-ordered in the plaid she had so wanted looked out of place when it finally arrived. She came to believe that her decision to marry George was just another example of picking the wrong blouse or ordering the wrong meal. If she had only given it more thought, she might have chosen better.

"I don't believe you," she said.

"That's your problem," he said. "Well, what is the point of the damned story?"

They were getting ready for bed. He was untying his laces. Instead of taking off one shoe at a time, he untied each shoe first. Then he took off his left shoe. Always his left shoe first. So many routines. So many habits. Always the same black socks. The same hairstyle. The same breakfast every morning. Shredded wheat and raisins with skim milk. The same foreplay over and over. No eggs or butter. No rear penetration. Nipple manipulation followed by oral sex followed by some perfunctory kissing. No conversation during sex. No bacon. No joy.

"The point is that it takes so little to be happy that I wonder why we fail at it so miserably," she said.

"I'm sorry you feel that way," he said.

The same answers for everything. He stood and undid his belt, unzipped his pants, and stepped out of them. Once she had loved the long leanness of his thighs. Now she turned away and sighed. His hand on her shoulder was a surprise, and not only because it was unexpected. It was heavy with sadness.

"What?" she said.

"Why do you always think the worst of me?"

It was such a sincere question, and she had no answer for him. She remembered her aunt Rachel saying that she knew her husband did not love her anymore when he started to complain about her cooking. Nothing tasted right to him. Everything had either too much salt or not enough salt. Or the meat was too dry, and the rice too wet. Kaye had been stunned at the nuance of her aunt's observation. But her aunt and uncle stayed together; her aunt always laboring in the kitchen, believing that if her cooking improved, her husband would love her again.

"Kaye?"

She patted his hand, and he moved toward her, taking her in his arms. Once she had savored his touch, hungered for it when a day passed without him. She rested her head on his shoulder and tried to relax as his hand reached under her nightgown. It had been weeks, maybe months, since they had made love. It was almost as if she wished she felt shy instead of tense. But she was tense. His touch seemed invasive, and her face burned with the shame of that truth. And still she allowed it because not to might have invited some dialogue, and the idea of talking was unbearable to her right now. They would have talked in circles. *Circumlocution.* SAT word. When she had tested Ruby on her SAT words, Kaye played a game with herself, grouping words that applied to her marriage and to George. *Circumlocution, evasion. Saturnine, sanctimo-nious, punctilious, illusory.* So many words. Charlie used to make up the definitions when she tested him. He never studied. He would repeat the word after she said it as though he were a contestant in a spelling bee. "Bucolic. Let's see. Bucolic. An alcoholic who has made progress." She always laughed, which only encouraged him. Words drifted through her thoughts now: *arable, askance, avuncular, atavistic, arcane* . . . George's heavy breaths grew deeper and shorter as he moved inside her, and she rested her hands on his damp back. *Braggart, blithely, cloying, cogent* . . .

*   *   *

FRANK was not particularly handsome. In fact, the first time Kaye met him, she thought he looked like a child's drawing of himself. His head was too round, as well as fairly bald, and he had jug ears that were useful for resting the arms of his glasses. While his smile was disarming, showing strong white teeth, his nose and eyes were quite ordinary. But somehow, he was so present. They met at one of Barbara's publishing events. For the last few years, Barbara had dragged Kaye and Ellen to the Romance Writers Convention. Grudgingly, they accompanied her to cities where the crazed fans gathered to meet their favorite romance writers. It was all sort of silly and fun, but it was also a little alarming. Barbara Shore was in-deed a favorite in Atlanta, a fact that was reinforced when they were greeted at the airport by banners that read *Atlanta Welcomes Barbara Shore* and another that proclaimed *Atlanta's Favorite Heroine is Bar-bara Shore*. The first day of the conference, Barbara autographed copies of her two most recent books, *Wanderlust* and *Half a Heart*. Women, and a handful of men, waited in a line that snaked around the ballroom. Some of the women, obviously first-timers to the convention scene, came with shopping bags filled with Barbara's books. They gushed at Barbara, quoting lines from her novels and asking her the same questions that everyone asked. *Where do you get your ideas? Are any of the stories based on actual experiences? Is there really a Quentin?* Barbara answered all the questions the same way she always did, with just enough evasiveness and seductiveness to titillate her readers and to satisfy her publisher. Franklin Fiske, new to the company, had been sent to keep a watchful eye on Barbara, as well as to meet her needs. "He doesn't look as though he could meet any of *my* needs," Barbara had said as she watched him walk away. Then she added, "Though he does have a very cute rump." Actually, Kaye thought Frank was cute enough, though she kept it to herself. He met up with them at the bar later that night, and Kaye was jealous when he talked to Ellen. Frank made it clear that he did not care for the name Franklin even though it paid homage to his mother's admiration for President Roosevelt. Kaye had two Bloody Marys, one too many for her. When Ellen went to the washroom, Kaye slid over onto the stool, right next to Frank. For the remainder of the evening, Kaye focused all her attention on him. They had very little in common. He was from the Midwest, and she was a native New Yorker. He was Lutheran; she was Jewish. He came from a large, close family, and she had one estranged brother. Frank had never married, and she felt as if she had never been single. He favored sweeping historical sagas (something she not only disdained but abhorred), and she loved mysteries. Thai food was his go-to comfort food while Kaye often dreamed about anything Parmesan. By the end of the night, the only interest they seemed to share was in each other.

Reluctantly, Barbara and Ellen left their slightly tipsy friend, but only because she was adamant that she was not drunk. Frank assured Barbara and Ellen that he was a gentleman and that no harm would come to their friend, who giggled at this promise, horrifying Barbara and Ellen and making Frank smile so broadly that it made Kaye giggle more. Somehow his face had already endeared itself to her, and she smiled much too fondly at him. They talked for hours. She talked mostly about Ruby and Charlie. And Frank talked about the children he had never had. Yes, of course there was Oliver, his nephew who was entering his third year at the University of Michigan. They were very close, but an uncle was not the same as a father. And he knew that his sister Ginny had given him full access to Oliver as a token of love. Kaye tried to point out that Ginny's offering was pure love, the most generous kind. Frank agreed, but he so hated the role of the poor bachelor. Well, no one likes to be pitied, she agreed. They had another round of drinks, switching to martinis, a drink Kaye had never liked but suddenly found irresistible. And as she sucked on her olive and reflexively puckered her lips, Kaye realized that Frank was watching her.

She began to go on about some nonsense that had to do with James Bond and the way he liked his martinis. "You know," she said. "Shaken, not stirred." And then she just had to mention George. She had avoided any mention of her marital status, and Frank was discreet enough to steer clear of the topic, though she saw how he noted her gold and diamond wedding band set, the only good jewelry she wore. So it seemed as good a time as any to point out that George just loved James Bond movies, all of them and any of them. She went on and on about how he knew they were sexist, but he just couldn't resist the intrigue and well, George said no one could deny that James Bond was just so damned cool. Kaye knew she was making a fool of herself, but she carried on, avoiding eye contact with Frank, who quietly sipped his own drink. She gulped down the remainder of her martini and said, "Well." Frank set his own glass on the bar and leaned over, kissing her full on the mouth. He kept his hands at his sides, and she gripped her glass with one hand and held on to the counter with the other. It was quite a long kiss for two strangers, and much more intimate than anything she had shared with George in the longest time. "Frank," she said when the kiss ended. But he held up his hand before she could say anything else and suggested that they call it a night. She agreed, but in the elevator, he kissed her again. This time, he did not keep his hands at his sides, pressing her flat up against the rear elevator wall and pushing against her. When a moan escaped from her open mouth, she said, "Was that me?" There was so much wonder in her voice that Frank laughed and pulled her even closer.

The elevator stopped at his floor, but he pushed the button down to the lobby again, and they rode up and down four times, kissing like teenagers, only better. By then, she had forgotten not only that elevators had cameras, but that she had a husband. She pointed up to the eye of the camera, and Frank bowed deeply to the mechanical eye. They were fortunate that it was so late that no one was around, and except for the desk clerk's discreet disregard each time the elevator stopped and the doors opened, they were alone. It all felt very sexy and very dangerous. "I feel like I'm in one of Barbara's novels," Kaye said. To this Frank responded, "Oh, dear. That's not at all the feeling I was going for." For the first time, Kaye felt ridiculous. A middle-aged married woman, clothes and hair completely disheveled, making out in a hotel elevator. "Look," she said. "I think I'm too drunk to make any decisions." He said, "Who's asking you to make a decision? I just want to take you to bed. Sadly, I'm too old for elevator sex." Her cheeks flushed bright red, and he kissed her again, but lightly this time, smoothing down her hair with an expression of concentration that made her breath quicken again. "May I see you to your room?" he said. "No," she said. "You go on." The last thing he said before the doors closed was, "Room twelve twenty-four. Make a right off the elevator."

When she got off three floors later, she straightened her dress and wiped under her eyes for any mascara smudges. Ellen was asleep. A hot pink satin eye pillow decorated with bright blue wide-open eyes was in place, creating a weird effect, especially when coupled with white-cotton-gloved hands folded on top of the blanket. The room was thick with the scent of roses from an aromatherapy oil burner that she never traveled without. Kaye sat in a chair and put her face in her hands. Five minutes later, she was knocking on Frank's door. "I have to be back before Ellen gets up," she said. Frank nodded. "I work fast," he said. She noticed that a bottle of champagne was chilling in an ice bucket. "I was optimistic," he said, taking her in his arms. He touched her cheek with the back of his hand and murmured, "Such soft skin. I can't wait for the rest of you." She undid her own dress and unhooked her bra with one hand. It was important to her that he saw her in the light. Her underwear was uninspired: plain, pink cotton briefs that could not have been flattering. Gallantly, he put his hand out for support, and she stepped out of her underpants, holding his gaze the whole time. It was a test, and she wanted to see if he flinched. After all, she was not young. But there was only pleasure in his mild eyes. When she was fully naked, he pushed her gently into the chair directly behind her. Quizzically, Kaye primly crossed her legs and folded her hands in her lap. Then, Frank kneeled in front of her. First, he unfolded her hands, and then he uncrossed her legs. By the time she felt his warm breath on her inner thighs, she was ready. Unashamed, she eagerly arched herself forward and held his head. There was so much pleasure that she felt it was almost too much. Even more amazing was that Frank knew when it was too much without having to be told. It seemed nothing short of a miracle.

He stood and she stood with him, unbuttoning his shirt and helping him off with his trousers. But he stopped her when she prepared to reciprocate and murmured, with great urgency, that he was no longer of an age when it was possible to wait. Pulling her along by her hand, he sat and motioned for her to join him. He laughed when she said she did not know if she could manage such a position. But he helped her, and she straddled him, rocking gently first, tasting his sweat for the first time as she licked his shoulder, and then forgetting everything as he moved her hips with such need that in the end there was nothing more they could do than sit, wrapped around each other, silent and exhausted. Finally, she found the energy to ask, "Why me?" He wrapped a strand of her hair around her ear and shook his head in disbelief. Kaye was suddenly acutely aware of everything she stood to lose.

*   *   *

BARBARA swore that no matter how hard she tried, she just could not see the attraction. Still and all, she said, she was glad for Kaye. A fling might help her put her life in some sort of perspective. Ellen was less enthusiastic. She felt responsible, as though somehow on her watch, Kaye had wandered off and gotten hurt or lost. "I'm not a child," Kaye said, "and you're not my babysitter." It was a little awkward for the rest of the trip. Frank was working, and Barbara made that very clear. She could be extremely territorial. Ellen talked even more than usual when Frank was around, batting her eyes at him, practically hypnotizing him with her double lashes. Kaye and Frank managed a few clandestine meetings, but mostly they just met at the bar and talked. By the week's end, they were fast friends. Kaye told him it was great to have met him. And she told Barbara and Ellen that it was over. They had agreed to remain good friends. That's all. Just friends. Barbara thought it was for the best, and Ellen was so relieved, exonerated at last. Neither of them suspected that Frank and Kaye were having dinner on Wednesday night at his apartment in the city, nor that she was forever changed.

*   *   *

THAT was six months ago. The magical labyrinth of intrigue pulled Kaye into its core. After the first few lies, it became easier, and then easier still, to fabricate her new life. Truly, she never meant for it to go this long. And she always meant to tell Barbara and Ellen, especially Barbara. But then Frank felt his job might be in jeopardy. Barbara could be so unpredictable, and Frank thought she was too volatile to be trusted with a secret of such magnitude. Kaye bristled at this analysis of Barbara, even though it was hard to ignore the truth in it. Still, Kaye suffered, imagining Barbara's humiliation over such a betrayal. Oddly enough, however, after a time, Kaye found that deceit brought its own challenges, and she found that she was caught up in the life she had invented. Frank found her fascinating as only someone from a completely different background could. It was as though she were some odd creature from another world. She had a yeshiva education, something that Frank could not believe. And she spoke Yiddish, German, and Hebrew with the same ease with which she could turn a phrase in English. Each time they met, he would ask her to translate something into Hebrew or Yiddish. He was less interested in her fluency in German. That seemed more average. He wanted to meet her mother, but Kaye refused. And he wanted to meet Ruby and Charlie, and Kaye said no again. And then he wanted her to leave George, and the answer to that was also no, though that was something she could not explain as easily or reasonably as the other nos. Frank said he loved her. She said she loved him. Certainly, she loved his humor and his spontaneity. Once he left a beautifully wrapped box on her pillow. It was the book on how to make mixed drinks that she had been reading at the checkout counter in Gristedes. That afternoon he made them grasshoppers. He loved her new, short haircut, claiming it gave him faster access to the nape of her neck, a spot he found completely irresistible. And when she woke, bathed in the sweat particular to women of a certain age, he referred to her as glazed, rather than sticky, the way George would have described her.

There was no reason not to leave George. Their marriage was muddled by history, weakened by unresolved bad feelings. But from time to time, George seemed as if he were fighting his way off his own dimly lit planet. Like just the other night. She picked him up from the train, watching him step onto the platform, his brown briefcase in hand. He looked well, very fit and attractive, and he slid into the car with an unusual amount of energy. After he kissed her proffered cheek, he began to speak without any prodding at all. "There was a fellow on the train with me; you know the kind. Very conservatively dressed, yet surprisingly bearded," he said. "Lawyer probably, maybe one of those civil rights lawyers. He caught my attention because he had an orange butterfly clip in his beard. You remember those, don't you? Ruby used to wear barrettes just like that. I wondered if he knew the clip was there, or if all day everyone around him had pretended not to see it. Maybe his little girl had put it there just before she kissed him good-bye and made him promise that he'd wear it all day." He shook his head, as if he were alone, remembering something he had once promised Ruby. And then he looked up, eyes a little moist, and sighed. "I was sort of jealous. Not only because his daughter was still a little girl but because he actually wore the clip all day. I probably would have taken it off and put it back on before I came home. But that guy had courage." George did not say his lack of courage was probably the source of all his failings. But then, there was no real need to. Kaye understood, and she stroked his hand. He smiled sort of vaguely, lost in his own reverie, absent to her once again. Nevertheless, Kaye counted it as a small victory and enough of an offering, not to explain why she stayed, but to explain why she did not leave.

* * *

WHEN her children were grown and out on their own, Kaye left her job as a school psychologist and decided to see private patients full-time in her home office. She loved her office, decorating it with framed pictures that covered practically every inch of wall space.

There were photographs of her family and photographs of strangers, treasures she had acquired at flea markets and in the secondhand shops she loved to prowl both in New York and whenever she was abroad. There were a few framed posters as well, chronicling favorite museum exhibitions. But Kaye's favorites were the framed postcards, a collection that represented an interest that began on one of her first antiquing excursions with George in upstate New York. It had been summer, and the children were away at camp, leaving Kaye feeling especially lonely and vulnerable. She loved poring through the bins of old postcards, reading the inscriptions and imagining the lives of these no-longer strangers. Most of the cards were ordinary, greetings from places no one really wanted to visit with kitschy pictures of buxom women and alligators. But one card caught Kaye's attention, and she peered closely at the faded writing. *The disconsolate figure you see before you is I, agonizing over your absence. Will we ever see each other again?* There was no salutation, no closing. She turned the card over and studied the bucolic scene of a lone figure on a park bench. The card was dated *13 June 1919.* The words reached out to her across time, and she began to cry. George rushed to her side, asking what was wrong. Was there anything he could do? He had meant well. He always did. But she said no and paid for the card. How could she explain that she felt closer to the man in the picture than she did to her own husband?

The framed card hung now in Kaye's office. After much consideration, she had decided to keep the inscription hidden. She knew what it said, and that was enough. The words were her secret, and the faded picture was enough of a curiosity to interest her patients who seemed drawn to the lonely figure. Kaye's practice was small, but energetic, her patients mostly locals from the neighboring villages, adolescents and women. Today, Kaye was listening to Zoë elaborate once again on her affair with her best friend's husband. Just that morning, he had been over to ostensibly drop off a casserole dish Zoë had borrowed. He had pulled Zoë into the bathroom, and they had sex in the shower. Kaye asked, "Weren't you afraid you might get caught?" Zoë looked incredulous. "Absolutely," she said. And when Kaye asked her why she continued to carry on this way, the plaintive reply was, "I can't stop." As the session came to a close, Kaye felt compelled to ask, "Is it true love?" Shaking her head, Zoë said, "How would I know?" Kaye had no answer. But she did say that some believed only true love could diminish the loneliness everyone fears. "Well, then it isn't true love," Zoë said. "I'm still lonely." Kaye looked up at her favorite framed postcard and said, "I'm afraid we're out of time."

After Zoë left, Kaye wrote down a few notes in the patient's file and sat staring at the postcard. The only two times she had ever been entirely free from loneliness were during her pregnancies, first with Charlie and then with Ruby. Loneliness. The silent killer. That was Kaye's definition of loneliness. Last summer, she had read George an article about the number of old men who die in heat waves. Locked up in their apartments, sealed out from the rest of the world, these old men died unnoticed and alone. George had stared at her afterward waiting (it seemed to her) for her to say that this would never happen to him.

When she told Barbara the awful statistics, she had shrugged and said, "They probably deserved it." Ellen had been shocked, as always, at Barbara's irreverence, especially for the dead. "It wasn't the heat, you know," Kaye had insisted. "It was the loneliness. Doesn't that make you want to cry?" Instead of answering, Barbara raised her eyebrow and held her tongue. In a questionable show of re-spect for the dead, they were all silent until Ellen saved them from their faltering sincerity, regaling them with the story of a new cli-ent who wanted his entire apartment done in a safari theme right down to the china. Gold-trimmed service for eight with painted giraffes, zebras, and tigers on every plate, bowl, and cup. Ellen had unsuccessfully tried to save the fellow from his own bad taste. As she listened, Kaye was ashamed that she had not saved George from an image of himself locked away in a steaming hot apartment, forgotten by everyone. She could have saved him with a kind word or two, but then the moment passed, and it was too late. It was there, and then it was gone. Just like that.

Five

THE legend of Queen Zenobia was worthy of its place in history. As beautiful as she was strong, Zenobia was believed to be a descendant of Cleopatra. Queen Zenobia spoke five languages, led her own army, employed a Greek philosopher as her counselor, and governed her people as though they were her children. Zenobia's people were wealthy and educated, their architecture prized, and their queen loved and respected. Initially, Barbara thought to take *Zenobia* as her sobriquet, but when she learned that *Delilah* meant "the weak" or "the longing," there was no longer a choice. Erotic tales of passion were meant to weaken resolve, just as Delilah had softened and weakened the strength of the great warrior Samson. He opened his heart to the temptress Delilah, casting aside his Nazarite vow and betraying the source of his superhuman strength, only to learn that without God's presence, he was nothing at all. Barbara saw the story of Samson and Delilah as a modern-day romance of lust and greed. It was yet another story of a clever woman who knew that most men would do anything for sex even if it meant denouncing Jehovah. Queen Zenobia was not the stuff fantasies were made of, at least not the fantasies of men. Delilah, on the other hand, was proof that men just never learned.

* * *

JUSTINE would have been the least horrified to know the truth about her mother's secret identity, except perhaps for Michael, who would likely have made the situation work for him. Justine had a sense of humor about most everything. Not so with Daphne, who was almost entirely humorless and infuriatingly self-righteous. Justine claimed that not only did Daphne invariably miss the point, but then she refused to ever acknowledge that she was wrong. She had been studying international banking in London when Roger died. After the funeral, Daphne returned to London to complete the last few weeks of the semester and then came home to live with Barbara. It had been a difficult arrangement. Daphne insisted on correcting everything Barbara and Justine said and did. At first, Barbara tolerated it. After all, Daphne had just lost her father, and Barbara was the parent. But when Justine stormed into Barbara's bedroom one morning and asked if she still had any contacts with Daddy's former business partners, Barbara knew it was time to move Daphne out. Poor Daphne was devastated. Wasn't she a good daughter? Hadn't she given up everything to come home and take care of her mother? But when Barbara asked her what exactly she had given up and why she didn't go back to it now that Daddy was dead and buried, Daphne fell into a sobbing heap. Immediately contrite, Barbara was heartbroken for her girl who was still her little girl in spite of everything. Somehow Daphne never seemed to measure up to her own expectations, and Barbara knew that, unlike Justine (who though equally goal oriented had a sardonic sense of reality), Daphne would be forever disappointed. So, like a good mother, Barbara reassured Daphne that she was a wonderful daughter and that her return had helped the family heal. They were all grateful to have her home, Barbara said, improvising on the truth just a little, but enough to assuage her previously bad behavior and give Daphne a reason to feel benevolent.

*   *   *

SOMEHOW, they got through those really hard months after Roger's death. Daphne found a job in a midtown bank. She moved in with Michael, who was gracious for the first few months. Then, one night he phoned Barbara, whispering, "How long does it take to kill someone with arsenic?" Beautiful, beautiful Michael. In some ways, it seemed wrong that Michael was the most attractive of her three children. "All those gorgeous features and magnificent curls wasted on a boy," passersby said when he was still in the stroller. It was nonsense, but it certainly did not make his teenaged sisters very happy as they struggled with acne and awkwardness while Michael sailed through blemish-free and innately suave. Now, of course, Justine found Michael's striking appearance intensely funny and teased him about his Roman nose, his porcelain skin, and his pouty lips. She never missed an opportunity to tell him how hot he was. But Daphne bristled each time Michael was complimented, noting that she had very similar features and no one paid her as much attention. "That's because everyone knows you're so modest, Daph," Justine explained. All in all, Barbara thought, her children had turned out quite well. Michael taught math in a private Manhattan high school and subsidized his income with tutoring. He regaled them with stories of all the mothers who tried to seduce him, as well as some of the fathers too. He changed girlfriends so often that Roger had been prone to ask, "So, what's the flavor of the month, sport?" Even though Barbara found the question coarse, especially for a father of two daughters, she tried to stay out of their relationship. Michael already questioned his father's business ethics, and she did not want to do any more to compromise their connection. While Michael could make Barbara fairly swoon with nothing more than a peck on the cheek, it was Justine's approval and love that Barbara worked to win and to sustain. Justine was born with a steely resilience that people believed was a form of self-protection, a way to compensate for the challenges of her cerebral palsy. But Barbara scoffed at this notion. The cerebral palsy was a mere afterthought. She was self-deprecating about her condition without being maudlin, a tough balancing act.

Nothing stood in Justine's way, although since Roger's death a sort of quiet had settled over her. She seemed incredulous that he was no longer available to her. Two years later, and she still turned at the scent of a cigar and often thought she had caught sight of him in a crowd. When Barbara listened to Justine's tales of how she had followed a man three blocks because he was wearing his baseball cap at the exact same angle that Dad always wore his, Barbara was amazed. It was so unlike Justine to be so sentimental.

Sometimes Barbara felt more alone with her children than she did when she was by herself. They loved her and showed her affection, but she often felt as if they would rather be somewhere else, with someone else. She never said this to them, knowing it would only make them defensive. And since Roger's death, they had been deliberately attentive. Michael would call on a Sunday and ask if she would like to come into the city to see a movie. When she said that there was an abundance of movie theaters not more than ten minutes away, Michael always countered with, "Yes, but your favorite Chinese restaurant is here, and I'm treating." He was seductive, her Michael, and she fell for him anew each and every time.

Her daughters, different as they were from each other, were

equally puzzling. Justine said she had never been in love. She never confided in Barbara, nor did it seem in anyone, though she had friends, good friends. Ruby and Justine had been friends since they were little, but Kaye occasionally mentioned that Ruby often found Justine distant. That worried Barbara, and when she could no longer restrain herself, she would ply Justine with questions, asking her if she was depressed, or if she might want to talk to someone, or even if there wasn't someone, anyone out there who tickled her fancy. Once, after enduring an endless barrage of these questions, Justine had said, "Am I supposed to tell you every time I get laid?" Such relief had washed over Barbara that she had blurted out, "No, but I'm delighted to hear that you are." Michael later reported to Barbara that Justine had told him that they had the strangest mother in the world. Roger's death had not brought Barbara and Justine any closer, though she phoned more often and even encouraged Barbara to date. "Really?" Barbara said. "Thank you." Justine laughed and said, "Just don't ever ask me to double."

Barbara hoped Daphne was not as hard to please in bed as she was everywhere else. Boys were always interested in Daphne. She resembled Barbara, though shorter and with a more athletic build. There was something so compact about Daphne. Once she had a boyfriend, Dutch he was called for some forgotten reason, who named her Pocket Girl. "I could slip Daphne into my pocket and no one would ever know," Dutch said. When Barbara first heard this, she had been certain that Daphne would chafe at the comparison, but she had seemed flattered, rubbing against him the way a cat who wanted more food might. It had shocked Barbara to see Daphne in this first real sexual role. Her skin seemed luminescent, lit by some inner heat, and whenever Barbara found the pair, they were intertwined. Barbara found that she sought them out, almost as if she might acquire some of their fire for herself and Roger. His hands were imprinted on her body like the stretch marks on her belly. It was all different from when Barbara and Roger had first met. Their heat could no longer burn anything. Their sex had become a series of moves that were notable mostly for their comforting sameness. Dutch and Daphne stirred Barbara's memories, reminding her that women might spend their entire lives longing for good sex if they never had it, or dreaming about it if they had.

It was exactly such fanciful wanderings that had led to Barbara's foray into writing erotica. She first became obsessed with ordinary words that had the potential to excite. What began as a diversion from her formulaic romance novels soon became a preoccupation with finding ways to cushion everyday words in ultimately titillating sentences. *Wetness, moistness, soft, hard, length, width.* This was the simple language of erotica that when matched to a character's earthy desires became the stories women wanted to read.

The stories were tame at first. *Dawn's painted fingernails were surprisingly gentle as they penetrated her own moist flesh.* Then Barbara became yet bolder. *Annabelle drew his large hand to the wetness between her legs, letting her thighs fall to either side. "Fuck me," she said in a throaty voice that she had never used before. He turned her around and prepared her with his tongue, running it along the backs of her thighs and then spreading her gently with his hands, pushing his tongue in deeper as she urged him on again.* When Barbara realized that her identity was safe and that her own mother was long dead, there was nothing to hold back. *Morning was best for making love. Eyes still crusted with sleep, Lenore reached for Kyle. He was still soft, but only briefly. As her mouth closed around his cock, he stirred faintly. She used one hand to firmly press along his length the way he liked it and the other hand to find the groove just beneath his erection. He reached down for her, but she was too aroused, too ready. Ignoring her resistance, his fingers found her, and she moaned that she was going to come. His determination aroused her even more, and he encouraged her,*

saying, "Come on my hand." She already had, so that when he finally en-
tered her, she could barely do more than allow it. Barbara wrote her first
drafts in longhand on lined yellow legal pads. She often became so
engaged in her own words that her breath quickened and she had
to stop writing long enough to take care of herself. It was an odd
way to pass time. A middle-aged woman wearing cotton briefs and
one of her deceased husband's dress shirts, writing erotica at the
kitchen counter.

Sometimes Barbara worried that she could die in the middle of
the night, and no one would know until perhaps a day or two later
when someone finally came to look for her.

"The smell would definitely draw attention within a few days,"
Albert said.

She was on a date. Periodically, she forced herself to accept a
date. Somehow everyone in her building knew a great guy who
wanted to date a woman just like her. Most of the time she was
able to beg off with some lame excuse that she was already seeing someone or that she was still in mourning. Internet dating
had been a disaster. All the men whose profiles were interesting
looked like Willie Nelson, and though she had nothing against
Willie, he was just not her type. At least not for another fifteen or
so years. She learned the language of the Internet, developing a
special fondness for profiles that began with *ISO*. The abbreviation
seemed as urgent as any SOS might. *ISO FRIDA KAHLO* caught
her immediate attention. Momentarily, Barbara considered dyeing
her hair black and tying it up in two braids. The unibrow would
be more of a challenge, though worth the effort to find her Diego
Rivera. Then there was the profile that read *FEATURES OF RE-
NAISSANCE CHRIST*. She would have to say that one was her
favorite until the accompanying photograph revealed yet another
Willie Nelson lookalike.

Albert was the nephew of Mrs. Haggerty from 14A. She had started badgering Barbara exactly one year after Roger died. This last time, Mrs. Haggerty had accosted Barbara in the laundry room, promising her that Albert was the man of her dreams. Albert had never been married (always suspicious) and loved action movies and the outdoors. "He's a real catch," Mrs. Haggerty said. "You'll see as soon as you meet him." Barbara agreed, surprising herself as well as Mrs. Haggerty.

"The smell?" Barbara said. "That wasn't really my point, but I guess I would start to smell by the second day."

He smiled brightly. Albert was pleased with himself.

"My aunt tells me you're a writer," Albert said.

"Yes. I'm a writer."

"So, what do you write?"

Barbara studied the menu very carefully. This was the part of the conversation she hated. Albert was a nice man, but not for her. She looked up, steeling herself for the inevitable.

"I write fiction."

"Ah, I see. What's your genre?"

Barbara wondered if he had crammed for their date, like a contestant on a quiz show.

"Romance. I write romance novels."

"Is there a lot of sex?" he said.

Albert smiled and winked. She smiled and winked back.

"Just between the women," she said.

Albert knocked over his water. Barbara had the napkins ready and waiting.

"Shall we order?" she said.

Poor Albert. He was a perfectly nice man. He was even quite handsome and reasonably tall. They ordered. She went with the sea bass, and he chose the lobster. They talked politics. He was informed and not a Republican. He did enjoy the outdoors, camping especially, and hiking. Barbara hated anything that was even remotely like nature. She even disliked the color green. Albert, to his credit, laughed when she said that. Why had he never married? Of course, he said that he was waiting for a woman like her to come along. After their decaf cappuccinos, they agreed it was late. He declined her offer to split the check and held her coat. Barbara did not even mind that he put his arm around her as they waited for the car. She had written a really torrid chapter that day, and it might be interesting to have a real live partner instead of a legal pad, a pencil, and her own inspiration.

"I really enjoyed dinner, Barbara," he said, drawing her closer.

"Thanks, Albert. I did too."

The valet brought their car, and Albert held the door for her. As they drove off, he asked if he could see her again.

"I don't know," she said.

He reached a hand across and placed it on her knee. She squeezed her thighs together.

"I'd really, really like to get to know you," he said.

Barbara patted his hand and moved it off her knee. She had felt a slight flutter when his hand made contact with her leg. *Yvonne was glad she had not worn stockings. She moved her thighs and arched herself forward, inviting his hand to explore further up her bare skin. "You're so ready," he said, moving his fingers inside her, rubbing her clitoris with his thumb. "I'd like to do you right here." She leaned over and kissed him, pushing her tongue into his mouth as he rubbed her faster and more furiously until she came.* It had been a long time since Barbara had been with a real man instead of one she had created, one who always knew how to do everything perfectly.

"I had a very pleasant time," she said.

"Pleasant?"

It had been an awful choice of words, and she was already sorry. Now she would have to make it up to him.

"I meant that in the nicest possible way," she said.

"Even in the nicest possible way, it's pretty insulting."

He sulked for the rest of the ride home, and she abandoned her efforts at conversation. When they got to her building, he pulled into one of the twenty-minute parking spaces and started to get out of the car.

"You don't have to see me up," she said. "I'll be fine."

"It's late. I'd rather see you to the door."

They were silent in the elevator. Barbara had her key ready. He walked her to the door.

"Well," she said, "thanks so much for dinner and for the good conversation."

"Yes, it *was* pleasant."

A sense of humor. Barbara was impressed. That deserved at least a kiss, and she owed him something. She reached up to kiss him, but he kissed her first. She wished he had waited for her lead. The kiss was too orchestrated and too hopeful. *Yvonne grazed his lips with hers and felt his need as he pressed against her. She licked his lips and reached down for him with both hands, rolling his hardness between her flattened palms.* Every word of the scene in her head was better than anything that was happening. Gently, she placed both hands on Albert's chest and stepped back.

"Thanks again," she said.

"What's the matter?" Albert said. "Was the kiss unpleasant?"

He was playing on her guilt, but she was immune to such artifices. A manipulative mother and three children had steeled her to take on any challenge with resolve.

"I'm really tired, Albert, and I just met you."

It was unlike her to be so forward on the first date, but he was so sweet and his eyes promised so much. She just knew he would be a great kisser with those beautiful, full lips. All through dinner, she watched him take bites of his food and then chew and swallow. His throat was long and thick, and she imagined herself naked, gripping his width as she rode his equally long and thick cock.

"I understand," he said, kissing her cheek. "It was nice to have met you."

As soon as she was safely inside her apartment, Barbara waited until she heard the elevator stop and the doors shut. Then she took off her clothes and slipped into one of Roger's one hundred percent cotton shirts. She still sent them out to be laundered. Silly habit. After she fixed herself a mug of hot tea, she sat at the counter with a fresh legal pad, a few sharpened pencils, and a new plastic cigarette.

Yvonne loved the excitement of first dates. All through dinner she wondered if she would let him come home with her. He was smart, and she liked that. She also liked his biceps when he took off his jacket and rolled up his shirtsleeves. It was evident that he was trying to impress her, and it was working. "So, you're in advertising," Clyde said. She smiled and leaned all the way over so he could see her cleavage. "Yes, I am," she said. "How am I doing?" Clyde laughed and squeezed her knee under the table. Yvonne loved men with big hands. She parted her legs, inviting him to explore, and he slid up her thigh as though her skin were made of glass. His fingers entered her, and she leaned over even further and touched the tip of her tongue to his lower lip. "Let's go," Clyde said. Gripping his wrist through the silk of her skirt, she said, "Not yet. Not just yet. I want to be sure I'm making the right decision." He nodded, acquiescing to her wisdom.

Barbara wrote furiously, biting down hard on her plastic cigarette. Her heart was racing. *I love you, Clyde.* She realized it was no longer Yvonne speaking. Barbara stopped writing until her heartbeat slowed, and she felt drowsy, just like Yvonne after she took Clyde home for the night.

* * *

"REMEMBER that guy you went out with who would sing all the time?" Kaye said. "That was really weird."

"Do I remember?" Barbara said. "He took any word from a sentence and matched it to song lyrics. When I told him that I didn't think it was going to work out, he left me messages for weeks. *They say that breaking up is hard to do. Now I know. I know that it's true.* When I called back and told him to stop, he left me a new message. *Stop in the name of love.*"

"I love that song," Kaye said.

"What made you think of him?"

"I don't know."

They tried to walk early on most mornings, but it was raining hard. Instead, they put on an exercise channel and ate muffins and drank coffee while they watched.

"These muffins are good," Kaye said. She took another big bite and peered at the television screen as she washed the muffin down with the strong black coffee. "Did you call Ellen?"

"I did. She was still in bed," Barbara said, picking up a muffin crumb from the counter with a moistened finger. She pointed at the screen. "I'm exhausted just watching them."

"I still can't believe that you went out with that guy. It's not at all like you to give in to pressure."

"You never met Mrs. Haggerty."

"And I hope I never will," Kaye said. "When did you speak to Ellen?"

"Yesterday . . . yes, yesterday afternoon."

"Yesterday. Love was such an easy game to play—"

"Stop! I can't take it."

"Sorry. It is kind of fun, though."

"You see? That's what my life is like." Barbara got up to pour herself another cup of coffee. She was exhausted, though she had slept well. "More coffee?"

"Sure."

"He was actually a pretty nice guy. He even knew the difference between fiction and nonfiction," Barbara said. "And he had a sense of humor."

"So? What's the deal? No spark?"

"Spark? You must be joking. I was glad I could follow the conversation. Based on that alone, I even thought about letting him come back here."

"Oh?" Kaye said. She turned off the television. "And then what happened?"

It would have been so easy to tell Kaye about Delilah. It would have explained so much, but instead Barbara just shrugged. Delilah's stories were so intimate, so personal. The Delilah persona had become Barbara's diary, and no one willingly shared her diary, not even with a best friend.

"I guess I chickened out," Barbara said. "I did kiss him, or at least, I let him kiss me."

"How was that?" Kaye said.

"Let's just say that it didn't make me gag. That's good as far as I'm concerned."

"Sorry. It should be more than that, especially the kissing," Kaye said. "The kissing usually tells everything."

"Where were you last night, anyway?" Barbara said.

"Last night?" Kaye blew on her coffee, though it was no longer hot. "Why do you ask?"

"Because I called, and George said you were out."

"Out?" Kaye said. "Last night?"

"Out. Last night." Barbara turned to look at her oddly. "You okay?"

"Oh, I went to the mall with Rose. You remember Rose, don't you?"

"The woman you did that stuff with for the Breast Cancer Walk?"

"Yes, that's Rose."

"But I called you at eleven thirty," Barbara said.

"We went out for coffee," Kaye said. "You sound jealous."

"Yes, Kaye, I'm definitely jealous of Rose," Barbara said. "Actually, your husband was the one who sounded jealous."

"George? Jealous?"

"Yes, George."

"Oh, he's fine. He just doesn't like it when I go out without him. I told him to get some friends."

"Or at the very least, a twenty-two-year-old girlfriend," Barbara said.

"That would be fine," Kaye said.

"Would it be?" Barbara said. "I don't believe you."

"Oh, I don't know. I guess sometimes it seems like it would."

"You wouldn't be jealous?"

"I guess, or relieved. I don't know anymore."

"I understand," Barbara said.

"So, how's the new book going? What is it a sweeping saga of this time?"

"It's the same sweeping saga, just different characters and a different setting," Barbara said.

"Sounds suspiciously like life," Kaye said.

"It is life, only an improved version," Barbara said.

Kaye walked over to the window and drew back the curtain.

"It stopped raining," she said. "Want to walk?"

Barbara immediately turned the television back on and smiled.

"I'd rather watch," she said.

"Now, put that in one of your novels," Kaye said. "You'll pick up a male readership."

"Do I want that?" Barbara said.

And she already was considering the possibility, already writing the scene in her head. *Lydia was the one who suggested a threesome with her sister, though everyone would probably guess it had been his idea. Not that he didn't love the idea, of course. Cheyenne was as beautiful as Lydia with even larger breasts . . .*

Six

SOON after Bill was out of her life, Ellen discovered a cable station that featured a program aptly called *Animal Miracle Stories*. It fascinated her, though she had no pets of her own. Bill had been allergic to cats, and he disliked dogs. As Ellen became more and more engrossed in the feats of ordinary household pets, she realized that Bill's dislike of animals should have alerted her to his shortcomings. How could anyone resist a beautiful yellow Labrador like Misty? In the middle of one very cold winter night, Misty woke from her cozy spot at the foot of her owner's bed and realized that something was terribly wrong. The astonishing dramatization showed how after some preliminary sniffing, Misty sensed that her owner was in trouble. Amazingly, Misty dialed 911, alerting the local police to the situation by barking into the phone. Within minutes, an ambulance was on the way, and Misty (obviously, no ordinary Lab) was invited to ride in the ambulance with her grateful owner. Ellen clutched her pillow to her chest and sobbed as she watched Misty receive a medal from her community volunteer ambulance corps. Ellen would not have been any prouder if Misty had been her dog.

Misty was the start of Ellen's addiction to *Animal Miracle Stories*. She found herself thinking about the show while she was at work or on the way home from the grocery. She eyed dogs and cats with new interest, wondering about each one's potential for heroism. The story of Jewel, the tabby who woke her owners and prevented the death of their newborn from SIDS, sent Ellen into hysterics until it was certain that the infant was out of danger. Oh, to have such a cat. Ellen was overcome with envy. Even more inspirational was the story of Gismo, the cat who found her way back home after an absence of eight years. Gismo's family had been forced to relinquish her after their son developed a serious allergy. Apparently, Gismo never quite adjusted to her new life because she traveled more than two hundred miles, hoping to be reunited with her original owners. Such devotion, Ellen marveled. Such loyalty. She was filled with the most unimaginable longing to be so loved, so wanted. After the Gismo episode, Ellen decided there was something worrisome about the feelings these segments provoked. It was late, but she had to talk to someone. She called Kaye, but George said she was out. Hesitantly, she called Barbara, who was unusually sympathetic, though she asked Ellen if she had first phoned Kaye.

"You did," Barbara said, "didn't you?"

"Yes," Ellen admitted. "It's not that I don't trust you, but you can be so hard sometimes."

"Maybe it's a defense mechanism?"

"I don't think so," Ellen said. "Do you?"

"No," Barbara said with exaggerated sadness. "I think I'm just a bitch."

"So, you're not offended?"

"Of course I'm offended." Barbara dragged hard on her plastic cigarette. "Shouldn't I be?"

"Are you smoking?" Ellen said.

"Plastic. Have you seen that show about freaky accidents? I'm not really sure what it's called, but I watched it all the time after Roger died."

"No, I never saw it. Is it good?"

"Good?" Barbara said. "There was this one kid who survived lightning that came up through the ground. He was virtually electrocuted, and he lived."

"That is fantastic," Ellen said. "But not more fantastic than Gismo. Can you imagine how much that cat must have loved her owners? Can you imagine anyone loving you that much?"

"No, I guess not. I mean, I love my kids that much, but I don't think they love me that much back."

As soon as the words were out, Barbara wished she could take them back. References to children were always painful for Ellen, but lately it seemed hard for her to breathe when there was even the slightest suggestion of babies or children in general.

Ellen went on as if she had not heard. "And that tabby who saved the infant. Well, *that* was truly inspirational."

"I'm sure it was," Barbara said. "But I still think the show about freaky accidents and their survivors is much better."

"You never saw my show," Ellen protested.

"Your show?" Barbara said, laughing. "Well, in that case, you never saw mine."

"I guess." Ellen sighed. "So you don't think I'm crazy?"

"I never said that," Barbara said.

"Do you think I need antidepressants?"

"I think everyone needs antidepressants."

"I think I need something," Ellen said in a voice so small that she barely heard herself. "I definitely think I need something."

"Have you spoken to Bill recently?"

"No, not for a while."

Ellen had called him at the office a few times, but she always hung up before Lisa, his secretary, answered. It was just too humiliating to speak to her. Instead, Ellen e-mailed Bill if she had to share any information. His responses were curt, businesslike, and without any trace of remorse or affection. Sometimes she stared at the computer screen, wondering how it was possible that this was the same man who had cut the crusts from her sandwiches after she had oral surgery and who brought her chamomile tea on a tray before bed, rubbing the back of her neck with so much enthusiasm that it made her wonder how it came to pass that she was lucky to finally be so loved. Now he sent her e-mails that had neither a salutation nor a closing. He never even signed his name anymore. It was all about facts and numbers. The messages were so terse that they felt like an assault. She recoiled when she read them. Once or twice, she had even covered her eyes, peering through her fingers.

"I'm sorry," Barbara said. "He treated you very badly."

"Yes, I know he did." Ellen swallowed hard, trying not to cry. "Tell me about another freaky accident. A really gory one."

Eager to oblige, Barbara told Ellen about a young electrician who lost his balance on a ladder and immediately dropped his electric drill, basic safety protocol for even the most amateur apprentice. Regrettably, he could not regain his balance and fell, landing squarely on the drill. It pierced the back of his skull and came straight through his forehead. A team of skilled emergency room doctors managed to remove the drill and save his life. The drill had missed his brain by millimeters. It was a true freaky survival story, Barbara noted in her final summation.

"I have to give it to you. That *was* freaky and fantastic," Ellen said. "I am genuinely impressed."

"I told you so," Barbara said.

"I still think my show is more uplifting."

"Uplifting is good, but I would rather be wowed than be uplifted."

"If you say so. " Ellen cleared her throat and said, "You never liked Bill, did you?"

"This is a bad idea," Barbara said.

"Just answer the question," Ellen said.

"It's such an unfair question," Barbara whined. If Kaye had been there, she would have given Barbara a warning look. But without Kaye, Barbara was left to her own poor judgment. She should have insisted that she liked everything about Bill, but that was not her way. "I guess I didn't like that he was so fussy about everything."

"What do you mean by fussy?"

"Everything had to be so perfect. Even you. It always struck me as sort of degrading."

"Gosh, Barb, I'm always so surprised at how uncharitable you can be."

"You asked me," Barbara said. "Isn't there anything about him that you didn't like?"

It was so silent on the other end that Barbara thought they had been disconnected. But it only took her seconds to realize that the silence meant that Ellen really still loved William Formerly Known as Bill. So when she finally answered, it was evident that she had struggled to think of something that might be considered damning, something that would exonerate her as the ill-used wife, the one who was always the last to know.

"He didn't care for animals," Ellen said. She sounded pleased with herself. "I don't trust people who don't like animals."

"That's the best you can do?" Barbara said.

"What do you want me to say? You want me to say that I don't like Bill because he betrayed me and then left me? Isn't that sort of obvious?" Ellen said. "That's not the worst of what Bill did to me.

The worst is that I let the years go by and gave in to his insistence that we didn't need to be parents. He said his life was complete with me at his side. We had each other, he told me. We didn't need children. And now he's going to have a baby, and I'm alone, truly alone."

"I'm so sorry, Ellen."

"That's all right. I'll think of something else to do with my life."

"Ellen, do you want me to come down there? I can call Kaye, and we can pick up some food and head down."

"Thanks, but no. I'm fine. I just felt I was headed for a melt-down," Ellen said. "Anyway, Kaye probably isn't even home yet. She's been so busy lately. And when we do speak, she seems so distant."

"She has been, hasn't she?"

"She gets like this sometimes. But never like this," Ellen said.

"Maybe it's us," Barbara said. "Maybe she's sick of hearing us complain. She listens to people's complaints all day long."

"True, but she complains too . . . though not as much lately . . . ," Ellen said. "Anyway, how are your kids? I haven't seen them in ages."

After Barbara quickly brought Ellen up to date, they agreed to meet on the weekend for dinner, maybe a movie.

"You'll be all right," Barbara said. "It's hard to start over, but you're smart and strong."

"I think I need a miracle."

"I didn't know you really believed in miracles."

"All reasonable people believe in miracles," Ellen said with conviction.

She had evidently given miracles a great deal of thought.

*   *   *

THE last time Ellen went out to dinner with Bill alone before the black-tie catastrophe, she felt apprehensive in a way that could only, in retrospect, be acknowledged as a premonition. In their favorite Chinese restaurant where large bowls of noodle soup were the house specialty, the commotion was always a bit alarming. Amid the cacophony of hastily spoken Cantonese, the crash and clang of dishes, and the blur of waiters and waitresses scurrying with plates of steaming food, Ellen noticed a young woman thoroughly absorbed in her bowl of soup. She was probably just thirty, if that, and she was dressed demurely in a pale yellow sleeveless blouse with a round collar (the sort they had called a Peter Pan collar in Ellen's day). The young woman was thin, but not skinny, her neck long and exquisite, rising from her jutting collarbones (the top few buttons of her blouse were open) like a piece of modern sculpture. Soft, dark curls framed her brow, but the rest of her hair was pulled away from her narrow face, revealing enormous brown eyes accentuated by thick though shapely eyebrows. Although she was beautiful, this was not what held Ellen's attention. The young woman's unhurried solitude was compelling. Totally committed to her bowl of soup, she lifted spoonful after spoonful to her full lips, parting them widely to receive the broth studded with broad noodles, broccoli, carrots, pea pods, tiny ears of corn, tofu, shrimp, and chicken. Ellen watched these delicate morsels disappear between the young woman's lips until she looked up and their eyes met. She neither smiled nor looked defensive. She had a bowl of soup to finish, and she was diligent in her task. Her temerity endeared her to Ellen, who suspected that in similar circumstances, she would have been reluctant to meet the eyes of a stranger, fearing everything from pity to loathing. After all, the sight of someone eating alone in a restaurant was generally more discomfiting than inspiring.

Several months later, Ellen was having dinner alone in the same restaurant. She waited for her bowl of soup to be served, remembering the young woman who had eaten every drop, even unabash-edly tilting the bowl on its side to scrape up every last morsel. Bill had noticed her too, looking away in discomfort. Ellen now real-ized that the young woman was probably the same age as his Daisy. Ellen had said that she admired the girl, emphasizing how awkward it could be to eat alone in a restaurant. She never really liked to eat alone herself, she said, and Bill had nodded without much enthusi-asm. But she had persisted, almost driven by his already foul mood. Did he ever eat alone in a restaurant? The question had hit a nerve, and Bill, inexplicably irritated, jumped up and excused himself. And then Ellen had known that his reaction was not really about her questions or her endless musings, but about the future she was going to inherit as a result of his selfish folly.

"Soup?" the waiter asked.

"Yes," Ellen said. "Thank you."

He asked if she wanted another bottle of Tsingtao, but she said no thank you. It was a large bottle, and she still had some left. The waiter was not listening anyway. She stared into her soup, remem-bering. Sometimes Ellen thought it must be easier to be widowed than a woman scorned. Widows were treated reverentially, but wives who had been replaced by younger and firmer flesh were carefully scrutinized to see what part they had played in the aban-donment. She smiled at the waiter, who gruffly asked if she would like anything else.

"Just some more tea, please, and some of those almond cookies."

He whisked away her bowl and utensils, wiping the table with a cloth that seemed to come from nowhere.

"Ellen? It is Ellen, isn't it?"

She gazed mildly into the eyes of a stranger, a rather handsome man, wondering how he knew her name. Ellen was feeling a little sleepy from the beer, a little groggy in general.

"Do I know you?" Ellen said.

"Anthony," he said. "Anthony Masters. You look terrific."

Ellen did indeed look terrific. Barbara always said Ellen was a classic beauty. She dressed in the fashion of women who came from old money. It was a look she had acquired by studying her clients. She favored slim-cut pants, tailored jackets, and silk blouses, but she looked well in dresses and skirts, wearing them with reasonably high heels, just high enough to show off her shapely legs. That evening, she was wearing a black skirt, a black silk blouse, and black-and-white stadium pumps. Her only jewelry was a pair of sizable diamond studs and an expensive watch that had been last year's Christmas present from Bill. Men found Ellen's restraint irresistible, even proper. Bill had always told her that every man dreams of bedding a lady and inspiring her to be unladylike.

Anthony Masters. The name meant nothing to her, and his face was an even greater mystery.

"I'm sorry," she said. "I'm not very good with names."

"It's been a very long time."

"Oh?"

"Thirty years, at least."

"Really? You're from Connecticut?"

"Actually, no. I'm from Rhode Island. We met a few times at U Conn. I was Sam Benedict's roommate."

It was a name she had not heard spoken out loud in so long that it seemed as though he had never existed. The last contact Ellen had with Sam was when she saw his signature on the relinquishment papers, terminating his rights as Faith's father. His signature guaranteed that there would be no problems later on. No one even spoke his name out loud then. She saw her parents exchange glances as she docilely signed all the documents. Her parents had appointed an attorney to contact Sam. He had not even known Ellen was pregnant. She overheard the attorney tell her parents that it was a standard line. Ellen had not argued; there was no point. Later, when she was able to be alone with the attorney for a few minutes, Ellen asked if Sam had wanted to contact her. The attorney shook his head and smiled, assuring her that the young man had been very pleasant. After all, it was for the best, the lawyer insisted. They were both too young. He had done hundreds of these adoptions. "You're doing the right thing for you and for your baby," he assured her. She noticed that he never made eye contact with her, not even once.

Ellen had actually forgotten that Sam's last name was Benedict. And she was stunned that this man remembered her. She searched his face for something familiar, but there was nothing. Ellen and a few other local girls had traveled the thirty or so miles to Storrs, desperate to escape the tedium of weekends at home where there was one movie theater and nothing much else to do except drink beer or smoke pot down at the beach with the same people you had known since kindergarten. When one of the girls, Marcy, met a boy from the University of Connecticut on the train, she invited Ellen and a few other girls to accompany her to a fraternity party. Marcy had lied about her age, so it was easy for all of them to pretend they were older. They drove to Storrs for the weekend in Marcy's parents' car, allegedly attending a college recruitment weekend. They had a great time and spent the night in the room of the boy Marcy had met on the train. He gave up his room to them because his roommate was in West Virginia for a family funeral. Ellen remembered that Marcy's friend had been a gentleman. She felt light-headed and sick to her stomach as she remembered the party and how stupidly she had behaved. It was possible that Anthony knew what had resulted from her night with Sam, but it was also possible that Sam had never said anything.

"You were Marcy's friend," Ellen said. "She met you on the train. We stayed in your room."

Anthony smiled. "Yes, that was me." He shook his head. "You look exactly the same."

"You were a real gentleman then too." She held out her hand. "I'm flattered that you remember me."

"You were the prettiest girl there," he said. "Everyone thought so."

"Everyone was very drunk." She looked past him and asked, "Are you alone? Would you like to join me for some tea?"

"Yes to both questions." He slid into the booth across from her. "What about you? What are you doing here all alone?"

Ellen signaled the waiter for another cup, holding hers aloft. He brought one almost immediately, and she noticed that her hand shook as she poured the tea. Hoping to distract Anthony, she pushed the plate of almond cookies toward him.

"Have one," she said. "It will be one less that I eat. I'm crazy for them."

Anthony obediently took a cookie and bit into it. Then he took a big gulp of the hot tea, draining the small cup.

"So, you never answered my question," he said.

"I live in the neighborhood. This is a favorite local haunt."

"Married?"

"Yes," Ellen said. "I'm married." She stared at him, daring him to ask if she had any children. "What about you?"

"Oh, I've been married." He held up three fingers. "This many times."

"Why?" she said.

"I keep hoping to get it right."

"I see. And do you live in the city?"

"Actually, no. I still live in Rhode Island. Newport."

"Lovely there. We used to spend a week there in the summer."

"It's even nicer off-season."

"I'm sure." Ellen was beginning to regret her invitation. She was running out of conversation. "So what do you do?"

"I'm an attorney. Estates, wills, that sort of thing."

And you're in town on business? All the way from Rhode Island?" Ellen said. "New York is full of attorneys."

"Well, this was a special favor for an old family friend."

"How sweet." She looked at her watch. "It's so late. I hadn't realized . . . early morning meeting tomorrow."

"With?"

"Oh, I'm an interior designer."

"Interesting work. You look the part."

"Is that a compliment?"

"Definitely." Anthony reached into his pocket and took out a business card. "If you're ever in Rhode Island, with your husband, your whole family, of course."

"Thank you," she said. "I'll keep it in mind."

"Do you go home much?" Anthony said.

"As little as possible. We're a very dysfunctional family."

"Welcome to the club. I'm afraid it's not terribly elite."

Ellen nodded to show her agreement, and then took out her credit card and placed it on the tray the waiter had left with her bill and a packet of fortune cookies. She held up the tray to get the waiter's attention.

"Are you going to eat those?" Anthony said, pointing to the fortune cookies. "I'm crazy for them."

"They're yours." She pushed the cellophane packet toward him. "Just keep your fortune to yourself. I've had enough surprises for one day." She caught his injured look. "Oh, not you. I'm sorry. That came out all wrong."

"No offense taken." He opened the packet and broke one of the cookies in half, reading the fortune before popping both halves into his mouth. "Stale. I hate that. You know Sam Benedict died."

Ellen looked around frantically for the waiter who had still not taken her credit card. She needed some air.

"Was that in your fortune cookie?" she said, sounding more flip than she had intended. Mean, really. It was a dreadful response. "I'm sorry. I don't know why I said that."

"It's all right. It was a real tragedy. He left behind a wife and three children. The family was devastated."

"I can imagine," Ellen said. She paused while the waiter finally took her credit card and the check. "Poor family. What did he die of?"

Just as Anthony was about to answer, Ellen decided she would rather not know and said, "Actually, I don't want to know."

Poor Anthony seemed just slightly taken aback, but he was so well mannered that he seemed more concerned with her discomfort and smoothly changed course.

"I never had any children," he said. "My second and third wives each had kids, but I never see them now."

"I'm sorry. That's very sad. And so is the news about Sam. Frankly, I don't think I would have recognized him if I ever saw him again." The waiter brought back the check with the printed credit card receipt and waited while she added a tip and signed. She acknowledged his thanks with a cursory nod and said, "Well, it's been interesting to see you."

"He would have recognized you."

Ellen looked up. She had been folding her receipt and placing it in her wallet. She was momentarily confused. "Who? Who would have recognized me?"

"Sam."

She touched the teapot. Surprisingly, it was still hot, and she left her hand there, suddenly feeling cold.

"I didn't mean to upset you," Anthony said. "I was stunned to see you."

"I don't have any children, if you were wondering."

"I was."

"So, that's all settled now." She stood and held out her hand. "Good luck to you, especially if you get married again." Her coat was hanging on the rack in the front of the restaurant. "I'd better be going."

"Yes, and thank you. I probably will get married again. I'm an optimist."

"How unfortunate," Ellen said, smiling wryly at this very nice man. "I'm glad for you."

They walked to the front of the restaurant together, and Anthony held her coat. They shook hands again, promising to stay in touch even though she had not given him one of her business cards. She got a cab right away. As soon as she settled into the darkness of the backseat, Ellen cried for Sam Benedict, who had died, and then for their daughter and all the unknowns in their lives.

Seven

THURSDAY was Kaye's regular day to drive down to visit her mother, Gertie. When Ruby and Charlie were little, Kaye used to go more often, leaving them with their grandmother several times a week. It was a good arrangement for everyone. Gertie loved her grandchildren and escorted them through Manhattan's busy streets, introducing them to neighbors, shopkeepers, the man at the newspaper stand, waiters and waitresses in her favorite hangouts, and even the police officers who slowed down as they patrolled in their cruiser to say hello. "Who needs Disney World," Gertie said, "when you can walk the streets of Manhattan?" The children seemed to agree. When Kaye came to pick them up, they regaled her with tales of their adventures. For Kaye, it was a joy to watch her mother with her grandchildren. She indulged them as she had never indulged Kaye or Solly. There was no time or energy for such nonsense when Gertie was a younger woman. She had two children to raise and a husband to keep house for with no help from anyone. But Gertie's causes took up most of her energy. Homelessness, the neighborhood watches, and Israel led the long list of her concerns. She was on countless committees, attended endless meetings, and could always be found with a clipboard and a petition in hand, going door-to-door, getting signatures or collecting money for something.

Gertie was one of the children of the famed *Kindertransports*. Her Hungarian parents had relinquished their two daughters to Great Britain under an agreement that allowed ten thousand unaccompanied Jewish children safe passage. Gertie was only eight years old when her smiling parents said good-bye to her and to her older sister, Bernice, and stood waving until they thought the girls could no longer see them. But Gertie saw. Her elegant mother, who had dressed for the occasion in her fur stole, had told her girls that it was a special day, a day to celebrate freedom. But when Gertie saw her father brace her collapsed mother, it was evident they would never see each other again. Later, Gertie and Bernice would learn that their parents had died in Auschwitz, just days before the liberation. The two sisters eventually left England and made their way to America when they were eighteen and twenty, accepting scholarships to Barnard endowed by one of many anonymous sponsors.

Kaye had heard the stories so many times that she often did not know where her own memory really began and her mother's took over. Gertie claimed the stories were intended to inspire courage in her American-born children and to teach them that true love is unselfish. But in Kaye's childhood dreams, she was often the little red-cheeked girl with the stitched knapsack, waving good-bye to her mother for the last time. It was all confused in her head, and she had nightmares that shook her and made her muffle her screams in her pillow. Her brother, Solly, used to console her, bringing her a glass of water when he heard her cries in the middle of the night. He was a good older brother, protecting her from the tough Irish neighborhood girls and holding her hand when they crossed the street. Gertie told them, "I have two eyes in my head. One for each of you." Izzy, their father, always added, "And I have two fists, one for each of you." He would brandish his clenched fists at them and send them scattering, screaming and pretending to be scared. Of course, it was all a game. Izzy never raised a hand to either of them. Gertie was the one who gave them an occasional pinch or slap and then only if they were, as she explained, asking for it.   .

Izzy was long gone, having succumbed to heart failure when he was merely sixty. Ruby and Charlie were still babies, and they had no memory of their grandfather, who had found every detail of their existence a phenomenon. "How did they come to be so beautiful?" Izzy always marveled. "And such geniuses?" Gertie had remarried twice, both times to survivors. She claimed there was no way to live with someone who had not directly experienced the Holocaust. For a time, she dated a very nice man who had been one of the American soldiers who liberated Bergen-Belsen, but this did not qualify him for marriage. "I should marry a man," she said, "who thought he saved the Jews with Hershey bars?" Gertie was a woman of strong opinions. Once her mind was made up, there was no way to persuade her to change. Ten years after Izzy's death, she married Morty, a Communist who still attended party meetings and spoke six languages. Solly was horrified, but Kaye convinced him that it was good for all of them. And Morty was a decent man even though Ruby and Charlie did not care for him at all. They claimed he smelled like mothballs. Kaye actually liked Morty. He was articulate and clever, and he adored Gertie. They were the same age, seventy, and it was clear the sex was still good. Once Kaye walked in on them in the kitchen. Morty was standing behind Gertie while she was chopping vegetables for soup. He was nuzzling her neck and fondling her breasts through her blouse while she kept chopping and laughing. "Oh, Kaye, darling," she said when she realized Kaye was frozen in the doorway. "Sorry," she said, even though Morty continued his hold of her breasts, clearly determined not to relinquish his bounty until Gertie shook him off. After Morty died, Gertie was inconsolable. Then she had her eyes done and seemed to recover. She looked great, and a year later she was married again. This time it was to a survivor of the Warsaw Ghetto Uprising. Chaim was a dear, and Gertie seemed very happy until she caught him in their bedroom with Aunt Trudy during a Passover seder. "A *chutzpah*," Gertie said, "in my bedroom." Though Chaim pleaded and begged and swore it would never happen again, Gertie divorced him and never spoke to Aunt Trudy again. The truth be known, Gertie never cared much for Trudy. She was Izzy's sister, and it was a relief to have an excuse to be rid of her. By then, Gertie was seventy-nine, and she said if she wanted a man, she would take a lover. No more marriage for her.

Gertie lived alone in the same apartment where she had raised two children and outlived two husbands. She refused all help, except the cleaning woman who came once a week to straighten up and do some laundry, maybe a few errands, but only if the weather was bad. This arrangement was agreeable to Gertie because she felt she was helping the young single mother from El Salvador. Every morning, weather permitting, Gertie went to the gym, lifted weights, and rode a stationary bike. Then she did her shopping, alternating between the greengrocer and the fishmonger (as she still called them), and once a week she went to the kosher butcher for a pullet to make soup for her grandchildren, and occasionally for a little beef or lamb for a nice stew, especially in the winter. She was active in the Democratic Party, played bridge two or three times a week, volunteered in the local public school as a mentor, and came in to read with children. Ruby called her a few times a week, and they had lunch together at least twice a month. Charlie took her to the opera and to the theater several times a year. She sent money to every *Kindertransport* organization that had her on its mailing list, but she refused to attend any reunions and declined to correspond with anyone from that time in her life. "What's done is done," Gertie said. Her sister Bernice had returned to Great Britain, finding America too big and too loud. She married and raised a family, but her relationship with Gertie was strained at best. Bernice felt too great a need to revisit their years after they said good-bye to their parents, and Gertie felt that good-bye was good-bye.

So this was Kaye's legacy. It was a formidable task to live up to Gertie's forte as a survivor. Her intensity and forcefulness made any sign of weakness seem shameful. Gertie faced aging as she had faced everything else, taking it on as a challenge. Her struggle, she said, was to remain human until the very end. Her kitchen windowsill was lined with bottles of vitamins that promised to stave off memory loss, heart disease, arthritis, and poor circulation. She ate lots of green vegetables and fruits, excluding refined sugar and white flour from her diet. She thought depression was nonsense and indecisiveness a character flaw. And she thought adultery was a luxury for the weak, a consequence of an undisciplined life. If women wanted to fool around with different men, that was fine, but you had to wait for your husband to die and marry a new one. Marriage, according to Gertie, was a commitment, a promise.

Kaye shared her mother's beliefs about marriage and had never been unfaithful to George until now. And Kaye had certainly never expected to fall in love with anyone else. Soon after Kaye started to see Frank, she began to lie to her mother. First, Kaye began substituting their weekly visits with additional phone calls and begging off visits with the excuse that she had an extra patient load that she had taken on for a sick colleague. Some of it was true, but most of it was a way to avoid her mother's scrutiny. Kaye spoke quickly and in a high-pitched voice whenever she called Gertie, who never, by the way, questioned Kaye's absence or challenged any of her excuses. All Gertie ever told Kaye was to take care of herself and to be smart. Kaye found both requests impossibly intimidating.

It had been almost three weeks since Kaye had driven to her childhood neighborhood in the Fort Washington section of Manhattan. The neighborhood had remained fairly stable, even enjoying a rebirth as savvy buyers swarmed uptown, eager to escape the prohibitive cost of real estate that a fifteen- or twenty-minute subway ride could reduce. Now the apartments that had once seemed dark and cavernous to Kaye were at the center of price wars that made her head spin. Gertie had bought her apartment as soon as the building went co-op, and it had been a sound investment. She had two bedrooms and a sunken living room the size of most city dwellers' apartments. Gertie had wisely never tampered with either the wall sconces or the period plaster moldings that were intertwined like rope around the living room walls. Most of her old neighbors either were dead or had moved to Florida. For a while, Kaye had been determined to have Gertie move as well. George and Kaye had even flown down to Fort Lauderdale and driven to various senior communities. They were all very nice, and the people who lived there were tanned and pleasant. But Kaye could not imagine her feisty mother basking in the tropical sun. She did not even like to spend a weekend with Kaye in suburbia. "It's only twenty minutes by car, Mom," Kaye argued. That did not matter to Gertie. If she could not get there by subway, she was not interested in going. End of discussion.

There was no traffic as Kaye breezed down the parkway. The river was beautiful on this clear morning, and the George Washington Bridge looked stately in the distance. Adjusting her headset, Kaye pressed a button on her cell phone and waited for her mother to answer.

"Yes?" Gertie said.

"Mom?"

"Kaye? Where are you?"

Though Gertie had become a whiz on the computer they had bought for her two years ago, she resisted the cell phone, claiming it was not such an advantage to be reached at all times. In fact, her number was the only one Kaye could still call and reach a busy signal.

"I'm in the car, Mom. It's Thursday."

"I know what day of the week it is, Kaye."

"Should I have called first?"

"You're calling now," Gertie said. "I'll put up a fresh pot of coffee. Did you eat yet?"

"No, Mom, I haven't eaten. Would you like to go out?"

"What out? I'm already scrambling the eggs."

Kaye laughed because it was probably true. She could hear the dishes rattling in the cupboard.

"I stopped for some bagels," she said. "And those cinnamon buns you love."

Gertie was the same size that she had been when she married Kaye's father. Trim and compact, she had never battled weight the way Kaye had most of her life. Gertie claimed Kaye had her mother's beauty and her father's appetite.

"Thank you," Gertie said. "I'll be happy to see you."

Luckily, Kaye found a parking spot right in front of the building. She smiled because it had been her father's favorite spot, right next to a streetlamp and directly under their living room window where he could check on the car during the night. They had all teased him that he loved his cars more than his family, and he never argued. Kaye gathered her bags and paused for a moment, taking a deep breath before entering the apartment building. She always felt a little bit like Alice must have just before she fell down the rabbit hole. There was a sort of hallucinatory effect that occurred each time Kaye stepped into the lobby of the building. Maybe it was the memories of the boys she had kissed in the elevator, or the sound of her angry footsteps echoing in the hallway as she raced out of the apartment, slamming the door and shouting something horrible at her mother. Today, however, it was none of these. It was Frank. Kaye felt that her mother would see the imprints of his hands all over her daughter's body, the mark of his lips on her cheeks and lips.

Gertie answered the door, wiping her hands on a dish towel. Kaye swore that if she pulled back her mother's skin just ever so slightly and dyed her gray hair brown, fifty years would drop away like nothing. The house smelled exactly the same, fragrant with whatever soup she was cooking, and filled with sunlight. Gertie eschewed drapes and curtains, grudgingly yielding to blinds or shades and only then as a bow to modesty. The windows were always clean, and the shades always up, inviting sunlight to wash over the rooms.

"There's my beauty," Gertie said, tucking the towel into her waistband to free her arms for a hug and proffering her face for a kiss. "Ah, it's wonderful to see you."

"Hi, Mom," Kaye said. She wanted to hug her mother more tightly, but she suddenly seemed so breakable in her arms. Three weeks was not very long, but Gertie looked older, frailer. "You look thin."

"I do? Come in, come in. Don't stand in the doorway. The coffee is going to run over. Come, come."

Gertie still perked coffee on the stove, replacing her coffeepot every few years with exactly the same one. Ruby swore that Gertie must have bought a hundred of them at one time and kept them locked up in a vault somewhere.

"The coffee smells great," Kaye said.

She set her bags on the counter and smiled at the set table. If Kaye closed her eyes, she could pretend she and Solly were at the kitchen table doing homework, waiting for their father to return home from work. Gertie would shout to them to keep an eye on the soup while she was out on the fire escape smoking a cigarette. Even though Kaye and Solly each had a desk in the room they shared, they preferred the kitchen, where pots bubbled on the stove and the phone rang incessantly, always for Gertie.

"So?" Gertie said. "Sit. The eggs are ready. Sit."

"Aren't you going to have something?" Kaye said.

"No, no. I had my breakfast at five. I'll have some soup in a little while. I made mushroom barley. You'll take some home for George. He loves my mushroom barley."

Kaye lowered her eyes and nodded. She felt her cheeks grow hot, and she busied herself with the plate of eggs. They were delicious, and she was hungrier than she had thought. There was one slice of toasted rye bread, no butter. Gertie did not believe in butter.

"Tell me something new," Gertie said. "How is Barbara? Is she dating anyone special?"

"No, no one special."

"But she goes out? A young woman shouldn't be alone."

"What about an old woman?" Kaye said.

"When I meet an old woman who's alone, I'll be sure to ask."

Gertie reached over for Kaye's hand and held it for just a moment before pulling away and wrapping both hands around her steaming mug of coffee.

"What about Ellen? I always liked that Bill," Gertie said, shaking her head. "Who would have figured him for such a louse?"

"Didn't you always tell me that you wouldn't put your hand in the fire for any man?"

"Yes, but Bill, he was always such a gentleman. I don't know." She sighed. "You know, I heard that Chaim died. Your Aunt Trudy sent me a note. She knew I would hang up if she called."

"Really? I mean about Chaim. That's sad. I liked him in spite of his weakness for women."

"He was a great lover, that Chaim." Gertie's voice got a little dreamy. "I think about him a lot just before I go to sleep." She waved her hand. "What's the use? An old woman like me, remembering what it used to feel like to be desirable."

"I bet there are a lot of men out there who would still find you desirable."

"Oh, really?" Gertie laughed and waved her hand. "Nah. I'm too old for any more nonsense."

"You still dream about sex, apparently."

Gertie looked over the top of her glasses at Kaye and said, "Are you working now, darling? Or is this about you?"

It was uncanny how well Gertie could always cut to the heart of a conversation. Kaye's father, Izzy, used to say that Gertie was like a surgeon, except her tongue was the knife. She slashed through empty dialogue with precision, getting right to the wound, ever confident that exorcising the infected area was the fastest way to heal.

"What if it is about me?" Kaye said.

"What if it is about me?" Gertie said.

"Okay," Kaye said. "You first. Tell me about growing old."

"Growing old? I'm already old. The funny thing about it is that you're never really different on the inside. It's always a surprise to remember that I'm eighty-two. I can't imagine such a thing. When did it happen? Sometimes, just before I open my eyes, I think I hear your father snoring, and then I wonder why I didn't hear you cry or why Solly didn't bring you to me. He used to take you out of the crib and bring you to my bed. Then I used to nurse you and play with his hair. Such a time it was, all curled up with my family. I thought I was the only mother in the world. And now it's gone. A dream."

Nodding, Kaye swallowed hard. She remembered her own children small and warm and in love with her. They were so perfect, so incredibly beautiful. And their eyes followed her wherever she moved, latching on to her as if they knew that as long as she was in their sight, they were safe.

"Remember when everyone had a potato baker?" Gertie said.

"What?"

"A potato baker." She stood and rummaged around in a cabinet until she produced hers, a worn and very familiar flat metal apparatus that was placed over a gas burner. "No one even knows what a potato baker is anymore. Everyone uses the microwave. You can't make a good baked potato in the microwave." She rubbed the tired cover of the potato baker and then looked up brightly. "How long are you staying?"

"Long enough to have a good baked potato," Kaye said.

While Gertie washed two large Idaho potatoes, dried them, and then made holes in them with a fork, Kaye talked about her work and how frustrating it was when a patient did not seem to be making progress or when it was clear that someone would never get it, never be able to take that next step.

"Never? It's not a word I'm familiar with." Gertie turned the flame on under the potato baker and adjusted the flame under the pot of soup. Using a wooden spoon, she stirred the soup and then brought a spoonful to her mouth, blowing first on the thick broth. After she tasted it, she said, "A good soup can be better than sex." She sat down again across from Kaye. "You seem impatient. Not just with your work, but with life."

"Maybe just a little. Maybe I need a potato baker."

"I don't think you would use it."

"You underestimate me, Mom," Kaye said.

She squirmed a little under her mother's gaze and tried to make a joke, suggesting that if any of life's ills could really be solved with the purchase of an inexpensive utensil, the government should provide one for every family.

"I never underestimate you, Kaye," Gertie said, ignoring her joke.

"I was just teasing, Mom."

"You never just tease, my darling daughter. More coffee?"

"No, thanks. So, have you been feeling well?"

"Me? According to my age, I'd say I'm doing well. I feel very good."

"You look very good," Kaye said. "For an old lady."

She meant it. Gertie was wearing the earrings that Ruby had brought back from Mexico. Each small gold disc had a tiny turquoise stone in the center, setting off Gertie's eyes. She wore her silver-gray hair short with the front pieces tucked behind her ears, giving her a sort of irresistible gamine quality. Charlie teased her that she was a fox, and she loved it. Today she was wearing a black velour pantsuit and her favorite necklace, a gift from Charlie. It was a silver pendant with the Chinese symbol for individuality. She wore it all the time, claiming that this year she was going to have it tattooed on the back of her neck. Kaye knew this was a real possibility.

"You look troubled," Gertie said. "Beautiful, but troubled."

Kaye ran a hand through her hair. It had grown back some, but it was still really short. She had just had the color done the other day, adding some highlights.

"Do you like the color?" Kaye said, pointing to her head.

"Yes, I actually do. It flatters you."

"Did you speak to Solly this week?"

"Yesterday. He calls once or twice a week. He doesn't sound happy. Do you speak to him?"

"Not too often," Kaye said.

Solly had moved out to Los Angeles a few years ago, and since then their relationship had been tense. When he announced his plans to leave New York, he also announced that he wanted to move Gertie to a senior residence. Not surprisingly, he wanted Kaye to make the arrangements, and she refused, accusing him of trying to make it easier for himself to leave without having to worry or feel guilty about Gertie. It had never been right between them after that. He soon divorced his second wife and did nothing to mend the miserable relationship with his children from his first marriage. Now, Gertie said, he was living with a woman who barely spoke English.

"They're probably better off," Kaye said.

"Another joke?"

"Yes, Mom. Another joke."

Gertie folded the dish towel and then unfolded it before looking up into her daughter's face.

"I read an interesting article the other day," Gertie said, holding Kaye's eyes in a steady gaze. "Online." She emphasized these last words as though she could not believe it herself. "A friend of mine from my book club sent it to me."

Kaye did not even know that Gertie had joined a book club.

"We read a lot of short stories. It's easier for people our age. Less to forget. Anyway, one of the stories we read was about the Berbers. I had trouble understanding the relationship between the husband and the wife, and my friend thought this article would help."

"Did it?"

"That's not the point. Apparently, when the Ait Hadiddous of the Berbers are going to marry, they find it a great advantage to delay sex. They bind the fingers of the groom for seven days before the wedding so that the bride can get used to her husband. She has to feed and care for him for a week to build trust. After that, the groom's fingers are freed, and the marriage is consummated."

Gertie looked expectantly at Kaye.

"What?" Kaye said.

"Trust. It's all about trust," Gertie said.

"Trust? You're describing the rape of a fifteen-year-old by a man forty years her senior. That's trust? That's criminal."

"Culture defines everything, Kaye. And you're missing the point."

"As usual, right? You were going to say, as usual."

"I don't have to say it. I know you'll say it for me."

"I don't want to argue with you," Kaye said.

"Then don't."

Gertie rose, pressing down with both hands on the table for support, and Kaye's heart lurched.

"Are the potatoes done?" Kaye said. Her voice was ridiculously cheerful. She sniffed at the air. "They smell good."

"No, they're not nearly done. They take a long time this way," Gertie said pointedly. "That's why they taste so good. Time adds value to things. We misjudge the value of time."

Kaye checked her watch. It was only a little past one.

"Are we still talking about potatoes?" she said.

Gertie continued to fiddle with the dials at the stove.

"The soup is done," she said.

They were ignoring each other. It was definitely time to go.

"Do you have to leave?" Gertie said, but she did not sound disappointed at the prospect.

"I should get going. Would you like to come home with me?"

"The potatoes aren't done," Gertie said by way of explanation.

"I see."

"Let me prepare a container with soup for George."

"Thank you. He'll enjoy that," Kaye said. "I'm going to use the bathroom."

When she came out, there was a small shopping bag on the kitchen table. Gertie was on the phone. She had her back to Kaye, giving her a chance to assess her mother's frame. Her back was still straight, and she seemed quite steady on her feet. Gertie had turned on her radio station. It was as if Kaye had already left. Kaye waited as her mother said good-bye to the person on the other end.

"Sorry," Gertie said. "Bridge tonight."

"Where?" Kaye said. She worried about her mother walking around at night alone. "In the building?"

"No, on the moon. Worry about yourself," Gertie said prophetically.

"Don't you worry about me?"

"Not as much as I used to."

"Is that a joke?" Kaye said.

"Don't forget the soup," Gertie said.

She walked Kaye to the door. Kaye put the shopping bag on the floor while she hugged her mother and kissed her on each cheek.

"George is a good husband," Gertie said.

They were holding hands, but they were not looking at each other. Not really looking.

"Yes, he is a good husband."

"Give him my love."

"I'll do that. Talk to you in the morning, Mom."

"I love you."

"I love you too."

As Kaye pulled out of the parking spot, she wished that her mother had confronted her, had asked why she had been visiting less frequently. It was not until Kaye was on the highway that she realized she had left the container of soup by the door. More evidence of Kaye's growing discontent. At least, that was the way Gertie would see it. But she would say nothing, not about the forgotten mushroom barley soup or about Kaye's recently inconsistent behavior. Gertie would place the container in the freezer, adjust the flame under the potato baker, and wait.

Eight

IN the expanse that Roger's death had left, Barbara found a nagging reminder of all that she had taken for granted. Roger had taken care of her, and she missed that. He made sure that her car was serviced and that the gutters were cleaned. He stopped for milk on the way home, picked up the pizza in the rain, glued the stone back in her earring, and hung the new mirror in the foyer. And the children, their children. It was always Roger's first question when he called or came home. He always wanted to know if she had spoken to any of the kids. No one else listened with as much interest to Barbara's recounting of how Justine had patiently explained to a co-worker that cerebral palsy was not a disease, or to how Michael had lifted a sixth-grader into the air and turned him first to the right and then to the left to demonstrate that a straight line remained a straight line no matter which way it was turned. And absolutely no one in the world felt as much sympathy for Daphne as her daddy when Barbara told him how Daphne had phoned semihysterical because not only was her order from Victoria's Secret late, but her favorite bra had been discontinued. Only Roger would cluck his tongue over his poor Daph and tell Barbara not to worry because Daph was really a good girl. And Barbara would sigh and say that he was much too kind.

In Roger's absence, Barbara worried about what would happen if she woke in the middle of the night with a sharp pain in her chest. There was no one on the other side of the bed to rouse, no one who could call an ambulance, no one to offer reassurance that it would all turn out fine. The apartment seemed hollow sometimes, as if she could not fill it up fast enough with new memories to soften out its edges. Even when she called the answering machine to pick up messages, her voice sounded tinny, echoing ominously in the still-unfinished space she now called home. Justine had first commented on this, saying, "It sounds as if you live in a cave, Mom. Unroll a few carpets and hang up some pictures. It's been two years. You're getting creepy." So Barbara promised.

The very next morning, Saturday, was fortuitously wet and stormy, preventing even the hardiest soul from an energetic walk. Barbara started with the living room, rolling out the area rug Roger had insisted they buy when they visited Turkey. The deep red and gold hues of the intricate pattern immediately warmed the room. She hung the walls with some favorite prints and two of the oils by Outsider artists that they had only fairly recently begun to collect. There were many framed photographs of the children that she hung without any devotion to a specific order. Desperate to fill the emptiness, she hurriedly unpacked boxes that had become part of the living room décor, stoic sentries to her past. The pieces filled her with nostalgia, not necessarily for Roger, but for the comforts family life promised.

The apartment's second bedroom served as her office. Barbara needed to hang up all the framed book jackets and press releases;

they were all leaning against a wall just begging for attention. There was a desk that had started life as white Formica. Barbara had rescued it from the sidewalk, refinishing and painting the former eyesore an intense shade of green. The desk now faced the river, the main reason she had finally decided on the apartment. Without any curtains or shades, she was free to gaze and did just that as she sipped her second cup of coffee and pretended she was smoking. An incomplete manuscript was waiting for her, and she had already ignored the last message from her editor about the urgency of getting her next romance, *Beneath the Silk Coverlet*, done by the month's end. She was late with the first draft. But Barbara was more interested in working on Delilah's latest piece, *Paradise Found*. Aimee, the heroine of *Paradise Found*, was far more interesting, far more provocative than any of the characters in her latest romance, set in Victorian England. When Barbara had last left Aimee, she was servicing Victor, the doorman, on her kitchen table.

Aimee's legs were wrapped around Victor's trim waist. She was gripping his buttocks, kneading his flesh with just the right amount of pressure when . . .

"Mom?"

Justine shook Barbara's shoulder, a little harder than necessary actually. Barbara was wearing her favorite noise-blocking headphones and was totally immersed in Aimee and Victor's next position. Barbara, startled and slightly dazed from too much sex, quickly realized that Justine was staring at the computer screen. Barbara quickly saved and clicked the button to make the screen go dark. Then she assessed the situation from Justine's point of view. The room was strewn with crumpled newspaper and half-unpacked boxes, abandoned relics of her good intentions before lust had overtaken her senses. It was late morning though just on the cusp of afternoon, and Barbara was still in her pajamas, a pair of worn sweatpants and a pink T-shirt with the faded sequined proclamation

Drama Queen Rehab stamped across the chest. Barbara's uncombed hair was held back with a frayed and stained terry cloth sweatband. She was wearing a pair of too-large sheepskin slippers that she had found that morning stuffed with knickknacks. It seemed such a fortuitous discovery because her feet had been unreasonably cold. The slippers must have belonged to Roger or Michael; they were huge on her, making her look rather clownish. Empty coffee cups were stacked on the floor next to her desk, with a plate of toast crumbs and a stack of dirty plates she had collected this morning, intending to take everything to the kitchen until the amazing bulge in Victor's pants had distracted her.

"I rang the bell," Justine said. "I knocked too. I hope you don't mind that I used my key. I thought that you might be hurt or something. I forgot about those stupid headphones."

She was flustered. Barbara could see that right away. Generally unfazed by most everything, Justine had seen too much on the computer screen to fully compose herself on such short notice. She hardly ever read Barbara's books, claiming they were too formulaic for her taste (though Daphne loved all of them), and, anyway, romance was highly overrated. Barbara never took offense at these criticisms. None of the heroines in any of her romance novels were ever as bold as Aimee. Instead, there were a lot of heaving cleavages and pounding hearts, and men who knew the art of a strategically placed kiss.

"That's fine, honey," Barbara said. "I was up early, unpacking and hammering. I wasn't expecting anyone. I got bored with unpacking, so I decided to do some work." She smiled. "My editor has been pressuring me."

"Oh." Justine's mouth formed a perfect little O and held it as if she were about to blow smoke rings. She did not smile back. "What's the name of this book?"

"Since when are you so interested in my writing?"

Justine shrugged. "Just curious, I guess. It looked a little racier than the junk you usually write."

"Thank you, Justine."

"I'm sorry. And I'm sorry if I scared you. I thought you might be dead. Anyway, nice shirt. I know that was never mine."

"Daph's, probably."

"Or Michael's." Now she smiled. "So, what's the name of the book?"

"Actually, it's *Paradise Found*," Barbara said. "Clever, right?"

"Especially since ninety percent of your readers won't get the joke."

"Don't be mean. It makes me miss your father."

Justine leaned her brace against the wall and took off her jacket, throwing it on the chaise that was in the far corner of the room. Barbara took advantage of the moment to give Justine the once-over and decided that she looked very fit, quite striking actually in her short skirt, dark tights, and fashionably pointy-toed boots. The green cable-knit sweater made her olive skin look even more olive, but it also set off her eyes. Her hair was pulled away from her face with two different barrettes, one tortoiseshell, and the other black with a sprinkle of sequins. She looked well, happy actually, and Barbara realized she must be involved with someone.

"I'm hungry," Justine said. "I didn't have breakfast. I wanted to surprise you."

"And you did."

"Apparently more than I realized."

Justine was naturally confrontational, and Barbara knew that it was best to just allow her daughter's editorial style to take its own course. She loved a good fight, and if Barbara were foolish enough to take her on without some preparation, the results could prove disastrous.

"What's your pleasure, darling?" Barbara said. "French toast? Pancakes? Eggs?"

Justine started to cry. When Justine cried, it was truly a flood. Barbara had never known anyone to cry the way Justine did. Her eyes just seemed to overflow, splashing great drops of water onto her smooth cheeks. She had cried like this even as a baby, startling Barbara enough to tell the pediatrician about it. Of course, the doctor had laughed, claiming that it was a first for her. A mother who worried about the intensity of her baby's tears. But Barbara thought that Justine's tears were meaningful, symbolic really. How else could a child who had been poked and prodded by innumerable strangers since birth make her fears known in any other way without losing dignity? She had never been one to wail or to throw a tantrum. And she cried so rarely, but so fully. Even now, Barbara was tempted to cup her hands beneath her daughter's eyes and capture the tears the way one might reserve rainwater in a cistern.

"What is it, honey?" Barbara said, rising from her chair so quickly that she stumbled. She embraced Justine and drew her head down. She was so much taller that it was difficult to reach her any other way. "Tell me what's wrong."

"I think I'm in love," Justine said between sobs. "I've met someone."

"That's wonderful. But why are you crying?"

Justine shook her head, helpless, unable to get any words out.

"Come, let's sit down," Barbara said. She reached for the brace that had fallen to the floor and handed it to Justine. She shook her head and made her way to the chaise, waving away her mother's offer of help. As soon as she was seated, she placed her face in her open palms and rocked slowly back and forth.

"Whenever you're ready," Barbara said. She knelt in front of Justine and stroked her hair. "I'm listening."

Justine lifted her tear-stained face and said, "I'm so stupid."

Barbara waited. She folded her hands in her lap.

"His name is Clifford." She laughed. "It's such a silly name. Don't you think?"

"No, it seems like a good enough name."

"He works at the station. He's very funny and very smart," Justine said. "And he's older than anyone I've ever dated."

"Oh?" Barbara said.

"He's thirty-nine."

"Aren't we all?"

"Well, he's really thirty-nine. And he's a musician. He plays cello, and he sings. He's in a choir."

"Well, this all sounds very nice."

"And he's married."

Bingo. Barbara steeled herself for the inevitable. Justine would tell her that he was very unhappy in the marriage. His wife was cold, frigid really, possibly even a lesbian. They had tried counseling, but it was hopeless. It was only a matter of time before he would have left her anyway.

". . . and he doesn't love her anymore. It's been unraveling for months, even years. Still, they have two children, and I feel awful about that. Really ashamed of myself."

Children. This was even worse than Barbara had first thought.

"Aren't you going to say anything, Mom?"

"What should I say?" Barbara said. "It's not as if I'm going to tell you to bring him home for dinner."

"Why not?" Justine said, immediately defensive. "I love him."

"That's your problem." Barbara stood.

Her knees ached from kneeling, and she wished Justine would leave, actually wished she had never come. It would have been nice to get back to Victor's incredibly huge tool, which grew in Barbara's imagination by the minute. She was too old and too tired for this parenting nonsense. The only men she liked were the ones she created, and only then because they were so good in bed without any coaxing or instruction. And she could make her imaginary men say whatever she wanted to hear.

"That's it?" Justine said.

"Listen, Justine, you're a grown woman with an adult problem. I'm your mother. You don't want my advice."

"What is your advice?"

"Get out of this relationship now. He's never going to leave his wife and his children. He'll do it as long as he can get away with it, which translates into until his wife confronts him. The thrill is that it's illicit, which translates into dangerous. Have you done it in the office yet? In his car? Standing up? Sitting down? Of course his wife is a shrew. He's at the office screwing a little twentysomething while the wife is home running after two toddlers and sitting on a cold bathroom floor half the day singing potty training songs to a two-year-old. Don't be a fool, Justine."

"I've never known you to be quite so mean, Mother."

"No? Well, that's the only good news I've heard from you today."

"He loves me. He tells me so all the time."

"When, Justine? When you're leaning over the desk with your butt in the air or when he's hammering it into you before he goes home for lamb chops, roast potatoes, and string beans and a drawer full of clean socks and underwear?"

Shocked into silence, Justine looked ready to cry again. Just as suddenly, however, she rallied and flung a comeback at Barbara.

"You and Dad weren't exactly role models for a perfect relationship."

Just that morning on public radio, Barbara had heard about a man who believed that he was missing internal organs, and another man who tried to commit suicide because he thought he was already dead and no one would believe him. There was also an account of a pregnant woman who hungered for plaster, and yet another woman who ate cloth. These bizarre stories had comforted Barbara, made her feel that her worries were normal. And now this. Justine and a married man. Justine criticizing her own parents' marriage, blaming them for her naïve stupidity. At least Justine did not crave charcoal for breakfast, Barbara consoled herself.

"Perfect?" Barbara said. "Well, I'm sorry about that. I never cheated on your father and, as far as I know, he never cheated on me. We had a lot of rough times, but most couples do. Maybe we stayed together for the wrong reasons, and God knows your father didn't always make the best business decisions. Still, we were equally devoted to our children. I think you're way out of line here, Justine. I'm not judging you. I just hate to think of you as the other woman. It won't end well for you. I can guarantee it. Sooner or later the betrayed spouse finds out, and it's awful. If you don't already, you will feel guilty and used and humiliated." She picked up Justine's brace from the floor and leaned against it. "Here. Let's go into the kitchen. I'll put up a pot of fresh coffee and fix us some breakfast. Pancakes sound good to me."

Justine stared at the floor. She looked exhausted.

"I just hope the sex is good," Barbara said.

"Mother!" Justine said. "What is it with you and sex? Are you trying to shock me?"

"Maybe. Now go and wash your face. I'll meet you in the kitchen."

"Don't tell Daphne or Michael," Justine said.

"Why not? Embarrassed?"

"Of course I am." She sniffled. "I'm not a complete slut. Don't you think I feel awful about this? Not only is he married, but he has two children."

Justine appeared so uncharacteristically vulnerable that Barbara restrained herself. It was evident that Justine knew she was in over her head, but she was in love the way that only a young woman could be, helplessly and foolishly.

"I won't say anything to Daphne or to Michael, honey, but I have to say one thing to you before we move on from here. Be careful, Justine."

Justine nodded and looked away. For just one second, Barbara thought to say that it was all right and that love was something that just happened to all of us. But Justine was smarter than that even if she was in love.

"I'm sorry, Mom."

"I love you, Justine. I always love you."

The downstairs buzzer rang, and they jumped simultaneously.

"Are you expecting anyone?" Justine said, wiping the tears from her cheeks. "I look awful."

"You look fine. And no, I wasn't expecting anyone."

Barbara buzzed back, asking, "Who is it?" Kaye's muted voice answered back, and Barbara buzzed her in, shrugging at Justine. Then Barbara kissed her once on each cheek before hurrying off to answer the door.

Kaye looked awful.

"What happened?" Barbara said. She pulled her inside by the sleeve of her coat. "Kaye? Did something happen? Are the children all right? Did something happen to George? Is it Gertie?"

"No, no," Kaye said. "Everyone is fine. Really. I just wanted to see you."

"That seems quite popular this morning."

Kaye looked around the apartment. "Am I interrupting something?"

A toilet flushed. The sound came from the bathroom in Barbara's bedroom.

"Oh, dear," Kaye said. "I am interrupting something. I should have phoned."

"It's Justine. She made a surprise visit of her own."

"Is she all right?"

"That depends on your point of view," Justine said as she walked in. "Hi, Kaye." She kissed Kaye once on each cheek. "How are you? It's good to see you."

"Good to see you too, sweetie," Kaye said, hugging her tightly. "I've missed you."

"She's been awfully busy lately," Barbara said sarcastically. "You know, working late at the office."

"Is that good?" Kaye said. She was holding Justine's hands and smiling. "I hope they're paying you overtime."

"There are some benefits," Barbara said, "but none of them are really long-term."

"Just ignore her," Justine said to Kaye. "Mother thinks she's so clever when she tries to be funny."

Barbara shrugged. "I'm not trying to be funny."

"I guess I picked a bad time," Kaye said, looking back and forth between mother and daughter. "Wonderful to see you, Justine. You look terrific. We'll catch up another time."

But Justine would not let go of Kaye's hands. Then, with as much dignity as the occasion called for, Justine looked into Kaye's shiny eyes and said, "I might as well tell you myself, since Mother will tell you anyway as soon as I leave. I'd rather you hear it from me and tell me what you think rather than talk about me behind my back. I'm having an affair with a married man. I'm not proud of myself, but it is what it is. Now you know what you walked in on."

"Well done," Barbara said. "Impressive."

"Barb," Kaye said pleadingly, looking at Barbara with clear disapproval. "Just try to listen for now."

"I'm not trying to impress anyone," Justine said. She had dropped Kaye's hands and faced Barbara, glaring at her. "Your attitude and observations are ridiculous."

"Is that so? Now *that's* funny, because I'm not the one who thinks her boyfriend is going to leave his family for an office fling."

"He loves me," Justine said.

"He loves to screw you, and then he goes home to his wife and kids. Grow up, Justine. Men don't leave their wives for a little office tail."

"Barbara," Kaye said. "Is that really necessary?"

"You tell me, Kaye. Are you suddenly an expert on infidelity?"

Even Justine was rendered speechless, but she recovered quickly, ignored her mother, and turned to Kaye and said, "It's all right. I should never have told her. I don't know what made me think she would understand. At least I got to see you. I haven't seen you in ages. I spoke to Ruby the other night. We're planning to have lunch this week. You look very well, by the way." She kissed Kaye's cheek and said, "I'm afraid I have to run."

Barbara watched this exchange in stony silence, disregarding the imploring stares that Kaye threw her way over Justine's shoulder.

"Don't leave like this, Justine," Kaye said. "Please."

Justine hesitated, hoping her mother would take the opportunity to reconsider her sharp words and soften her predictions just a little. But Barbara's stubbornness was as legendary as her sense of the ironic. She handed Justine her coat and waited, eyes locked on her daughter's face.

"Good-bye, Kaye," Justine said, keeping her eyes level with her mother's unflinching gaze. "I'll see you soon."

"Barbara," Kaye said, pulling on her friend's sleeve. "This is wrong. You've done many foolish things in your life."

"Nothing like this," Barbara said.

"Really?" Kaye said. "Is that how you wound up pregnant and married by the time you were nineteen?"

"Roger wasn't married," Barbara said. "I might have been careless, but I wasn't entirely naïve."

"Regardless of the circumstances," Kaye said, "love is its own aphrodisiac."

"Now there's a phrase I could turn into a novel," Barbara said.

"Well," Kaye said, looking at Justine, "at least it's not personal."

Justine smiled, but weakly, and put on her coat and her scarf.

"I'm sorry, Mom," she said. "It's not about you."

"If it were about me," Barbara said, "I wouldn't be so angry. This can only end badly, and you'll be hurt."

"I guess I stand warned, then," Justine said. She played with the fringes of her scarf and then took her gloves out of her coat pocket. "Have you ever had an affair, Kaye?"

Barbara and Justine turned to Kaye and waited, never anticipating the flood of indignation that accompanied her response.

"Me? An affair? You must be joking. Who would have an affair with me? I'm a middle-aged crone. Really, Justine. It's such a silly question. I'm flattered that you think—"

"I don't mean now, Kaye," Justine said, looking at her strangely. "I mean ever, like *in the past* ever."

"Oh," Kaye said. "Oh, well, that makes sense. I mean the question. No, I can't say that I ever did have an affair." She laughed a bit too shrilly. "No one ever asked me, of course. Not that I would have if anyone had asked." This confession had clearly drained her, and she became flaccid, like a deflated parade balloon. "Well, then, enough about me."

"Yes," Barbara said, narrowing her eyes and giving Kaye a look that suggested she had made a fool of herself, "enough about you." She turned to Justine. "Stay. Please. I'll make you that coffee I promised, and the pancakes too."

"Yes, do stay," Kaye said, almost begging. "It's not good to walk away with unresolved feelings toward each other."

Justine laughed and said, "I'll stay because I'm hungry. I think I've resolved enough feelings for one day."

"Good," Barbara said. "I don't want to hear any of the details. I don't think I can bear to know more than I already do."

Kaye was already helping Justine off with her coat and smoothing down her hair. "You can tell me everything instead," Kaye said. "Ruby is so tight-lipped about her life."

"You're pretty open-minded for a middle-aged crone," Barbara said. "I actually think I'm more interested in your life right now, Kaye."

"Yes," Justine said, turning to her mother. "And maybe you can tell us about your new work. Whatever I managed to read on the screen before you caught me was very different from your standard romance novel fare."

The three women were immediately locked in a moment, just on the threshold of the door to the place where secrets were stored, jolting Barbara into a memory of Roger's Aunt Millie, an artist who had painted pysanky, Ukrainian Easter eggs. Pysanky dated back to pagan times when the painted eggs were believed to have talismanic powers. The first time Barbara visited Millie in her studio, she invited her to paint an egg of her own, and guided her through the intricate process. Over tea and biscuits, they waited for the egg to dry. When Millie declared the egg ready, Barbara reached out to pick up the painted egg, but was swiftly intercepted by Millie's agile hand. She explained that painted eggs were like secrets. As she rolled the egg in a thick wad of cotton and expertly placed it in a white box, Millie said that after a painted egg was entrusted to another, it had to be handled with complete caution, just like a shared secret. Confused, Barbara said she thought that secrets must be guarded and never shared. But Millie shook her head and said that secrets were more powerful when they were shared.

"Barb," Kaye said. "Are you working on something different?"

It was an opportune moment for Barbara to come forward to

tell them about Delilah. It would be a relief after all this time. Barbara looked from her friend to her daughter and said, "No."

"I don't believe you," Justine said.

"Then don't," Barbara said.

"Just like that?" Justine said.

"Just like that," Barbara said. She turned to Kaye. "Did you have something you wanted to tell me?"

"No," Kaye said.

Justine looked from one woman to the other and said, "I'll make coffee. You two stay and talk."

In the kitchen, she measured out coffee and poured water into the coffeemaker. While she waited, she loaded the dishwasher, scraping the stack of soaking plates. She heard her mother's slightly demanding tone and Kaye's even response. Their words were muffled; they had reflexively lowered their voices. It took Justine back to all the times she and the other children had been strapped into the back of the van, returning home after a long day at the beach or an outing to a museum. Subdued by exhaustion, most of the others fell asleep, but Justine and Ruby always listened to their mothers' voices, sometimes pitched high with excitement and laughter or quiet with something that felt like longing. Barbara's inner life was still a mystery to Justine, who found her mother more cautious than ever, more secretive. The difference was that now Justine was busy with her own secrets.

What surprised Justine, however, was that Barbara and Kaye kept some secrets tightly wound from each other, as if exposure would unravel everything in their lives. As she set three mugs on the counter, Justine called out that the coffee was ready. She poured for them, insisting it was her pleasure. Barbara asked if she remembered Aunt Millie, and Justine said, of course she did. Aunt Millie had given her one of her beautiful painted eggs. Didn't she remember how she had cried when Daphne broke it? Barbara didn't remember that. They talked about Aunt Millie, about how sad it was when arthritis made it impossible for her to paint. Barbara said nothing about what Aunt Millie had told her about secrets. It would have been an invitation to share something more of herself. And she wasn't ready to do that. Not yet, anyway. Justine sensed that her mother was holding back, but she was quiet, listening again, hoping to learn more about the lives of the two women she thought she knew so well, and the secrets they kept even from each other.

Nine

MARISOL was recommended to Ellen by one of the buyers in her office. Although quite young, Marisol was reliable and hardworking. She had been cleaning since she left home in the Dominican Republic two years earlier at seventeen, often working seven days a week to save enough money to go to school. She wanted to learn to read and write English fluently, as she was practically illiterate in Spanish. Her father had denied all his daughters any formal education, claiming that learning to read and write would only enable them to exchange love notes with boys. And everyone knew that boys were only interested in one thing. Marisol giggled behind her hand when she told this to Ellen, and Ellen surprised herself by giggling along. It was hard to resist Marisol's expansive nature. Every Monday she came to clean the apartment, and every Monday Ellen was newly struck by Marisol's beauty. She braided her curls into a single plait that hung down her narrow back almost to her waist. Her only jewelry was a pair of small gold hoop earrings and a gold cross on a gold chain that nestled in the hollow at the base of her throat. A starched white blouse and ironed jeans were her unofficial uniform. Her sneakers were always clean, and her unpolished nails noticeably manicured. What really struck Ellen, however, was that Marisol always wore makeup. It seemed odd at first that she would wear lipstick, eye shadow, and a light touch of mascara. At first, this meticulous grooming effort to clean for six hours worried Ellen, and she expected to be disappointed in Marisol's performance. However, not only did Marisol's work surpass Ellen's expectations, but Marisol won Ellen's heart. The gentle grace of this young girl was humbling. Soon Ellen understood that Marisol's preparations gave her work dignity. She might have been illiterate, but she had a job and was sought after because of her efficiency. Several months after Marisol had been working for them, Ellen offered to give her English lessons. For a moment, Ellen thought she might have offended Marisol. She hung her head and stared, motionless, at the floor. Concerned, Ellen touched her arm and said her name very softly. In excruciating slow motion, Marisol lifted her head. The perfectly smooth dark skin on her cheeks was streaked with tears. She clasped her folded hands to her chest and mumbled in Spanish, a prayer it seemed. With her usual dignity, she offered to pay Ellen, who thanked her but refused, saying that it would be good for her own soul to do something for someone other than herself. Marisol shook her head vehemently, adding that Miss Ellen was a wonderful and kind person. Pleased, Ellen impulsively hugged Marisol, who seemed desperate to be held. It was a telling moment. Marisol so clearly longed for her mother, any mother really at that moment, and Ellen so clearly longed to offer a mother's comfort.

Bill, of course, disapproved. He maintained that Ellen would be crossing a line that would have dire consequences. Ellen regarded him with cool disdain. Dire consequences? She thought good deeds brought spiritual reward, not the wrath of the Almighty. They sparred in this manner for weeks until Bill finally withdrew. It was evident that Ellen's mind was made up. She searched the Internet for appropriate materials, pored over educational catalogs, and visited several bookstores until she was satisfied that she had enough to begin Marisol's lessons. Ellen planned for the first lesson as though she were planning a party. She bought marble composition books, pencils, and index cards. Although it was prematurely optimistic, Ellen bought several easy readers to tempt Marisol once her confidence was firmly established. Their first lessons went extremely well—so well, in fact, that Ellen found she had underestimated Marisol's determination and ability. In no time at all, Marisol was combining sounds and forming words, moving from basic primers to more complex exercises. She grappled with grammatical constructions, wondered over how little phonetics governed the rules of English spelling, and was elated when she met success. Ellen matched Marisol's excitement and pleasure with heady enthusiasm. There was something about the sight of Marisol poring over a blank page in her composition book and filling it with words and then full sentences that made Ellen feel she had finally accomplished something worthwhile.

Every Monday Ellen timed her arrival home to coincide with the end of Marisol's workday. Ellen quickly changed out of her business clothes and fixed them sandwiches. Marisol especially liked it when Ellen placed a few potato chips alongside the sandwich. The first time Ellen did this, Marisol clapped her hands and said it was fancy, just like in the diner. The flush of pleasure that this gave Ellen was even more touching than Marisol's delight. Such a small gesture, and yet it was one of the countless niceties that Ellen had imagined she would have performed as a mother. A note in a lunch box, a book of poetry with favorites checked in the index, homemade marshmallows on a wintry afternoon, tiny foil hearts spread over a red tablecloth on Valentine's Day. Ellen knew they were silly fantasies, but she could not escape them. The idea of her own little girl doing homework at the kitchen table, chattering about her day while Ellen prepared their dinner, was an image that she had permanently etched into her consciousness. The evenings Ellen spent with Marisol did not make up for what had been lost, but they allowed Ellen to practice the maternal feelings she so longed to share.

The day that Ellen had been alternately working toward and dreading finally came. She knew it would. Marisol shyly announced that she had started taking a class at the local community college. "Oh?" Ellen said in her best surprised voice. Marisol wanted to learn to read and write in Spanish, and Ellen spoke only enough Spanish to say *hello*, *good-bye*, and *thank you*. The boy's name was Carlos. He was twenty-two, and he had a green card and a job. He planned to go to college and become an accountant. Marisol said he was very smart. And handsome. When Marisol said that her father had been right after all, she giggled. She and Carlos passed each other notes in class, and now they were in love. Ellen said how wonderful that was, and gave Marisol a congratulatory hug. Wonderful. Ellen wished her all the best. Really. Marisol and Carlos were getting married next month and moving to New Jersey. He had family there. She was so grateful to Miss Ellen. Really. The next time Marisol came would be the last. There was so much to do before the wedding. Ellen gave her an envelope with an extra hundred-dollar bill and pretended that she was really, really happy, though once again, she felt that terrible emptiness that comes with an irreplaceable loss. Bill could not believe what he heard. Irreplaceable? There were millions of young illegal girls out there looking to clean for cash. And Ellen said that, of course, that was true. How foolish of her. Later that night, after Bill's snores signaled a deep sleep, she got up and sat at the dining room table, arranging and rearranging the pencils, pens, index cards, and miscellaneous school supplies she had kept in a blue plastic box marked *Marisol*.

*   *   *

FOR some time after Marisol left, Ellen cleaned the apartment herself. It felt like penance, though she did not know what she had really done wrong. Still, it was oddly satisfying to wipe down the furniture and move the mop around the wooden floors. This fascination did not last long, and she hired an older woman this time. Bertha was Polish and very stern, but she cleaned like a professional and kept her distance. And she never asked about The Mister after all his things seemed to have just vanished one week.

Practically everything Bertha owned had been purchased from the Home Shopping Network. Bertha proudly revealed this one day after Ellen politely complimented her on a vinyl alligator tote that she used to carry her sensible work shoes and the no-frills cleaning supplies in foreign containers that Bertha evidently preferred to all the products Ellen stocked. Although Ellen hated anything alligator, genuine or fake, she felt like talking. The morning was a lonely time for Ellen, the time she most missed Bill's company. He had always made the coffee, fixing it just the way she liked it in a French press with lots of warm milk and a half teaspoon of sugar. After he left, Ellen switched to tea. It was just too painful to prepare her own coffee. Bertha looked stunned when Ellen admitted that she had never even seen the Home Shopping Network. As soon as she finished her duties, she would fix The Missus a coffee and introduce her to the wonders of HSN. Bertha called it HSN, and said it with such authority and respect that Ellen was immediately chagrined. While Bertha worked, Ellen halfheartedly went over some plans for an office she had just been hired to redo.

True to her word, Bertha finished her work and made the coffee, adding steamed milk and a dusting of cinnamon. Ellen pretended to be absorbed in the work she had spread out across the dining room table, but she covertly watched as Bertha set the mug on a tray with a napkin, the sugar bowl, and a few dark chocolate–covered biscuits, Ellen's favorite. After Bertha set the tray down, Ellen urged her to pour herself a cup of coffee as well. Bertha said yes as though it were a question, and Ellen nodded emphatically and said, please, please so that even Bertha could not resist. She poured herself a cup and added three heaping spoons of sugar with an almost apologetic little smile and a shrug that made Ellen laugh as she pushed her papers to the side, and pointed to a chair. There was no television in the dining room, but Ellen thought it would be better if they had their coffee first.

Bertha's English was wanting, but she was able to explain that she had left a family back in Poland. Two daughters and a son. From this proximity, Bertha was much younger than Ellen's initial assumption. Ellen was able to understand that Bertha's husband had been injured in a factory accident, and so it had been decided that she would come to the United States and work for a few years. Yes, it had been hard to leave her family, but the first two years she lived with a couple in Connecticut, caring for their two young children. That had filled the loneliness quite a bit. When the couple relocated to California, Bertha declined their offer to accompany them, even though she loved the children. She was afraid of being too isolated. She had made a few friends in New York, and she had some family in Brooklyn. Waving her hands, Bertha said California was another country. Too far. Ellen nodded. She understood. With the money Bertha sent home, her daughters could attend the best schools, and her son was able to marry and buy an apartment. American money could buy a great deal in Poland. Then Bertha smiled sheepishly and said that after she had discovered HSN, she began to put a little aside for herself each week. At first, no one noticed, but then her husband began to ask if she was all right. Did she have enough work? Was it time to come home? Bertha said she told him everything was fine. And it was except for her addiction. Yes, some of her purchases were for her family. Like the set of nonstick pots she would take home when she visited at Christmas. And the matching flannel shirts and down vests she bought for her husband and son. The girls, her daughter-in-law included, would get three-piece mix-and-match outfits in different colors. Wash and wear. That was the part Bertha found most impressive. She had made all her children's and husband's clothes (even his suits), but since discovering HSN, well, it was liberation she had never believed was affordable. When they had finished their coffees, Ellen suggested they move to the study.

Within an hour, Ellen was hooked. The hostesses were so familiar, all of them. And they seemed to care so much about the people who phoned in. Everyone was so proprietary about the products. And the hostesses were so nice to each other. It felt as though Ellen had a new family. She could see what had attracted Bertha. Everyone was so friendly, and they were available twenty-four hours a day, seven days a week. By the time Bertha gathered her things to leave, Ellen was already fantasizing about a new career, selling polyester blouses with bold animal prints. After Bertha left, Ellen practiced in front of the mirror, holding up one of her own garments and practicing clever descriptions like the one offered by the hostess with the Texas drawl who pointed out that sometimes when there was an animal print, the colors fought each other. But not so with these fabulous pieces. She laughed so viewers would know she meant to be funny. Ellen practiced on, holding the shirt against her body, turning for the imaginary cameras. Many of the item descriptions were kernels of homespun wisdom, something a grandmother or a favorite aunt might share. Ellen's eyes welled up when one cheerful blonde said, "When you get a hug in this shirt, not only do you feel good, but the person who hugs you feels good too." And even though she had no intention of sending it, Ellen ordered the shirt for her mother for Christmas. The purchase was just part of the fantasy of having a family that shared holidays and thought of each other while watching the Home Shopping Network.

Ironically, the very next day Ellen received a call from her brother Hugh. She had decided to work from home again. She was feeling a bit out of sorts, maybe fighting a cold or something. Her head ached, and she was chilled. The fleece blanket that Mary, Ellen's favorite hostess, had said could double as a sort of shawl would have been perfect. Mary had bought one in each color for her children. Ellen wished she had one, but instead she pulled on another pair of socks and an extra sweater. As she rummaged through the kitchen cupboards searching for honey, the phone rang. Hugh's voice resonated on the machine as if he were the Wizard of Oz. Ellen stopped her search and listened.

Hugh was the oldest of the four siblings and the kindest. All three brothers had remained in the community where they had been born and raised. It boggled Ellen's mind to think of this, but it was also enviable. All their lives, their routines remained the same. They shared coffee at the same diner every morning, went to church together on Sunday, never missed a dance at the VFW, and attended all the high school sporting events with matched enthusiasm. Hugh had become a police officer, though he had retired from the force years ago. Since then, he devoted all his time to his bait and tackle shop, Hooked. He had never been mean to her. Mostly, though, she was grateful for his consistent intervention when the other two, Owen and Andrew, were downright cruel. Hugh left a rather brief message, saying it was nice to hear her voice even if it was only a recording, and would she please call him back as soon as possible. It was a matter of some importance. He spoke softly and with a gentleness that touched Ellen. They had not spoken in months, maybe even a year by now. She knew that one of their parents must be ill, not dead, or his message would have had more urgency.

She stared at the phone while she ate a bowl of cold cereal with a sliced banana. Bill had hated when she ate standing, and now she did it all the time. Hugh had three children, and Ellen searched her memory for their names. His wife's name was Maureen, and their daughters were Sara, June, and Christina. Before Ellen rang him, however, she washed her face and combed her hair. For a moment, she stared at herself in the mirror over the sink. Hugh always told her she was pretty. He was the only one. Ellen opened a pair of new eyelashes and expertly applied them. Then she randomly picked a lipstick from the basket on the vanity and covered her lips in fire-engine red. Better, she thought. Less haggard. She took some of the color from her lips and smudged it on her cheeks. Even better now.

Hugh's number was on the phone, and Ellen wrote it down on the back of an envelope. He answered on the first ring.

"Ellen?"

"Caller ID has ruined the element of surprise," she said.

"At least I answered," he said. "How are you, Sis? It's been forever."

Ellen smiled. He always called her Sis, rarely Ellen, unless it was as a reprimand. And there was no judgment in his tone about screening her calls, only affection. "I just needed a minute," she said. "Whenever I hear your voice, I'm always sorry that we don't speak more often. And, in answer to your question, I'm well. How are you?"

"I'm well too."

"And Maureen? And the girls? Sara, June, and Christina?"

Hugh laughed. "Had to look that up, huh?"

"No, actually, I just had to brainstorm a little."

"They're far from girls anymore."

"I know. I remember. They're all married, some with practically grown kids of their own. You're the only one who invites me to anything. And I know about all the grandchildren as well. I have a collection of birth announcements from your family alone."

"Yes, they all have girls and boys of their own now. I'm a grandfather seven times over. Just had a new one last week. A boy. His name is Hugh. After me. I was tickled. We already have a little Maureen."

"How nice for you and Maureen. I'm really happy for you both."

"So, do you remember your brothers' names?"

"In spite of all my efforts to forget, yes. I remember their names."

"Ellen," Hugh said. "They're old men now."

"Not that old."

Their collective past silenced them momentarily. Then Hugh spoke, quietly explaining that Mother's emphysema was really bad now. She had an oxygen tank, and the doctors did not have much hope for any successful outcome.

"Is she still smoking?" Ellen said.

"Ellen," Hugh said again, his voice even heavier with reproach. "You should come see her."

"Why? So she can tell me I'm a whore and my husband is old enough to be my father, no, wait, I think she said grandfather."

"How is Bill?"

Ellen walked into the study and pressed the remote, turning on the television. It was already on HSN, and she hurriedly hit the mute button. The hostess was holding up a velour jogging suit in bright red. On the rack behind her were several identical suits in royal blue, lime green, orange, and your standard black and brown. Ellen checked the bottom of the screen for her size. She always checked. It reassured her.

"Sis?" Hugh said. "Are you there?"

"Yes, I'm here. But Bill isn't. He left me about four, no maybe five months ago. Seems he was having an affair with a little twenty-something in his office. They're expecting their own little bundle of joy soon."

"Oh, Sis, I'm so sorry. How have you been managing?"

"Well, I've moved on from *Animal Miracle Stories* to the Home Shopping Network, or HSN as I now call it."

"Maureen loves HSN."

Somehow that did not surprise Ellen, though she did not say so.

"I'm sorry about Bill. I was never crazy about him," Hugh said. "He always seemed a little stuck up; like he thought he was too good for us."

Ellen knew Hugh was just trying to say the right thing and make her feel better, but his *us* did not include her. It never had.

"It's fine. These things happen to women my age."

"Well, you didn't deserve it. You're a good person."

"Oh, I'm fine, Hugh. It's just another adjustment. I've had plenty of those, and a childhood that prepared me for the worst."

"You didn't deserve that either, Sis. None of us did."

"I'm not so sure of that," Ellen said and laughed. "Owen and Andrew were pretty horrendous individuals."

"They didn't set you on fire or anything," Hugh said. "Remember the Carson boys? They set their sister on fire. And the family cat as well. Those boys were half mad, I swear."

They both laughed at the absurdity of this comparison, also intended to make her feel better.

"Well, it ain't much," Hugh said, "but it's something."

Ellen gazed over at the television screen. The hostess was pointing to a model in a black jacket with a faux fur collar. It was actually very pretty. The model turned, halted, and turned again.

"How's Dad?" Ellen said.

"Old and frail, like Mother," Hugh said. "But he doesn't have emphysema. Just a touch of diabetes and the usual arthritis and a flare-up of gout now and then."

"Well, it ain't much, but it's something."

"It's not good to be so bitter, Sis. It's bad for your heart."

"Is it?" Ellen said. "It can't be worse than having your baby snatched from your arms and taken away. Can it, Hugh?"

"You were just a child yourself. Besides, times were different then."

"I think about that baby girl every day of my life. Every single day."

"I'm sure you do."

"Thank you for that, Hugh." Ellen said, more gently now that he had acknowledged her pain. "So, how are our brothers?"

"Our brothers are well. They have grandchildren of their own. Owen's wife, Nelly, had breast cancer, but she's doing fine. And Andrew is still in real estate. There's quite a market up here now for your Wall Street types and their second homes."

"And how's your shop? Are you still enjoying it?"

"I can't complain. It's a nice life. I think about you a lot, though."

Tears sprang to Ellen's eyes. She often wondered if anyone thought about her, ever.

"That's sweet, Hugh. Why don't you and Maureen come and visit? I'll get tickets to a show, a musical. The tree will be up in Rockefeller Center before you know it. You can stay with me. I'll wine and dine you both."

"Let me talk to Maureen. She might enjoy an outing. We could take the train."

"I'm here," Ellen said. "My work is flexible. Any time you want to come is a good time."

"So, how are you managing now with Bill gone?"

"You mean financially?"

"Yes, do you need anything? I'm pretty well fixed, you know. I can help if you ever find yourself short."

Ellen stared at the television screen and saw that the hostess was holding a tunic against her body and demonstrating how it could be worn either with or without a belt.

"Thank you, Hugh. I really appreciate your concern, but money is the only thing I don't have to worry about. I have a very successful business. I got the apartment, the car, the investments. Bill was happy to just get out with as little fuss as possible."

"He's a fool."

"But a happy fool."

"He's a fool. Trust me."

"I do."

"Then come and see Mother, Sis. Before it's too late. I don't want you to have any more regrets."

"Any more than I already do?"

"It wasn't your choice to give the baby away. It was a decision that was made for you."

"And now you think I should come see the folks who made that decision?"

"Ellen, they're still your parents. Dad will be ninety next month. And Mother is not far behind. We're planning a party for Dad. Will you come? That way you can see Mother and celebrate Dad's ninetieth with the whole family."

"Will she make it another month?"

"I hope so."

"See? And I don't know what to wish for."

"Ellen."

"Sorry. You're much kinder than I am. You always have been."

"Nonsense," Hugh said. "Just promise to come. And promise to wear those false eyelashes, so I'll be sure to recognize you."

"Promise."

"Sis?"

"Yes?"

"I miss you."

"I miss you too, Hugh."

"It's not normal the way we live. A brother and a sister should stay close. You're my little sister. I was supposed to take care of you."

"You did. You really did. You were the only one."

Hugh was suddenly quiet. When he finally spoke, his voice was level, "I tried to talk to Mother way back then. I tried to tell her that we should keep the baby. I said that it would be nice to have another girl around the house."

Way back then. They never spoke about way back then. She was stunned.

"Sis?"

"I'm here. I'm okay. I'm okay."

"I shouldn't have told you."

"No, I'm glad you did."

"I'm sorry, for that and for this now. It doesn't make a difference anymore."

"But it does. It means a lot to me."

"Mother slapped me. It was the only time she ever hit me. She told me I was too soft. 'A man shouldn't be soft' is how she put it."

"And now you look after her," Ellen said.

"She's my mother. Yours too."

"Whatever."

"So you'll call me, right?" Hugh said. "And let me know about the party?"

"Yes, and you'll let me know if you and Maureen would like to visit?"

"Yes, I promise."

For the rest of the day, Ellen stayed on the couch and dozed. When she opened her eyes, the hostess was talking to another equally exuberant woman. They were wearing matching ponchos this time, one in moss green and the other in purple. The sound on the television was still off, and the remote was nowhere in sight. Ellen concentrated on their lips, trying to make out the gist of their banter. She definitely liked the moss green better than the purple. The hostess turned and then sat while the other woman stood and did several silly pirouettes. Ellen went to the kitchen for her purse and took out her credit card. Back in the study, she dialed the number at the bottom of the screen, ordering several ponchos in all the colors. She would need gifts for her sisters-in-law and nieces when she went to her father's party.

Ten

THE lecturer explained that the Incas sent their messages and kept their records by a complicated system of differently colored strings called *khipu*, tying groups of knots at intervals. Unfortunately, no one had yet been able to decipher the meaning of the string configurations. Kaye pretended to listen and to take notes, but she doodled instead. When she signed up for the lecture series, Patterns of Communication: Its History and Relevance to Contemporary Psychotherapy, she had anticipated some illumination or at least a better grasp of the struggle to be understood. But Kaye knew that even if the mystery of the strings was ever fully decoded, there would be no answers to the really important questions like what made a fifty-two-year-old married mother of two grown children embark on an affair that was guaranteed to have disastrous consequences. Even now as she contemplated her future, she could only think about the way Frank held her head when he kissed her, supporting her skull as though she were an infant.

It was as though Kaye had lost all ability to reason. Frank's kisses obliterated all rational thought. She could not get enough of the way he tugged at her lower lip with his teeth or the way he always surprised her with his tongue. It made her feel like a teenager, the preliminary dry humping and the urgency that prefaced the feeling of flesh against flesh. But Frank was not a frustrated boy begging for relief. Restraint was no longer called for, and Kaye made no attempt to show any. She was the one who was reckless, the one who slipped Frank's hand under her skirt in a taxi, parting her legs and placing a hand on him so efficiently that by the time they reached his apartment it was all they could do to make it inside. Even when he protested that he was too old for such games, he seemed delighted by her need and eager to please, although he occasionally told her to be realistic, making them both laugh over his honesty.

Frank wanted Kaye to leave George, insisting it was the only way to start anew. But Kaye protested, arguing that she could not leave George. He was her husband. They had a family. The children would be devastated. The children were not children anymore, Frank pointed out. She wanted to tell him that he did not understand about children, never having had any of his own. But she was afraid to hurt him. It was certainly true that Ruby and Charlie were adults, but Kaye knew that most children did not care about their parents' happiness, not really anyway. Children just wanted to know that their parents were always exactly as they had left them. Change was the enemy. Sex, particularly illicit sex, was impossible to fathom. Sometimes Kaye wondered what her children would think if they knew what she was hurrying off to in the middle of the day. She imagined the horror they would feel if they could hear the words she whispered to Frank. *Faster, harder, more.* Once, while Frank expertly held her hips, she had moaned, urging him on, and then turned and asked him what her children would have thought if they saw her. Frank had gripped her tighter, pushing himself even deeper inside her and said they would probably be surprised that their mother knew so many dirty words. It was funny, but it was untrue. Still, she could not resist Frank, or the way he made her feel. It was really all about that after all. His attentiveness was an aphrodisiac. The way he observed how the color of her eyes changed against a new sweater that he also noticed. His pleasure at the noises she made in the back of her throat when he kissed her neck. He told her that she was sexy, and that he loved the taste of her. They were made for each other. He told her so every time she called his name, holding him with her legs as if she were afraid he would escape. And when he said that he was hot for her, she laughed but was secretly delighted.

It did no good to obsess, as she often did, about what her life would have been like if she had met Frank first. It did no good to think about the trips they might have taken together (George did not like to travel), or the books they would have shared (George did not read fiction, finding it superfluous in light of all there was to learn about the past and the future), and the meals they would have cooked together ("Not interested," was how George put it when he was asked). When Kaye allowed her fantasies to wander, these were the places she went, the places she could never share with George. But her children brought her musings to an end. Ruby and Charlie were her prizes, the rewards of her years with George, and she could not have loved them more. Her Charlie was so unlike his sister, the quintessential hippie. Charlie was more interested in Wall Street and stock trading than in saving the world. Although he had a brilliant mind and was a voracious reader, it was money that intrigued him. *Let others save the world,* he always said. *I'll do my best to pay for the expenses.* After Ruby announced that she had been accepted to a program to study midwifery, Charlie had scoffed at the plan, claiming it was a feminist cop-out for someone too lazy to do medical school. When Kaye scolded him for being too judgmental, he said that it was kinder than Ruby's response. She had e-mailed him, calling him a fascist-warmonger-misogynist-pig. Charlie was most impressed by her use of hyphens, suggesting the combination might qualify as a neologism. Should he expect to see it in the Sunday *Times*? Her two-word response, according to him, was disappointingly unoriginal. They had always clashed.

Conservative Charlie was a surprise to everyone, especially as his parents had been political activists in the sixties and his grandmother had practically been a revolutionary. Sometimes Kaye believed this was the real reason behind his tendency to take a more measured approach to just about everything. Theirs was a family with very established criteria. A liberal point of view was the standard, and Ruby and Charlie had been raised to express themselves freely and without fear of criticism, even if, as was the case with Charlie, the point of view did not reflect Kaye and George's. In spite of some of Charlie's views, George was quick to note that at least their boy was not a registered Republican. This gave Kaye and George some comfort, though Ruby was convinced her older brother was a closet Republican. The fights around the dinner table had been passionate, but Kaye worked hard to make sure that they always ate as a family, and that Charlie helped with the washing up.

These were Kaye's children, but they were also George's children, an inescapable and firm truth. And George was a good father. Ruby said he was the most handsome man in the world, and Charlie said he had never met anyone as smart as his dad. But at the core of this family unit was Kaye, mediating and adjusting, mending and urging. She was the one who forced dialogues, who planned events, who reminded one of the other's birthday, suggesting gifts and ideas. Kaye was, as George was not reluctant to point out, the brains behind the whole operation. She feared that if she was not at the helm, her family would shatter. It was her job to keep them together, and she took the job very seriously.

After the lecture was over, Kaye was meeting Ruby for tea at a place in Chelsea they both loved. The first time Kaye had brought Ruby for tea, she had been as delighted as a little girl, though she was already in high school. They had sampled several teas, punctuated with darling (as Ruby called them) sandwiches. When their waiter brought the three-tiered tray for them to choose, Kaye suggested that he might want to leave it. Ruby and Kaye ate everything and then moved on to the clotted cream and jams and tiny muffins and scones. It was all deliciously decadent. For a period of about two years, Ruby refused to take tea with her mother, insisting it was far too bourgeois for her plebeian tastes (Ruby's description entirely). During that time, George had referred to Ruby as the Plebeian Police. Whenever she came to visit, Kaye and George scurried around the house removing all evidence of their bourgeois lifestyle, including copies of *People,* name-brand products, any clothes with designer labels, and any DVDs that were not foreign or independently made. It was easier to do this than to listen to Ruby's tirades against the Establishment and to endure her long-winded lectures about how they were conspiring with the enemy by supporting large corporations. Fortunately, this period did not last as long as her punk rock phase (during which she pierced her lip, her eyebrow, and her nose), and she turned her attention to ecological concerns. As with anything Ruby set her mind to, she was completely committed and tended to bully others to follow suit. At first, George had been inclined to hide the paper towels, napkins, and tissues that were not planet friendly if Ruby was paying a visit. But Kaye refused to be browbeaten by her own daughter.

To Kaye's surprise, she arrived at the restaurant to find Ruby already seated and happily engaged with a pot of tea and a book.

"Hello, dear," Kaye said.

Ruby looked up, smiled widely, and stood to kiss her mother.

"You look terrific," Kaye said. She ran her hand over Ruby's wiry curls. "I *love* your hair."

"It's all about the hair, isn't it?" Ruby said. "Try some of this tea. It's ginger peach and yummy."

As if on signal, the waiter brought another cup and saucer and handed Kaye a tea menu. Ruby introduced him, saying, "This is Steve." Kaye nodded and ordered black chai, but poured herself a little from Ruby's pot just to taste.

"Very yummy," Kaye said. "How are you?"

"I think I'm all right."

Kaye smiled. Ruby was such a serious girl these days. Somehow the earnestness that had replaced her flighty approach to almost everything had also calmed her. Almost immediately after she sat down, Kaye noticed Ruby had stopped biting her nails. They were still short, but they were also perfectly groomed, covered with polish that had just a hint of pink in it. Kaye knew better than to say anything. Even a positive remark would likely be misinterpreted.

"Well, you look swell," Kaye said. "Truly, you do."

Anything more would likely have been seen as criticism of how Ruby looked before. Steve set her pot of tea down and turned over her china cup. He was marvelously efficient in the way that only someone who considers himself a professional can be. Apologizing for the interruption, he backed away, forewarning them that he would return with their sandwiches momentarily.

"Thanks. You look quite swell yourself," Ruby said. "What's new with you?"

"Not much, really. Same old, same old."

"How's Barbara?"

"Barbara is wonderful if not a bit worried about your pal Justine."

"Ah," Ruby said. "My pal Justine. Now there's a story."

"So you know?"

"Not only do I know, but I've actually met the fellow in question."

"And?"

True to his word, Steve returned with a beautifully arranged tray of crustless sandwiches and left without further conversation, giving them privacy. Ruby took one of each kind of sandwich and arranged them on her plate. She bit into a watercress-and-avocado combination, and made appreciative noises as she chewed.

"I'm so glad they use cloth," she said, wiping her mouth. "It makes the dining experience completely satisfying." She smiled. "And no guilt."

Kaye laughed and poured herself some more tea and then bit into a sandwich and said, "So you were just going to tell me about Justine's whatever-you-want-to-call-him."

"I guess I'd call him her lover. What would you call him?"

"The same, I guess."

"The lover's name is Clifford, and he's a pretty nice guy. I don't approve of their relationship. I'm fairly certain that Justine will get hurt. He's having a fling even though he tells her how much he loves her. But she loves him more. And he has a wife and kids."

"So why doesn't she get out now?"

"Why?" Ruby looked incredulous. "C'mon, Mom. You know why. The sex is great. It's almost always about the sex, especially in this kind of relationship. Secret lives make for great sex. Everyone knows that."

Instead of responding, Kaye signaled the waiter. He was at her side almost immediately, offering the next course. Kaye took a much too large serving of clotted cream and then selected the largest scone from the tray. Ruby smiled and said she was much too full already, but she would love another pot of tea and maybe just some fresh fruit.

"No dessert?" Kaye said, trying not to seem too surprised. Ruby had never dieted, having been blessed with lean genes from George's side of the family. "That's a surprise."

"I'm trying to go vegan," Ruby said. "The cream is a no-no."

"That's a shame," Kaye said, licking her fork. "It's delicious."

"It will take its toll."

"I think it already has." Kaye smiled. "So where do you see this relationship with Clifford going?"

"Oh, I think that eventually Justine will give him an ultimatum. They'll have sex a few more times after that. It will make it even worse because that will be the best sex of their relationship. It always is. Parting sex is so poignant. That's what makes it ferocious. You know, in a savage sort of way. After that, it will burn out. Justine is smart. She'll realize the guy is a dog and has to be shown the door. And that will be that."

It did not take much effort to read between the lines. Ruby was even more complex than Kaye had always suspected. And secrets were apparently not Kaye's exclusive domain.

"And how long will all this take?"

"Most? Maybe another month or two."

"I see," Kaye said. "You seem very knowledgeable about this subject."

"I am," Ruby said in a way that made it clear she would say no more for the moment.

Kaye discreetly signaled for the check. Within moments, they were outside. It was cold and almost dark, though it was not yet five. They walked down the steep stairs and stood facing each other on the street.

"Ruby, I don't know what to say or what to ask." Kaye fussed with Ruby's scarf. "I'm at a loss."

"It's late, Mom. I should get going." Ruby kissed her mother's cheek. "Don't worry so much. I'm all grown up." Her smile was, as always, just a little lopsided, making it difficult to know how serious she really was at any time. "I love you."

"And I love you," Kaye said much too solemnly for the occasion. "I really do."

"It's okay, Mom. I'm really okay. Sometimes it just feels good to grab on to a secret and hold on. Maybe it makes us feel special in some weird sort of way. Don't you have any secrets?"

For one completely crazy minute, Kaye thought she was going to tell Ruby about Frank. Ruby suddenly seemed so wise, as though she would completely understand why her mother was having an affair. Blessedly, Kaye returned to her senses and behaved like a mother.

"Of course, Ruby. You're right."

Apparently some people were better at keeping secrets than others. Mistaking her mother's restraint for injured feelings, Ruby seemed to reevaluate her position on secrets. In what was clearly a weak moment, Ruby rolled her eyes. This was followed by a dramatic wave of hands and an exaggerated sigh.

"His name was Gabe," she said.

"Whose name?" Kaye said. She was confused, lost in her own reverie of deception and subterfuge. "Who's Gabe?"

"The man I was involved with." Ruby looked sorry she had even mentioned his name. "The *married* man. The reason I am so knowledgeable about Justine and what will happen with Clifford."

"Oh, Ruby, I'm so sorry. I should have known what you meant. I've been distracted lately. I'm sorry. Gabe. Well, I guess there's no point in asking why you never brought him around. Did he hurt you, darling?"

Ruby shook her head and laughed, holding up her hands in what seemed like despair, but was really irritation.

"Hurt me? I guess so. I met him in a bar. He didn't tell me he was married."

"What did you do when you found out?"

"Nothing. I did nothing." Ruby wiped at a stray tear. "I don't feel good about what I was doing, but he told me that his wife wasn't interested in sex anymore."

"Did he really?" Kaye said. "He sounds like a really clever fellow."

Ruby did not miss the sarcasm; she simply chose to ignore it.

"We had great sex," Ruby said. "He seemed genuinely unhappy with his wife and genuinely horny."

Kaye bristled. "Why are you telling me this? This isn't my business, Ruby."

"Isn't it? You have a husband. Do you know where he is all the time? You need to keep an eye on Dad. He's very handsome. Lots of my girlfriends would go for a guy like him. He's smart and funny, and he's sexy too. Mostly, he's unavailable, and that has an allure all its own."

Finally, Kaye understood. Ruby could never have imagined that her mother might be having an affair. But Ruby's daddy was another story. Ruby was warning Kaye about what could happen if she did not pay closer attention.

"Did you want to marry Gabe?" Kaye said.

"I don't know. It doesn't matter anymore. I gave him an ultimatum, though. I wanted him to choose, and he did."

"I'm sorry, Ruby."

"Yeah, well, whatever. It was good for a while."

"That's important."

"I guess so," Ruby said. "But not important enough, right?"

They walked to the subway together. Kaye pressed three twenties and a ten into Ruby's hand in spite of her protests, and they kissed good-bye, promising to have dinner the following week. On the way to the train, Kaye thought about one of her patients, Ariel. She was divorced, had remarried, and was now recently widowed.

In her very first session, Ariel, thirtysomething by her own definition, had described how several years ago she had traveled to a
gorge of cedars and olive trees in the northern Galilee town of
Amuka to pray at the tomb of Yonatan ben Uziel, a rabbi who had
been dead for more than two thousand years. Ariel had explained
that although she was not superstitious, her parents, distraught that
she had not remarried after her first disastrous attempt, had insisted
that she make the pilgrimage. Rabbi Yonatan, a disciple of Hil-
lel, the revered Talmudic sage of the first century BC, was believed
to study Torah with so much burning passion that if a bird flew
overhead, it would be instantly incinerated. Although he had died
a bachelor, folk legend evolved around his inexplicable ability to
intercede on behalf of those desperate to find love.

On the anniversary of his death in the Hebrew calendar, thou-
sands of pilgrims flocked to his tomb to recite psalms. Ariel described how she had wrapped her wish for a husband in a red silk
scarf and hung it from an olive tree branch alongside countless others. Within three months of her visit, she was married to a man she
met at the tomb. Their first child was born just weeks before their
first wedding anniversary. Regrettably, two years later, her wonderful husband unexpectedly died. Now Ariel was fighting depression
and considering a return to Rabbi Yonatan's tomb. Should she return to the tomb and ask for another husband, adding that this time
good health must be a prerequisite? Kaye said she did not see any
reason why it would be wrong to return to Rabbi Yonatan's tomb,
or to ask for a healthy husband this time around. Relieved, Ariel
said she would consider making the pilgrimage one more time.
Her loneliness was terrible.

Kaye imagined herself moving along the sun-baked walk that
twisted up to the ancient stone-block structure that housed the
tomb of Rabbi Yonatan. Joining the throngs of young hopefuls who
had never found love or who had missed opportunities, as well as

parents who worried that their children were still alone, Kaye saw herself draping a scarf from one of the olive tree branches. Tucked inside the scarf were several written notes. The first was a plea for Ruby, a hope that she would recognize true love when it came her way. The second note was for Charlie, for a good woman who would love him. And the third note was for George, an entreaty that he would forgive her after she left him.

Eleven

ONE of the junior editors at Barbara's publishing house, Patricia, swore that her uncle Kenneth would be perfect for Barbara. Kenneth was divorced from his first wife and left a widower by his second, so he was a stranger to neither relationships nor sorrow. It seemed a perfect combination. Of course, Patricia failed to mention that Kenneth liked to abbreviate everything. That was not the worst part of his affectation. After the abbreviation, he said the words in full, prefacing them with "you know." He was looking for an SO ("you know, a significant other") who could make him LOL ("you know, laugh out loud"). By the time the entrée was served, Barbara had a headache. When Kenneth took her home and asked if he could see her again, she almost said. "N-O, you know, no." Instead, she told him that she had been wrong. It was too soon after her husband's death. She simply was not ready to date. Kenneth understood. It had taken him a good month or two after his beloved Lauren passed to even think about dating, much less about sex. He asked Barbara how long it had been since her husband passed. When she told him the truth, he offered himself. The first time was the most difficult. If anyone knew that, he did. Thanking him for his generous offer, Barbara said that she had slept with a lot of men since Roger's death; she just had not dated any of them.

Grateful to finally be home, Barbara threw her bag and wrap on the counter and checked her messages. There was Kaye, sounding serious and asking Barbara to call, no matter how late it was; Daphne, sounding typically weepy; and her aunt Faye, sounding disappointed. It was too late to call Aunt Faye, an aged aunt of Roger's who kindly checked in from time to time. And Daphne, well, it was never a good time to call Daphne. Anyway, Barbara was starving. Even the food at dinner had been unsatisfying. After she changed into sweats, she stuck some leftover Chinese food into the microwave and dialed Daphne's number. Her machine picked up after the second ring. Poor Daphne was worried that callers might be too easily discouraged if there were too many rings. Barbara left a message, saying she was in and available, no matter what time Daphne needed to call. The call to Kaye could wait because she had been inexplicably lax herself about returning calls. In fact, she had been downright inattentive. Whatever she was going through, Kaye had distanced herself enough to make it clear that she did not want to talk about it. Except for that one time she had shown up on Barbara's doorstep visibly weepy and overwrought, Kaye had maintained a sphinx-like profile.

After she poured herself a generous glass of wine, Barbara arranged the brown rice and vegetables, chopsticks, and a bottle of water on a tray. Her desk was a mess, but she cleared a space for the tray and turned on the computer. Under her pseudonym, Barbara had created a website: www.delilahsdivulgences.com. It was a place for women to anonymously share their sexual exploits. Barbara had concluded that universally, women remembered all the incredible sex they had ever had. And Delilah's fans were proof of just how willing and eager women were to share. The response was overwhelming. Barbara weeded through these submissions, culling them for details of what made women tremble. Invariably, the women's stories were not as much about sex as they were about how men made them feel. All the messages had one common denominator. A woman would agree to practically anything if a man showed he had some tenderness, some ability to nurture something other than his own base inclinations. A man who said, "You look tired. Let me finish up," was guaranteed a night of pleasure unlike anything he had ever imagined. It was that simple, and all the e-mails Barbara received confirmed this.

At the core of all the great sex women wrote in about was a man who knew how to do the laundry without being asked, or how to change a diaper without making a face. The husband who volunteered to do the grocery shopping with the kids in tow on a Sunday morning so his wife could have the morning to herself received (according to the account his wife shared on the website) an evening of sex that began under the dinner table with her bare foot on his groin (as he urged the children to finish their macaroni and cheese), and ended with her kneeling at the foot of the bed, pressing her face into the coverlet while her husband satisfied a long-awaited fantasy.

When Barbara had downed the last mouthful of food and taken her final sip of wine, she decided to take a break and call Kaye. It was late, but Kaye had said to call, no matter how late it was. It was eleven thirty, but George sounded wide awake when he answered, and Barbara realized she should have phoned Kaye's cell phone.

"Hi, George. Did I wake you?"

"Hey, Barbara," he said. "No, not at all. Everything all right?"

He really was a nice man, although she harangued him unmercifully at times. Good husband material even if he was not the most interesting person in the world. There was a lot to be said for good husband material.

"I guess," she said. "Kaye left me a message."

"Oh? Well, she isn't home yet. I think she went shopping with Ellen. They were going to try to get tickets to a show or have dinner. Something like that."

"You weren't invited?" She was trying to be funny, but she immediately regretted her words and added, "Me neither."

"Well, I don't think it's quite the same, but thanks anyway."

George cleared his throat, and Barbara wished again that she had remembered to call Kaye's cell.

"Can I give Kaye a message?"

"I guess so. Just tell her I called."

"Good enough. How are the kids?"

"Good. Everyone is good. And your kids?"

"Busy with their own lives. As it should be, right?"

"Absolutely," Barbara said, wanting nothing more than to end this conversation. "So you take care."

"I have been. Actually, I've been working out."

It was a totally random comment, but clearly an effort to keep the conversation moving. She listened to him talk about the gym he had joined as her thoughts wandered to his biceps. He had very well-developed biceps, and lately she had been giving biceps a lot of thought. Strong biceps were highly underrated. For some time, hands had been the featured body part in her imagination. She stared at men's fingers, imagining them curved, running along the length of her legs; then, she imagined them rigid and inside her, finding the places she liked to have probed. Before fingers and biceps, it was an even more primitive absorption, and she often found herself in a trancelike state, staring at men's crotches while she rode the train. One man who had been the object of her shameless scrutiny had even pressed his card into her hand as they stepped onto the platform in Grand Central Station, urging her to call, anytime, really.

"You should try it," George said.

Barbara realized she had missed a whole section of their conversation.

"I will," she said. "Definitely."

"Really? You will? That's great," he said. "I think you'll love it."

"I know I will," she said, hoping she had not agreed to bungee jumping or swimming with the dolphins. "As soon as the winter is over."

George's silence told her she had missed an important cue.

"So what were you talking about?" she said.

"Skiing." George sounded slightly irritated, like a sulky adolescent. "A very popular winter sport."

"I'm sorry, George," she said. "I have a lot on my mind."

"It's all right. I guess I was going on a bit."

"No, not at all. I would like to go skiing. I've never been."

"Really?" He brightened. "They have day trips, you know. Maybe we could all go."

"Maybe. Let's talk about it."

They said their good-nights and Barbara felt miserable for him. His loneliness was so evident. Barbara dialed Kaye's cell and went immediately into voice mail. Annoyed, Barbara left a message, asking Kaye to call back, pointedly adding, "Tonight, please. It's urgent." Less than a minute passed before Barbara's phone rang and Kaye's voice, heavy with sleep and concern, was asking what was wrong.

"Where are you?" Barbara said.

"What?" Indignation altered her tone. "What's going on? You said it was urgent."

"It is urgent. Are you with Ellen?"

"Did something happen to Ellen?"

"I thought you were with Ellen. George told me that you were shopping with Ellen today, and then the two of you were going to take in a show and dinner."

"When did you speak to George?"

And then Barbara knew. She recognized the nervous edge that always accompanied the unveiling of a lie. Roger's voice had always sounded the same when he came home too late or too drunk, or when the bills could not be paid. Somewhere between the anxiety and the defensiveness was the hope that the con might go on just a little bit longer, just long enough to figure out how to avoid exposure. A drum roll should have accompanied this confrontation with Kaye. Something, anything, to mark the event. It was clearly a juncture in Kaye's charade.

"What difference does it make when I spoke to George?" Barbara said.

"I was just asking."

"Where are you, Kaye?"

"That's not really your business, is it?"

"I'm asking you to tell me the truth."

"The truth? That's new for you, considering you've always given truth a bad name."

"I've changed, and apparently so have you."

"I have to go now, Barbara."

"Is it Frank? Have you been seeing Frank all this time?"

"I have to go," Kaye said.

Somewhat stunned, Barbara realized that Kaye had actually hung up. Barbara poured herself another glass of wine. There was a bowl of artificial fruit on the counter. Pears. They were all pears, red ones and so real looking that people were always fooled unless she forgot to dust them. Roger had always teased her about the pears, claiming it tickled her to put one over on some unsuspecting fool. She hotly denied this, but he was right. They were so dusty now that only a real fool would have been deceived. There were twelve pears in all. They had been an impulse purchase at some crafts fair together with the brilliantly red rattan bamboo bowl that held them. Moistening a piece of paper towel, she wiped each pear and then the bowl. Just as she set the bowl back in its place on the counter, the phone rang.

"I'm sorry I hung up on you," Kaye said. "I don't know why I did that. I've never done anything like that before."

"It's okay," Barbara said. "Apparently you're doing a lot of things you've never done before."

"Do you think it's apparent to everyone?" Kaye asked.

Barbara knew exactly what Kaye was asking. "You'll have to work that out with George, honey. I can't help you with that."

"I need to see you."

"Now?" Barbara looked at the clock. "It's past midnight. Can't it wait until tomorrow?"

"No. I'll lose my nerve. I already phoned Ellen and asked her to meet me at your place. Do you mind?"

"Of course not," Barbara said. "Drive carefully."

*   *   *

IF Kaye was, as Barbara suspected, at Frank's place, it would take better than a half hour to arrive. It was unlikely that there would be any traffic at this late hour, even on a Saturday. Barbara put up a kettle of water and measured several spoons of black tea into the infuser of her favorite teapot. It had been another impulse purchase. It seemed a long time since she had bought anything just because she thought it was beautiful. The teapot was made from unique, mineral-rich clay that was found in the Yixing province of China. This particular type of pot, with a reclining and laughing Buddha carved into its handle, was a replica of a design that dated all the way back to the Ming dynasty. With each brewing, natural oils from the tea were absorbed, seasoning the pot and intensifying its color and finish. Whenever Barbara lifted the lid of the teapot, she inhaled the mingled scents of teas, as well as the memories that accompanied the numerous cups of savory liquid that she had shared with others or enjoyed alone.

Kaye arrived first, hugging and apologizing simultaneously. By the time Barbara took Kaye's coat and hung it in the front closet, Kaye was already in the kitchen, pouring the tea.

"I'm so sorry," Barbara said. "I had no right to attack you."

"No, no, it's my fault. I should have been more forthcoming. This is a terribly awkward situation on many levels." She smiled very slightly. "Having an affair requires a lot of planning. That's never been my strong suit. Planning."

"No, I guess it hasn't," Barbara said. "So, it is Frank then, isn't it?"

"Most definitely." Her cheeks were flushed, and her eyes shone over the rim of the cup as she sipped her tea, nodding her acknowledgment. "Most definitely." She saw Barbara's expression and said, "I'm sorry."

"I feel sort of like the cuckolded husband."

Kaye reached over to pat Barbara's hand. "I'm sorry. You shouldn't."

"I shouldn't? You lied to me. You shouldn't have lied to me."

"I'm sorry. You're right. But aren't you the one who is so cynical about the people who insist on the truth all the time?"

"This is different, Kaye. This is between us. Anyway, I think George knows, or at least suspects."

"Tell me what he said." Kaye swirled the tea around in her cup and picked out a stray leaf. "How bad is he?"

"He seems sad." She folded the towel into a neat square and rested both hands on top. "And very lonely."

Kaye shook her head and said in a not-to-be-mistaken tone of defiance, "I refuse to feel sorry for him. George had plenty of opportunities to make our marriage work. I tried everything. We did the counseling route. You know I tried. All these years I hoped to make a life with him. That's why I'm so surprised by your attitude." She held up her hand as she saw Barbara was about to respond. "Let me finish, Barb. I'm happy now, and I'm not going to apologize for it. Beyond that, there isn't much else to say."

"Are you really happy, Kaye?"

"Don't you think I know when I'm happy?"

"I don't know. Sometimes we all get confused."

"I'm not confused, Barb. I'm happy."

"Really?" Barbara said, "I guess I underestimated Frank."

"I guess you did. He's good to me, and good for me."

"Well, that doesn't make me feel any better," Barbara said.

"It was never my intent to deceive you. Under the circumstances, we thought it would be easier for you to work with Frank if you didn't know. And we were just not ready to make our relationship public to anyone."

Barbara reached over and placed a hand on Kaye's arm.

"Don't tell me you've become one of those people who begin every sentence with *we*. I'll have to kill myself. I can't take it."

"Don't be unkind, Barb. You'll regret it later. You always do."

"I know. I promise that I'll try to deal with this. But Frank works for me. You should have considered that."

"Actually, Frank doesn't work for you. He works for your publisher. But I knew you would feel this way. If you must know, Frank wanted to tell you, but I insisted we wait."

"If you say *we* one more time, I'm really going to have to do something drastic."

"Oh, grow up. I don't have to tell you everything I do or whom I sleep with. Do you tell me everything? Do I expect you to tell me everything?"

"This is different."

"That's just plain silly. Why can't you be happy for me?"

"I *am* happy for you."

"This is happy?" Kaye shook her head and folded her arms across her chest. "Listen to me. I'm going to go forward with my life."

"What does that mean?"

"I asked Ellen to come over because you are my two best friends. Frank has asked me to marry him, and I said yes. That's why I left you a message earlier. I wanted to tell you my good news."

"Good news? Let me guess. You asked Ellen to come over because you can't decide who should be your matron of honor, so you want us to decide. Right?"

Instead of answering, Kaye pursed her lips and poured herself some more tea.

"I'm sorry," Barbara said. "I just think you're moving too fast."

"Too fast?" Kaye sounded incredulous. "How much time do we have left? What should I wait for? My children are grown up. I have a successful practice. George will be fine. He'll meet someone who can make him happy. I'm just not that person."

"What about Gertie? She loves George."

"This is ridiculous. You're telling me to stay with George because my mother loves him? I can't believe you."

"What about your children?" Barbara said. "How will they feel when they find out?"

"My children are adults," Kaye said. "I've been a devoted mother. I know they will be hurt, but it's my turn now. I love Frank, and I want to be with him."

"Kaye, listen to what you're saying."

"I *am* listening to myself, Barb. *You're* not listening. I am in love. I may never feel this way about anyone again. I can't miss this opportunity for a better life."

"What's wrong with the life you have?"

"George never makes me feel the way Frank makes me feel."

"Too bad," Barbara said. "And how long will that last? Have you weighed all this nonsense against the life you've made with George?"

"Of course I have," Kaye said. "And it's not nonsense. It's not that I don't care about George. I really do care about him. I love George."

"Then think this through, Kaye. I'm not telling you to end your affair. Let it play itself out. Have a double life. Men do it all the time. This whatever-you-want-to-call-it with Frank won't last forever."

"How do you know?"

"Because I know men, and I know Frank Fiske."

"What does that mean?"

"Kaye, do you really think you're the first woman Frank has had an affair with since he came to work for my publisher?"

"I never thought about it," Kaye said. "And I don't care, anyway."

"Well, you should think about it, and you should care." Barbara said. "What makes you believe you can trust Frank to be faithful? Men like Frank are rarely faithful for long."

"He loves me."

"So does George."

"I'm going ahead with my plan."

"You do realize that if you go through with this, the fallout will be extensive."

"I don't have a choice."

Barbara threw up her hands in surrender and said, "I think it's a mistake. I love you, Kaye, but I can't support you in this."

"Then don't. I stand forewarned. Now let me make my own choices."

Barbara arched her brow and was about to have the last word

when the buzzer rang. Without even bothering to ask who it was, Barbara buzzed back to let Ellen in and opened the door to wait for the elevator. When the elevator arrived, the door opened and Ellen stepped out, looking so wan and stunned that Barbara turned to call out to Kaye to come quickly. Together, they ushered Ellen inside. Ellen leaned on Barbara and squeezed Kaye's proffered hand. "My father is dead," she said and burst into tears.

Twelve

"I DON'T think I've ever seen you without false eyelashes," Barbara said.

Kaye shot her a disapproving look and ushered Ellen to a counter stool, murmuring condolences and rubbing her back. No one was more appearance conscious than Ellen. As smart as Ellen was, she still believed a really flawless haircut and the right shade of lipstick could make a bad situation better. She was unabashedly candid about this. Barbara and Kaye owed the several really excellent pieces of clothing in their wardrobes to Ellen's taste and knowledge. Thanks to Ellen, Barbara and Kaye each had two good pantsuits (single-breasted, never double-breasted); two traditional suits (one with a pleated skirt and one with a pencil skirt); five pairs of slacks (two black, one gray flannel, one brown tweed, and one tan); a well-cut blazer; a tweed jacket, a trench coat, and a dark wool overcoat; two pairs of boots; three good pairs of pumps in black, brown, and navy; and several pairs of dress shoes that Ellen called two-hour shoes. In addition, Ellen insisted on three good white blouses, a selection of dark silk shells, one really good cashmere sweater, and scarves galore. With unwavering patience, Ellen tried to teach them how to wear these scarves to achieve different looks. Neither Barbara nor Kaye, however, could achieve the right combination of effortless elegance that made a scarf a worthy accessory. A crowning achievement had been a visit to an eyebrow expert, someone Ellen felt was more important than a family physician. But Ellen had given up on her friends' hair. Barbara changed her color and style according to her moods, and Kaye's last haircut had been catastrophic, pushing Ellen to resign from her role as the self-proclaimed haircut supervisor. "I wash my hands of your hairstyles," she had told them both. "You are dangerously on your own."

"Horrible, right?" Ellen said, smiling wanly through her tears. "What a sight I must be."

"You look just fine." Kaye said. "Don't pay any attention to her."

"I'm sorry," Barbara said more to Kaye than to Ellen. "I was just surprised. I didn't mean anything." She turned to Ellen. "I'm actually more surprised at how upset you are. I barely knew you had a father." Kaye glared at her. Using her hands and face, Barbara said, *What?*

Ellen sighed deeply and dabbed the corner of her eyes with a tissue. Her mascara was smudged, and without any lipstick she looked truly bereaved. "It's true. It's just that I was so surprised when my brother Hugh called," she said. "We had just spoken a few weeks ago. He called to invite me to Dad's birthday party. Did I mention that to either of you? I guess not. I've been so busy at work. Anyway, I said I'd think about it, but I had made up my mind to go. I just never got the chance to call Hugh back and tell him. Dad would have been ninety, and I haven't seen the family in ages." She blew her nose. "I feel so stupid. It's not as if we were close or anything. In fact, I was going to ask you both to come with me. I couldn't bear the thought of going alone."

"And we would have come," Kaye said gently. "This must be such a shock."

"It's not really. I mean he was old. Hugh wanted me to come to the party because he was worried that Mother's death seemed imminent. She has terrible emphysema. My father had a little diabetes and some arthritis. Hugh said that occasionally there was a flare-up of gout, but he was otherwise in remarkably good health for someone his age."

Barbara concurred that ninety was quite old. She had lost both parents by the time she was thirty-five. Of course, she said, losing a parent was difficult no matter how old one was.

"That's the point, isn't it?" Kaye said. "It's another rite of passage."

"Love those rites of passage," Barbara said. She suddenly brightened. "But hey, now we can go with you to the funeral and meet your family, minus Dad, of course."

"Is something wrong with you?" Kaye said.

"I don't think so," Barbara said. "C'mon, it's not like Ellen was close to this guy."

"It's still her father." Kaye put her arm around Ellen and hugged her. "When is the funeral?"

"I really do want you to come with me. I cannot face these people alone. I'm not sure when it is, though. Hugh said he would call with all the details. They'll wake Dad for at least two days, if not three. I wish he had died after the birthday party. At least I would have had a chance to first see my family under a less awkward circumstance."

Kaye and Barbara looked at each other quickly and except for Barbara's slightly arched brow said nothing. They knew very little about Ellen's early life. She was closemouthed about the person she had been before she reinvented herself as an interior designer and lauded hostess via marital connections and obligations. She hated when Barbara referred to her as a socialite, but there was some truth in it. Much of her life before she came to New York was a mystery. They knew she had a strained relationship with her brothers and parents. She almost never saw them and, unlike Kaye and Barbara, Ellen never shared any warm memories or displayed any family pictures.

"Are you all right?" Ellen said to Kaye, suddenly remembering there had been another reason for meeting. "Why did you ask me to come here?"

"Never mind that now," Kaye said. "My news can wait."

Barbara had folded her arms across her chest, silently watching them. Ellen caught her expression and decided not to be persistent.

"Are you sure?" Ellen said. "My father isn't coming back any time soon."

"My news can wait," Kaye said.

Ellen blew her nose. "I can't remember the last time I spoke to my father. And I haven't been home in almost two years. I feel so guilty. I didn't think I would, but I do."

"Guilt? Now there's a time-honored concept," Barbara said.

"Since when do you believe in guilt?" Kaye snapped. "First the truth and now guilt. A complete transformation."

"I didn't say I believed in it." Barbara's tone was cool and even. "I merely acknowledged its existence."

Ellen looked from Kaye to Barbara. "Why do I feel like I missed the first ten minutes of the movie?"

"Whatever it was, it can wait now," Kaye said. "Your news is more significant."

"I see," Ellen said. "So, you're telling me that I won the disaster contest? How nice for me. I haven't won anything in a long time." She sipped her tea. "You asked me to drive up here for a reason. I'd like to know what's going on."

"Anyone for toast?" Barbara said.

For the first time since she had arrived, Kaye was grateful to Barbara.

"That sounds good," Kaye said. "With lots of butter?"

Before long, they were eating buttered toast in the warm kitchen as if it were any other late night. But it was not any other late night. Barbara and Kaye had learned that Ellen had a father, and now he was dead. Kaye had called in her two dearest friends to hear her confession. And Barbara had discovered, yet again, that she was not nearly as brave as she had hoped. Kaye took advantage of the lull to satisfy the initial intention of their get-together. She put her arm around Ellen and told her everything. Ellen nodded, leaning her head in toward Kaye as she admitted that her relationship with Frank had not ended after Barbara's convention. Kaye slowly revealed that she was planning to leave George and move in with Frank, and eager to begin a life that she had only imagined was possible. Throughout all this, Ellen and Barbara listened quietly. Barbara played with the remaining triangle of toast on her plate, crumbling it into tiny pieces. And Ellen, though not typically one to respond to anything quickly, seemed unusually restrained.

"You're angry with me," Kaye said.

"Me?" Ellen said. "I'm not angry. I don't know quite what to say just yet."

"I'm happy, Ellen." Kaye began collecting the dishes, scraping the plates and stacking them. "This is good for me."

"Leave the dishes," Barbara said. "I'll do them in the morning."

Ellen looked at her watch and said, "It is the morning. It's almost two." She turned to Barbara. "Did you know all along?"

Barbara snorted. "Of course not. That was the purpose of this little meeting."

"We can get through this without being mean, Barb," Kaye said.

"I'm not being mean."

"When you preface your descriptions of people or events with a diminutive, it's your way of being condescending," Kaye said. "In my book, condescending is mean."

"In *your book*?" Barbara said. "Is there anything in *your book* about betrayal and family and loyalty? Or does *your book* skip those chapters?"

They all just stared at each other. If they ever quarreled, it was never about anything any one of them would be likely to remember. But this was different, and Ellen, anticipating what she would have to face in the days ahead, spoke up.

"We need to call a truce until after the funeral," Ellen said. "I cannot get through the days ahead without both of you firmly in place, concentrating on me. Is that clear?"

Without looking at each other, Barbara and Kaye nodded obediently.

"I know there is a lot to absorb here," Ellen said, measuring her words carefully, "but if we fall prey to judgments, we'll be lost." She took Kaye's hand. "I'm happy that you're happy. I really, really am, but I would be lying if I didn't admit that it's hard to separate those feelings from my sadness. I feel sad about George and about Ruby and Charlie. Their family will be torn apart, and that's just sad. That doesn't mean you don't deserve to be happy, but how different is this really from what Bill did to me? And you and Barbara were merciless. Maybe he really fell in love with Daisy. Maybe she gives him what I couldn't."

"Oh, Ellen." Kaye pulled her into an embrace. "I'm sorry. I didn't mean to open up old wounds."

"Old wounds?" Ellen laughed. "These are far from old. It doesn't take much to open them, so don't worry. If you want to see old wounds," she said, prophetically, "wait till you meet my family."

*   *   *

THE funeral was set for Wednesday. Hugh called early the next morning, causing Ellen to bolt upright in bed and shout *yes, yes* into the phone as though someone else had died. He apologized profusely. He had not even expected to find her home, thinking she would be out jogging or something. He thought everyone in New York jogged or went to the gym on a Sunday morning.

"So you didn't want to speak to me?" Ellen said, finding the wherewithal to disguise her overreaction with humor. She could not have slept more than three hours, and those hours had been filled with pouncing jaguars and baby chicks turning into rats. "Avoiding me already? I thought you were my only ally." Hugh's laugh warmed her, although she burrowed down into the covers anyway. Since Bill had left, she was cold almost all the time, especially first thing in the morning. "What time is it anyway?"

"A little after eight and I am your ally, Sis. I just wanted to be sure you had the information. Are you sick?"

"No, just exhausted. Why are you up so early?"

"Church. I'm waiting for Maureen. We go to church every Sunday."

"Jesus," Ellen said, and laughed, regretting both offenses immediately, "I'm sorry. Nerves, I guess. Or just irreverence."

Ever the consummate gentleman, or at least a seasoned diplomat, Hugh let it pass and said, "We've decided to wake Dad for two days. It's what Mom wants."

"And the fanfare never ends."

Although Hugh was a patient man, Ellen was evidently testing his limits.

"They've lived in this town their whole lives. A lot of people will want to come to say good-bye. That's the way it is when you stay in the same place for so long."

"I'm sorry. I didn't mean to sound critical. I just think wakes are a little barbaric."

"Well, that's the way we do it. And besides, it's a good way to accept that death is just another part of life."

"There should be an easier way than gathering around a made-up corpse for two days."

"So far we haven't come up with an alternative, Ellen. And no matter how much you balk at the arrangements, you need to pay your respects to your father."

"At least you didn't say *dearly departed*," Ellen said. "So when do the festivities begin?"

"Tomorrow," Hugh said. "Will you be driving or taking the train?"

"Driving."

"You're welcome to stay with us. We've got plenty of room, and Maureen would be pleased."

"Thanks, Hugh. I really appreciate the offer, but I think two of my friends will be coming along. Barbara and Kaye. Maybe we'll stay in a motel or in one of the inns."

"You're all welcome to stay with us. It's good to be with family at a time like this."

"I'll let you know."

"Ellen? Can I ask a favor of you?"

"Of course."

"Don't come up looking for a fight. Let's bury Dad and celebrate his life. His grandchildren loved him. There's no reason to taint the memory of their Pa."

"Pa? Is that what they called him?"

"Yes. Grammy and Pa."

"That's sweet," Ellen said.

"Ellen. Please."

"I'll call you later, Hugh. What time do you get back from church?"

"We go out for pancakes afterward at Phil's. Remember that place?"

"Sure do. Best burgers and pancakes around. Really good pie too. I remember how much I used to love their banana cream."

"It's still good. Phil's son runs the place now. He's serving a few more trendy dishes for the summer folks, but during the rest of the year, it's burgers, stew, and mile-high pancakes."

"Enjoy. I'll call you this afternoon."

"One more thing, Ellen."

"Yes?"

"You won't bring up the baby thing with Mom, will you? She's very fragile and what with Dad's sudden death."

"What baby thing, Hugh?"

* * *

AN art installation near Ellen's office had once exhibited a sculpture of two motorized hands, one of chalk and the other cloth. The chalk hand wrote, and the cloth hand followed, erasing the marks. Ellen had been mesmerized by the artist's intent, wondering if the goal was profundity or humor. The gallery owner had offered a third possibility, suggesting a combination of both. After all, there was an element of humor in all great truths, and what could be more truthful than a mistake that could never be erased, following one into eternity and beyond? Ellen had blanched, immediately worrying that her expression had given away her history, allowing her facial expressions to be read the same way FBI agents were taught to observe the tiniest flicker of an eyelid or a scarcely noticeable flaring of the nostrils. Any facial movement at all hinted at something that could be construed as a window into the person's life. It had been Ellen's lifelong goal to conceal her past, to keep her sorrow and shame private. Although she had considered purchasing the piece, she stumbled out of the gallery after her exchange with the owner. Feeling strangely violated, Ellen fled, walking backward at first because she was too afraid to turn around and leave herself even more exposed. She nearly knocked over another piece, apologizing profusely to the bewildered owner, who seemed suddenly delighted. Unable to return to her office, Ellen hailed a cab and went home, threw herself down on the bed, and immediately fell into a deep and troubled sleep. When Bill came home, she told him about her day, and he murmured *never you mind*, smoothing her hair and assuring her that it had been nothing more than coincidence. Calmer, but still unconvinced, she had taken comfort in his sympathy and pleasure in his kindness.

Now she had neither a child nor a husband. And she had to rally herself for the days ahead. She was grateful for Barbara and Kaye, but Bill would have handled the whole event with natural graciousness. He was always so good at easing awkward situations. The few times her parents had met Bill, she had seen her mother's grudging approval even though she had never said so much as a word to Ellen. Her father had called him a man's man, a comment that had sent Bill into peals of laughter when she told him this later. Her brothers had been uniformly polite even when their wives had flirted with Bill, clearly infatuated with his good looks and charming ways. Now she would have to not only face her estranged family, but field their questions about her missing husband. It all seemed so horribly unfair. In one of those knee-jerk moments that guaranteed regret, Ellen dialed Bill's number and promised herself she would not hang up, even if Daisy answered. In the first act of grace all weekend, Bill answered.

"It's Ellen."

"Ellen." He paused. "Are you all right?"

"I don't know."

Sounding genuinely concerned, he said, "Are you hurt?"

Unintentionally, she laughed, and said, "Indeed." Then, quickly, she told him about her father and about how much she dreaded going home for the funeral. Then she asked him if he remembered how hysterical she had been after the episode in the gallery, the one where she had seen those mechanical hands.

"Yes," Bill said. "I actually do remember. I went to the gallery the next day to have a look for myself."

Ellen drew in a sharp breath of air. She had never known that.

"I understood why you reacted so strongly."

"I'm sorry now that I didn't buy them. If I hadn't thought the owner was a crafty undercover FBI agent assigned to expose me, I might have."

"And why would she have been assigned to you, Ellen?"

"Why? Because I allowed my baby to be taken from me."

"Ellen."

She could see him shaking his head, and she began to sob, great, heaving expressions of grief. Through her sobs, she heard the sound of heels against what must have been ceramic tile. The sound pierced Ellen's heart. Daisy had entered the room. The heels had stopped *clip-clop*ping and were now replaced by a slightly nasal and plaintive barrage of questions from someone in evident proximity to Bill. Ellen sensed that he had immediately placed his hand over the receiver to muffle his words, and she strained to hear whatever she could. She had stopped crying the moment she heard the heels. It was too humiliating to do otherwise even if Daisy could not see or hear her. When Bill finally spoke, his voice was strained.

"Are you all right?" he said.

There was no point in apologizing, and no point in her making any comment about what had just happened. They were beyond the recrimination phase.

"I shouldn't have called you," Ellen said. "I'm sorry."

"No, I'm glad you called. I've been thinking about you."

Ellen said nothing. She did not trust herself to speak.

"Would it be all right if I came over?" Bill said.

She hesitated too long. She should have said no immediately, but the delay exposed her, made her vulnerable, and he knew it and seized his opening.

"Ellen?"

"I don't think so, Bill. It's a mistake."

"It's not. I hate for you to face all this alone."

She stiffened. "I'm not alone. I have friends, devoted friends. Friends who would never betray me."

"Of course. Of course. I know that."

Of course he knew nothing. As anticipated, Bill had either ignored or missed the point. It occurred to Ellen that behind every woman who has been betrayed is a confused man. A man who simply cannot understand why women must continue to carry on about something that is over and done. What really was the point of that? Even more fantastic was that men were so good at convincing women that it was a valid argument.

Ellen braced herself. She had made a terrible mistake, and she had to recover without further incrimination.

"I shouldn't have called. It was just all that thinking about the baby and all, and remembering that day in the gallery. You were so kind."

"I'm still kind."

"But now you're kind to Daisy, aren't you? Now it's Daisy that you love, right?"

It was the eternal question of the betrayed woman, and Ellen hated herself for asking. But, thankfully, she hated Bill more after she heard his answer.

"I respect her, but it's you I've always loved."

Barbara would later tell her that she should have asked him to come over and greeted him at the front door with a shotgun. "Right in the middle of the head," Barbara said. "Ka-boom!" At the moment, however, Ellen wavered. She was mortified by her own weakness, ashamed that she still desired him. But she was smart enough to know that she would bemoan her decision forever if she said yes. Every woman does each time she allows herself to be persuaded one more time by a man who has deceived her and broken her heart.

"Just for an hour," he coaxed. "One hour, Ellie. Sixty measly minutes. I'll time it."

Maybe, just maybe if he hadn't said *measly*, she would have agreed. *Measly*. When had he ever used such a word? It was so juvenile. And then she remembered who he lived with, and it all made sense. *Measly*, indeed.

"Another time, Bill. It's just too much for right now. You understand, don't you?"

"Fair enough," he said.

He hung up before she could say that he had lost the right to ever use the word *fair* again. Ever, ever, ever again.

Thirteen

IT would be at least a three-hour drive from the city to Ellen's childhood home in Connecticut. She would pick up Kaye first and then Barbara. It had taken a bit of doing to make all the arrangements. Kaye had to cancel several appointments and reschedule everyone for the following Friday, a day she did not normally see patients. Barbara's work made it less complicated for her to leave on sudden notice. She could always take her laptop and work in the car. Ellen had booked rooms for them at a local bed-and-breakfast. Her treat, of course. They would leave very early Monday morning. That would give them time to settle in, unpack, and get to the funeral home. It was Ellen's plan to return home on Wednesday as soon as the funeral was over. *Immediately afterward* was the way Ellen put it, and the way Kaye told it to Frank as they talked in bed Sunday afternoon.

"I guess she's dreading this," Frank said.

"I guess."

"I wonder what really caused the rift."

Kaye propped herself up on her elbow and said, "What do you mean?"

"Well, something really dramatic has to happen for a family to become so divided," he said. "Doesn't she have a lot of siblings?"

"Three brothers. She's the youngest."

"Think about it. The only girl, the youngest. The circumstances tell their own story. There must have been something that caused the family to part with such hostility. Do you think she could have been abused?"

"It doesn't always have to be something that dramatic, Frank. It's like erosion. A lot of different conditions can contribute to the deterioration and then to the collapse."

"I love it when you talk like a psychologist."

"Do you?" she teased, holding him at bay with her free hand. "Families are in crisis all the time."

"It must be awful to be so estranged from your family." He stroked her bare leg. "I can't imagine not speaking to my sister Ginny again, or not speaking to Oliver. It's unfathomable. I need them to remind me of where I came from."

Barbara's words turned over in Kaye's head, a nagging presence. What did she really know about Frank? She had never met any of his friends, and he took all his calls in another room, mouthing the word *business* to her as if it were a secret code to another dimension. He kept anything that was in the slightest way personal out of view, but he was almost predatory in his eagerness to know about her life. His hand inched up her leg, making its purposeful ascent with just the appropriate modicum of playfulness to distract her from her thoughts.

"Estrangement is more common than uncommon, especially these days," Kaye said. She placed her hand over his, trying to control his advances. "It's very sad."

"Very." Frank pulled her closer. "I'm not feeling very estranged from you."

"I'll have to go home soon," Kaye said. "I have to pack."

"I know," Frank said. He kissed her neck. "I'll miss you."

"Silly. I'll be back Wednesday." Her cell phone rang, and she scrambled to find it in her bag. It was George. She pulled the sheet around her naked body. "Hi. Is it really three already? I'm sorry. What? Yes, thanks. I really appreciate you picking up Gertie. Ruby's there already? That's lovely. Yes, get some lettuce if you can. Of course I'll drive carefully. Bye. Me too." She closed the phone and put her head in her hand. Her cheeks were flushed.

"Me too?" Frank said.

He hung his lip down in a way that Kaye wasn't sure whether she found endearing or revolting. Rather than think about it, Kaye dropped the phone into her bag and turned around. She was still holding the sheet crunched up around her breasts.

"Yes, me too. George said he'd like to fuck Frank, and I said me too."

Frank was momentarily dumbstruck, and then he laughed. She lay on top of him and covered his face in kisses as she pulled the sheet over their bodies. He had no way of knowing that she was thinking that this is what her mother must have meant when she had first warned Kaye that she was going to hell in a handbasket. And to think, back then it was because she had stolen a lipstick from Woolworth's.

* * *

"POOR Ellen," Ruby said. She was standing at the sink breaking up the lettuce with her hands. "She must be miserable. She's been through a lot."

"Yes, she has," Kaye said. "Make sure you get all the grit off. Boston lettuce is so sandy."

"I know how to wash lettuce, Mom," Ruby said.

"I didn't say you didn't." Kaye opened the oven door and checked on the chicken. "It was just a statement."

"It was the only kind that looked fresh," George said, trying to be conciliatory. "Sunday is a lousy day to buy produce. I should have asked you to pick some up in the city."

"What were you doing in the city again?" Ruby said. "You should move down there already. You're there so much."

"Am I?" Kaye said evenly, trying to remember to breathe. "I guess I'm so used to it that I never give it much thought." From the corner of her eye, she saw George gauging her reaction. "Did Charlie call and say what time he would be here?"

"No," George said. He came to stand behind Kaye, placing his hands on her shoulders, gently kneading in a protective way. "You look tired. You'd better brace yourself for the next few days."

She felt tense, and George's efforts were actually welcomed as she leaned back against him, surprising them both.

"Now that's what I like to see!" Gertie whooped as she entered the kitchen. "My children, happy and in love."

"Hi, Mom," Kaye said. She bent down to kiss her cheek. "I'm glad you decided to honor us with a visit."

"My pleasure," Gertie said. "How could I resist a chance to see my Ruby?" She held out her hands. "Look, she already did my nails."

Kaye took her mother's hands and admired the black nail polish.

"It definitely makes a statement," Kaye said. She rubbed her mother's hands. "Your hands are very cold. Do you feel well?"

"Old people have cold hands," Gertie said. "Poor circulation. Worry about yourself." She pulled her hands away and went to check the pot of soup on the stove. "I made a nice kidney bean this morning with broad noodles. Just the way my Ruby and Charlie like it."

Ruby smiled and wiped her hands on her apron. The apron must have been Gertie's idea. If Kaye had suggested that Ruby wear an apron, she would have made a scene. Gertie, however, could tell Ruby anything and expect compliance.

"Thanks, Mom." Kaye said. "What's new?"

"What should be new?" Gertie said. "Tell me, how's Ellen? George told me you were driving up with her for her father's funeral. I'm glad. No one should be alone at such a time."

"Oh, she's anxious. There are so many levels to this situation. It's hard to know what's really at the bottom of the whole family drama."

"Every family has its own drama," Gertie said. "No one escapes."

"True." Kaye took five plates from the cupboard and looked up at the clock. "Shouldn't we phone Charlie?"

"It's still early," George said. "He'll call when he's on the train. How about a glass of wine?"

"That sounds perfect," Kaye said. "Mom?"

"Sure, why not? I'm going to hell in a handbasket no matter what I do," Gertie said.

Kaye dropped the glass she was holding. It just fell out of her hand.

"Damn," she said. "I'll get it. It just slipped out of my hand."

"Happens," George said. He was picking up the big pieces while she stared down at the floor. "Careful. There are shards everywhere."

"I thought the expression was going to heaven in a wheelbarrow," Ruby said.

"No," Gertie said, shaking her head. "It's definitely a handbasket, and it's definitely hell."

"I think they both mean the same thing," George said without looking up. "I think it was the Grateful Dead who said, 'but at least I'm enjoying the ride.'"

The phone rang, and Ruby jumped to answer it. From her urgent whispers, Kaye could tell it was Charlie. Ruby and Charlie were cohorts only when they teamed up against their parents. Kaye didn't mind, and she knew George didn't either. They were glad for any excuse that brought their kids together. Kaye's only truly fond memories of Solly were the times they used to team up against one of Gertie's implacable rules or badger their father until he was worn down. He was always easier to handle, always more willing to indulge their whims even if it contradicted one of Gertie's communist principles, like rejecting commercialism. If it had not been for their father, Solly and Kaye would never have had any toys at all, or even a television set. As Kaye looked over her own family, George at her feet, Gertie at the stove, and Ruby on the phone, it was difficult to imagine leaving them behind even for sex that made her body tingle for hours after. Impulsively, she touched the top of George's head, fingering his hair between her thumb and forefinger. He paused, startled, smiled up at her, and continued with his task. Neither of them wanted to make too much of her gesture. And it was really more of a gesture than an overture, as Kaye would later rationalize. But for now, it felt natural to show her appreciation as he stood and swept the small pieces into a neat pile.

"Let's have that wine," George said.

"Yes, let's," Kaye said. She waited as he emptied the dustpan into the garbage. A pang of remorse coursed through her as she rummaged through one of the drawers for the corkscrew and handed it to him. "There's a nice bottle of white in the fridge." From the corner of her eye, Kaye saw Gertie watching. "Thanks again. I don't know what happened. It just fell out of my hand, I guess."

"Happens," George said. "No big deal."

Ruby had disappeared, but she returned now, looking decidedly more cheerful. Charlie's arrival must have been imminent.

"Can I take the car?" Ruby said, untying the apron strings behind her back and pulling it over her head. "I have to pick up Charlie."

George took his car keys from his pocket and handed them over without any of the usual warnings. Everyone was clearly in a generous mood, and it was all because of Kaye. She was there, and she was oddly content. Something she had not been in months. Her mood always set the tone for the family.

"Tell him the soup is ready," Gertie said. "And I brought those little rolls he likes."

"I'll tell him, Grandma," Ruby said, planting a big kiss on her grandmother's cheek. "I'll be back in a flash."

As soon as the door slammed behind her, George popped the cork and poured them each a full glass. He raised his glass and said, "To us. To our family."

Kaye clinked her glass against his and then against her mother's but said nothing. As Kaye took a long and thirsty sip, she looked up and saw her mother watching her with knowing and disapproving eyes.

* * *

CHARLIE had an ease around everyone that neither of his parents could take credit for. It was as natural for him to join a group of strangers and make everyone comfortable as it was for someone to fix a car engine or sing an aria in perfect pitch. Charlie's personality was his gift, and Kaye could not have been any more in love with him. Ruby generally resented this truth, but today she seemed not only resigned to it but equally enamored of Charlie's seductiveness.

"There's my grandson," Gertie said. She opened her arms wide, and Charlie, stooping to her height, embraced her. "Let me look at you."

"Let me look at *you*," Charlie said. "Did you grow?"

Gertie laughed and pushed him gently, pressing both hands against his chest.

"I mean it," he said. "You look statuesque."

"Statuesque," Gertie said, mocking herself. "You're a funny boy."

All this while, Kaye was studying her son. Charlie was rarely dressed casually. George always teased him that he had asked for a tie for his third birthday. It wasn't true, but it could have been. He was dressed in casual chic this evening in dark perfectly pressed jeans, white shirt, and tan sweater topped off with a black suede jacket. He looked elegant. He knew exactly how to wind his black-and-white striped scarf around his neck, right down to the way it was tucked into his jacket. Even Ellen was impressed with Charlie's fashion sense.

"No coat?" she said.

Charlie turned and smiled. "Ah," he said. "The voice of reason that is the background music of my life." He hugged her tightly, and she inhaled his scent, smoky cologne that barely masked the somewhat damp and woodsy scent that always took her back to the loft she had briefly shared with an artist in Chicago. She was there working at part-time jobs and completing her dissertation. He, Mario, was in terrible need of money, and she, needing a cheap place to live, had pulled his phone number from the community bulletin board in the student center. The arrangement was cramped, but agreeable. They kept different hours. Mario worked through the night and slept until midafternoon. Kaye was out most of the day, went to bed early, and got up at dawn to do her work. One day she had come home from class to find the floor strewn with drawings of naked men and women having sex in every imaginable position. She was shocked only when closer examination revealed that she was the woman in the drawings. Mario, still asleep beneath the patchwork quilt he had made himself, welcomed her when she slipped under the covers, pressing her nakedness close to his. From that day on, they adjusted their schedules to accommodate their sex. When the summer was over, Kaye moved back to New York and married George.

"You smell good," Kaye said, accepting his kiss on her cheek and then protesting the several days' accumulation of stubble that grazed her skin. "You need a shave." She ran the back of her hand along his jawline. "Or not. I like the look." She kissed him. "It's good to see you."

"I'm sorry. I've been too busy," Charlie said. He set his leather knapsack down on the counter and hugged his father. "Nice to see you guys." He opened the oven door. "I'm starving."

"When aren't you starving?" George said. "Help me with the table, and give me some good stock tips. My own judgment is faulty."

George draped his arm around his son's shoulder as they moved off to the dining room. In the kitchen, Ruby dressed the salad, chatting on about her classes, describing mucus plugs and the benefits of raspberry tea to speed up labor. Gertie stirred the soup, tasted it, and added a pinch of coarse salt. She laughed when Ruby said that sex also hastened labor, stressing that stimulating the nipples was especially helpful. Kaye and Gertie exchanged the knowing looks of women who had been pregnant. Stimulating nipples and having sex, Gertie patiently explained, were not exactly what women about to give birth wanted to do. They argued these points while Kaye transferred the roasted potatoes from the pan to a serving plate. She looked over into the dining room at George and Charlie. As Charlie amicably folded napkins, George set out the plates and silverware. They were talking stocks and sports, and Kaye remembered how at birth Charlie had looked so much like George. Their likeness had soon faded, but Kaye had recently learned that this was actually an evolutionary phenomenon. At the time, however, she had not known this and had meant only to tease George that their likeness would dispel any future doubts about paternity. But poor George, confused and in a haze of new-parent bliss, had asked if he had anything to worry about. Kaye had quickly reassured him. In fact, she distinctly recalled that she had said, "Oh, never! Never, never, darling. There would never be a reason for such concern." *Never.* In retrospect, it seemed like something only a young woman would say.

"Mom?" Ruby was standing at Kaye's elbow, easing a slice of potato out of the pan. "So, so good. Are you all right?"

"Don't get oil on your blouse," Kaye said. "Yes, of course, I'm fine. Put this on the table, please."

"You seem to sort of fade out every now and then."

"Where's my mother?" Kaye said.

"Bathroom. You see? I was asking you a question."

"And I answered. I'm fine." She saw doubt in Ruby's eyes. "Really. Stop acting like an old lady."

"Something wrong with old ladies?" Gertie said as she reentered the kitchen. She checked on the chicken and nodded approvingly before she turned off the oven. "Let it rest a few minutes before we serve it. So, who's acting like an old lady?"

"Apparently I am," Ruby said.

"Good for you," Gertie said.

Kaye smoothed her mother's hair, an unusually affectionate gesture. They had never been particularly demonstrative, at least not spontaneously. Gertie was not aloof, but she was self-contained in the way of her generation. Except, of course, with her grandchildren.

"Let's eat," Kaye said. "Ruby, put out some of those rolls your grandmother brought. I'll serve the soup. George? Is the table set?"

"All systems go," George called to her from the dining room. "Don't forget the wine."

"Got it," Kaye answered.

Gertie expertly cut the chicken parts while Ruby held the platter. Their heads were close, and Kaye overheard pieces of their conversation,

"Solly always had to have the wings, so I made two chickens every Friday to keep the peace."

"My teacher says it's best to keep moving as long as possible when you're in labor . . ."

"I love the skin, but my doctor says not to eat it . . . What does he know?"

"There's never too much garlic . . ."

"Your mother looks well . . . I've been worried too . . ."

"Let's eat," Kaye said, hastily. "It's getting late."

Charlie came in to carry the platters. Ruby followed with the bread and more wine. And Gertie stood guard by her soup while Kaye ladled it into bowls, which Charlie carried into the dining room. The kitchen was fragrant with all the good smells, and the voices of her family seemed to harmonize. Kaye thought about Frank, eating alone in his apartment, listening to the radio and probably reading. She felt sad for him, though she knew he was fine. Her hands shook a little, and her mother, eyes never leaving the pot of soup, said, "You have a wonderful family, Kaye. Two beautiful children and a good husband."

"Are you having soup, Mom?"

"Just a little," Gertie said.

They continued in silence, but as Kaye absentmindedly adjusted the flame under a pot, her sleeve came dangerously close. Gertie intercepted, pulling at Kaye's arm and warning her daughter that when you play with fire, you can get burned.

"Let's eat, Mom," Kaye said.

"What? No thank-you?" Gertie said. "I'm trying to save your life."

Ruby stepped up behind them and said, "Is that it?"

"That's it, honey," Kaye said.

"Everything okay?" Ruby said, looking from her grandmother to her mother. "You guys look grim."

"Not at all," Kaye said. "Right, Mom?"

"Whatever your mother says," Gertie said, coolly. "She knows best."

"If you say so," Ruby said.

As soon as Ruby was out of earshot, Gertie reached for Kaye's arm. "Kaye," she began. "I only have your best interest at heart."

"Thank you."

"Don't be foolish."

"I'm not sure what you mean."

"Really?"

"Really," Kaye said. She emptied the potatoes into a yellow stoneware bowl trimmed in robin's-egg blue that had been a present from Ellen. "Really, really."

"Then it must be too late," Gertie said.

There was so much sadness in her voice that Kaye felt like crying. She turned away and washed her hands more carefully than necessary. Gertie watched and waited.

"Let's go eat, Mom," Kaye finally said. "Everyone is waiting."

"Me too," Gertie said. "I'm waiting for you to come to your senses."

Wordlessly, Kaye led the way into the dining room, carrying the bowl and wondering how many different ways there were to justify what coming to one's senses really meant.

*   *   *

THE suitcase was open on the bed, and Kaye was searching through her closet for her beige silk blouse. She had already found her black suit and hung it from the hook on the inside of the door. The suit really needed to be pressed, but she was too tired. She would hang it in the shower tomorrow morning and hope for the best. Ellen had phoned during dinner to say she would be there by eight. And Ellen was never late.

"Dinner was wonderful," George said. He was already in bed, propped up against two pillows, reading. "The kids look good."

"Yes," Kaye said, still rummaging. "I have to clean out this closet. I don't wear half these things. I thought Charlie looked a little tired, though."

"He's been working hard." George put his book down and raised his arms, folding his hands behind his head and interlacing his fingers. "He's young. He can handle it."

"I wish he'd meet a girl."

"I think he meets lots of girls."

"You know what I mean. I worry that he'll never settle down."

"He will," George said. He stretched his arms in front of him and yawned. "Charlie has a lot of time before he needs to settle down. You don't seem as worried about Ruby."

"I worry about Ruby." She knew she sounded defensive. "I really do, but differently. Ruby is a fighter."

"And Charlie?"

Kaye finally plucked her blouse from the closet with a small shout of triumph and held it up to the light, checking for stains. "Charlie? He's a lover." She laughed. "Lovers move through the world differently." She hung the blouse on the hook over the suit. "They need more care, more understanding." Smoothing the front of the blouse, she felt George's hands wrap around her waist. "Oh, I didn't even hear you."

"You seem to know a lot about lovers," he murmured into her neck. "I hope that's good news for me."

Slapping his hands lightly as they inched up and under her nightgown, Kaye felt slightly faint. Only this morning, she had been meeting Frank's thrusts, and now George was running his thumbs over her breasts and pressing into her from behind with unavoidable urgency. And she liked it.

"My mother is right next door," Kaye whispered.

Gertie had agreed to spend the night, and George would take her home in the morning. She was sleeping in Ruby's room. Charlie and Ruby had taken the train back to the city. They had looked so sweet, standing huddled on the platform. Charlie had protectively put his arm around her as they waited.

"I won't make any noise," George said. He was pulling her nightgown up over her hips. "Not a single peep." He maneuvered her against the closet door and pulled her hips toward him as he worked himself against her. "Shh, quiet."

She realized he was referring to her breathing, which had become labored as she arched herself to meet him, moaning loud enough to be heard from another room. Carefully, he led her to the bed and eased her onto the coverlet, turning her over. He never shaved on Sunday, and the stubble grazed the skin on the inside of her thighs, making her gasp. As her pulled her nightgown up over her head, she giggled, imagining her mother on the other side of the wall, listening. The laughter caught in Kaye's throat as George's mouth found her. Minutes later, she was returning the favor, running her tongue in circles and telling herself that none of this should be happening. It was wrong. Two different men in one day. But then George was ready, and he positioned himself, lowering himself slowly as he bent over to kiss her, first on the mouth and then on her neck. She told him to hurry. There was no way of knowing when that handbasket to hell or that wheelbarrow to heaven was finally coming for her.

Fourteen

AT eight sharp, Ellen pulled up to the front of Barbara's building. Two coffees and a bag of bagels were carefully positioned on the backseat. Ellen was already having her coffee, returning it to the cup holder between sips. She popped the trunk for Barbara and waited while she positioned her suitcase and garment bag. When Barbara was done, she closed the trunk and rapped on it twice. As she slid into the front seat, she turned around, sniffing eagerly.

"There are bagels too," Ellen said.

"Any whole wheat?" Barbara said, searching the bag.

"Yes. They should be marked."

"Do you want anything?"

"Plain with cream cheese, please."

"A very sensible and Protestant choice," Barbara noted.

"I'm a lapsed Catholic, not a Protestant."

"Same difference," Barbara said as she handed Ellen half a bagel in a napkin with an extra napkin for her lap. "These look good."

"Thanks." Ellen smiled. "For everything."

Barbara reached over and kissed her cheek.

"My pleasure, for everything."

"I can't tell you how much it means to me that you and Kaye are coming with me."

"We try to never miss a funeral."

"Well, this one will be memorable."

"Oh?" Barbara tried to sound as casual as possible. Ellen was so rarely forthcoming about her past or her family that it seemed as though the slightest indication of interest would scare her off. "What are you anticipating?"

"Everything and nothing," Ellen said. "I'm probably overreacting as usual."

"I've never really known you to overreact."

"Really? Tell that to my family."

"I will if you want me to," Barbara said.

"I'm sure you would."

It was a dark, chilly morning, and a cold rain had just started to fall. All of Ellen's memories of home were shrouded in exactly the same darkness, though she knew it was a trick of her imagination.

"Is there anything I can do?" Barbara said.

"You're doing it." Ellen gave Barbara a sidelong glance. "You don't need to be so cautious with me. I'm not quite as fragile as you seem to suspect."

"I don't think you're fragile, Ellen. I just know that your past is a no-trespassing zone, and I've always tried to honor that."

"Thank you."

"Thank you? That's it?"

Ellen laughed. "If you're expecting me to spill my guts on this trip, you'll be disappointed. At best, I can promise you a glimpse of my history. My family will speak for itself."

"Most families do."

"Ah, wisdom from a woman without one."

"What can I say?" Barbara said. "I got lucky."

"Sadly, there is some truth in that. Except for my brother Hugh, there's no one in my family I really care about."

"Then why are you going to the funeral?"

"Hugh asked me to, and I guess it seems like the right thing."

Barbara snorted. "The right thing? Now there's a concept I could never quite sink my teeth into. What does that even mean?"

"You know what it means, Barbara. A person's father dies, and the appropriate response is to attend the funeral and pay one's respects."

"Did you respect him?"

"It doesn't matter," Ellen said. "It's not about my father. It's about me. I'm going for myself. I need to do this. I feel compelled to make an appearance."

"And you're curious."

"A little, I guess. Wouldn't you be?"

"I've been curious about you for years," Barbara said.

At the red light, Ellen turned and acknowledged Barbara's comment with a slight shrug. But that was all. Silence. It had been her only defense against her mother's daily verbal assaults. Nothing was ever good enough for her. Nothing was ever right. She had to rearrange everything, make everything better. Her mother's mouth was set in a perpetually bitter line, and she was always at Ellen about something. Early on, Ellen had learned how to steel herself against her mother's diatribes. Ellen would hold still, regulate her breathing, and remain silent, implacable. It was the only way to endure the attacks. The slightest indication of weakness whetted Alice's appetite. The approach worked until Ellen found out she was pregnant. She cowered under her mother's rage and took cover in her room, forcing a chair under the doorknob at night for fear that her mother might come in and kill her and her unborn baby. Alice approached the debacle as simply another mess that only she could right. And when Ellen told her mother that she wanted to keep the baby, Alice's response was no different than if Ellen had announced she would not do one of her chores. Alice simply set her mouth in an even tighter line and made it quite clear that it was not up to Ellen to decide. Alice was obviously the only one in the family capable enough to fix what Ellen had broken. Ellen's transgression was unforgivable. That was the final verdict, and Ellen's father went along without any protest. He never spoke to Ellen about the matter except to say that her mother knew what was best. Even when Ellen begged him to intervene, he said, "I'm sorry. I can't." And he never did.

The light changed, but Ellen did not notice until Barbara pointed up and said, "Green."

Sighing heavily, Ellen drove on. She wanted to tell Barbara and Kaye about Faith, but it felt like such a fiercely private sorrow that if she shared it, she might come apart. Somehow her ability to keep Faith's existence to herself held some sort of mystical power, like not telling your wish when you blew out the candles, or the wish wouldn't come true. Ellen had convinced herself that if she carried her sorrow alone, she would be recompensed in some magical way. Still, she knew Barbara needed some explanation, some reason for why Ellen had felt the need to escape her home and her family.

"I don't mean to be so tightlipped about my past," Ellen said. "I just don't know any other way to be."

"That's ridiculous," Barbara practically sputtered. "It's all part of that stoic Protestant nonsense."

"I told you, I'm not Protestant," Ellen said.

"Well, you might as well be for all the difference it makes to me."

"You're so egalitarian." Ellen pulled up in front of Kaye's house. "Should I get her?"

"I'll get her."

As Barbara turned to open the door, Ellen touched her sleeve and said, "Let's talk about something else on the way up there."

"Sure. How about Kaye's reckless infidelity?"

"Perfect."

The streets were busy already with school buses and children. The rain had started to fall more steadily, and a flurry of umbrellas had suddenly appeared. It seemed as though they had opened all at once; the colors were reassuring, almost hopeful. Ellen was momentarily sorry that she did not believe in signs.

"There's Kaye now," Barbara said. She waved and opened the window. "Need help?" Kaye had a small overnight case and a garment bag. She shook her head as Ellen popped the trunk open again. George had come out on the porch as well, and he walked toward them, his step jauntier than it had been for the last few months. Ellen and Barbara exchanged looks. Kaye busied herself, stretching out her garment bag and smoothing it down with both hands.

"Hey there, ladies," George said. He walked around to the driver's side and kissed Ellen. "I was sorry to hear about your father. Are you all right?"

"I'm fine, George. Thanks. It's really not a great shock. *That's* still to come."

"Let's hit the road," Kaye called out rather abruptly, slamming the trunk shut. "Time to go."

"Looks like my better half is in a rush," George said. He opened the back door for Kaye and stepped aside, so she could slide in under his arm. "You in?"

"I'm in," she said.

When George folded his long body over to reach in and kiss Kaye, Ellen and Barbara stared. He held the back of her head as he kissed her, letting them know that he had reclaimed his wife. Awestruck, they watched as Kaye kissed him back, even holding his arm as they said good-bye.

"Well, good luck," George said.

"I'll call you tonight," Kaye said.

Ellen and Barbara said good-bye in matching small voices, looking straight ahead as Ellen pulled away from the curb.

"Don't say a word, either of you," Kaye advised as she turned around to smile and wave.

"His better half?" Barbara said. "Boy, is he deluded."

"I warned you, didn't I?" Kaye said.

"You slept with him, didn't you?" Barbara said, laughing incredulously. "You're a little slut. A real backdoor woman. Go figure."

"He *is* my husband, you know," Kaye said. "It's legal."

"Legal, but not ethical," Barbara countered. She turned around to hand Kaye a container of coffee. "What the hell has happened to you?"

Ellen glanced at Kaye in the rearview mirror. She was blowing on her coffee and apparently considering Barbara's question. After several sips of coffee, Kaye finally said, "I don't know. I really, really, really don't know."

"Well, that's commendably honest," Ellen said.

"So what?" Barbara said. "What *is* the sudden deal with honesty?"

"So nothing," Ellen said. "It was just a comment."

"Might I point out that I can hear both of you?"

"Sorry," Ellen said.

"Don't you find this a little weird?" Barbara said, directing her question at Ellen. "Would you have slept with Bill after he started sleeping with Dixie?"

"*Daisy.* And I did sleep with Bill after he took up with her." Ellen shrugged. "It just happened."

"Like a safe falling on your head? Now, that's something that just happens. But we aren't cartoon characters." Barbara shook her head. "You both seem very casual about this. I don't get it."

"There's nothing to get," Kaye said. "I love George. I love Frank too. Actually, I slept with both of them yesterday." She opened a bagel to peer inside. "Is this plain cream cheese?" Without waiting for an answer, she took a bite. "It was sort of weird to feel like a man. I'd have to say it was empowering on some level."

"I don't think I've ever done that," Ellen said. "Slept with two different men in one day."

"I have," Barbara said. "Actually, I slept with them at the same time."

"Get out," Kaye said. "What was that like?"

"Satisfying. Of course, I was only seventeen, and I wasn't married to either of them." She gave Kaye a meaningful look. "And it was just part of experimenting."

"So, I'm experimenting too," Kaye said, licking cream cheese off her lips. "George is a very good lover, but Frank talks more. I like that. He tells me how it feels while we're doing it, and he's hornier. George is very contained, but very thoughtful."

"Too much information, Kaye. Anyway, look at Ellen," Barbara said, pointing at Ellen's beet-red face. "I can't believe it. You're embarrassed."

"Am I?" She touched one cheek and then the other with the back of her hand. "I guess I am." She shrugged. "So what? I can't be embarrassed?"

"Didn't you ever have any careless flings?" Kaye said. "You know, a one-night-stand sort of thing? I remember a week in college that I slept with a different guy every night. That was intense."

"And dangerous," Ellen said, clenching the wheel. "For your information, I knew many men before I met Bill, but I was never immoral."

"Immoral?" Kaye said. "That seems very judgmental."

"I'm sorry," Ellen said. "That wasn't my intent."

"Well, I wasn't immoral or judgmental. I was just pregnant,"

Barbara said. "I loved Roger. Or at least I thought I loved him. No, I loved him. Maybe not. I was so young. Who really cares anymore?"

Ellen was quiet, staring resolutely at the open road. She was pale now that her blush had faded, and she seemed waiflike, lost.

"You okay?" Kaye said, leaning forward to touch Ellen's shoulder. "We seem to have hit a nerve."

"No, no nerve," Ellen said. She kept her eyes on the road. "I'm fine. Just a little tired and a bit anxious."

Barbara and Kaye tacitly agreed this was more than tired and anxious. They knew that they had somehow come closer to the source of Ellen's sadness than they had ever been before. Inadvertently, as is the nature of most discoveries, they had found themselves at a precipice, dangling dangerously between curiosity and allegiance. It was certain that one misstep could have irrevocable consequences. Kaye, who had never been a risk taker, now moved carefully toward the edge, inching her way forward with the studied exactness of her professional skills and her new bold disregard for propriety.

"Would you like me to take the wheel for a while so you can rest?" Kaye said.

Ellen raised her eyes to the rearview mirror and shook her head.

"I'm fine," she said. "Driving helps me take my mind off things."

"You mean the funeral?" Kaye said.

"Yes, there's that too," Ellen said.

"So it's more than the funeral. It's really your family."

"Well, of course it's my family."

Kaye said, "No one's family is perfect."

"Well, that may be true, but my family is so far from perfect that it's scary."

"You sound so hurt whenever you talk about your family," Kaye said. "It's painful just to listen to your voice."

Ellen was silent, but then she shook her head and laughed.

"Are you playing psychotherapist with me?" she said. "You're very good."

"Thank you," Kaye said. "But I wasn't playing psychotherapist. More like concerned and loving friend."

"And what's your story?" Ellen said, reaching out to pinch Barbara's arm. She had been looking out the window, pretending not to listen. "You think that I'll reveal my innermost secrets if you make yourself invisible?"

"Ouch," Barbara said, rubbing her arm where Barbara had pinched her. "No, I was just trying to be respectful."

"Of what?" Ellen said. "Kaye's interrogation strategies?"

"Maybe," Barbara said. "What's wrong with that?"

"It's shifty," Ellen said. "And I don't like being played."

"It's not like we planned it or anything," Kaye said.

"Oh, please, let's just not do this," Ellen said. "I have the same advice for each of you. Mind your own business."

"You are our business," Barbara said. "You're our friend, and we love you."

"We really do," Kaye said.

But Ellen had nothing more to share. She turned on the radio and drove the rest of the way without speaking to either of them. Barbara fell asleep, and Kaye made some business calls. Before long, they were turning off the exit to the place where Ellen's steely resolve to hoard her grief and shame had been forged.

*   *   *

"You shouldn't have booked a suite," Barbara said. "We could have all stayed in one room."

"Well, this is like one room," Ellen said. "I'll sleep on the pullout in the living room."

"My kids used to love these suites," Kaye said. "They always felt like they had their own apartment." She sounded wistful. "Why do we always want to be at a different place in our lives than we are?"

"I don't know," Ellen said, "but I wish it were three days from now."

"You need to change your attitude," Barbara said. "Something wonderful may come out of this experience."

"My mother could die too?" Ellen said. "Then I wouldn't ever have to come back here."

"Charming sentiment," Kaye said. She hung her garment bag on a hook at the back of the closet door and opened the zipper, peering inside to assess the wrinkles. "I love this suit. I bought it at a great sale last year. I've worn it a million times."

"I'm going to put my things away," Barbara said. "What are our plans?"

Ellen had plopped herself down on the couch with the remote in hand, and immediately found the Home Shopping Network. She was automatically mesmerized by the hostess's description of a filigree cross that she promised was both substantial and elegant. Ellen leaned forward; she wanted to hear every word Jodi, the hostess, said. Jodi was one of Ellen's favorites. She exuded warmth and compassion. Ellen trusted Jodi.

"Ellen?" Barbara said.

"Isn't that cross beautiful?" Ellen said. "Jodi says it's substantial and elegant. It really is, don't you think?"

"Jodi?" Barbara said. "You want to know what I think? I think you're nuts."

"You have no sense of what a cultural experience these shows are." Ellen sounded genuinely indignant. "You can't simply dismiss them based on snobbery."

"Why not?" Barbara said.

"Okay, girls," Kaye said. "Let's try to be tolerant of our various addictions. Ellen, can you tell us what plans you made with your family?"

"It's not an addiction," Ellen said. "And I haven't really made any firm plans as of yet. I should phone Hugh." Ellen clicked the remote, silencing Jodi. "Do you think those folks are actors or real people?"

"I still hold with my first assessment. I think you're nuts," Barbara said. "And who uses the word *folks*? Who are you? Did you fall into some sort of time warp when we crossed the state line?"

"I'm not talking to you anymore," Ellen said. She took her cell phone out of her bag and pressed the directory until she came to Hugh's number. "But for your information, I bought presents for my family on the Home Shopping Network. Ponchos for all the women and an animal-print blouse for my mother."

"What did you get your father?" Barbara asked. "An animal-print shroud? Imagine selling *that* on HSN."

"You can buy a casket online," Kaye said. Seeing their looks of disbelief, she added, "No, really. One of my patients had a casket delivered overnight."

"That's really good to know," Barbara said. "Was someone dead, or was it for her?" She turned to Ellen. "Now that would have been a thoughtful hostess gift to send to your family."

Waving her hand in dismissal, Ellen waited for Hugh to answer. "Hugh? Hi, we're here. In the hotel. No, it was an easy trip. Less than three hours and only because of some construction. You're at the funeral home now? Oh, I see. No, that makes sense. Yes, my friends are with me. I'll let them know. Thanks, Hugh. What? Yes, of course I know where Flannigan's is, the funeral home as well as the bar." She laughed. "Absolutely. I won't confuse the two. We'll be there in a half hour. Bye." She closed the phone and her eyes at the same time. "So, are you ready to meet Dad? He's all decked out and ready to be viewed. He'll be available to the public after four, but Hugh wants us to come there now."

"Is the whole family there?" Kaye said.

"Seems that way. Everyone except Mother," Ellen said.

"How is she doing?" Barbara said.

"I guess we'll find out soon enough," Ellen said. "Are we ready?"

"So it's Hugh and Maureen, Sara and Alan, June and Timothy, and Christina and Patrick," Kaye said.

"Very impressive," Barbara said.

"How do I look?" Ellen said. "Do you think I should put on some lipstick?"

"Why not?" Barbara said. "Your father will probably be wearing some."

"And yet another totally inappropriate sentiment," Kaye said. "Let's go and get this first part over with."

"Yes," Ellen said, checking her hair in the mirror. "Let's."

* * *

THE funeral parlor was an old Victorian home with a wraparound porch. Carefully tended plants in macramé holders were cleverly interspersed to provide just enough coverage for privacy, yet still the opportunity to look out over the manicured grounds. Elegant dogwoods surrounded the porch, and it was easy to imagine the heartbreak the flowering pink blooms might cause in the spring when grieving friends and family noted the beauty their newly departed loved ones would be missing. The setting was ideal, and the Flannigans had done everything to maintain the image of austereness and intimacy that was crucial to their business. Three generations of Flannigans had served the community, catering to their losses and easing their suffering at the wakes that typically took place in the local pub owned and run by yet more Flannigans. Ellen had dated one of the Flannigan boys in high school. He had been a nice boy, Liam Flannigan, and she had heard from Hugh that Liam, or Will as he was known, had grown up to be a nice man. He ran the pub with his wife, Eileen. Local news appealed to Ellen. Most of the boys and girls she had grown up with had stayed, many moving in with their parents and then taking over their homes after they died. Ellen knew she could never have stayed. Not even if she had never had Faith, not even if it had been possible to keep her.

"Well, if you have to have a funeral," Kaye said, "this is as good a place as any."

"I can't wait to see what it's like inside," Barbara said.

Ellen pulled into the parking lot. She rested her head on the wheel for a moment before she quickly checked her face in the visor mirror.

"You look great," Kaye said. "As usual."

"Too much makeup?" Ellen said.

Kaye and Barbara shook their heads.

"You're sure?" Ellen said. She smacked her lips together. "I don't want to offend anyone."

"I'm positive. You look fine."

"Come on," Barbara said. "Lead the way."

The porch was empty except for two men dressed in almost identical black suits, white shirts, and thin black ties. Ellen gave them a perfunctory glance, assuming they worked there, and then looked away. She was still unprepared to come face-to-face with anyone she knew. One of the men, however, turned and called her name.

"Ellen?"

At first she thought about not turning around. She could have kept walking, and it would have been clear that she was not, indeed, Ellen, but something about the man's voice compelled her to stop. It was Owen's voice. They had shared a bedroom, because he was the next youngest. At night, he had terrorized her with stories of murder and kidnappings. He had always been a sullen and angry boy, and by adolescence prone to fits of uncontrollable rage that she had always suspected were alcohol provoked. She could not remember the last time she had even spoken with him.

"Hello, Owen," Ellen turned, but she did not smile. "It's me. Is it you?"

"Always a wiseass," Owen said, putting his cigarette out with his heel, then bending down for the stub and flicking it into the bushes all in one deft movement. It was agility left over from his days as a star soccer player. It was, according to Hugh, the last success Owen had known. "Still pretty though, too."

"Thank you," Ellen said.

Neither made a move toward the other. Kaye and Barbara silently waited to be introduced. The man Owen had been talking to before the women arrived stepped forward and placed his hand on Owen's shoulder.

"I'm going to head inside," he said. He smiled at Ellen. "I guess you don't remember me. I'm Louis Flannigan." He put out his hand. "I hung out with Hugh's crowd. I'm sorry about your dad. He was a good guy. He used to take us fishing."

"Of course I remember you now," Ellen said. "I'm so sorry. I'm a bit overwhelmed." She turned to Kaye and Barbara. "These are my dear friends, Kaye and Barbara. They were kind enough to make the trip with me."

There was lots of handshaking and additional introductions all around.

"Where's your husband?" Owen said. "Working?"

Without any hesitation, Ellen said, "Yes. Unfortunately, he had a case that took him to Chicago. He was so sorry that he couldn't come. He even asked Kaye and Barbara to attend in his place, so they could look after me. He's such a sweetie."

"Such a sweetie," Barbara echoed.

"A real dear," Kaye said.

"I'm sorry I won't have the chance to meet him," Louis said. He smiled again at the women. "It's good to see you, Ellen, even under these circumstances, and a real pleasure to meet you ladies. I have to get back to work now. See you inside."

That explained the almost identical black suits. Owen was working for the Flannigans. It seemed an appropriate career move.

"Should we go in?" Owen said. "You'll have to see Dad sooner or later."

"I'm ready," Ellen said, too brightly.

"Let's go," he said. "I'll show you the way." He held the door for Kaye and Barbara and took Ellen's elbow as she passed. "I'm sure Dad will be happy to finally see you."

Barbara and Kaye were just over the threshold. Barbara stepped forward and slipped her arm around Ellen's waist. Almost instantly, Kaye flanked Ellen's other side. Owen, smart enough to see that he was outnumbered, as well as outwitted, waited until there was a safe distance before he followed them into the viewing parlor, where the rest of the family had gathered in force, not so much to view the dearly departed as to anticipate Ellen's arrival.

Fifteen

IT was a shock to see almost her entire family all at once. It was likely that Louis had forewarned them because they had gathered in front of the coffin like a Greek chorus, ready to offer commentary on the forthcoming reunion. Ellen hesitated, but she was propelled forward by Barbara and Kaye's steady grip. When Hugh emerged from the back of the throng, smiling generously, Ellen was so overcome with relief that she broke free of Barbara and Kaye and threw herself on him as if he had come to rescue her from a burning building. His bulk steadied her, and she closed her eyes, grateful for his presence.

"Ellen," Hugh said, "it's been much too long."

His embrace was genuine, and she was touched by the way he released his grip but held her hands, keeping her at arm's length to fully assess her appearance.

"Still too skinny," he said, shaking his head. "Never could get you to eat a damned thing."

"That's not at all true. It's good to see you, Hugh," Ellen said. She turned to look over her shoulder, and Kaye and Barbara stepped forward. "These are my friends, Kaye Lerner and Barbara Shore."

"Finally we meet," Barbara said, shaking Hugh's hand. "Too bad it has to be under such circumstances, but . . . well, it's nice to meet you anyway." She shrugged and nodded at the rest of the family, who remained silent, but cordial. In fact, they seemed eager to be introduced, anticipating their turns with patient politeness. "We've heard a lot about your father." The group seemed to take a collective breath, releasing it only when Kaye reached for Hugh's hand, introduced herself, and then stepped forward into the crowd like a seasoned politician, asking everyone's name and even kissing one or two babies. As each family member was introduced and then stepped aside, the coffin was fully exposed.

"Oh, dear," Hugh said, "we forgot all about Dad. He would certainly have had something to say about that." He held out his hand as if it were necessary to introduce the deceased and said, "Here's Dad."

Everyone stepped aside, allowing Ellen to pay her respects, though she would have been just as happy to keep her distance. Nevertheless, she knelt in front of the coffin, pressing into the padded bench for stability, and leaned over to peer inside. Hugh Sr. was wearing his Sunday best. His good blue suit had been freshly cleaned, and he looked surprisingly dapper in a white shirt and a red tie decorated with little golf balls. In fact, a golf club and a fishing rod rested alongside his body, together with several family photographs, a bottle of Black Label, a Bible, and a worn-out Yankee cap. A rosary had been placed between his clasped hands even though he had never attended church unless it was for a special event or the occasional bingo game. Ellen crossed herself and pretended to pray, because so many pairs of eyes were on her. She lost her balance as she tried to stand, and Hugh was quick to grab her arm and say a few consoling words, believing that she had been overcome by emotion. Indulging this misconception was easier than correcting it, and Ellen waited until she was safely off the bench before whispering, "Dad played golf?"

Hugh started to laugh and then seemed to think better of it. "He took it up fairly recently," he said. "Maybe in the last six or seven years. I think he just loved driving around in that cart. We had some fun with it, and it was more exercise than waiting for the fish to bite." There was no recrimination in his tone, but it was evident that he had a lot on his mind. "He mellowed in these last years, Ellen. There was a lot he was sorry about. I think he would have liked you to know that."

"He could have phoned me," Ellen said. "He could have written me a letter."

"Dad? A letter? You know that wasn't his style. Fancy-boys write letters. That's what he would have said. I think he was waiting for you to come home."

"That's very sweet, Hugh." She was unmoved by Hugh's sentimentality, impressive as it was, considering that their father had rarely shown them any affection. "Well, I'm home now." She turned around. Most everyone had either taken a seat or wandered off into the lobby, forming small groups that merged, then divided, and then reunited again, reminding Ellen of the slides of amoebas she had studied in high school. She scanned the crowd for Kaye and Barbara, but they must have slipped out for some air or to use the washroom. Turning her attention back to Hugh, she asked, "Those photographs. Who picked them?"

"I did," Maureen said. She had been inching up on them, waiting for an opportune moment to interrupt. "It was hard to find old family pictures where everyone didn't look positively grim." Before Ellen could respond, Maureen said that she had made a really good pot roast with the little potatoes that Dad had been so fond of, and why don't you and your friends join us for dinner later?

"There's fresh apple pie, too," Maureen said. "You can talk to your nieces and get to know your nephews-in-law and their kids. They only have one great-aunt."

"That sounds very nice," Ellen said. "I'll have to check with my friends, but I'm sure they would be happy to get a front-row seat to my family." She placed a hand on Maureen's arm and in a voice that implied they were confidantes added, "It was Owen, wasn't it, Maureen? He picked the photographs, didn't he? You had nothing to do with it." Ellen shook her head. "I don't know why, but Owen wouldn't miss an opportunity to remind me of my loss. I'll never know why he hates me."

Maureen's fair skin colored, and her freckles stood out across the bridge of her nose and her forehead.

"I don't think it's you he hates, Ellen," Maureen said.

"I'm not so sure of that," Ellen said.

Maureen looked imploringly at Hugh, who held Ellen's gaze with impassive remoteness.

"It's time we took our seats with the rest of the family," he said, pointing to the clock on the back wall. "I can see that people are beginning to arrive."

It was an oddly defining moment in Ellen's homecoming. For all his warmth and sincerity, Hugh, the family's new patriarch, was every bit his father's son. If she had permitted any expectations that her oldest brother would openly acknowledge the family's continued complicity in her sadness, she would be disappointed.

"This isn't the time, Ellen," Hugh said so softly that both she and Maureen reflexively angled to hear him. "I am begging you not to make a scene. We have to conduct ourselves with some dignity here. The people in this community expect something from this family, and we have to deliver."

"I understand," Ellen said.

Responding to her evidently patronizing tone, Hugh's temper

flared. He ignored Maureen's pleading look, and said with more sharpness than he had evidently cared to expose, "This isn't about you now, Ellen. It just can't always be about you. We have to bury Dad. It's our job."

"And I'm glad to help," Ellen said, coolly smiling through her unflappable veneer. "Just lead the way."

Maureen was stunned by such bold disrespect and stepped away from Ellen as though mere proximity would link them, an association Maureen clearly now wanted to avoid. Even Hugh was taken aback by Ellen's insolence. He put his arm protectively around Maureen, excluding Ellen even further, and led his wife away. Ellen watched as they fended questions from the rest of the family, who discreetly looked in her direction and then solicitously ushered the new family patriarch and his wife to the seats of honor directly in front of the coffin. Barbara and Kaye were still nowhere in sight. The crowd had thinned as everyone found seats. Only a few stragglers, mostly young mothers with restless toddlers to chase after, congregated in the rear. No one looked Ellen's way, and she felt more forlorn than she had since first anticipating what it would be like to return to her home and to her family. She turned to look at her father again and moved toward the coffin, reaching in for the framed photograph that had been strategically placed where it would be immediately noticed. The photograph had been taken only days after Faith's birth and Ellen's return home. It might have been Easter because there was a lot of food on the table, and everyone was wearing church clothes except for Ellen. She was struck by the photograph because she was not wearing her own clothes. Nothing had fit her yet, and she had been forced to borrow a skirt from her mother, a plaid cotton horror with an elasticized waist, and a blouse that buttoned over her still-engorged breasts. When Ellen had complained about how awful she looked, her mother had told her that it would do her some good not to think of herself as so high and mighty all the time, adding that if for once she had thought of someone besides herself, she might not have to pump her breasts instead of helping around the house like other girls. And when Ellen had been dragged to the table by her father for the clove-studded Easter ham, he warned her not to make a scene in just the same way that Hugh had just urged. Then she had complied, tucking her blouse into the elasticized waist of the skirt and standing, unsmiling, next to her mother's chair while Andrew, who had recently developed an interest in photography, placed the camera on the tripod, set the timer, and raced back into the picture, taking his place next to Owen. All of them were grinning, probably at Andrew's quick return, except for Ellen. She had her hands on her hips, jutting her breasts at the camera, and a smirk that dared anyone to question the reason for her altered appearance. It inspired her now to see her younger self, so full of determination and willfulness. Only Owen would have been mean-spirited enough to suggest that picture.

"You all right?" Kaye said.

Ellen whipped around. She had not heard Barbara and Kaye's approach. Barbara took the photograph from Ellen's hand and studied it. Ellen decided not to say anything about her confrontation with Hugh.

"You look awful in this picture," Barbara said.

"Thanks," Ellen said, adding lightly, "That's probably why my dear brother Owen picked it."

"He's a real charmer," Kaye said. "What's his story?"

Ellen shrugged and took the picture back from Barbara, who said, "How old were you? Seventeen?"

"Thereabouts," Ellen said. She set the photograph back exactly where it had been before, careful to avoid any contact with her father. "It was a long time ago. That I'm certain of."

"Are you sure you're all right?" Barbara said.

"Yes," Ellen said. "I'm fine, really. Actually, I think I'm going to go to see my mother."

"She's not coming here?" Kaye said.

"Hugh said she wasn't up to it. She'll come tomorrow, for the closing of the coffin and the funeral."

"Do you want us to go with you?" Barbara said. "I can't imagine having any more fun than I'm already having, but I'd be willing to try."

"No, but thank you. I can drop you off at the hotel. I won't be long."

"Are you sure it's a good idea?" Kaye said.

"I'll be fine," Ellen said. She smiled at their worried expressions. "You look like a pair of bookends with those faces. I know what I'm doing."

"Whatever you say," Barbara said. "By the way, so far I like your father best."

"That's just because he can't talk back to you," Ellen said. "Oh, and Maureen invited us for dinner."

"Are we going?" Kaye said.

"Sure. I'll come back for you."

"The fun just never ends," Barbara said.

Their attention was suddenly diverted by Owen's entrance. He walked somberly toward the front row and took his place near Hugh and Maureen and their children and their spouses, along with Andrew's wife, Pamela, and their four sons. Hugh caught Ellen's attention and motioned for her to sit. Just as she was about to protest, she thought better of it and looked apologetically in Kaye and Barbara's direction, taking the seat between Owen and Hugh that had been held for her.

"I think I'd like to go see Mother," Ellen whispered to Hugh.

"Not now," he said. "Your place is here now."

She folded her hands in her lap and stared at the coffin. Suddenly, she remembered the photograph and the headstrong resolve of the girl in the photograph. Ellen patted Hugh's hand and told him he was right. She would stay an hour and greet those who had come to pay their respects. And then she was leaving. She wanted to see Mother alone, without his supervision. Owen tried to pretend he was not listening, but he was. Ellen was sure he had warned Hugh that Ellen would be nothing but trouble. She was sure Owen had said, *Her and her fancy friends and all their fancy ideas.* Ellen turned and saw that Barbara and Kaye had taken seats in the rear. As soon as she had their attention, she pointed to her watch, and held up one finger. They nodded. Clearly angry, Hugh moved his hand out from beneath hers, and Ellen gathered herself together and stared straight ahead, pretending not to be afraid, just like the sixteen-year-old in the photograph had so very long ago. It had been a lie then, and it was a lie now.

* * *

STILL protesting Ellen's decision to see her mother alone, Barbara and Kaye reluctantly agreed to be dropped off in town. Up until the last moment, they insisted that Ellen should be accompanied, if only for moral support. They even offered to wait in the car while she went inside, but Ellen was intractable. This was something she had to do alone. Of course, she said, between kisses and hugs, they were the best friends in the world and absolute dears to worry about her so much, but she would be fine. She would phone as soon as she left her mother. It wouldn't take more than an hour. There was nothing to really say to each other, not before and not now.

The back door was open as always, even though there was a spare key in the barbecue. Everyone in the neighborhood knew where everyone else kept a spare key. Ellen opened the door and was immediately pulled back into her childhood by the smell of cooked cabbage and old coffee. She recoiled momentarily, considering the possibility that she had made a mistake after all. Suddenly, she felt unprotected and wished Barbara and Kaye were waiting outside. The sound of an unfamiliar voice distracted her, and she remembered Hugh telling her that they had hired an aide to stay with Mother ever since she required oxygen. The voice Ellen heard now was soft and almost pleading, urging Alice to drink it all down, dear, like a good girl. Ellen shut the door with more force than necessary, hoping to alert them that someone had come in.

"Mr. Hugh? Did you forget something?"

A woman appeared in the kitchen doorway, looking surprised but welcoming. She was close in age to Ellen, but older in every way. In fact, oddly enough, she resembled Alice more than Ellen ever had.

"Oh, hello," the woman said. "I'm Janet." She held out her hand. "Are you Ellen?" Then, seeing Ellen's surprise, added, "Mr. Hugh phoned to tell us to expect you, but he thought you might be a while."

It was a family that did not care for surprises.

Ellen took Janet's hand, unprepared for the strength of her handshake, and said, "Yes. I'm Ellen."

"Your mother is in the living room. She's expecting you." Janet led the way, as though Ellen would not know where to find her mother. "She's watching television. She loves her stories."

"Yes, she always has." Ellen said. "We always knew never to disturb her when her stories were on."

"Well, some things never change, do they?"

"I guess not." Ellen smiled to mask her annoyance at Janet's proprietary tone. She acted as if she knew Alice best, which of course she probably did. "Thank you."

Stepping into the living room and seeing her mother in a wheelchair jolted Ellen. She had not expected to feel much of anything except anger, but she was startled by how feeble her mother appeared. A green oxygen tank was attached to the back of the wheelchair. As Ellen approached, her mother turned slightly to the side, revealing part of the clear plastic tubing that ran into her nostrils. Her hair was entirely white now. Ellen was glad to see that her mother had eschewed the do-it-yourself dyeing product that always produced terrible results, mostly because she refused any help from Ellen. All of Ellen's girlfriends helped their mothers dye their hair. The girls would trade secrets, talking about which colors to mix for a more natural result. But when Ellen had offered to help her own mother, Alice had scoffed, saying that she wouldn't trust Ellen to frost a cake much less apply dye to anyone's head. Ellen's revenge was the awful color her mother's efforts produced. It was almost impossible to lose sight of Alice anywhere. One only had to look for a head of brash red hair to find her in even the densest crowd. It was difficult now to reconcile that mean-spirited woman with the fragile white-haired remnant of what had once been her mother.

"Ellen is here, Alice," Janet said. "She's here for a visit."

"Hello, Mother," Ellen said. She stepped forward and bent over low to kiss Alice's cheek, noting as always the absence of any scent. It was as though her mother's skin were a barrier, unable to absorb smells of any kind. No one ever told Alice that she smelled good. She claimed it was an asset, because she didn't need folks rooting around her like a bunch of pigs on a hunt for truffles. "Am I interrupting?" Ellen asked, referring to the television program, but Alice seemed to think there was some deeper relevance to the question. She shook her head and smiled slightly. Not knowing what else to ask or to say, Ellen said, "I'm sorry about Dad."

Alice neither acknowledged her daughter's condolence nor offered one in return. Instead, she curled the index finger on her right hand and motioned Ellen to come closer. Obligingly, Ellen moved next to the wheelchair, placing both hands on the armrest and stooping alongside her mother.

"Janet," Alice said, scrutinizing Ellen's face. "Make us some tea, would you, dear?"

Her voice was raspy and unfamiliar, and the tenderness this provoked in Ellen was equally unexpected. Before Ellen could act on her feelings, Alice said, "You still drink tea, don't you? Or do you only drink champagne now with all your fancy ways? I see you still wear those trashy false eyelashes."

Reflexively, Ellen stood and stepped away from the wheelchair. Neither age, nor illness, nor time could disguise the real Alice. It was almost a relief. Ellen knew how to conduct herself with this woman. She stood and reached for the bag she had brought. The goal was to ignore the bait. Just soldier on and complete the mission. That's what Bill would have said. Ellen missed Bill now. He would have done this with her, stood by her side throughout the funeral, intercepted her family's aggressions, eased her mother's indifference, and possibly even quelled her hostility. Instead, he was probably picking out a layette with a girl who was young enough to be his granddaughter. Ellen felt as though she might come undone if her mother uttered one more unpleasantry. Adeptly, Ellen mounted her own attack.

"I have a present for you, Mother."

"Oh?"

"I bought it on HSN."

Alice's eyes flickered with interest, just as Ellen had anticipated.

"It's an animal print. You've always been rather fond of those," Ellen said. "I remember you had a knitting bag in a leopard print."

"Your trouble is you remember too much," Alice said. "You always did."

It was amazing how Alice could twist something as potentially gentle as a childhood recollection into ammunition for an assault.

Ellen breathed in through her nose and closed her eyes slightly, forcing herself to stay calm. If she allowed herself to be lured into a confrontation with her mother now, the only choice would be to leave. Ellen was too weak to sustain her mother's vitriol, which seemed to have grown proportionately stronger as she grew weaker.

"Do you still knit?" Ellen asked, forcing herself to be pleasant. She opened the bag and took out the blouse, shaking out the wrinkles with both hands. "You were very good at it, as I recall."

"You should have hung whatever that is on a hanger as soon as it came. You would have hung it up if you had ordered the blouse for yourself. You never would have left it in a bag if it was for you."

Undeterred, Ellen smoothed the fabric. Tears stung her eyes, and she felt foolishly adolescent, a young girl still trying to win her mother's approval. Just as Ellen raised her head, Janet returned with a tray. She set it down next to Alice and poured her tea.

"Are you all right, dear?" Janet asked, looking pointedly at Ellen. "You haven't gone and let your mother upset you, have you? Her bark is even a bit sharper these days, isn't it, Alice?" Alice didn't respond, but she took a sip of tea from the steaming cup Janet held to her lips and accepted the biscuit with a tremulous hand. "She can be perfectly wretched sometimes. Can't you, dearie?"

Ellen watched in amazement as her mother accepted Janet's critique without the slightest objection.

"I think she considers it a bit of sport to give others a tongue lashing whenever she can get away with it." Janet gave Alice the cup to hold herself and then fussed a bit with the oxygen tank. "The trick is to stand up to her. Let her know that her nonsense won't be tolerated. That's what I do, right, dear?"

Alice had closed her eyes for a moment, and the cup wavered precariously. Ellen took it from her mother's hand and held it to her lips just as she had seen Janet do, but Alice shook her head and turned away.

"She's tired. She should have her nap pretty soon," Janet said. "She has to get her rest if she's going to attend the funeral tomorrow."

"I'm going to the wake tonight," Alice said. "I'll be a good girl and get my rest now."

"We'll see," Janet said, winking at Ellen. "First, let's see if you can be a good girl."

As Ellen watched this extraordinary exchange play itself out, she took on her own role as the feckless interloper with much greater gusto than she would ever have believed possible. If nothing else, Ellen told herself, she could live up to all the terrible stories her mother must have shared about her one and only daughter.

"Well, Mother," Ellen said, "I should let you take your nap." She placed the blouse on the table and turned to Janet. "I bought this for Mother on HSN. I can return it and get her something else if she doesn't care for it."

"I saw a fake fur the other day that would look smart on me," Alice said.

"Did you?" Ellen said.

"Oh, what do you need a fur for?" Janet said in her most take-charge voice. "Even a fake one. You hardly go out at all anymore."

Alice laughed so companionably that Ellen was startled. She could not recall her mother ever having girlfriends. She had tended to her family, overseeing their lives with military precision. Dinner was at five every day except for Sunday, when they ate at two. The menu was as unwavering as her attitude toward strangers and anything even remotely foreign. Now she had a girlfriend, and it softened the lines around her mouth and eyes and made her seem more likeable, more approachable. But the door to this side of Alice would forever be closed to Ellen. She would always be a stranger to Alice, an intruder who had almost fractured the family's good standing in the community and brought shame to them all. Fortunately, Alice had been able to outwit Ellen's bad judgment by convincing everyone that the family was better off without her. What had always amazed Ellen was how willing her family had been to let her go.

"I'll keep an eye out for the fur, Mother," Ellen said. "Perhaps you'll have a reason to want to go out then."

"Janet says I don't need it," Alice said, dismissing Ellen's suggestion. "Janet knows."

Janet took up her position behind the wheelchair and gripped the handles. "There's a good girl, then," she said, smiling kindly at poor Ellen's incompetence, her inability to have even the most benign conversation with her own mother. "Off to bed with you now." She unlocked the brake and inclined her head toward Ellen. "I hope we'll see you later. You can let yourself out. You know the way, don't you?"

"Indeed," Ellen said. She gathered her coat and her bag. "It was a pleasure meeting you, Janet. Thank you for taking such good care of my mother." She bent over and barely kissed her mother's cheek. "See you soon, Mother."

Alice nodded, and Janet moved one hand to squeeze Alice's shoulder in commiseration. Ellen could leave now, virtuous in the knowledge that she had not made her mother into a liar. Her daughter was indeed temperamental and unpredictable, downright unreasonable actually. It was no one's fault but her own that the family, especially her own mother, had chosen to let her go her own way. Ellen's intrusive presence had confirmed this. Her and those trashy false eyelashes and her fancy ways. Poor Alice. Poor, poor Alice.

Sixteen

"YOU'RE not still planning on going to dinner at your brother's house, are you?" Barbara said.

Ellen had phoned from the car to recount the details of her meeting with her mother, omitting some of the more embarrassing high points.

"Only if you both go," Ellen said.

"We'll do whatever you want us to do," Barbara said, "but don't you think it will just be more of the same?"

"Maybe, maybe not," Ellen said and laughed. "I survived my mother, so dinner should be a snap. Don't you think?"

"I suppose. What are you doing now?"

"I think I'll head back to the funeral home. It's early yet, and I should be there. The evening viewing doesn't begin until seven. Maureen expects us at five. It will be a quick dinner. I don't want to do anything more to antagonize these people."

"I don't think you really have to do anything to antagonize

these people, honey. They just don't like you," Barbara said. "And I mean that in the nicest possible way."

"Thanks. Where's Kaye?"

"Taking a nap."

"I won't be long."

"Be careful. These are angry people."

"I'll be fine."

She pulled off her headset and turned her directional on. It was strange to be back home, navigating the streets she had once biked and walked. In spite of the town's provincial stance, it had been a nice place to grow up. Ellen fondly remembered riding her bike to school and greeting almost everyone she met along the way. Unfortunately, her good years had been short-lived. By the time she entered adolescence, her need to escape created a counterpoint to the nagging familiarity of everyday life. After Faith was born, Ellen's determination to abandon her bucolic surroundings took on new dimensions. She longed to wake up a stranger, to move through unknown streets, and to meet new neighbors. The place she dreamed of would allow her to remain a mystery as long she chose to, speaking to no one, avoiding all contact unless she decided otherwise. The wish to escape her surroundings, her past, and her family was all she thought about. When she finally decided to leave, encouraged by her family's disregard and the belief that Faith would never know where to find her anyway, Ellen had rolled all her memories into one miserable collection. Now it seemed easier to divide those memories into before Faith and after Faith just to remind herself that once she too had been a girl who eagerly read mysteries and romances, kept a diary, listened to the Beatles, had friends, loved pizza, earned good grades, and was more or less a normal teenager. In a way this eased Ellen's heart, just knowing that she had not been born doleful and isolated. She moved through the streets of her childhood and saw herself as she had been, accepting that her loss had rightfully and profoundly altered her future.

The parking lot at Flannigan's had thinned out quite a bit since Ellen had left. She spotted Hugh's car with its *I Climbed Grandfather Mountain* and *Honk If You Love Jesus* bumper stickers. Owen's car had a National Rifle Association bumper sticker that practically shouted its message: *Guns Don't Kill, People Do*. Somehow, especially on Owen's car, Ellen did not find that at all comforting. She pulled into a spot and checked her face in the rearview mirror. *Haggard* would be the best word to describe her appearance and her mood. She applied some fresh lipstick, ran a hand through her hair and fluffed her bangs just enough for that casual tousled look her stylist loved a little too much, and took a swig of cold coffee from the foam cup she had yet to discard from breakfast. The weather had turned warmer, and she left her coat open as she strode toward the funeral home. A lone figure, a young woman, sat huddled on the front steps. As Ellen approached, she saw it was one of her great-nieces, though her name was impossible to recall. The girl was dragging hard on a cigarette, but she tossed it to the ground as soon as Ellen neared, uncurling her body and standing up, showing her surprising height. She threw her shoulders back, and Ellen did not know quite what to make of the young woman who loomed over her. She was beautiful, though in a self-conscious way that came across as confrontational. Careful not to scrutinize her too closely, Ellen held out her hand and said, "I know you're one of my great-nieces, and I'm ashamed not to know your name. I'm your great-aunt Ellen."

There was a moment when the young woman stared into Ellen's eyes as if trying to decide what to make of this infamous great-aunt whose disappearance had reached mythic proportions in family lore. Then, the young woman—Lorelei, it turned out— smiled and offered her hand.

"Everyone calls me Lori," she said. "I'm Sara's daughter. Hugh's granddaughter."

"I didn't realize Sara had such a grown-up daughter," Ellen said.

"I'm sixteen." Lori took a pack of gum from her coat pocket, offering Ellen a stick before putting two pieces into her own mouth. "I'm not supposed to smoke, of course. I'm not supposed to do anything."

"I remember sixteen," Ellen said. She took a stick of gum and put it in her pocket for later, a habit that had always annoyed Bill. "You're very tall."

"I'm five-ten-and-a-half. I'm probably going to grow another half inch, maybe an inch. Everyone says I should model, but I don't think I'm pretty enough. Grammy says you don't have to be pretty, just tall and thin." Lori laughed. "That's her idea of a compliment."

"I remember those compliments too," Ellen said. "Do you have another cigarette?"

"Sure." She hit the pack against her wrist. "Here. Need a light?" Ellen nodded, and Lori expertly lit the cigarette with a fluorescent orange lighter. "Let's move around to the other side. They might be coming out soon."

Ellen thought Lori was a knockout. She was wearing red pumps, black fishnet stockings, and a very short black leather skirt that peeked out of her coat as she walked. The skirt was topped by a black sweater. The whole outfit was clearly intended to be noticed. Lorelei tolerated Ellen's once-over and smiled.

"My mother freaked out over the red shoes," Lori said. "That's why I came outside."

"Is that why you wore them?"

"Probably. My grandfather says I remind him of you."

"Oh?" Ellen dragged hard on the cigarette. She had quit years ago, but once in a while she bummed a cigarette and enjoyed every drag. "That can't be a compliment." She made a face. "Or maybe it is."

"It depends on his mood."

"So what do you want to do with your life?"

"Fashion," Lori said. "I know, me and a zillion other people. Still, I'd do anything in fashion that does not involve modeling. I feel like everything I say should have quotation marks around it. You know, it all seems so obvious."

"I actually love the red shoes. And I think you're way too hard on yourself."

"Well, thanks, Aunt Ellen. I appreciate that. I really do. I think clothes are costumes. I take that very seriously."

"And you should." Ellen reached into her purse and pulled out a card. She scribbled her home phone number on the back. "I'm not a fashion designer, but I know lots of people in New York. If your parents approve, you're welcome to visit me anytime."

"Thanks." She looked impressed as she read Ellen's title on the card. "You never had any kids, right?"

Whenever she was faced with this question, Ellen hesitated. It was an impossible question to answer without divulging too much. But she had a daughter, and so each time Ellen denied this, she felt that much further away from the possibility of ever finding Faith. Still, Ellen nodded, almost apologetically, and shifted the conversation back to Lori.

"Do you have a boyfriend?" Ellen said.

Blushing furiously, Lori said she did, and he was wonderful. Ellen took this to mean that they were having sex, and she felt a chill run through her though the sun was beating down on them. The boyfriend's name was Luke, and he was a senior. He planned to major in art in college, which Ellen assumed translated into sensitive and romantic.

"He sounds wonderful," Ellen said. "He's a lucky boy."

"I'm the lucky one," Lori said, as though only she could render the final verdict. "See? That should have had quotation marks around it." She laughed. "He wants to marry me."

"I'm sure he does." Ellen threw the cigarette butt to the ground and stamped it out with her heel, grinding more than necessary. "Love can be stronger than the will to live."

Lori stared at Ellen, savoring this explanation, knowing she would repeat it to her friends when she told them about her Great-Aunt Ellen from New York.

"I'm glad I remind Grandpa of you. He loves you, no matter how it seems. And I think you're beautiful and mysterious. I've always wanted to get to know you. I knew Grammy was wrong. She never says anything nice about you except that you're too smart for your own good. As if that's a crime, being too smart. I know you have a big secret. I know because the adults whisper about you sometimes and stop as soon as any of the kids walk into the room."

"Everyone has a big secret, honey."

"Not this big," Lori said. "And I can see it in your eyes anyway. Your secret. And if you don't mind my saying, you should wear greens. It would pick up some of those flecks in your eyes and overshadow the darkness." She looked Ellen up and down, approving her clothes. "You have good taste. A little too classic for me, but sharp. I'd lose the turtlenecks if I were you. Go for a boat collar. Something gently scooped. It will make your neck seem longer. But you look great, really you do."

"Thank you." Ellen kissed Lori's cheek. She smelled like patchouli. It was deliciously exotic and must have driven the family mad. Lori's ambition to be different and her honesty must have made her suspect at all times. For Ellen, the combination worked. "You smell wonderful, and I've loved talking to you. But I'd better get inside before they send out a search party."

"I understand." Lori reached for the sleeve of Ellen's coat as she stepped back. "I'm really good at keeping secrets, Aunt Ellen. If you ever need to share, it will be safe with me."

To deny that she had a secret would have been yet another offense to Faith. Ellen unwrapped the stick of gum that she had taken from Lori earlier and chewed it several times before answering.

"Thanks, Lori. I know I can trust you."

As she followed Lori into Flannigan's, Ellen wondered if Faith was tall and thin like her cousin Lorelei. At least that would have been nice to know.

* * *

THERE were a few stragglers left in the viewing room. Ellen stood in the doorway and stared at her father's coffin. Hugh and Owen were saying good-bye to guests, thanking them for coming and sharing final words about Hugh Sr.'s many kindnesses. Although she could not hear what anyone said, Ellen could imagine. Her father had been a devoted member of the community, offering his time to many charitable activities, including the Rotary Club. Just as Lori came up behind Ellen, Hugh turned and saw them together. He was not smiling as he approached.

"Where have you been?" he said, directing the question at both of them. "We were waiting."

"I went to see Mother," Ellen said. "I haven't been gone that long."

"And you?" Hugh said. He appraised Lori's outfit, trying not to grimace at her red shoes. "Your parents called your cell."

Lori was the same height as her grandfather, but she seemed smaller as she rubbed his shoulder with hers and said, "I was outside smoking, Pops. I turned my cell off." She kissed his cheek. "Don't tell on me. Mom already freaked out over the shoes, but you like them. Don't you?"

It was evident that she was a favorite by the way he simultaneously embraced her and sniffed at her hair, pronouncing that she had better do something to rid herself of the stink of cigarette smoke.

"Will do, Pops," Lori said, turning and blowing him a kiss as she loped off to the bathroom.

Ellen turned to watch her go and then said, "I like her."

Hugh snorted and said, "Now there's a surprise. She's a handful for sure."

"I didn't realize Sara had a teenaged daughter."

"Sara will be forty this summer. I had her when I was twenty-five, and she had Lorelei at the same age. It's nice to have kids when you're young." He caught himself too late and said, "That was remarkably insensitive of me."

"It's all right, Hugh. It's not your fault."

"How did your visit with Mother go?'

"She's still a lot of laughs," Ellen said, looking past him at the throng of mourners, all of whom looked vaguely familiar. "I don't know how you do it."

"Someone has to. Actually, Maureen does more than I do. All the gals do, and the grandchildren, except for Lorelei. She drops by occasionally, but never with a good result. Oil and water, our Lorelei and Mother."

"No wonder she reminds you of me."

"Did she tell you that?" Hugh said, and then without waiting for an answer added, "She would. She holds nothing back, that one."

"Why should she?" Ellen said.

"Because it makes life harder when you have to let everyone know how you feel all the time."

"Harder? For whom, Hugh?"

Hugh seemed about to answer then seemed to think better of it and said, "Are you and your friends coming for dinner?" He checked his watch. "We need to get going. I'm just going to say good-bye to Dad. Do you want to come with me?"

"Yes to dinner," Ellen said, "but no to Dad. Say good-bye for me. We spent enough quality time together. And please tell Maureen that I'll bring dessert. Dad's favorite, éclairs."

She kissed his cheek and left. There was no need to wait for his answer. She knew exactly what he was thinking,

* * *

"SO you're the romance writer," Maureen said. She set a bowl of mashed turnips next to the bowl of string beans and moved things around to make more room. "May I serve you?"

"No, thank you," Barbara said. "I'll help myself. And yes, I am the romance writer."

"I enjoy your books," Maureen said.

"Our Barbara is very talented," Ellen said.

"I never even knew you read any of them," Barbara said.

"I don't," Ellen said.

"That's not true," Kaye said, lifting a piece of pot roast from the platter and passing it to Barbara. "We read all of Barbara's work. Well, most of them anyway, and then we pretend to have read the rest. They're a bit formulaic and after a while so predictable."

"Thank you, my dear," Barbara said with pointed wryness. "Just what the world needs, more critics."

"Oh, but that's what I love about them." Maureen said. "They always seem like old friends. The characters, I mean. It's as if I know all of them."

"See what I have to put up with?" Barbara said as she speared some pot roast. "This looks great. I hardly ever eat meat anymore, so this is a real treat."

"Are you a vegetarian?" Maureen said. "Lori's a vegan, and it drives us all crazy."

"No. I'm neither, but I try to stay away from red meat," Barbara said. "High cholesterol and all that. So, did you read my last book?"

"Which one was that? *Wanderlust*?" Maureen said.

"Actually," Barbara said, "the last one was *Half a Heart*. I'll send you a copy."

"Oh, thank you. What's it about?" Maureen said.

"Oh, the same thing the last one was about," Kaye said.

"I think we get the point." Barbara used her sternest voice, though it was obvious she was not offended. She had no illusions about her romance writing. It was exactly as Kaye had described. And thank goodness for devoted fans like Maureen, who expected nothing more than what they received. "I guess my work is a little bound by its predecessors. Regardless, my stories pay the bills."

"Is there a lot of sex in your novels?" Lori said. She ate a string bean with her fingers and smiled, all innocence, at her mother's disapproval. "Is that a bad question? I'm sorry. I never read romance novels. They're all so derivative."

"Well, that's fine," Barbara said. "Romance novels seem to appeal to middle-aged women. There is some sex in my novels, but it's all very veiled if you get my point."

"Of course," Lori said.

"What do you like to read?" Barbara said.

"Mostly science fiction these days. Last year I was into the Victorians. Those Victorians were really horny even though they put skirts on table legs. Or maybe it's because they put skirts on table legs." She laughed at her own joke. "Anyway, all those repressed feelings produced some seriously memorable erotic literature."

"More of anything, anyone?" Maureen said. "Our Lorelei has always been a bit too highbrow for this family."

"I think we're good, honey. Everything is delicious," Hugh said, trying to silence her. "Lori's just smart, that's all."

"I brought a few desserts. I couldn't resist those éclairs," Ellen said, following Hugh's diversionary strategy. "I was happy to see that Artuso's was still open."

"Oh yes," Maureen said. "Their grandson is in the business now. He went off to some fancy cooking school, but he came back home."

"By the way, that was a veiled message," Lori said. "You can leave, but you must come back. And furthermore, Nana's talking about the Culinary Institute. That's her idea of exotic, sort of like going to Paris."

"Don't be fresh to your grandmother," Sara said. "Excuse me, Barbara. I didn't mean to cut you off."

"Why is that being fresh?" Lori said.

"It's your tone," Sara said. "It suggests that you are superior, or that you at least think you are."

"Aunt Ellen invited me to visit her in New York," Lori said mildly, knowing full well how this news would be received.

"Aunt Ellen?" Hugh said.

"There's no need to say it that way, Hugh," Ellen said. "For your information, I prefaced the invitation with a warning that parental approval was mandatory."

"When Pops says 'Aunt Ellen' with a question mark, it really means who does she think she is stepping into our lives and making waves. Right Pops?"

"Lorelei!" Sara said. "On the night before we bury your great-grandfather, can't you find it in your heart to show a little respect?" Then Sara turned to Ellen and said, "I'm sorry. I know your invitation was meant well—"

"I understand your concerns," Ellen said, waving her hand, more in a show of sympathy than protest. "I only invited Lori because she expressed an interest in a career in fashion design, and I happen to know a number of people. I meant no harm to anyone, especially not to Sara and Alan, and especially not to Lori."

"We can vouch for Ellen's reliability," Kaye said. "My children adore her. They always considered it a treat to spend time with her. In fact, they still do, and they miss her when they don't see her."

"My kids call her Aunt Ellen," Barbara said. "And they are equally wild for her. She dotes on them and indulges them shamelessly—"

"Enough," Ellen said. "I feel as though I'm being eulogized. Let's save it for tomorrow."

"I was just going to tell them how you took the kids to porno movies and bought them drugs," Barbara said. "But don't mind me."

"I'm sorry," Sara said to Ellen, and then, turning to Barbara, added, "We know that Ellen is very responsible and loving. It isn't that at all."

"Is it her friends?" Barbara said. "Bad influence?"

"Of course not," Sara said.

"She's just kidding, Mom," Lorelei said.

"I knew that," Sara said, though it was clear from the blush that spread from her neck to her ears that she had not known that at all. "Let's have some dessert." She turned to Ellen one more time. "I'm sorry."

"No need to be," Ellen said. She reached over and touched Lori's hand. "If your parents approve, my invitation still stands."

Lori acknowledged this with a victorious smile and continued to help her cousin with her shoe. It had somehow become unbuckled, and Lori was trying to find the hole. Little Alice had her foot in Lori's lap and seemed quite content with everything, the arguing, her big cousin, and even her new great-aunt.

"I'll put up a pot of coffee," Maureen said. "I think we could all use a cup."

"I could use an éclair," Kaye said, "or maybe two."

Barbara stood and began to collect dishes while Ellen gathered the used plates within her reach. When she had a reasonable stack, she followed Barbara into the kitchen. Maureen was filling the electric coffeepot with water and looked up only as they entered. Kaye was on their heels, and the three friends formed a formidable front against Maureen's aloofness.

"I was just wondering about something. If I had children," Ellen said, "would anyone have objected to my invitation?" She had positioned herself directly in front of Maureen right by the sink, blocking any possible escape. "It's because I don't have children, isn't it?"

"Of course not," Maureen said. She set the pot on the counter and looked unflinchingly into Ellen's face. "All of us know that had you been given the chance you would have been a terrific mother. Right now, we're all a little on edge these last few days. I'm sorry if anyone hurt your feelings. I am truly glad that you came. It's good for all of us to be together."

And then Ellen began to cry. And no one was more surprised than Barbara and Kaye when with a heart-wrenching sob, Ellen fell into Maureen's arms and was immediately and knowingly embraced. It seemed such an unlikely choice when Ellen's two best friends in the whole world were right beside her, but then so much was a mystery. Kaye and Barbara stood quietly waiting while Maureen whispered words unintelligible to them but evidently not to Ellen, who soon composed herself.

"Sorry," Ellen said to everyone. She dabbed at the corners of her eyes. "I guess coming home is a little overwhelming."

"It's okay," Barbara said. "Do you want us to wait outside?"

"No, I'm fine now," Ellen said. She squeezed Maureen's hand. "I'm fine. I was just caught a little off guard."

Maureen had prepared serving plates for the pastries, and Kaye offered to help. Barbara loaded a tray with cups and saucers, as well as dessert plates and silverware, all according to Maureen's gently delivered directions.

"I have the milk and sugar," Ellen said.

Suddenly, the kitchen was filled with helpers. All the children seemed to enter at one time, carrying dishes and platters and bowls of leftover food, competing with each other for counter space. Lori was directing the children, showing them where to put things, taking care that nothing broke and that everyone had a turn. Everything seemed so normal that no one wanted to end the charade, at least not yet. There was something wonderfully soothing about the noise and the commotion, and the feeling of physical closeness in that space that was too small for so many people. They fell into a rhythmic orchestration, like synchronized swimmers, acutely aware of each other and of the illusion that they were just another ordinary family.

Seventeen

TWO entirely separate, yet equally dramatic, events occurred on the morning of Hugh Sr.'s funeral to overshadow even the penultimate closing of the coffin. First, Alice arrived with her oxygen tank and Janet in tow and proceeded to rail against Ellen almost immediately. Second, Bill, who had walked in before anyone arrived and taken a seat in the last row, rescued her. No one, least of all Ellen, could have imagined what was waiting for her as she alighted from her car, slung her good black bag over her shoulder, adjusted the belt on her coat, smiled at her two best friends, and strode purposefully ahead of them and up the steps of the funeral home. She heard her mother's shrill lamentations before even crossing the threshold and told herself that it was wrong to be cynical. It was possible that her mother was capable of love, that she had truly loved her husband of more than sixty years and that it was her right to mourn. But it was not until Ellen was only steps away from the room that she could actually hear herself vilified. *That Ellen has no business here. She's not part of this family . . . it was her choice to leave*

us behind . . . near broke her father's heart that Ellen never forgave us . . .
This litany of seeming agony was intermittently interrupted by
Maureen's insistent demand that Alice pull herself together, Janet's
more gentle urging, and even Owen's persistent *stop it*s and *that's
enough now, Ma, you're embarrassing everyone.* (In fact, he was really
talking about himself, because it was his place of work, and his family, who would be the topic of conversation later when the other
employees gathered on the back porch for a cigarette break.) Ellen
did not hesitate. She could have. She could have turned and fled,
and no one would have thought any less of her, as most of them
did not think much about her at all in the first place. In that regard
Alice was right. Ellen was not a genuine part of the family. But
Ellen persevered, and it was duly noted even by those who were
guilty of previously slanderous comments. Later they would discuss
her grace under fire, her remarkable self-control, even her kindness
as she moved toward her mother in an attempt to quell the diatribe
so reminiscent of the innumerable attacks that had shaped their
history. Alice, however, would not be silenced. The moment she
saw Ellen, it was all Janet could do to keep her charge still. Those
present who needed some explanation for Alice's terrible behavior
justified it by saying that she was so overcome with grief.

Nothing, however, could have prepared Ellen for her rescuer.
Bill seemed to come from nowhere. Suddenly, he was the hero in
this family drama, distracting even Alice with his stage presence. He
stepped up, took her hand, bent in so low to her face that his words
were audible only to her. Whatever he said, it quieted her, and she
hung her head nodding and sniffling into the tissue that Janet had
hurriedly pressed into Alice's hand before backing away in deference to Bill's expert handling. All of this unfolded in a matter of
minutes: Alice's hysteria, the family's attempts to calm her, Ellen's
determination to tolerate her mother's rage, and Bill's appearance
all occurred in such a series of perfectly timed steps that there was

no opportunity for Ellen to be any more stunned than she already was. In fact, she was genuinely glad to see Bill and said so (much to Kaye and Barbara's dismay). Bill took Ellen's elbow, led her away from Alice, offered his condolences to each member of the family (by name), and then warmly kissed Kaye on each cheek. Barbara sidestepped his attempt to kiss her, held out her hand, and said, "Bill. What a surprise."

"You look very well," Kaye said.

"Thank you," Bill said. "It's nice to see both of you."

"Barbara, dear," Ellen said quickly, suspecting that Barbara's unrepentant tongue might suddenly strike, "would you keep an eye on Bill while I join my family?"

Clearly injured, Bill said, "Don't you want me to be at your side?"

It was such a telling moment. Bill genuinely believed he still had a place at Ellen's side, and she so clearly would have liked him to be her husband during this stressful time. In spite of his abandonment, in spite of his treachery, Ellen wanted him next to her. But then she looked over at the hand Bill had placed on her shoulder. She stared at the familiar hairs that covered his knuckles, the well-manicured nails, and then at the thin white line where his wedding ring had once been. She might have forgiven all if it had not been for that white line.

"It's not necessary, Bill," Ellen said, oozing politeness, "but thank you for offering."

Then Hugh beckoned to her that it was time. He also nodded at Bill, who looked imploringly at Ellen, but she shook her head and whispered something to Kaye. Bill was led away by Barbara and Kaye, looking like a sullen child. Ellen took her place next to Hugh. Maureen was on his other side. Their children and grandchildren were in the row behind. Andrew and Pamela looked somber, and even Owen was demure. Alice was eerily quiet as Janet held her hand. The priest stepped to the front of the room and stood before the coffin. The prayers were brief and familiar. Ellen crossed herself along with everyone else and waited as the priest told them to line up and say good-bye to Hugh Dougherty, Sr. It was so quiet that she felt sleepy. Hugh asked if she was all right, and she said, yes, just tired. He told her it was a bad time to close your eyes for too long, and he winked. She smiled and slipped her arm through his, feeling the wool of his good suit. She watched as he stepped up to their father's coffin and touched the old man's hair, smoothing it down ever so gently. Then Hugh kissed his name-sake and convulsed into sobs. Maureen rushed up to stand beside her husband, and they said good-bye together. Hugh turned and looked at Ellen, inviting her to join them. She was relieved not to have to face the moment without some support. Maureen smiled indulgently at her sister-in-law and then kissed her cheek, leaving brother and sister alone to say good-bye to their father. As soon as Maureen moved away, Hugh whispered to Ellen that their father had not been a bad man, only a foolish one. Hugh wanted her to forgive Dad and to tell him that she loved him.

"I won't," Ellen said.

"You need to," Hugh said.

She looked at her father's face, wishing she felt some love, even a little tenderness. Anything, even regret, would have been wel-comed. But where any of those feelings should have been, there was only gaping space.

"I can't," she said. Instead, she reached a tentative hand inside the coffin and touched his hard, cold cheek with the back of her hand. The best she could do was try not to let her revulsion show. "Good-bye." She looked up at her brother. "I'm sorry. That's all I have."

Hugh shook his head and shrugged as if to let Hugh Sr. know that there was nothing more to be done. Ellen was Ellen, after all.

In spite of that, Hugh took Ellen's arm, and they stood together, waiting side by side as everyone else filed past the coffin. Lorelei had brought a book, though Ellen could not see what it was. She was moved by the girl's gentleness and impressed that she kissed her great-grandfather's cheek. Finally, Hugh, Andrew, and Owen surrounded Alice's wheelchair and pushed her up close enough to the coffin so that she could reach in and touch her husband's face. Ellen could not make out what any of them were saying, but Alice seemed comforted. Each of her boys kissed her cheek, and she smiled very slightly. When they moved the chair away from the coffin, Alice looked up and unintentionally caught Ellen's eye for just a moment before they each looked away. When the last person had moved past the coffin, the funeral director came forward and took his place at the foot of the bier. He would close the coffin after everyone except the family left the room.

As soon as everyone had filed past the coffin and left the room, the funeral director reached up to pull the coffin lid down one last time. Hugh took a deep breath, Owen bit his lower lip, and Andrew blinked several times. Ellen closed her eyes, waiting for the final thud. When it came, she felt nothing. She took her place, last in line behind her brothers, walking in single file behind the bier.

Kaye and Barbara were in the parking lot, leaning against Ellen's car. Bill was in his car on the other side of the lot, talking on his cell phone and keeping a lookout for Ellen. As soon as he saw her, he got off the phone and stepped from the car. She waved, just to let him know that she had seen him, but she walked toward Barbara and Kaye.

"How was it?" Barbara said. She had her plastic cigarette in her mouth. "Are you all right?"

"It was fine, and I'm fine. It's almost over."

"Did you know he was coming?" Kaye said.

"Bill? No, of course not." Then, responding to Barbara's questioning expression, Ellen explained, "But I did call him to let him know that my father had died."

"Why?" Barbara said.

"I guess I felt lonely." Ellen shrugged. "It was one of those bad ideas."

"You still love him, don't you?" Kaye said.

"Did you see him with my family?" Ellen said. "I miss that."

"He's good," Barbara acknowledged. "Especially for a low-life—"

"We're only saying nice things about people today," Kaye said in a saccharine singsong. "Remember our agreement?"

"Actually, I don't," Barbara said, but she pressed her lips together in uncharacteristic obedience.

Louis Flannigan was in the parking lot, urging people to get into their vehicles. The hearse was waiting, and they needed to get to the church. There was another funeral immediately after Hugh's. One of the village trustees had passed the day after Hugh, and his family had decided to wake him for only one day. His funeral was scheduled for one o'clock. It was almost eleven.

"Do you want me to drive?" Kaye said.

"I'm going to drive over to the church with Bill," Ellen said.

"Are you sure?" Barbara said.

"Yes," Ellen said. "I need to speak to him, and this is as good a time as any. If I don't, I'll just have to deal with him later on in the day. I'd rather get it over with."

"Well," Kaye said, "if you're sure."

"I'll be fine. Please don't worry."

"Want a drag?" Barbara said. She offered her plastic cigarette to Ellen. "It's not bad."

"Thanks," Ellen said. "I'll mooch a real one from Lorelei after this is over."

She knew they were watching her as she walked toward Bill's

car. Bill opened the door for her and waited as she fastened her seatbelt.

"All set?" he said.

"Fine," Ellen said.

Bill turned the ignition on and looked over his shoulder, easing into reverse before he said, "I'm so glad you called to tell me about your father."

"I didn't ask you to come to the funeral."

"That's true, but you did call me."

"It was a moment of weakness, Bill. I knew coming home would dredge up all sorts of feelings about the baby."

Bill looked confused.

"Which baby?" he said.

Ellen was incredulous at her own stupidity. Bill had not given any thought to how painful it must be for her to come home. He had not given any thought to the baby she had lost because he was too preoccupied with the mess he had made of his own life. "Which baby do you think I mean, Bill?" She forced herself to keep her voice low, but she felt like screaming. "Surely not the baby you're having with Daisy."

"Of course not," he said. "Of course not. I'm just a little off my game. I knew exactly what you meant."

"Don't lie, Bill. It just makes it worse."

"I'm sorry. I really am. If you want to know the truth, I'm not at all happy with the idea of this baby."

"I'm really, really not interested in talking to you about this."

"Believe me, Ellie, I know."

He patted her arm, and she stiffened.

"Is that really necessary?" he said. He put the car in park, waiting to join the line. "I miss you, Ellie. I made a mistake." He reached over so deftly that she had no time to object as he nuzzled her neck. Her resolve weakened immediately, just like the women in

Barbara's romance novels. Bill knew exactly where Ellen liked to be touched and kissed. He knew everything about her. As she tilted her head to make his kisses easier to place, she thought of the empty closet in their bedroom, the vacant drawers in their dresser, and the sound of his keys and change as he emptied his pockets into the now-bare antique brass dish she had bought him for just this purpose. Then, she remembered that he had left the dish behind when he moved out, and she sat up and pushed him away.

"This is really inappropriate," Ellen said as she removed his hand. "Even for you, Bill."

"I want to come home. I'll make it up to you, Ellen."

The car behind them beeped. It was time to move out.

He looked so sincere as he fell into line behind the other cars.

"We were so happy once," he said.

"Once?" Ellen said. "*Once* is a time that is gone." She shook her head sadly. "*Once* belongs in fairy tales."

"I can be your prince again," he said.

"Poor Bill. The prince doesn't get to live happily ever after if he dumps the princess for a young little strumpet." The car behind them beeped again. Ellen lowered the visor and checked her lipstick. It was perfect. She smiled at Bill and said, "Drive."

*   *   *

HUGH'S eulogy was the most sentimental. He reminisced about the times he spent fishing and later playing golf with his father. Hugh called his father a man's man, someone who loved women but just did not know how to spend time in their company unless it was to go dancing. In his day, Hugh said, the old man had been quite a hoofer, taking the cha-cha and the mambo to great new heights. He paused as everyone laughed. Ellen was seated between Kaye and Barbara, who each held one hand, interlacing their fingers between Ellen's and squeezing at appropriate intervals. Andrew praised his father's values, his strong love of family, and his bond with his grandchildren and great-grandchildren. Even Owen said a few carefully rehearsed words. No one had asked Ellen if she would care to speak, and she understood even though it would have been nice to be asked.

She was stunned at how much her brothers had loved their father. As each son stepped down from the podium, he kissed Alice. Ellen literally sat on the edge of her seat, waiting for someone to say something about her father that made some sense to her. And then Lorelei took her place at the podium and smoothed out a piece of yellow lined paper. As the oldest great-grandchild, she had taken it upon herself to be the spokesperson for all the children. She looked out over the throng of familiar faces and smiled her lopsided grin. Instead of the fishnet stockings she had worn to the wake, Lorelei had succumbed to propriety and worn black tights. Her hair was pulled away from her face by a thick black headband, and without any makeup, not even lipstick, she looked about ten, maybe eleven years old. Ellen let go of Kaye's and Barbara's hands and leaned forward so as not to miss a word of her great-niece's eulogy. It was then that Ellen spotted the red shoes. All black was just too much for Lorelei. It was as though those red shoes grounded her, and she was able to explain why she loved her great-grandfather in spite of his cantankerous ways.

Lorelei referred to him as cantankerous, especially in these last few years. She said he would have loved her shoes. He would never have said so, Lorelei said, but he would have loved them. He would have told me, she said, not to let your Grammy see them. Lorelei laughed as she stepped out from behind the podium and gave everyone an opportunity to see her bright red three-inch platform heels that were a thrift store find. A wave of approval rippled through the crowd, and Lorelei inclined her head in appreciation. She was the final speaker. The priest gave one last blessing before it was time to move the coffin to begin its final journey. Everyone filed out behind the coffin and watched as it was lifted into the back of the hearse. People gathered in small groups, chatting and smoking until the funeral director urged them to please get into their cars and turn on their headlights. Ellen hurried over to Lorelei before she was whisked away by her parents.

"You did a grand job," Ellen said. She kissed Lori on each cheek. "I was very proud of you. Your great-grandfather would have been pleased. I know I was. I was especially glad to know that he would have loved your shoes. I love them too."

"Thank you, Aunt Ellen. It means a lot to me to hear you say that." She smiled and leaned in to whisper conspiratorially, "I'm dying for a cigarette."

"Me too. So what book did you give him on a permanent loan?"

Laughing at Ellen's irreverence, Lori said, "*Kaddish* by Allen Ginsberg."

Ellen laughed and shook her head. "Good choice."

"I used to read poetry to Gramps. He liked it. He liked Ginsberg and Frost and Roethke. He said their work was clean."

"He was right," Ellen said.

"Wonderful eulogy."

They both turned to Bill, who had come up behind Ellen like a strong gust of wind.

"Oh, Lori, this is Bill," Ellen said. "Bill, this is Lorelei. She's my brother's granddaughter, and Sara and Alan's daughter. I think you might have met her when she was a toddler."

"Pleasure," Bill said. "Please call me Uncle Bill."

Lorelei's gaze was expressionless when she held out her hand. She had already sized him up. She added that to the information she had gleaned from skilled eavesdropping, giving her more than enough ammunition to clarify her position.

"Thank you, Bill," she said, "and you may call me Lorelei."

So young and so smart, Ellen thought. With a single omission, Lori had made her allegiance clear. She was not about to fraternize with the enemy, no matter how charming he might be. Bill might have been a fool, but he was not stupid.

"Lorelei, then," he said. "I'm glad to meet you. I was impressed with your eulogy. I'm sure your great-grandfather would have been very proud of you."

"I'm sure," Lori said. She turned as her father called her name. It was time to get into the car. "I have to go." She kissed Ellen's cheek and said, "Will I see you back at the house?"

"Of course, dear," Ellen said. "We have a date, don't we?"

Lori tapped her pocket and said, "Definitely, Aunt Ellen."

Bill watched Lorelei lope off almost jauntily in her bright red shoes.

"Well, she's something," he said.

"Yes, she is certainly something," Ellen said.

"I can see a family resemblance."

"Oh, she's much taller than I am."

"You're funny, Ellie." Bill sounded wistful. "I miss that too."

The hearse was waiting, and a line of cars, headlights on, was forming. Stragglers hurried to their cars.

"We'd better go," Ellen said.

He put his arm around her and pulled her close. Ellen might have tolerated it all if only because she was too weary to do much else and because, in spite of everything, his arm felt so good around her shoulder. And he seemed so sincere. But then she turned and saw Lori watching them from the car. Her brow was furrowed, and she seemed overly observant. Ellen could have justified her behavior by insisting that she was showing Lori the importance of forgiveness. But Ellen knew this was a flimsy substitute for the truth. Ellen knew that if Lorelei had been her daughter, it would be more important to teach her that it was right to walk away from a man who had mistreated her than to teach her a simulated lesson about kindness. Ellen would have wanted her daughter to know that it was better to be alone than to be with a man who had blithely excused his infidelity by suggesting that it was her fault for never putting him first. Gently, but firmly, Ellen removed Bill's arm and walked on ahead, alone, and still intact.

Eighteen

O N the way back from the cemetery, Ellen settled into a state of focused calm that no one saw fit to disturb. In fact, none of them said much on the way to Hugh and Maureen's for the lunch that neighbors had prepared and set up. There was typical after-the-funeral food with unusually good coffee and wonderful desserts waiting for them. Everyone was exhausted and hungry, and it was a blessing to have it all ready. Barbara made small talk with the women while Kaye helped organize the children. They both made sure that Ellen was in their line of vision. She seemed weary as the afternoon wore on. While she helped serve and clean up, Barbara wondered about everyone's secrets. All these last long years of Alice's sickness, surely Hugh Sr. might have had a woman on the side. And his sons; were they all really such good family men? The women seemed so docile, so domesticated, but Barbara had noticed how Maureen had blushed when the priest whispered his condolences to her with his mouth right alongside her ear. Barbara was certain one of the grandsons was gay. He arrived with another young man who discreetly took a seat in the back, away from the disapproving glances of the family. The night before, one of the girls had talked about her English teacher. He had died suddenly. They said it was a heart attack, but he had been so young and so healthy. Foul play was suspected. And it made sense, after all. Two wives and two sets of children had shown up at the hospital. He had been living a double life in two separate communities only fifty miles apart. Maybe he knew his time was almost up. Maybe one of the wives had become suspicious. She could have found something in his trouser pocket, a slip from a strange cleaner, two ticket stubs from a movie they had not seen together. Perhaps the walls had started to close in on his two perfect worlds. Barbara looked around at everyone. Her secret seemed so tame in comparison to the secrets she fancied everyone else had. But then she reminded herself that whenever relics were finally unearthed and their mysteries revealed, it became apparent that since the beginning of time, everyone was essentially alike, searching for the same pleasures and dreaming the same dreams. And more than likely, keeping the same secrets.

*　　*　　*

THE Dougherty women loved their ponchos. Maureen slipped hers over her red hair and twirled around for everyone to see. She just adored it, she said, and it was something she would never buy herself. Hugh's body language, squared shoulders and deep scowl, suggested that he thought she was behaving a tad too silly, considering the reason they were gathered, but Maureen ignored him. Sara and June and Christina and even Lorelei shared Maureen's enthusiasm. Janet took Alice home for a nap, and all the guests were gone. Kaye and Barbara were clearing plates and glasses, wrapping up leftovers, and matching Tupperware lids to containers. Maureen, still wearing her poncho, began to give her girls instructions about what was still left to do.

"I think we're going to start heading home," Ellen said to Maureen and Hugh. "It's late, and we have a drive ahead of us."

"You could spend another night," Hugh said.

"We already checked out," Ellen said. "And our luggage is in the car, but thank you."

"You could stay here." Maureen said. "All of you. It's been fun." She hastily covered her mouth as if her additional indiscretion could be reversed, and then added, "You know what I mean." She squeezed Ellen's arm. "We never get to see you."

Ellen hugged her sister-in-law and said, "I promise not to let so much time go by again. But you know it works two ways. You could get on the train in the morning and even spend a day in the city with me. I'll take you to the theater and shopping."

"I'll wear my poncho," Maureen said, fingering the fabric and smiling. "I will. I'll come."

"I'll come with you," Lori said.

"That would be great." Ellen hugged Lori, and in the good-will of the moment said, "I think I'll just stop by Mom's and say good-bye. Janet sort of whisked her out of here before I could say a proper good-bye."

Neither Barbara nor Kaye offered her opinion, but it was hard to miss their matching stunned expressions. They could see that Ellen was practically giddy with the rush of warmth she was feeling from her family. But Kaye, recognizing the symptoms, knew for certain that it was impossible to obliterate years of resentment and disregard with a few days of carefully culled kindnesses. Poor Ellen was desperate for whatever it was that she felt she had missed over the years. Barbara would have been quick to tell her that family was highly overrated, a global conspiracy to make people feel bad about what they believed they were missing. And Kaye, though she felt differently than Barbara about the importance of family, would have told Ellen that when it came to family, it was best to let the past stay in the past and not to expect momentous change from the future. Such expectations would only bring disappointment greater than any she had already experienced. One of Gertie's favorite expressions was, "Let sleeping dogs lie." For years, it had bothered Kaye that her mother took this position so frequently, but as Kaye got older, it made more and more sense. Old conflicts were best resolved if they were not revisited. But it was too late now to reel Ellen back in off her cloud. She was in the throes of sentimentality, convinced that she had rediscovered at least some part of the family she had been estranged from all these years.

"... and they had these fabulous sweaters called the Hummingbird Series. I mean they actually only make about three hundred of them," Maureen said. "The designer said that once they make a design, they never make it again. That way there is only a limited number of sweaters with a specific design, so you'll never run into someone wearing the same thing."

"That's good news on several levels," Barbara said.

Maureen looked confused, but Lori laughed and Barbara quickly apologized, explaining that she had just been teasing. Embarrassed, Maureen hurried to her own defense.

"The hummingbirds happen to be made of sequins in very realistic colors," she said, almost pouting. "And the options of flex payments make it even more appealing."

"Definitely," Barbara said. "You can't beat those flex payments."

Kaye glared at her and then turned to Maureen, hoping to undo some of Barbara's damage. "Was that HSN or QVC? I usually watch HSN."

Maureen smiled gratefully at Kaye. They entered into a lively discussion of the pros and cons of each show while Ellen nodded appreciatively at Kaye and ignored Barbara. Before long, Maureen seemed to have regained her composure and was singing the praises of silicone bakeware. She had bought an entire set from QVC for a mere $29.99, and her corn muffins had never come out so moist. Forget about her banana bread and her oatmeal cookies, to say nothing of her piecrusts. Maureen's kitchen was spotless once again. The men were gathered in the living room, watching television with the children. All was right in her world.

"We really should get going," Ellen said, checking her watch. "I have to work tomorrow. I'm doing an apartment lobby in Tribeca."

"Cool," Lori said, even though she had no clue where or what Tribeca was. "I wish I could see it."

"You will," Ellen said. "I promise."

"You should never make promises," Hugh said, appearing suddenly in the doorway. "That's what Dad always said." He stepped over to Ellen and held her in his bearlike grip. "Don't be a stranger anymore, okay?"

Ellen nodded; then she kissed Maureen and Lori, and each of the children who dutifully came in one by one to say good-bye. Kaye and Barbara were not excluded from this seemingly endless display of maudlin affection that finally ended when Owen ambled in and crossed his arms over his chest, watching the scene before him with characteristic skepticism.

Ellen held out her hand to him and smiled. "Thanks for coming over to say good-bye."

He stared at her hand, shook his head, and pushed her hand away, hugging her awkwardly. Ellen kept her hands at her side, trying not to clench her fists, and pulled away as soon as she could without calling too much attention to her discomfort. Somehow she felt that Owen was still at the helm of her misery, and she could not pretend otherwise, no matter how conciliatory this last gesture might seem to everyone else.

"Well," Ellen said. "I'm really going now. Just a quick stop to see Mom."

"Are you sure that's a good idea?" Owen said.

It got so quiet in the kitchen that you could hear the telephone ring next door, and then Mrs. Mueller's muffled insistence, "Hold your horses! I'm coming." But no one in Maureen and Hugh's kitchen smiled the way they usually did when Mrs. Mueller's one-sided conversations could be heard.

"I just want to say good-bye," Ellen said. "I'm not going to fight with her. I'm too tired to fight."

"No harm in a quick good-bye, Owen," Hugh said pointedly. "Ellen's right."

"Suit yourselves," Owen repeated, directing his warning at everyone now. He zipped up his jacket and nodded at Barbara and Kaye. "Thanks for coming. Drive carefully, ladies. I'll be going. It's been a long day."

"We've all had a long day, Owen," Maureen said, touching his sleeve. "No harm in Ellen saying good-bye to Mother one more time."

Ellen smiled at Maureen and turned to Barbara and Kaye. "Ready?"

"We're ready," Kaye said, speaking for them both.

In the car, Barbara leaned forward from the backseat and put her arms around Ellen's neck, kissing her loudly on the cheek and said, "You deserve a medal just for coming." She leaned back and settled in. "That's a scary family."

"Oh, stop it," Kaye said. She was rummaging in the glove compartment for the roll of mints she had left there earlier that morning. "You've lost touch with family dynamics. It's easy to be critical when you don't have to deal with a family of your own."

"Ouch," Barbara said, clutching her chest and pretending to be wounded.

"You know I'm not trying to hurt you, Barbara," Kaye said. "But family is a lot of work. You don't have siblings or aged parents to deal with. It can be torturous." She turned to Ellen. "I think you're very brave and very smart. This was an important step for you. And I think your family tried very hard—"

"Especially Owen," Barbara said. "He's a regular doll."

"Owen is a troubled fellow," Kaye said, "that's for certain." She narrowed her eyes. "What was all that weirdness with him anyway?"

"I think he just likes to be a bully," Ellen said.

"Let me just say that I've never felt quite so lucky that I had parents who had the grace to die in a timely manner and the foresight to make me an only child," Barbara said.

"It's true that Owen's never been much different from how he is now," Ellen said, "but Andrew and Hugh were not terrible brothers. The four of us even used to play together sometimes."

"What did you play?" Barbara said. "Serial killer?"

"Don't listen to her," Kaye said. She had found the roll of Life Savers she had been searching for and popped one into her mouth, holding it out first to Barbara who took one, then handing it to Ellen over her shoulder, and then taking another for herself before putting the roll back in the glove compartment. Throughout this, Kaye waited patiently for Ellen's response. "Well? Are you going to enlighten us?"

"We played games," Ellen said, biting down on her candy and crushing it between her teeth. "We played Parcheesi, Monopoly, Knock Hockey. I was really good at Knock Hockey."

"Solly and I used to play poker," Kaye said. "We used animal crackers instead of chips."

"We played poker too," Ellen said.

Barbara had grown quiet in the backseat, listening to her friends talk about childhood memories that had been softened by time. In spite of her penchant for cynicism, she was drawn into her friends' stories. There was no point in reminding Kaye and Ellen that over the years the childhood stories that had occupied them most were those filled with details of disappointments and sorrows that seemed impossible to leave behind. Ellen had barely acknowledged a childhood at all, and now she shared dreamy reflections of a past that seemed more fiction than fact. And Kaye, sadly alienated from her only brother, now recalled a time when they had shared a room and suffered the uncertainties of the night together. Barbara supposed it was human nature to pick and choose memories.

"You're awfully quiet back there," Ellen said, lifting her eyes to the rearview mirror. "Feeling left out?"

"Not at all," Barbara said.

"That's it?" Kaye said. "No clever retort from the world's most well-adjusted only child?"

"None at all," Barbara said, "just enjoying listening to the two of you reminisce. It's a revelation."

"We're pathetic, right?" Kaye said.

"I don't think so," Barbara said. "I just think that all our lives are living laboratories. We sort of watch each other move through life and try to gather whatever we can through observations. It's all instructive, you know, being in love and not being in love, having a family and not having one. Even having children and not having them."

"Is that really necessary?" Kaye said.

"Kaye," Ellen said reproachfully. "Barbara isn't trying to hurt me. Is that what you think?"

"I suppose not," Kaye said.

Ellen reached over and touched Kaye's hand. "You're sweet to be so concerned, but it's our Barbara you're talking about."

"Thank you, Ellen," Barbara said. "For some reason Kaye always seems to think the worst of me."

"I'm sorry. It's true," Kaye said, turning around to face Barbara.

"I don't know why I expect the worst of others sometimes. Maybe I hope that way my own flaws will be ignored."

"What flaws?" Barbara said. "You mean your sanctimonious and saintlike perspective on just about everything from removing wine stains to understanding family dynamics?"

"You're so gracious," Kaye said, playfully trying to reach back and swat Barbara, but she was too quick. "I don't know why you always have to be such a bitch."

"Listen to me, my friends," Ellen said. "I couldn't feel any more loved than I do by the two of you. I know how cautious you are around me with any talk of children, and I love you both for that. But this is my private grief, and I am simply unable to share it."

"Unable or unwilling?" Kaye said.

"Secrets can be a real burden," Barbara said.

"That's so true," Ellen said. "Well, we have arrived." She pulled into her mother's driveway and sighed. "I'll just run in and say good-bye."

"Are you sure you want to do this?" Kaye asked.

"Are you sure you *need* to do this?" Barbara said.

"Absolutely," Ellen said. She ran her hand through her hair and reapplied lipstick without even looking in a mirror. "I'll be fine."

For just a moment, the three women seemed on the threshold of dropping all the deceptions that defined their inner lives. The energy in the car was charged with anticipation. Only one of them would have to be brave enough, and their sub-rosa lives would be liberated. Barbara could have identified herself as Delilah. Ellen could have told them about Faith and the lifetime of sorrow that had followed losing her. And even Kaye, who had been the first and only to confess her secret life, could have revealed that she had decided to end her affair with Frank because she could not leave George. She just couldn't.

Kaye and Barbara waited until Ellen turned from the porch and waved before entering her childhood home through the back door. Then, wordlessly, Barbara got out of the car, walked around to the driver's side, and took the wheel. She was about to say something to Kaye, but saw that she was gazing out the window into the fading afternoon light.

Nineteen

THE refrigerator door was covered in magnets. One, which identified the area as *Alice's Kitchen*, held a grocery list. Most of the magnets seemed to be souvenirs from grandchildren, party favors from weddings (featuring photographs of beaming couples), and opportunities to advertise clever adages about family and love, none of which Ellen had ever known her mother to practice. The kettle was whistling on the stove, and as Ellen walked over to turn off the flame, she read the unfamiliar script that must have been Janet's—*condensed milk, bananas, fabric softener, navy beans, Milk of Magnesia, yogurt, bird food stick, and eggs.* Ellen loved shopping lists. She covertly rescued them from empty carts and studied them the same way a detective would, hoping to glean some information from clues at a crime scene. Some of the more memorable lists were impossible to throw away, like the one that had ice cream and Slim-Fast on the same line, and the crumpled piece of paper on which someone had plainly written *FOOD*. Ellen suspected that if she took all the shopping lists Alice had written in her lifetime, the lack of variety itself would be a clue. Alice was never conflicted about anything, at least not in the way that a list that had Slim-Fast and ice cream suggested. She had certainly never written a list that included anchovy fillets or any fresh herbs or real butter. Her recipes never varied, so neither did her ingredients. She often said that if you stick to one path, you'll never get lost. And when Ellen once said that it was true, but it also meant that you would never see anything new, Alice scoffed at her. As far as Alice was concerned, there was nothing new to see.

"I thought you'd left already," Janet said.

Ellen jumped. Janet was wearing slippers that muffled her footsteps.

"You startled me," Ellen said.

"I'm sorry. I didn't know you were here. I was pretty startled myself." She smiled. "I didn't even hear the car."

"My friends dropped me off," Ellen said. She felt the need to apologize. "The door was open, so I let myself in."

"It's your house. You don't need to ring the bell," Janet said.

An awkward silence followed in which they sort of shuffled around each other, trying to mark a comfortable space.

"I came down to shut off the kettle," Janet said. "I forgot all about it."

"I took care of it," Ellen said.

"Yes, I see. Thank you."

"You must have added birdseed to the grocery list," Ellen said, pointing to the refrigerator. "Mother would never think of feeding the birds unless she planned to eat them later on."

To Ellen's surprise, Janet laughed, acknowledging what they both knew to be the truth. She touched the kettle with one finger to see if it was still hot and said, "You know, people do mellow as they get older."

"Not my mother."

"Well, it is harder for some than for others," Janet said with just a slight nod. She was trying to be conciliatory. "Would you like a cup of tea?"

Barbara and Kaye were waiting at the local coffee shop. She had promised not to be long, and they were expecting her to call.

"Sure," Ellen said. "Is Mother upstairs? I just wanted to say good-bye."

Janet was already filling the metal strainer in the teapot with tea leaves. This was also new. Alice had reused the same bag of Lipton's until the water was clear.

"She's resting, but feel free to go up and see her. I hope you like ginger. I've hooked your mother. She's rather fond of good tea now."

Ellen was amazed to think that this woman genuinely doted on Alice, even to the point of being protective. For Ellen, who had never shared a cup of tea with her mother or ever had the standard mother-daughter chat, it was hard to imagine that anyone could cross that divide and be welcomed in that space. Alice and Ellen had worked hard to keep their distance. When it was time for new clothes, Alice bought what she thought Ellen needed until she was old enough to shop on her own. Hugh Sr. took his only daughter for shoes, and this was one of Ellen's happiest memories. He seemed more relaxed whenever he was away from Alice. And Ellen could hardly blame him.

"Sugar?" Janet said.

"Yes, please. I like it sweet," Ellen said.

"Would you like a cookie? Peanut butter. Alice really loves peanut butter."

"Really? That's new too." Ellen pulled out a chair and sat down. The table was still covered with red oilcloth. Growing up, she had hated the feel of the plastic. It had never felt clean to her overly critical teenaged fingers. The oilcloth seemed to hold the smells of everything that Alice cooked, mixing the odors of boiled cabbage with sautéed onions and Duncan Hines cake mix into one horrible scent. "Mother never even bought peanut butter. She always said it was for white trash." She saw Janet color, right around the tips of her small unpierced ears, and knew immediately that it had been the wrong thing to say. Hoping to recover from this blunder, she tried to make it seem as though Alice's dislikes were simply a function of her unpleasant disposition. "She said the same thing about marshmallow fluff, fried chicken, and Jell-O, and who doesn't like fried chicken?"

"Well," Janet said, drawing herself up a bit and tucking a loose strand of hair back into her neat little bun, "she likes all those things well enough now. I suppose I've been a bad influence."

"I seriously doubt that, Janet. Let me try one of your cookies, please."

Immediately, Janet opened a tin and set two cookies on a plate.

"They're so easy to make," she said. "I could give you the recipe. My kids love them. My grandkids too."

Ellen added two heaping spoons of sugar to the tea Janet had just poured. The smell of ginger was sharp but fragrant.

"Delicious," Ellen said, biting into a cookie. "I'd love the recipe." She took another bite and swiped at some of the crumbs that fell onto her sweater. "I don't know why, but I just assumed that you didn't have a family."

"Well, I do." Janet took a sip of tea. "I'm a widow, two years now. My husband died of cancer. Prostate cancer to be exact. He went fast. He was a stubborn fellow, refused to see a doctor. By the time Hank finally went, it was too late. He was a good husband and a good father."

"I'm sure he was," Ellen said and then added, "I'm so sorry for your loss."

Without responding to this last statement, Janet went on with a summary of her life. "We had four children. I had my first when I was twenty, exactly nine months after we got married. Some folks thought the timing was a little fishy, but it wasn't." She winked. "We just had a busy honeymoon."

"What are your children's names?"

"I have three sons and one daughter. Just like your mother. The boys are Carl, Chris, and Alan; my daughter is Leona. I have seven grandchildren, but I won't run their names by you." Janet laughed and touched her hair again, though there wasn't a strand out of place. "I know all their names and birthdays. I never forget a birthday."

"You look very young. I would never have guessed that you have so many children and grandchildren."

"I'm fifty-two. I have good skin. It's genetic, and I put olive oil on for the night and wash with Noxzema morning and night. Noxzema is a good product. Your mother uses it now."

"Does she?"

Instead of answering, Janet sipped at her tea and broke off a piece of cookie. There seemed nothing more to say. In some odd way, Janet had stepped into the shoes that belonged to a daughter and taken full charge of Alice. *Jealousy* would certainly have been the wrong word to describe Ellen's feelings, but it was hard not to feel a twinge of something close to it, longing perhaps, but not jealousy. Ellen had come home looking for something—but not for her mother. That was for certain.

"I'm sorry about your baby," Janet said.

It was as though Janet had read Ellen's mind, and she was so startled that she neither looked up nor responded, certain that she had imagined Janet's words. Instead, Ellen stared into her teacup and said nothing.

"Ellen?" Janet reached across the table and touched Ellen's hand. "Did you hear me? I said that I was sorry about your baby."

Ellen looked up and nodded, still speechless.

"Your mother told me everything," Janet said. "It's quite unfor-givable, actually. As a mother, I can't imagine your sorrow. It's the one subject Alice and I cannot agree upon."

Ellen had begun to stand. Her hands were pressed firmly on the sticky red oilcloth, and she had risen several inches off the chair. Now, she sat down with a thump as though she were the clay pigeon on a skeet shoot and someone had taken a perfect shot. It was almost impossible to imagine her mother talking to Janet about Faith. Of course, Alice would not have called her Faith, but that was irrelevant. Alice had talked to Janet about The Baby. That would have been her name. The Baby. It seemed inconceivable to Ellen that Alice had talked to a seemingly perfect stranger about something so painfully shameful.

"Her name is Faith," Ellen said. "The baby's name. I named her Faith."

"Well, that's a beautiful name, and a very appropriate one under the circumstances."

"She was a beautiful baby."

"Yes, I know," Janet said.

"You know?"

"I've seen pictures of her. They're with all her papers. Didn't you know?"

Sometimes it seemed as though someone could spend a lifetime trying and failing to make something happen, to discover some truth, some cure. And then it could happen without trying, by pure accident, like the invention of the smallpox vaccine or the theory of gravity, and the world would never be the same. Perseverance, a desire to know more, and simply good luck could turn accident into discovery. Ellen had merely been sipping tea and nibbling at a peanut butter cookie when her entire life was suddenly redefined.

"No, I never knew there were any pictures of her," Ellen said.

She took several small sips of tea just to have something to do. "Do you know where they are?"

"Of course," Janet said.

"May I see them, please?"

"Why, certainly. Your mother keeps everything in your father's desk. It's always been there. Since forever."

Forever had never seemed quite so long to Ellen. She did not move, afraid that if she did, Janet would disappear along with the promise of what she had to offer.

"Just a minute, dear," Janet said.

There was a small rolltop desk in the hallway that had always been Hugh Sr.'s makeshift office. It was off limits to all the children, and Ellen had never dared explore its interior, especially not after Andrew discovered a box of condoms in one of the drawers and a catalog for porn movies, which he showed off to his friends whenever they were over. It went on for some time, and then Hugh Sr. caught Andrew in the act of displaying these treasures and promptly asked the boys to leave. As soon as they were gone, Hugh Sr. threw Andrew so hard against the wall that his collarbone broke. No one distrusted such injuries in those days, and certainly not in their community. Parents were expected to keep their kids in line no matter what it took, so a broken collarbone was as problematic as a splinter. Kids got hurt; accidents happened. Everyone knew that.

"Well, I found everything," Janet said. "I was surprised when your mother said you weren't interested in seeing the pictures or even in knowing what happened to your baby."

"Not interested?" Ellen said evenly.

She was afraid that if she did not mask her incredulousness, she would startle Janet and cause her to panic, like a spooked horse. It took all of Ellen's strength to remain calm and let Janet take the lead. When Janet held out a bulging manila envelope, Ellen wanted to grab it and make a run for it. Instead, she smiled benignly, pretending it was routine to see pictures of the daughter she had not seen since she was only days old.

"It seemed odd to me when Alice told me that you had made it very clear you wanted nothing to do with any of this information. I mean, for Pete's sake, even a sixteen-year-old feels like a mother after she has a baby. Am I right?"

Ellen nodded. This woman knew everything about what had happened. Janet had been fully taken into Alice's confidence, even if most of the information she had disclosed had been all lies.

"You take a look through those papers, dear," Janet said. "She was a real cutie pie, no doubt about that. Especially at her first birthday. Never mind her first Christmas. I tell you, it pains me to think what they did to you, and I told Alice so. Mr. Hugh, well, he was really quiet whenever the subject came up. Your daddy was the same way."

For a moment, Ellen thought she was holding a baby in her arms. She drew the thick envelope against her chest and squeezed her eyes shut as she began to rock back and forth, humming softly to herself. She heard Janet's voice continue to drone on until it must have become evident that Ellen was no longer listening,

"Ellen, dear?"

Ellen kept rocking.

"Are you all right?" Janet said. "Can I get you something? A glass of water? A fresh cup of tea?"

The rocking stopped.

"Yes, tea, please. I would like some more tea." Still clutching the envelope, she leaned over and peeked into her teacup. It was empty, but she could not remember having drunk any of it. She watched as Janet refilled the cup, surprised that the tea was still hot. It seemed as though so much time had passed. "Thank you," she said, though she made no move to drink any of it.

"Why don't you set the papers down a moment and take a

deep breath?" Janet said. She seemed genuinely concerned with Ellen's odd behavior. "I always suspected that Alice was misleading me." She wagged her finger at an invisible presence. "Shameful. Just shameful."

Ellen reached for the teacup and drank. She had forgotten to add sugar, but the tea tasted surprisingly sweet anyway.

"Good girl," Janet said. "Better now, right?"

She said this with such hearty approval that Ellen was pleased in spite of herself. It was no wonder that Alice was so fond of Janet.

"Much better," Ellen said. "Thank you."

She pushed the teacup to the side and then with both hands set the envelope down on the oilcloth. As soon as she undid the string and reached inside to withdraw the papers, she knew that from this moment on everything would always be different. There were several files, each one carefully marked in her mother's parochial school script. The file on top had *Pictures* written along the tab, and Ellen turned the cover carefully. And there it was, like the first breath someone took after being resuscitated. Her lungs burned, but the relief was so profound it was almost unbearable. Faith at one day old. Her face was as familiar as Ellen's own, yet as unique as a fingerprint. The full, moist lips that Ellen had kissed so deeply it had woken her infant daughter from a deep sleep. And skin so perfect that Ellen could not stop running the back of her hand along her daughter's cheeks and across her smooth brow. The next picture was of Faith at three months, and she had green eyes just like Ellen. Faith was wearing a pink T-shirt that had *Princess* written across the chest in red sequins, and her chubby hands were clutching a yellow rubber ball. A thin pink headband with a lone pink flower jauntily attached on the side adorned her bald head.

She was so beautiful that Ellen could not quite believe she was hers, and Sam's of course, though Ellen could barely remember what he looked like. Certainly he was responsible for the tiny cleft in Faith's chin and the wide-set eyes. There were dozens of photo-graphs. On the back of each photograph was a date and brief de-scription. *Joy Anne's First Birthday at Grandma and Grandpa Brown's country house; Joy Anne's First Christmas at home with the whole family; Joy Anne at Disney World for her third birthday; The first day of kinder-garten in the new dress Grandma Carver sent; Joy Anne and her new baby sister, Elizabeth Fay; Joy Anne loses her first tooth.* As Ellen studied picture after picture, only one thought raced through her mind and gave her the courage to go on. Faith had been loved. She had been given to parents who treasured her, who knew they had been given a gift unlike any other, and they had been forever grateful. This, however, was the piece of Ellen's past that she had never anticipated. Certainly, she had always hoped that she would learn what had happened to Faith, maybe even meet her someday. It had been impossible to completely abandon this dream. But never in all of Ellen's imaginings or musings had she ever thought that her parents had not only known who had adopted Faith, but had been instrumental in orchestrating that transfer. Ellen returned to the pictures with trembling hands.

The pictures told the story of Faith's life with increasing re-straint. As Faith moved into her teens, there were evident changes. There were still blurbs, though they were less detailed and almost ambivalent at times. *Joy Anne—Girl Scouts; Joy Anne merit badge swimming; Joy Anne's flute recital; Joy Anne wins sixth grade science fair.* It was as if it were too much trouble to write a full sentence. The Joy Anne in this last picture may have been the final one where she was clear skinned and open faced. The cleft in her chin was barely visible, and her straight brown hair was cut into a pageboy, framing her sweet face and setting off cheekbones that were Ellen's unmistakable legacy.

The last few pictures in the folder, however, told an entirely different story. One in particular stood out. There was no writing on the back; nothing, not even a date, and Ellen wondered why it had been sent at all. At first, Ellen thought that Faith might be dressed to attend a costume party. She must have been twelve or thirteen, maybe fourteen, and thin to the point of gauntness. Her hair was dyed electric blue. Even this did not bother Ellen, nor did the piercing above Faith's right eyebrow and the thickly applied black eyeliner that made her look more like a waif and less punk or Goth, the look that she had probably been going for. Ellen even smiled at the purple lipstick that Faith had so conscientiously applied; it was so reminiscent of Ellen's own tortured adolescence. The need to be different, unique even in some small way was so familiar. Ellen had distinguished herself with false eyelashes, an attitude, and then a pregnancy before fleeing and leaving everything except the pain behind. Suddenly, it all made sense to Ellen, and she thought she even understood why the Browns had sent this disturbing photograph. They had needed some answers too, some way to understand why they had stopped making Joy Anne happy. Ellen understood immediately because she knew what a broken heart looked like. It looked like a grief-stricken sixteen-year-old as she was forced to give up her infant. It looked like a teenager who wondered why her mother had not fought harder to keep her baby. Ellen could have been looking into a mirror as she stared into her daughter's eyes. Then Ellen remembered Janet and looked up to find her quietly waiting for Ellen to finish with the photographs.

"It's been quite a few days, hasn't it?" Janet said. "What with your father's funeral and now this."

"And now this . . ." Ellen echoed.

"There's more," Janet said. She stood and walked over to the sink. "There's so much more. I couldn't let it go on any longer." Her hands trembled as she covered her face, and she pointed at the file folders on the table. "See for yourself."

Ellen nodded, but she made no effort to continue her search.

The photographs had left her enervated, too weak to even think about what else there was to confront. More evidence of her family's duplicity, contracts that documented the transfer, the sale, so to speak, of Ellen's baby and proof of her family's indifference to the pain it would cause. Ellen knew exactly what the files contained. She could not look just yet. Instead, Ellen tried to absorb the images of Faith as her life moved across Ellen's consciousness like a parade, each picture more colorful, more spectacular, and more telling than the one before.

"I know there's more, Janet. I know. And I can't tell you how much I appreciate what you've done for me—"

"I didn't do anything I shouldn't have done ages ago." Janet opened her arms as if she wanted Ellen to step inside an embrace and offer forgiveness. But before Ellen could respond, Janet dropped her arms to her sides. She had merely been affecting a pose of shame, an act of contrition. A plea to be absolved of her guilt. "I'm so sorry, so very, very sorry," Janet said.

Their exchange was suddenly interrupted by a cry from upstairs. Alice was calling out to Janet.

"She has bad dreams," Janet said. "Terrible nightmares."

"She deserves them," Ellen said.

Clearly taken aback, Janet composed herself and quietly said, "I'd better go to her. She gets hysterical."

"Let me go."

"I don't think that's such a good idea," Janet said warily. "Certainly not in your state of mind."

"Are you afraid I'll kill her?" Ellen said and laughed. "I won't. I promise. Believe me. She's already ruined my life. I have no desire to let her finish it off."

"I think she's sorry for what she did. I know your father was."

Ellen put her glass in the sink and took another glass from the dish drain.

"Do you usually bring her water when she wakes up?" Ellen asked.

"Yes, and I usually sit with her a bit. Let me go, dear. You'll say or do something you'll regret."

Alice's voice rang out again. Ellen filled the glass with water and shut the tap.

"I really, really believe that she's sorry," Janet said.

Wiping the bottom of the glass with a dish towel, Ellen said, "And I don't really care."

There was no stopping Ellen. Janet called out from the bottom of the stairs, "Ellen's coming up, Alice. She's bringing you some water, and then she has to leave."

Ellen knew Janet was watching her as she walked up the stairs, one step at a time, careful not to spill any water.

Twenty

FROM time to time, the news featured human-interest stories about some victim's family who publicly forgave an offender rather than live with crippling hatred. Ellen had witnessed some of these astonishing reconciliations. She had even been deeply moved by the emotional response of a murderer, sentenced to life with no chance of parole, who bonded with his victim's family. Forgiveness could be a balm to someone who had finally confronted his wickedness, no matter what the future held. Sometimes the stories were so poignant that Ellen wondered why she could not emulate the high moral standards of those who found it in their hearts to absolve. It would have been such a relief to feel virtuous, to know that she too was such a genuinely good person.

Ellen pondered the merits of forgiveness as she noted the warning sign on her parents' bedroom door that oxygen was in use. The bedroom door was partially open, and Ellen could see her mother lying in bed. She was propped up on pillows, and one blue-veined hand hung down, opening and closing, turning from side to side—

gesturing, it seemed, to some nameless presence. Alice's mouth was moving in silent discourse with the same wrongdoer, whoever it might be. With her other hand, she kept tugging at the oxygen lines. The green tubes had somehow become tangled, and Alice was unable to make the appropriate adjustments. She was a pathetic sight, but Ellen was more pained by her own lack of pity. The door creaked as Ellen pushed it open. It had always creaked, swelling with damp weather and moaning at the oddest moments, frightening Ellen in the middle of the night. The good news was that Ellen was no longer frightened, not of the sound, or of her mother.

"Janet? Is that you?" Alice said. "What took you so long?"

Taking purposeful strides, Ellen was at her mother's bedside. After setting the glass down, Ellen began fussing with the oxygen tubes and adjusting the bedclothes. When Alice saw who had come to her rescue, her eyes opened wide, and she drew back reflexively. The once-commanding matriarch was now an old woman with skin so papery and dry that Ellen thought her mother might disintegrate like some creature in a low-budget horror movie. But Alice did not break apart. Instead, she narrowed her rheumy eyes and silently fixed Ellen with a beady stare.

"Relax, Mother. Let me untangle this one. I didn't mean to startle you."

She saw that Janet had pulled Alice's hair away from her face with a bobby pin. Maybe Janet had found it in her pocket at just the moment that Alice's hair had fallen across her eyes. The intimacy that this suggested shook Ellen a bit. She would never have touched her mother's hair, never.

"I thought you had left," Alice said. Years of smoking and bronchitis had entirely changed the timbre of her voice, making her sound oddly masculine. "That's all. I thought you were finally gone."

"Finally gone?" Ellen laughed. "Well, don't hold back, Mother."

"What do you want?" Alice said. "You did what you had to do.

You buried your father. You didn't have the decency to be a daughter to him, but you were there to see him put in the ground." She began to cough uncontrollably, reaching for the glass of water on her night table and then spilling the water on herself as she took a sip. "See what I mean? A good daughter would have helped me." She wiped her mouth with the back of her hand. "You were never a good daughter."

"You never treated me like a daughter," Ellen said.

"That's nonsense," Alice said. "I treated all my children the same. But you were a difficult child from the day you were born. Like that Lorelei who took such a fancy to you. No surprise there. Boys are much better. Boys are devoted to their mothers."

"That's nonsense, Mother. My friend Kaye is very close to her mother. I have other friends, women, who adore their mothers, and vice versa." Ellen had no idea why she was trying to defend herself. And she had never used the term *vice versa* in her life. She felt out of control. "It doesn't matter," she added lamely. "I haven't come to convince you of anything."

"Well, you couldn't have even if you tried." Her hand shook as she set the glass back on the table. "Girls. Too high-strung. That's the problem."

"Maybe you should have given me away too," Ellen said.

Alice had an infallible will. That had always been certain. She pulled the sheet up and dabbed at each corner of her mouth, smiling almost smugly.

"Janet hates it when I do that," she said, and did it again. "She can be really bossy."

Ignoring Alice's observation, Ellen said, "I know everything, Mother." She refused to cry, refused to show any weakness. "I saw the pictures. I know everything."

"Do you now?" Alice said. "Nothing new there, is there? You always knew everything."

"Stop it," Ellen said. "This is too important."

"It's over, Ellen. Let it go. I told your father that you were like a dog with a bone in its mouth. You just can't let anything go, can you? We did the right thing for you."

For a moment, Ellen wondered if she was dreaming. She had often had a dream similar to this in which she confronted her mother about Faith and demanded an explanation. Several times in her dream, Ellen would watch her mother's mouth move as she revealed Faith's whereabouts, but Ellen would be unable to hear and would wake sweating and screaming that Alice should speak up. Other times, Ellen would dream that her mother had hidden Faith somewhere and left clues to her whereabouts, riddles that Ellen was unable to solve. All of the dreams had been disturbing, leaving Ellen on edge for days, certain that there was something she had overlooked. But none of those dreams had been as frightening as the reality of her mother's sanctimonious cruelty.

". . . sixteen-year-old whore. That's what you were. With those false eyelashes and your tight clothes. Is it any wonder you got raped? You were always asking for trouble. That's for sure. Everyone knew it. They all talked about you, and I had to listen—"

"Shut up. Just shut up," Ellen said. She was not shouting, but Alice heard the rage and grew silent immediately. "I don't want you to say anything unless I ask you a question. Do you understand?"

More frightened than chastened, Alice set her thin lips in a straight line and waited.

"I wasn't raped," Ellen said. "Is that what you told everyone? You had them believe your poor daughter was raped. Well, I wasn't. I was drunk and young and stupid, and I had sex with a very nice boy who was also young and drunk and stupid. He's dead now. You don't have to worry about him anymore. Poor guy. Did you scare him into signing the rights to his baby away? I was a lonely kid who never felt loved. That was your fault, Mother. I never felt loved, but I knew how to love. And I would have been a good mother to a boy *or* a girl. I named her Faith. Did you know that? All this time, all these years, you let me believe that my daughter was out of my reach. How much did you get for her, Mother? How much was my happiness worth?"

Alice was nervous now. She strained her head toward the door, hoping to hear Janet. The doorway was empty, and Alice's eyes darted from Ellen to the doorway and back.

"Tell me," Ellen said. "I want to know how much you got for selling my baby."

"It was all legal," Alice said lamely. "Private adoptions are legal. They wanted a baby, and they got one. It was a win–win. And we got some compensation for our trouble. We deserved that after all the trouble you brought this family. It paid for a few things we'd needed for a long time. Washer and dryer, for one."

Ellen's chest hurt when she breathed, as though she were standing in the frigid cold. She never heard Hugh enter the bedroom. But suddenly he was there, pale and weary and ready to take his place in the tragedy that was their lives. He looked directly at Ellen, and then her body just yielded to all that loss and rage. Hugh caught her as she crumpled into a heap. He wrapped his arms around her and held her as she said *how could you have done this to me* over and over until the words were just one long wail of anguish. It was so, so sad. And for no particular reason Ellen remembered the girl in the next bed in the home. She had also given birth to a daughter. The fourteen-year-old mother, Penny, never spoke. She had wrapped herself in a cocoon of mourning for her imminent loss, refusing any comfort or help of any kind. The day Penny gave birth was the first time Ellen ever heard her speak. As she was holding her infant daughter, Penny looked at Ellen and said, "I named her Air because she is like a breath of fresh air." It was such an unusual name, especially in those years when the standard was traditional names, good solid family names. That was the first and last time they ever spoke. As Hugh embraced her, Ellen wondered what had happened to Penny and to Air, to all the girls and their babies, and to all their unfinished lives.

"I'm sorry," Hugh said into Ellen's hair. "I'm so terribly sorry."

"I told you she would never understand," Alice said, pulling the bedclothes around her and smoothing them down with both hands. "She was always on the hysterical side. I don't know what she expected from us."

"Mother, that's enough," Hugh said. "It's not the time."

"Well, I think—"

"I said enough now," Hugh said sharply. "You need to go to sleep. It's very late."

"I want Janet," Alice said, whining like a petulant child. "Janet puts me to sleep. She knows just what to do."

Hugh nodded. Ellen's body was limp in his arms, and he sort of dragged her to the doorway and shouted down the stairs for Janet. She must have been waiting for her cue because she was there almost instantly, immediately busying herself with Alice's medication and avoiding all eye contact with Ellen.

"Ellen," Hugh said, "let's go downstairs and talk. Come on. Let me take you downstairs."

But Ellen shook her head vehemently. There was something else she had to know, and she was not leaving until she had her answer. She swallowed and stood up straight, trying not to cry.

"Where is she?"

Hugh looked down at the floor and shrugged. He really did not know.

"Mother?" Ellen said. "Where is she?"

"How should I know?" Alice said.

"Tell her," Janet gently urged. "Tell her. It's the right thing to do, Alice."

"Tell her what? I don't know what happened to the girl after she moved away from here. That was ten years ago. Wild thing—just like her own mother. Ran off and broke her parents' hearts."

"Jesus Christ," Hugh said. He shook his head, running his hand through his white hair. He still had beautiful hair. "Jesus, Joseph, and Mary. What a fucking horror you are. A real fucking horror."

Alice and Ellen were equally shocked, but for very different reasons. Janet looked stunned for all reasons. Of course, Alice immediately started going on about how her son had spoken to her, asking Janet if she had heard the terrible things Hugh had said to his own mother. No one was really listening to her anyway, but Janet finally shushed Alice and told her to take her pills and just be quiet once and for all.

"She was living in town?" Ellen said. "She lived here all this time? And you knew?" She turned to Hugh. "You *knew* about it?"

"No, I didn't know. I really didn't. It was only recently that I learned any of the details about the adoption. I didn't know the family lived here. I swear."

Ellen believed him. She had to believe him. "Hugh, it's all right," she said. She had already started to plan. It was suddenly as if Faith were still here in town. Ellen felt as though she could walk out the front door and find her daughter, or at least find the remnants of the life she had fled. "Will you help me find her?"

Hugh said, "Of course, I'll help you. Of course I will."

Just before she had left to come to the funeral, Ellen had seen a woman on the news who had miraculously survived the mindless prank of a group of careless teens. One of them had thrown a bag of bricks from an overpass. The bricks had crashed through the windshield of the woman's car, forcing her off the road and smashing every bone in her face. After countless reconstructive procedures, the woman was able to return to a normal life. Yet what Ellen found almost unbelievable was the woman's testimony at the hearing. She forgave the young man and asked the court for leniency. The young man would have to have psychiatric counseling and serve six months in jail and three years on parole. After the hearing, the woman and the young man were caught on camera embracing. Tears streamed down his face as he proclaimed his love for his victim, calling her the most wonderful woman in the world. Ellen had to agree. The woman said that in forgiving the young man, she had actually freed herself.

Ellen approached her mother's bed and stared into her face. Alice had never been very pretty, but age agreed with her in the way it did with some men and fewer women. The wrinkles that lined Alice's brow and the concave hollowness of her cheeks made her features more interesting than when she had been young. A photographer would have been likely to find Alice a worthy subject. All these details, however, could not mask the reality of who Alice had been then, and who she was now. The common denominator was always the same. Alice had been a wretched young woman, and she was an even more miserable old woman.

Everything suddenly seemed so easy. Ellen knew exactly what she wanted to say, and she said it all in one great relieved admission.

"I'll never forgive you, Mother. Never."

Alice narrowed her eyes, ready to respond with some new defamatory variation of Ellen's worth. But Ellen was prepared and swift, and she brought her face close enough to her mother's face so that Alice knew enough to pull back, cowering at the scent of her daughter's steely hatred. Before she could say anything, Ellen felt her brother's hand on her arm, urging her away from the bed.

"Ellen," Hugh said. "For your own sake now, pretend she's a stranger."

"I don't have to pretend," Ellen said.

*   *   *

HUGH hovered in the kitchen doorway, unsure of what to say or do next.

"I don't know what to say," Hugh said.

Ellen thought he seemed older than he had just a day ago, and she was sorry for disrupting his life.

"I'm very thirsty," Ellen said.

Glad for something to do, Hugh asked if she would like a cup of tea.

"Just some water, please," she said. "No ice."

There was a pitcher of water in the refrigerator, and Ellen downed the glass while Hugh stood at readiness in case she wanted a refill. She shook her head, smiling to let him know she was all right and motioned for him to sit. He obliged, still holding the water pitcher, and pointed to the thick file that Ellen kept one protective hand on as she drank.

"I suppose you've seen everything in here?" she said.

When Hugh did not answer, Ellen pushed the file toward him, but he only stared down at it before he set the pitcher on the table at a safe distance.

"She's so pretty. Isn't she?"

"Of course she is. Why wouldn't she be?" Hugh said.

Finally, he opened the file and began to move through the pictures and documents with steady persistence, pausing very briefly to peer into his niece's eyes or to note a date or read the accompanying narrative. Ellen watched him, waiting for him to say something about the little girl who was his niece, but he said nothing until he was done. Then he closed the file and clasped his hands on top.

"Now what?" he said. "What do we do now?"

"When were you going to tell me?"

"Ellen . . ."

"When, Hugh? I need to know."

"I was going to tell you when you came up for the birthday party, and then Dad died and, well, things just got out of hand."

"Things have been out of hand for a long time."

"Yes, they have, and I'm sorry."

"I believe you," Ellen said.

Hugh dabbed at his moist eyes with a paper napkin. "Thank you. That means a lot to me."

"Does Maureen know?"

"Yes," Hugh said. "She wanted to tell you right away. I asked her to wait. It wasn't something to talk about over the phone."

"Who else knows?"

"I think Owen knows. I haven't talked to him about it, but he has a way of knowing things he shouldn't. He seems to thrive on the misfortune of others."

It was the first time Ellen had heard Hugh speak so disparagingly of Owen. First Hugh's attack against their mother, and now this. She knew he wanted to prove his loyalty, and it moved her. After all, she and Hugh were not of the same mind about most subjects.

"I have to find her," Ellen said.

"We'll find her."

"Joy Anne Brown," Ellen said. "Such a normal, almost ordinary name. Did you know the family?"

"No. I never knew them. Apparently, the Browns had moved here from the city. Dad said they were good people, already in their late thirties by the time they adopted Joy Anne."

"Faith. Her name is Faith."

"All right."

"I'm sorry," Ellen said. "It doesn't matter what her name is, does it?"

"Names are important." He reached over and patted her hand. "Faith or Joy. Everyone had so many expectations for such a tiny creature."

Ellen nodded, pointed her chin toward the upstairs, and said, "How did she manage to do so much damage? She wasn't that powerful."

"I think she was," Hugh said.

"Only because we let her be. She was always a fraud. We could have taken her on if we had worked together."

Hugh laughed, and then Ellen laughed too, sharing the image of their mother being set on by her children and husband, a sort of coup d'état, resulting in the establishment of a new, more popular regime.

"I'm telling you we could have taken her." Ellen said. "I wish we had. It would have been different for all of us."

"It can be different now, Ellen. This could be our second chance."

She was skeptical. Second chances were for optimists, people who believed in the essential goodness of others. Once, long ago, she had been such a person. Perhaps Hugh was still such a person. She smiled at his good intentions and his furrowed brow.

"I wonder if Faith knew," Ellen said. "I wonder if she knew that her biological family was close by."

"How would she have known that?" Hugh asked. "And if she had known, wouldn't she have come knocking?"

"I don't know. Who knows what she knew or what she thought? She seemed like she was happy. Don't you think she looked happy when she was a little girl?"

"Yes, yes, she does. " Hugh patted her hand, hoping to comfort her. "She looks like she was a happy little girl, and that's something, isn't it?"

"It is something, right?" Ellen said. "I just hope she was happy."

"You sound just like a mother," Hugh said.

Ellen lowered her eyes as they filled with tears, and she said, "Thank you."

"They say a mother's love is the strongest power in the world."

"Ours must have missed that lesson." She took Hugh's crumpled napkin and wiped her own eyes. "She certainly never behaved much like a mother."

"I think she's the exception, don't you?"

"I hope so."

"Just because someone is born with all the parts doesn't mean they all work," Hugh said. He rubbed his eyes. He looked weary with his family's secrets. "Do you remember when we had squirrels in the attic?" Hugh said.

"No, not really," Ellen said.

"It was the summer we finally insulated the attic."

"Ah," Ellen said dryly. "I must have had other things on my mind, like my expanding waistline. I do remember that there was some construction going on. Tell me about the squirrels."

"I remember those squirrels well only because the timing was so strange. After the installation was in, and the roof patched, it became clear that we had an intruder. I could hear the sound of chewing at night. It was an awful sound, but Mother took it as a personal affront. She called the builders back to assess the situation. There was a nest of torn fiberglass inside one of the vents, where a mother squirrel had evidently worked to make a home for her babies. The builder replaced the vent and nailed it shut."

Ellen felt more relaxed than she had all day. It was warm in the kitchen, and she yawned, covering her mouth with one hand.

"Are you getting the picture?" Hugh said.

"Not yet."

"The sound of chewing returned the very next morning. Dad was outside with Mother, pointing up at the place where the vent had been replaced. There was a squirrel, frantically spitting out pieces of wood as she tried to work her way back inside. The builder had nailed her babies inside."

"Poor thing," Ellen said. "What happened?"

"Mother started throwing rocks, forcing her to take cover in a nearby tree. I remember that Mother told Dad that eventually the squirrel would have to give up."

"What did Dad say?"

"He said it would never give up. No mother would." He paused and took a sip of water from Ellen's glass. "Mother laughed and said, 'Just watch me make her change her mind.' Poor Dad looked horrified."

"So what happened?"

"Dad called a trapper. He climbed up a twenty-five-foot ladder and took out four babies. He put them all in a trap in the woods behind the house. Mother wanted him to kill them, but he said it was against the law. He told her he was going to wait for the mother squirrel to find them and then take them all away to the other side of the river."

"She wanted them killed?" Ellen said incredulously.

Hugh nodded and said, "As soon as the trapper left, that mother squirrel made a beeline for the ladder, looking for her babies. When she saw they were missing, she flew down that ladder and went into the woods, scurrying up and down every tree until she heard them squawking in the trap and joined them. I swear, Ellen, in all my life, I never saw Mother look so dumbfounded."

In spite of herself, Ellen laughed. "Did she say anything?"

"Not a word," Hugh said. "She just stared."

Ellen leaned toward him and said, "Do you think she ever loved us?"

"Who knows? Besides, what difference does it make now?"

"I think it always makes a difference."

Ellen's cell phone rang then, startling them both with its repetitive chime and sending her across the room to retrieve it from her purse.

"Hello? Hello?"

It was Kaye. Ellen looked up at the clock over the sink. She had promised to be no more than an hour. That was two hours ago.

"Ellen?" Kaye said. "What's going on there?"

"I'm sorry. I should have called. I was just talking to Hugh, and I lost track of time."

"That's fine. Barbara or I can drive. You must be exhausted."

"I am. I'm utterly exhausted."

"We'll come and get you right now, honey. We had something to eat while we were waiting. Should we pick up a sandwich for you? You can eat it in the car."

"Yes," Ellen said. "I would like a sandwich, and some coffee, please."

"Sure," Kaye said. "Whatever you want. What kind of sandwich?"

"You decide."

"Okay," Kaye said. "I'll take care of it."

"I love you, Kaye. And I love Barbara too. Do I tell you that often enough?"

"We love you too, Ellen." Kaye paused, and then added, "That old bitch must have done some job on you."

"I'm all right now."

"You should have killed her if you had the chance," Kaye said.

"I had the chance," Ellen said. "Did you know it was an old wives' tale that you should punch a shark in the nose to fight it off?"

"I didn't know that," Kaye said.

"It's actually their eyes and their gills that are the most sensitive."

Hugh was staring at her, wondering what she was talking about. But Kaye understood.

"So next time put a stick in her eye," Kaye said.

"There won't be a next time," Ellen said, looking directly into Hugh's face. "I'm never coming back to this house again."

Shortly after she hung up with Kaye, Ellen gathered her belongings, kissed Hugh, and took the file that he had bound with rubber bands and then slipped into a plain brown shopping bag. As she hugged the package to her chest, Ellen imagined how that poor mother squirrel must have felt, worrying and worrying about how to get to her babies. Ellen wanted to believe that after they were reunited the trapper had indeed taken the mother and her babies to a safer place, a nicely wooded area where no one threatened them again. She sympathized with the poor mother's terror as she scrambled from tree to tree, trying to reach her babies as they waited to be rescued. Ellen understood. She was a mother too, and she was prepared to do anything to find her own baby, even if it meant climbing up and down trees or chewing down a house in the process.

Twenty-one

WHEN Ellen had first moved to Manhattan, she had dated a photographer who supported himself as an elementary school teacher. He was a nice man, but too earnest for Ellen, too much in love with her too quickly. Cyrus had been born in Queens to immigrant Haitian parents, and he had a chip on his shoulder about everything. Ellen, however, found him to be an ardent lover who rejoiced in pleasing her, and she found it unbearable to think of parting with his wolfish tongue. Nevertheless, after three months, Ellen could no longer tolerate his attitude—even if he was delighted to pleasure her until she had to beg him to stop—and she decided to break it off with him. On what she had planned to be their last day together, she accompanied him to Central Park to witness yet one more of his scientific metaphors. Cyrus was forever making points about how nature predicted human behavior, or the other way around. She could never remember. Silently, she watched as he removed several white sheets of paper from his knapsack (truthfully, she hated his knapsack—it was so obviously a statement about something) and randomly arranged miscellaneous objects. He placed a few coins on one sheet, some leaves on another, and his wristwatch on a third. He asked her for her necklace, a tiny diamond circle, but she had refused for no good reason other than it felt like too much trouble to take it off and then put it back on. It was a fairly reasonable predictor of what she thought of their future as a couple. While Cyrus set up the sheets of paper, positioning them in direct sunlight, she wondered how she was going to tell him that they were through. Interrupting her thoughts, he took her hand and stepped back. They watched as silhouettes of the objects suddenly took hold on the papers. Cyrus remained impassive when she smiled, but then he told her to look again. His intention had been different from what she surmised. The silhouettes had begun to darken until they disappeared as quickly as they had appeared, and the papers became almost uniformly dark. He said that without a chemical fixative on the paper, the images disappeared. Perhaps, Cyrus suggested, a bit too woefully to seem sincere, some things were just not meant to last. It was only then that Ellen realized that Cyrus was breaking up with her. Panic set in. Cyrus's extended metaphor left her unexpectedly wounded. She turned and fled the park, thinking sadly of the heat his tongue produced and already mourning the loss of his attentions. Human nature, Ellen eventually concluded, was far more intriguing than any of Cyrus's experiments.

As Ellen waited, she peered into the darkness, remembering Cyrus and studying the streets for imprints of her daughter's presence, as if somehow, by a twist of nature, something of her had been left behind. Ellen wondered if Faith might have crossed at this very intersection. Maybe she rode her bike along this particular road, or even took a book out of the library where Ellen had taken refuge many years before. It was in that very library where Ellen had first begun to research the impact of adoption on children. She learned that although most were grateful to have been raised in a loving home by parents who would have done anything to have a child, invariably even well-adjusted children reached an age where they just wanted to know about their birth parents, especially their mothers. More often than not, these children were aided in their search for information by their adoptive parents. Ellen hoped that Faith's adoptive parents had been sensitive, careful to explain that the decision to give up a child for adoption was always hard, and always an act of love. Ellen clutched the file and wondered as she had many times before what it would have been like if she had never signed the papers, relinquishing all her rights to Faith and agreeing to a closed adoption. What if all this time had not been lost, and they could go back. For a moment, Ellen believed Faith was actually sitting there, talking about school, maybe about a project that would require them to stop at the art supply store. They would go home and clear the kitchen table so that Faith could do her homework while Ellen fixed them dinner, something nourishing and wholesome, like soup or stew. In this fantasy, Ellen had raised her baby alone, avoiding that inevitable day when Faith would have to ask her adoptive parents why her birth mother had not loved her enough to keep her. Of all the scenarios that played in Ellen's head, this was the worst, the one that gave her the most pain.

Ellen spotted the car with Kaye at the wheel.

"Where do you want this?" Kaye said as she got out of the car and took the file from Ellen. "Can I toss it in the back?"

"What took you so long?" Barbara said. "You told us an hour." She took the bag from Kaye under Ellen's watchful eyes. "Are you all right?"

"There were unforeseen events."

"Unforeseen events?" Kaye said. She settled into her seat as Ellen took the wheel, then scrutinized Ellen's face. "Do you want me to drive? You look beat."

"Actually, you know," Ellen said, "I think I would like that."

Barbara held out a brown paper bag. "Chicken salad on toasted rye and a cup of chicken noodle soup."

"Thanks," Ellen said, but she made no move to get out of the car. In fact, she gripped the steering wheel with both hands and stared straight ahead. "Thanks." She nodded continuously, swallowing between nods until her shoulders heaved and she rested her forehead against the steering wheel, hunching forward.

"Ellen?" Kaye said. "What happened?"

"Is she crying?" Barbara whispered as if Ellen could not hear her. "I think she's crying."

"She *is* crying," Kaye snapped. "Ellen, honey, what is it?" She tried to pry her off the steering wheel, but Ellen had made her body stiff, like a child in the middle of a tantrum. "Tell us. You can tell us anything. You know that."

Ellen lifted her head and wiped at her cheeks with the back of her hands. Kaye and Barbara waited for Ellen to speak, but when she did it was only to ask if they had remembered coffee.

"Black with two sugars," Barbara said, passing a cup to the front. "I put them in already."

"Thanks," Ellen said. She tore off the perforated triangle and sipped gratefully. "Where is it from?"

"The diner," Kaye said.

"They always made good coffee. My dad said they put eggshells in the grounds before brewing."

"Why are you crying?" Barbara said.

"Barbara," Kaye said. "Let her be. She'll tell us when she's ready."

"She's ready," Barbara said. "Look at her. The crying phase is preliminary to the spilling-your-guts phase."

Even Ellen laughed, but she only shook her head and took several small sips of coffee. The windows fogged with their collective breaths, and they sat quietly, listening to the local disc jockey tease his guest, some former beauty queen who had gone on to become a Rockette.

"If we sit here long enough," Barbara said brightly, "we could die of carbon monoxide poisoning."

"That would be terrible," Ellen said. "Then I would never be able to find my daughter."

Kaye tilted her head to the left as if she thought she had heard something but could not be entirely certain. And Barbara came right out and asked Ellen what she was talking about, as if she had said she was moving to Thailand and having a sex change operation. Ellen set the container of coffee in the holder between the seats and shut off the engine, cutting off the radio host midsentence and beginning her own narrative in a carefully composed voice.

"When I was sixteen, I had a daughter. My parents forced me to give her up for adoption. I named her Faith. It didn't seem quite so dramatic at the time, but I know it is. It was a closed adoption. I was forced to agree to that as well. I just found out that my parents gave Faith away in a private adoption to a couple who lived right here. My parents sold my baby and never told me. They used part of the money to buy a new washer and dryer. That's her file back there."

"Oh, Ellen," Barbara said. "How sad."

Kaye, responding to Ellen's muted affect and her toneless account of the events, decided it was necessary to take a different approach to the tragedy that suddenly explained everything about Ellen. Clapping her hands, Kaye said, "You have a daughter. This is the most wonderful news."

"Yes, but . . ." Ellen said. "I don't know how to separate one reality from the other."

"You can't put them in the same category," Kaye said. "They are two entirely different realities."

"Selling a baby for a washer and dryer?" Barbara said. "You would have done better if you had been raised by wolves."

"I can't argue with that," Kaye said. "But you have a daughter, Ellen. Oh, I can't wait to meet her."

"How old is she now?" Barbara said.

"Thirty-two," Ellen said shyly. "My daughter is thirty-two." Then she shook her head, forcing herself out of the good feelings they were trying to impose on her. "But this is all nonsense. If, and it's a big if, I can find her, I can't barge into her life now after all these years and become her mother. She has a mother and a father. They raised her. If she had wanted to find me, I'm sure they would have helped her. Her adoptive parents certainly knew how to set that process in motion. They lived right here in town. They must have seen me."

"Are there pictures of her in here?" Barbara said. She touched the file with one finger. "Can we see her?"

"Sure," Ellen said. "Hand it to me. I'll show you."

As Ellen reached for the file, Barbara held it fast and leaned in close to Ellen's face. Then Barbara freed one hand to stroke Ellen's hair. Ellen started to cry again, and Barbara said, "We'll help you. We'll help you find Faith."

Barbara and Ellen were still holding the file across the car seat, and Kaye placed one hand on top of the file, so they were all touching it, all sharing the loss of what was inside.

"We'll do this together," Barbara said.

"Okay," Ellen said. She took a deep breath. "We can do it."

"We're going to love her as much as we love you," Kaye said.

"Thank you," Ellen said. "There was so much sorrow connected to this part of my life, but there was also so much shame. How could I have allowed them to take her away from me?"

"You were sixteen, Ellen," Kaye said. "You were a baby yourself."

"Still," Ellen said, taking her hand away and shaking her head.

"I should have taken her and run away. Some girls did that, you know."

"Not many," Barbara said.

"You were only nineteen when you had Michael," Ellen said.

"But I was married, Ellen. I didn't have to do it alone."

"I never even told Sam, Faith's father. He didn't know anything until the lawyers contacted him, so he could sign the papers."

"How old was he?" Kaye said.

"Eighteen? Maybe nineteen. He was a sophomore in college. I can barely remember what he looked like, though it came back to me when I looked at the pictures."

"May I?" Barbara said. She pulled the file out of the bag without waiting for an answer and rested everything on the seat. "Joy Anne?"

"Yes, her adoptive parents renamed her," Ellen said.

"I like Faith better," Barbara said.

"Me too," Kaye said.

"It doesn't really matter, does it?" Ellen said.

"Everything matters," Kaye said. "You should know that."

"Look at this one," Barbara said, turning the photograph over and peering at the date. "She's gorgeous. Look at that little cleft in her chin. Did she get that from her father? Oh, look at this! Joy Anne in the Girl Scouts. She looks happy." Barbara passed photographs to Kaye. "She's darling, Ellen. I love her. She's so cute."

Kaye was still on her first photograph, holding it up to the light as though she might discover something beneath the photograph, an underlying image of an earlier photograph, perhaps one that included Ellen as a very young mother.

"What are you doing?" Ellen said.

Kaye shrugged. "I don't really know. I feel like we have to go through all these papers and documents with a fine-tooth comb. We can't afford to miss anything, not one detail."

"Listen, Sherlock," Barbara said, "will you stop being so dramatic? We live in extraordinary times. Technology provides endless possibilities." She held up the last picture in the collection, the one of Faith where she seemed to know what she had lost. "This girl needs to know where she came from." She handed several photos to Kaye. "The only thing you need to know about this girl is right here in her face. There's a piece of her missing that needs to be reclaimed, and it's our crusade."

"Oh, Barbara," Kaye said, "talk about being dramatic." She looked through the pictures more quickly now. "She is beautiful, Ellen."

"She has a mother," Ellen said very quietly. "I can never lose sight of that, you know. I simply can't go barging into Faith's life. It's wrong, and you both know it."

"I disagree," Barbara said, holding up her hands, asking them to give her time to explain. "Think about this. This is a miracle, a fairy tale. You find out that the daughter you thought was forever gone has been right under your nose."

"Thank you," Ellen said. "I'm truly grateful for your optimism, but how will I ever make her believe that I've thought about her every day?"

"She'll believe you," Barbara said.

"I feel lost," Ellen said. "I've felt lost since the day she was taken out of my arms."

"And I think your daughter feels the same way," Kaye said.

"Thank you," Ellen said. "Both of you. Thank you, thank you, thank you."

"Let's go home," Barbara said. "I feel as if we've been away for years."

Ellen finally got out and switched seats with Kaye. As they drove away from Ellen's past, they talked about motherhood, newly liberated from the restrictions that Ellen's presence had previously dictated. For the first time ever, Kaye and Barbara were unencumbered by the fear of saying something that would remind Ellen she was not a mother. Ellen still listened mostly, though she sensed the difference in her friends' conversation, the absence of wariness, and the acknowledgment that it was safe to speak now because they had all felt the same inexhaustible love.

Twenty-two

DURING one of their hard times, early in their marriage and soon after Charlie's birth, George (in that placid sort of non-committal way that she hated) had informed Kaye that the trouble with her was that she wanted the glamour and none of the work. In that voice that made Kaye shudder, he said that it was impossible to be a great chef unless you knew how to cut the vegetables yourself. Furious, Kaye had thrown a plate at him, only reinforcing his claim that she was an irrational, hysterical woman who was unable to meet the challenges of her roles as daughter, mother, wife, and therapist. Between clenched teeth, she told him how much she hated him. By then, Charlie was awake and screaming, and everything else was put on hold. Now, all that was left was the memory of that rage. And (since she couldn't remember what they had fought about) the helplessness of feeling misunderstood.

Years later, Kaye, the therapist, recognized that she had married George (and he her) because they had found in each other someone who spoke to their weaknesses, rather than to their strengths. Kaye, spontaneous, disorganized, volatile, and promiscuous, saw in George someone who would help tame her passions and teach her how to channel her energy into good works. He was so calm, so thoughtful, so damned directed. She had felt certain that George would make her a better person, while George must have anticipated that Kaye's energy would fire up the evenness of his responses. Over the years, Kaye had counseled many couples in similarly frustrating relationships. The process was arduous and possible only if both embraced the work with enthusiasm and committed to expansive individual changes. Always, always, Kaye was clear on one point: The couple would have to help heal each other. In the end, Kaye believed that this was the truest love of all. And in the end, George was not her true love. Still, he was her husband, and there was something to be said for that. They had simply lost their charge. Two magnets left too close for too long. From a purely scientific perspective, it was inevitable.

Just as Ellen announced they were leaving Connecticut, finally entering New York State, Kaye's cell phone rang. They stopped for gas, and Barbara volunteered to take the wheel for the rest of the trip. George sounded tired, but he said he had some work to finish. She asked him if he had eaten anything, and he laughed and said he was fine. He had met Charlie in the city for dinner. They decided not to call Ruby because they wanted steak and beer, and Ruby would have nixed that plan in a flash. It had been a gloriously decadent meal. Kaye threatened to tell Ruby, and George laughed and said, "No matter. I'd do it all over again." Kaye called him a glutton, and he shamelessly agreed.

As soon as she said good-bye, Barbara noted that it had been a remarkably chummy conversation for someone who was spending her afternoons and weekends humping another man. Kaye asked Barbara if she was so charming with everyone or was it just with her closest friends.

"It's a legitimate question," Barbara said.

Kaye could see that Ellen, who was always so neutral, so fair, and so deliberately nonjudgmental, was a little skeptical as well, though she merely pursed her lips and kept quiet. Kaye was resolute, insisting that Barbara was intentionally argumentative and mean-spirited. Barbara laughed and agreed that both descriptions were accurate. "I'm just a poor widow with a good imagination," she said. "But I'm not the backdoor woman in this drama." Kaye was simply not yet ready to announce that she had decided to end her affair. Before long, Barbara pulled into Kaye's driveway behind George's car and weary good-nights were exchanged.

George had left the porch light on, and she was grateful. It was new for him to remember such details, especially because Kaye no longer reminded him, knowing he would say that if she wanted him to leave the porch light on or do anything, anything, all she had to do was tell him. For a long time, Kaye had believed that he just did not get it, did not understand why it was so important not to have to tell someone what to do. Just to have someone know what you need. He told her she was ridiculous, and sometimes she almost agreed. But she knew that George knew exactly what she meant, exactly what she was talking about. He just refused to change. Until now. The changes were so small, so imperceptible that Kaye might have missed them if she had ever really stopped looking for them.

"Kaye?"

George's sleepy voice called to her from upstairs. Dropping her keys and her bag on the hall stand, she called back that she would be up momentarily. The house seemed different somehow, and she looked around, remembering the way she used to feel when she came home from sleepaway camp to find that her mother had bought new pot holders or new sheets. Once, Kaye had even returned to find a new lamp in the living room. Every new addition, no matter how small, always seemed like an offense to her. The idea that her parents, especially Gertie, had actually had a life while Kaye was away for eight weeks was confusing. There was nothing new to catch Kaye's attention as she scanned the hallway, and then the dining room and the living room, but the proportions all seemed skewed, somehow altered, and she felt disoriented. A stranger in her own home.

"Kaye?"

She looked up the stairs and saw George at the top, rubbing his eyes. He was wearing sweatpants and a T-shirt, and he grinned sort of sheepishly and said that he had done the treadmill for an hour and fallen asleep almost immediately afterward.

"Buffing up?" Kaye said as she ascended the stairway.

"Should I be?" He walked down several steps to meet her. "I smell. I haven't showered yet. Sorry."

"Well, that's very welcoming."

They faced each other, George looking serious as he took in Kaye's expression.

"You're tired," he said.

"Yes."

"Was it awful?"

"It was . . . well, I guess you could say it was a lot."

He touched her cheek with the back of his hand and said, "I was going to have a shower. Would you like to join me?"

And Kaye, surprising herself, nodded.

"Good, it'll kill two birds with one stone," George said and laughed. "I'll smell better and . . ."

"And?" Kaye said.

He bent down low and kissed her, a kiss like one of the kisses they had first exchanged. A kiss filled with urgency and need, but also with the heat of uncertainty.

"And," he said, "I'll feel better."

"What about me?" Kaye said.

"I'll be sure to accommodate you."

"All right then. I'd like that." She hesitated. "I think we need to talk first."

"First? It will kill the mood, don't you think?"

Kaye laughed. "Yes, I guess it would." She placed a hand on his arm and rubbed back and forth, slowly but thoughtfully rather than suggestively. "But we have to talk about it sometime."

"Okay, then. Sometime we will."

She knew they would never really talk about it as well as she knew that George knew she had strayed. He might even suspect that she had been in love, or believed herself to be. She also knew that the subject would rear its ugly head in the heat of some future argument, shrouded in innuendo and sharp with unresolved pain. George would use it as ammunition against her, striking with precision, aiming to kill. But they would never really talk about it.

"Are you sure?" she said.

"I'm positive," he said.

He sounded weary, and her heart tugged. She had hurt him. Holding out her hand, she allowed herself to be led to the bathroom, allowed George to raise her sweater over her head and unhook her bra. She held his head as he mouthed her, tugging gently on her nipples just the way she liked. He licked the inside of her arm in the groove where it bent, and she murmured appreciatively as she kicked off her shoes and helped him with her pants and underpants, and then with his clothes. Their shyness made them more eager. And as they stepped into the shower, Kaye smiled because Mr. Mulligan just popped into her head. He had been her high school physics teacher. Mr. Mulligan had explained the phenomenon of gravity by demonstrating how a tiny magnet could lift a paper clip even though all the masses of the earth pulled it in the opposite direction. Mr. Mulligan had said that gravity was a lot like love. He had been met with thirty-two blank stares. Now, some forty-odd years later, Kaye finally understood what Mr. Mulligan had been talking about. She only hoped that Frank understood the laws of physics too. George wiped the soap from his hand before he eased it between her slippery thighs. Kaye stared up at him, then closed her eyes, and then her mouth, against the force of the water. She let George have his way with her, enjoying his ambitious efforts to please her. And he did. But Kaye knew that behind her closed eyes, she would always be remembering Frank and the way he said her name just before he collapsed against her damp skin. Now she had a new secret to keep, a reminder, like an invisible ribbon tied around her finger so she would never forget.

*   *   *

THERE was nothing waiting at home for Barbara except her computer. The apartment was eerily quiet and dark. In her rush not to be late, she had forgotten to leave any lights on. Now she went from room to room, flicking on every light, turning on the television in the bedroom and the stereo in the living room. Her office was as she had left it: the wastebasket overflowing, the shredder in need of emptying, coffee cups everywhere, and Post-its with hastily scrawled notes and reminders stuck to every available surface. A description of a girl she had seen in the market, a few words of a conversation she had overheard in the elevator, the Barbara Shore Fan Club's new website address, and a grocery list that she had still not filled. That meant no milk for her coffee. No coffee either, according to the list. The light on her answering machine was flashing, and she reached out to press the button. She had called her children before she left for Connecticut just to remind them she was going to be away. Michael had been out, so she left him a message. And Justine said to give her love to Ellen and to tell her she would visit over the weekend. Daphne pretended to listen, waiting for an opportunity to describe the great boots she had just bought and didn't even remember to ask about Ellen or to give condolences.

There were three messages. The first two were recorded announcements that she deleted midmessage, and the last was from Carli Kavanagh, webmistress. She sounded perky, one of Barbara's least favorite qualities. *Check your e-mail, Barbara, and call me. I put together a few possibilities for the proposal we talked about.* Barbara sat down at her computer. Carli was a very energetic and bright young woman. And Barbara was certain, based on Carli's title and the way she spelled her first name, that she was also an enthusiastic devotee of the exclamation point—the only potential obstacle to their working well together.

Carli Kavanagh had been dragged to the bookstore by her friend, a Barbara Shore fan, who never missed a reading. Barbara had liked Carli immediately because she had never heard of Barbara Shore and did not apologize for it. Instead, Carli rattled off the names of the female authors she loved, like Jane Austen and Dorothy Parker. No real surprises there. But then Carli alluded to a fondness for the erotica genre, quoting Anaïs Nin, and compelling Barbara to correct her if only to prove that just because she was a romance writer didn't mean she was not well read. Carli had blithely acquiesced to Barbara's greater knowledge, but not before slipping her a business card that touted the web-designing skills for which, according to her own estimation, she was already legendary. Yes, Barbara said, Barbara Shore had a website, compliments of her publisher, but Barbara had another project she was interested in discussing. Could she phone her later in the week? She would be interested in talking about what Carli had to offer in the way of graphics and strategic planning, online multimedia, and even some online PR. If Carli was intrigued, she didn't show it. She was all business. Very cool. Very impassive. She used all the active-listening skills the marriage counselor had valiantly tried to teach Barbara and Roger to use when, at Barbara's insistence, it was therapy or divorce. It was in an era long before savvy counselors realized that couples with longevity never paraphrased each other's words, especially not in the heat of an argument. Roger found the experiment amusing, and when she informed him that she had missed two periods, he said, "So, what I hear you saying is that you're pregnant again and won't be leaving me." He had heard right. She was too tired to leave, and too tired to chase after her rambunctious toddlers. But Roger, in spite of his shortcomings, truly loved her and knew she would not be tired forever. He knew he would have to make changes or lose his family. He agreed not to conduct any business from home, not even phone calls. His associates were never to drop by, not ever. And Roger would be home to have dinner with his children. Now Carli promised to be equally accommodating to Barbara's needs. Carli shook Barbara's hand and even promised to read one of Barbara's romance novels, laughing gratefully when Barbara said not to bother.

The very next morning, Barbara called Carli and came right to the point. "Come on," Carli said. "Be serious." Of course she knew Delilah. Every girl in the world knew Delilah, and yet wasn't it wonderful that no one knew *her* identity? Carli loved that. It made it all so mysterious, and so much more interesting. Didn't Barbara think so? Barbara didn't hesitate. She was afraid she would lose her nerve if she did, so she said it fast, the same way she had told Roger she was pregnant. *I'm pregnant. I'm Delilah.* Different words, yet the same impact. Carli lost her cool, dropped her business persona, and said *shut up* so many times that Barbara actually did.

Carli had a million questions. ("Really a million, Barbara!") Should she call her Barbara or Delilah? Barbara said she preferred to be called Barbara because it was her real name. Really young in spite of her polished veneer, Carli missed the sarcasm and just kept going. Did anyone else know? Where did she get her material? Was she really planning to come out on the Internet? It was all so fantastic. How did she know so much about sex? Had she ever really had sex as great as the sex she described? Finally, Barbara told Carli to take a breath. If this was going to work, Barbara explained, she needed someone serious, someone she could rely on. In slow and elaborate detail, Barbara explained her dilemma. None of her friends knew about Delilah. Her own children did not know she was Delilah. Exposing herself would mean that her career as Barbara Shore was over. That was a lot to give up. She had invested years in her image as a romance writer. That life would be over. A closet full of high-collared and long-sleeved old-fashioned romantic getups might have to be replaced by plunging bustiers and satin and lace merry widows. Barbara had not worn a garter belt since middle school. Barbara paused, but Carli missed that one as well. She was awfully young. Barbara asked her how she would feel if she found out her mother wrote erotica under a pseudonym. Carli giggled and said her mother didn't even know what erotica was. Barbara answered that her own kids would probably give the exact same answer. Neither of them said anything for a moment, and then Carli asked Barbara what she had in mind for Delilah.

The culmination of Carli's imagination and computer skills was now in full view on Barbara's screen. Although some of the images were a little scandalous (a pair of full and pouting painted red lips that showed just enough white teeth to see exactly what was gripping the unusually thick pencil and yet more graphic images of tangled male and female legs, taut with exertion), they were exactly what Delilah needed for her debut. Slowly, savoring each frame, Barbara clicked on images, scrolling down to read well-matched excerpts from her novels. Carli was a pro. She had also sent a Power-Point marketing presentation. This weekend, Barbara would call her children together to tell them about Delilah, but first Kaye and Ellen would have to be told. And Frank Fiske, too. Some would be hurt by Barbara's revelation; others would be delighted. Good and bad. Win and lose. Barbara Shore's fans would be stunned by the news, but Delilah's fans would be exonerated. Great sex would have its day, and it would have nothing at all to do with romance, not one damned thing.

*   *   *

SINCE Bill had moved out, Ellen had dreaded coming home to the empty apartment. It always seemed to mock her loneliness. Bill's office stripped of all his personal possessions, except for their wedding photograph and another photo of them on top of an elephant in New Delhi. Ellen had left these in the otherwise bare room. It reminded her of a furniture showroom. They could have been any generic couple inside a frame, selected to give shoppers a sense of reality. The empty closets suddenly seemed vast, and the freezer that held a bottle of vodka, two bags of coffee beans, a few Lean Cuisine dinners, and several containers of sorbet were a little too much reality for Ellen sometimes. Without even removing her coat, she filled a mug with water and put it in the microwave, reading the mail as she stood by the counter, waiting for the water to boil. Bills and advertisements, and a thank-you card from a satisfied client. She stared at the folder she had placed on the counter. With one arm, she pushed everything—dishes, mail, pill bottles—to one side and removed the contents of the folder. Pursing her lips, she arranged the photographs in chronological order. Next, she began going through all the papers, one at a time, taking notes, writing down phone numbers, and making lists. Periodically she glanced at one photograph or another and felt her stomach flutter with anticipation and fear. Ellen had been preparing for this every day since she had signed away her rights to Faith. And then Ellen remembered the necklaces. She went to her bedroom and dug around at the back of the dresser until she found the small box she had hidden there years ago after a trip to Berlin. Inside the box, nestled in a bed of thick white cotton, were two tiny silver acorns on delicate silver chains. She had accompanied Bill to Berlin, where he had business that he had promised would not occupy all of his time. Of course, she had spent most of her days alone in museums and galleries, or prowling the shops. Charmed by the display of silver acorns in a jewelry store window, Ellen had stepped inside to inquire about them. The shopkeeper had explained that in Germany, where oak trees were considered sacred, the acorn was a symbol of good luck, as well as of rebirth. Ellen had only been half-listening to him drone on in his stilted English. She already knew she was going to buy two, one for herself and one for Faith, but the shopkeeper droned on with his prepared account of how ". . . the rebirth of life in the coming of the Christ child is also represented in the acorn. Bearing a tiny seed that will produce a mighty oak, the acorn reminds us that great results can be born of humble beginnings." When he was finally done, Ellen, dazzling him with her smile, said she would take two of the silver acorns. The shopkeeper added two silver chains, *ohne Entgelt,* free of charge.

Perhaps it was just a bit too optimistic, a bit too premature, but Ellen lifted one of the necklaces and stood in front of the mirror while she closed the clasp. The tiny acorn settled right between her collarbones, in the base of her throat, moving imperceptibly with her pulse. Ellen felt like a warrior, donning her armor for battle, readying herself for what was yet to come. The fight of her life, for sure. She leaned in to stare in the mirror at her false eyelashes. There was a time when she would have fervently denied that she never left the house without her false eyelashes. It was too vain, too superficial to admit. Now there was nothing left to hide. Tilting her head from one side to the other, she paused, stood up tall, shoulders back, eyes straight ahead. She blinked at her reflection and decided she would definitely get a full set of those mink lashes no matter what they cost. The real ones, not the synthetic kind. And maybe she would get a pair for Faith too. The real ones. Only the real ones.

Twenty-three

IT seemed like a portent when Kaye heard the impassioned pleas of a doomsday apologist recounting how an asteroid with the potential to annihilate the earth and its inhabitants had only recently missed its target by a hairsbreadth. Through telescopic eyepieces, amateur and professional astronomers had actually seen the deadly asteroid as it whizzed past this unsuspecting world. He urged listeners to heed the reports or the implications of these observations. "This is not the hysteria of quacks," he said. To herself, Kaye acknowledged that no matter what one believed, it was foolish to ignore warnings, especially because (according to quacks and scientists alike) another asteroid would be headed our way before long. Great changes were imminent, and the naysayers would be forced to realize their folly because even if one disregarded the voices and the signs, they were still present.

If George believed in signs, he chose to ignore them all. He was glad to have Kaye back, both from Connecticut and from the gray area where she had hovered all the last months. He loved her, plain and simple. That was how he always put it to her. *I love you, plain and simple.* Kaye knew he meant it as a compliment, but it grated on her. But George said she was his girl, his one and only. And she believed him. What mattered to George was that his thumb fit perfectly in the scar on Kaye's arm, and that he could recount the details of how she had acquired the emergency room stitches as well as if it had been he instead of Kaye who had ripped his flesh on the schoolyard fence.

George often told Kaye that he wouldn't have changed anything about their lives; he would do everything over exactly as they had done it. She didn't tell him that she would have changed everything and done everything differently. Who wouldn't? Obviously not George. He was resolute. He loved her. He loved their children. He would change nothing. And because she knew he meant what he said and because of the way he placed his finger in her scar and smiled because the fit proved they were meant to be together, she simply could not leave him. She could not leave him even if she had never felt with him the way she felt with Frank. Not ever. Not even for a moment.

Frank had to be told in person. It was the only decent way to tell him that she just could not leave George. Manny the doorman was not at his usual post when she arrived, so Kaye glided blithely through the entrance and into a waiting elevator. She rang Frank's doorbell and waited.

Frank paled when he saw her.

"Was I expecting you?" he said. "How did you get upstairs?"

If she had not come to end their affair, she would have answered seductively, dangled the key he had given her as a gift just a week after they met, and told him that he was lucky she hadn't let herself into the apartment. She would have pressed against him, asking if he had to be expecting her. Teasingly, she would have asked if he was hiding someone in his bedroom. She would never have doubted that he was happy to see her. And she had yet to doubt it now. Poor Kaye, she was still new to the ways of duplicitousness, hers and others.

"Where was Manny?" Frank said. "And how did you know I was home?"

Frank was not playing any game that was familiar to Kaye, and she was suddenly taken aback by his tone.

"I called the office," she said. "Samantha told me you were working from home today."

"Samantha had no business telling you that."

"I said I was your sister," Kaye smiled. Yesterday, Frank would have found that droll (his word). But now he seemed completely irritated both by Kaye's lack of self-control and by his secretary's stupidity. He touched the white stubble on his cheek. The white was new, and it had tugged at her heart the last time they had been together. He had rubbed his rough cheek along her bare skin, making her laugh and shout in protest. He was getting older, finally ready to settle down, and he wanted her. He loved her, found her winsome. No one had ever found her winsome before.

"You called the office? I thought we agreed that was a bad idea."

"We did, and it is. I'm sorry."

She was still standing in the doorway, and he was still blocking the way.

"May I come in?" she said. "You're acting awfully strange. I need to talk to you."

Was it her imagination, or did he seem nervous? A boulder from space was heading toward her, aimed directly at her heart, and she had not even noticed, had not even felt the wind in her face.

It was not until Frank stepped out into the hallway that she realized he was wearing what seemed to be a skirt. She covered her mouth with her hand to stifle a giggle.

"What are you wearing?" she said, reaching for the fabric between thumb and forefinger. "Is that a skirt?"

Frank said, rather stiffly as he stepped out of her reach, "It's not a skirt, Kaye. Don't be so provincial. It's an Indonesian sarong."

Amazing how winsome could turn into provincial in a heartbeat.

"Well, why are you wearing it? And why won't you let me inside?"

"I can't let you in now, Kaye. Suffice to say that I wasn't expecting anyone."

"Suffice to say?"

"Kaye, listen to me . . ."

The funny thing was that she still believed there was some other reason that Frank, wearing an Indonesian sarong (that she had never even known he owned), was keeping her at bay in his hallway. She still did not suspect anything, even though the only reason she had ever known Frank to take a day off from work was to spend it making love to her and feeding her spoonfuls of his delicious jambalaya, the only dish he cooked well enough to serve company.

"What's that I smell?" She sniffed at the air. "Is that shrimp?"

"Yes."

"I smell garlic." She sniffed again. "And shrimp. Are you cooking?"

"Yes, Kaye."

A neighbor walked by and stared at Frank's sarong.

"It's Indonesian," Frank said, pulling the knot at his waist as the neighbor hurried past. "And it's very comfortable."

"You're making jambalaya," Kaye said as awareness dawned on her. "You son of a bitch. You're making jambalaya."

"Now, Kaye," Frank said, "you need to lower your voice. It's nothing. She's just a girl I met. It's not serious."

"A girl?"

"Yes, a girl."

"How old?"

"What difference does it make?"

"I want to know."

"Twenty-six. She's twenty-six."

"Good Lord, Frank. Did you promise to make her crappy little novel into a bestseller?" When Frank cleared his throat and squared his shoulders, Kaye knew she was right.

"You did, didn't you? You deliberately misled her."

"This is none of your business, Kaye. And I would like you to lower your voice, please."

"You're so deceitful."

"I'm so deceitful? I'm not the one who's married. I'm not the one hiding a husband in the wings."

"I never hid him, Frank. Never. You knew from the very beginning that I had a husband."

"And I begged you to leave him. I asked you to marry me."

There are moments in life when telling the truth is just such a loss of a great opportunity, such a waste of a perfectly timed dramatic moment. There would have been nothing gained by telling Frank the truth about why she had come unannounced to see him. Not now. Kaye never even had to think about what to say.

"I know, Frank. And I came here to tell you that I was leaving George. I came here to accept your proposal and to tell you that I want to spend the rest of my life with you."

"Kaye—"

"No." She covered his mouth with her hand. "Don't say anything. It's all right. How can I compete with a twenty-six-year-old?" She hung her head. If only she could make herself cry. "I can't, Frank. I'm just a middle-aged woman who thought she had found another chance at love."

"I don't want it to end this way between us," Frank said. "I really, really love you."

"But not as much as you love a young girl in your bed, right?"

"It's not that, Kaye."

"It isn't? Tell me what it is then, Frank."

"I don't know what it is." He ran his hand through his hair. "Can we talk about this over dinner later in the week?"

"I don't think so, Frank."

Frank did not like to be refused. He grew impatient with Kaye's lack of cooperation and made a decision. She could read it in his expression, in the way he gathered himself (and his sarong) and made a mistake that would erase everything good that had happened between them.

"Look," he said. "The truth is that I never promised you anything, did I?"

Kaye had steeled herself for this exchange, but nothing could have prepared her for such indifference. With one simple question, Frank had exonerated himself. How lucky for him. Unfortunately for him, Kaye decided that his luck had just run out.

"No, you never promised me anything, Frank. You are quite right. And it was foolish of me to think you were different."

"I'm begging you," he said. "Let's not end it this way."

"Don't beg, Frank." Kaye wrinkled her nose as if against some offensive smell. "I hate to see a man in a sarong beg."

"Don't be vicious, Kaye. It's not attractive."

"Really? I think I look my best when I'm vicious. It gives me such a glow."

"When did we move in this direction?" Frank shook his head sadly. He was the victim. "I would never have predicted this would happen to us."

"You should have anticipated this the minute you tied that sarong on to come out and answer the door." Kaye felt tears where she wanted anger. "And you brought a child into your bed." She shook her head. "I'm so disappointed."

"Twenty-six is hardly a child, Kaye. You were a mother at twenty-six, weren't you?"

Kaye dismissed this fact with a wave of her hand and pointed to the sarong. "The things men will do to bed a young girl. You look like a fool, Frank. I never figured you for such a fool. You must have some idea of how perfectly ridiculous you look. Don't you?"

He grabbed her arm, hard, pressing down on the exact spot where just hours earlier George had so lovingly rubbed his thumb against her scar.

"Let go," she said. "You're hurting me."

"This isn't over," Frank said. He let go of her arm. "We have to talk about this."

"I don't think so," Kaye said. "I think we're quite done."

She started down the four flights of stairs. Anger replaced sadness as she thought about what Frank had blurted. *I never promised you anything, did I?* Suddenly, the fervent warnings of the doomsday apologist made great sense. Kaye stepped out into the sunlight and into a cab that seemed as if it were miraculously waiting for her. At that moment, it felt as if all the planets were in alignment and everything was going according to plan. Kaye settled into the back-seat of the cab, envisioning how her good fortune would translate into the perfect headline: *Earth Escapes Brush with Killer Asteroid.* Poor Frank. He had never been a great fan of astronomy. He never even liked to read his horoscope. Maybe he would from now on.

*   *   *

SHE called Barbara from the cab, whispering so that the driver would not hear.

"How old?" Barbara said.

"Twenty-six," Kaye said. "Apparently she's your publisher's newest shining star."

"Clementine Green."

"You know her?" Kaye had stopped whispering. "Seriously?"

"I know of her."

"Is that her real name?"

"Green?"

"Very funny."

"Why are you mad at me? I wasn't humping Clementine during company time."

"Do you think he shouts, 'Oh, my darling Clementine' at the penultimate moment?"

"God, I hope so," Barbara said. "That would be so great. Assuming, of course, there is a penultimate moment."

"He was wearing a sarong," Kaye said.

Barbara howled so loudly that Kaye had to hold the phone away from her ear. The driver looked at her in the rearview mirror.

Kaye had never felt as foolish as she did now. In the bed where she had allowed herself to forget she was a wife and a mother and a daughter, there was now a child the same age as Ruby. It was so insulting now to think of how she had been replaced. Women simply became invisible. Maybe that was the reason some old women dyed their hair orange and wore large pieces of costume jewelry. At least people noticed them. At least they were no longer invisible. Kaye had always felt just a little sorry for the old women in the nail salon who insisted on blood-red talons. She told herself that she would never call such attention to herself, but she wasn't at all sure about that anymore. Now she understood. No one wanted to be invisible. Those colorfully painted nails could be waved about like so many distress flares, demanding attention. She could see herself in the future; she would be one of these women someday, wearing garish clothes and too much lipstick. She sniffed loudly.

"Are you crying?" Barbara said. "Oh, Kaye, don't cry."

"Why not?" Kaye said. "I feel so stupid."

"I'm sorry you were so disappointed."

"He told me that he had never promised me anything." Kaye sniffed again. "Can you believe he said that to me?"

"I can believe it."

"It's awful to feel invisible," Kaye said. "When did we become so invisible?"

"I see you."

"What do you see? A stupid middle-aged woman who had an affair and was replaced by a girl half her age before it was even over?"

"Well, that too. But wait, I also see my wonderful and brilliant friend who is kinder than anyone I've ever known—"

"And fatter. Let's not forget fatter."

"Actually, I've known people much fatter than you."

"I love you, Barb, but I'm still sad."

"You have to learn something new today, something you never knew before. Remember the story about Merlin the wizard and King Arthur? No? Merlin told King Arthur that the best defense against sadness is to learn something new."

"Maybe Merlin could have helped me not feel so invisible."

"We don't need Merlin for that, sweetie. We need a good plastic surgeon."

"Clementine doesn't need one," Kaye said.

"She will. You can be sure of it," Barbara said. "Where are you now?"

"Approaching Grand Central. I think I can make the next train," Kaye said. "You know, Barb, you're very smart for someone who writes such dumb books."

Barbara could have slipped right into that opening and told Kaye about Delilah. Instead, Barbara said, "I knew you would never leave George. Not even for great sex."

"Why do women remember all the great sex they've ever had?"

"Because they've had so little of it."

"See? I said you were smart."

The driver pulled over. As she rushed down the steps and into the terminal, Kaye realized that she had already learned something new. There was nothing genuinely attractive about an overweight, middle-aged, balding man in a sarong.

*   *   *

AT George's suggestion, Kaye invited Barbara and Ellen for dinner on Saturday night. Gertie was coming for the weekend, and Justine and Charlie said they would come, especially after they heard that Ruby, Michael, and Daphne had all accepted Kaye's invitation. It had been ages since they had all been together, and it would be good for all of them. Barbara said she would bring dessert and bread and wine. And Ellen offered to make salad and another vegetable dish. Maybe some corn pudding, even though it didn't really count as a vegetable, not with a whole stick of butter and a half cup of heavy cream. Of course, Gertie was making soup, and Kaye would make some salmon in her special dill sauce.

"Do you think I should roast a chicken?" Kaye said. She was writing out her shopping list while Gertie chopped celery and carrots for the soup. "I'm worried there won't be enough or that not everyone likes salmon."

"So roast a chicken. Roast two. You'll have it for the next day, or one of the kids will take it home."

George had picked Gertie up last night on his way home from the city. She had bought everything she needed for her soup in her own neighborhood, insisting that whatever Kaye bought in those fancy markets of hers had no taste. Kaye had woken to the smell of onions cooking and found Gertie in the kitchen having her second cup of coffee and a boiled egg.

"The coffee smells good, Mom."

"Of course it smells good." Gertie smiled. "It would be better if you let me bring you a percolator, but it's still good. Let me make you some scrambled eggs."

Kaye never ate so early, but she said yes because she loved to watch her mother beat the eggs into froth. When she was done, she wiped her hands on the dish towel that was tucked into her waistband and turned the heat up under the frying pan. Without asking, she toasted a piece of rye bread, cut it into triangles and set it alongside the eggs.

"More coffee?" Gertie said.

"Yes, please."

Gertie smiled and nodded as Kaye ate.

"Good, right?" Gertie said. "You should eat in the first half hour after you get up. It gives you energy."

It was the same speech Kaye had heard for more than fifty years.

"I know, Mom."

"So, tell me about Ellen. A daughter. I'm happy for her. Between you and me, I'm happy it's a daughter and not a son. She has a better chance with a daughter. If it were a son, and he had married a prize like the ones Solly married . . . well, what's the use? Right?"

"I'm sorry, Mom. About Solly."

"What can you do? Life never turns out the way we think it will."

"No, it doesn't," Kaye said. She took another sip of the strong coffee. "It surely doesn't."

"I guess life surprised you too."

Kaye looked up. Gertie had resumed chopping. There was no point in asking her for her recipes. She never wrote anything down. If you asked her how many potatoes, she said, "To the eye." How long should you cook the onions? "Until you put a dent in them."

It was the same with everything. Gertie insisted that she never tried new recipes because each time she cooked something, it was a little bit different than the time before. A new recipe each time. She said she cooked the same way a child made lemonade, adding sugar until it tasted good.

"Am I right?" Gertie said.

"Yes, you're right."

"So, he hurt you? This surprise of yours?"

Kaye knew there was no point denying anything. She shook her head. "Not really. He embarrassed me."

"Ah, that can be worse sometimes." Gertie wiped her forehead with the back of her hand, and a strand of hair fell over her eye. "Are you all right?"

Kaye put down her pencil and stood up. She practically towered over her mother now. Bending over, Kaye took the stray piece of hair and wound it behind her mother's ear. Then she kissed her mother's forehead and said, "Is this where you hide your third eye?"

"What hide?" Gertie said, and they both laughed. But Gertie was not easily distracted. "I didn't hear an answer."

"Sometimes it's just easier to be a different person with different people than it is to change."

"I understand," Gertie said.

She was about to say more, but George walked in.

"Am I interrupting?" he said.

"Of course not," Gertie said. "Can I make you some scrambled eggs?"

"I'd love that." He kissed Kaye's cheek and poured himself a cup of coffee. "Either of you beautiful ladies need a refill? No? Well, I'm just going to get the paper."

Gertie waited until George was out of earshot and then said, "Do you know when a poor man is happy?"

"When he loses something and finds it," Kaye said. "You've told me so a million times."

Gertie smiled, pleased, and then set to beating two more eggs into froth. If Kaye wondered (and she did) who her mother thought was the poor man in the current scenario, she didn't ask. *Better not to know everything,* Gertie would have answered.

Twenty-four

IT had always seemed to Barbara that new love was so heart-stopping not only because of the ever-present fear that the love might not be requited, but that the love might end. This fear, according to Barbara, was intensified if great sex was involved, the pursuit of which (also according to Barbara) was not unlike the quest for the Holy Grail.

"Disappointment and sex are not exactly strange bedfellows," Justine said.

"Heartbreak," Ruby said. "That's what you get if you look for good sex and spiritual satisfaction."

"I have a theory about the Holy Grail," Charlie said. "Did you know that legend claims the Grail was kept in a mysterious waste-land and guarded by the Fisher King, who, by the way, had a wound that would not heal?"

"Are you suggesting the wound was a broken heart?" Ruby said.

"Well, mere speculation on my part," Charlie said. "But who's to say what's right or wrong?"

He was growing a beard, hoping to make his boyish appearance more mature. Instead, according to Ruby, it made him look like a boy wearing a fake beard.

"And we welcome your interpretation," Michael said with an ironic half bow. "Very clever on your behalf."

"You know us Wall Street types," Charlie countered. "We have to be clever about everything."

"That must be quite a burden," Michael teased. "So how's the corporate world taking that pathetic attempt at a beard?"

Rubbing his face with exaggerated thoughtfulness, Charlie said, "They love it."

"Seriously?"

"Well, I haven't gotten any flack yet, so I'm going to see it to completion."

"I like that spirit," Michael said. He slapped Charlie on the back. "You'll be shaving in a week's time. Trust me."

"I'm not as one-dimensional as your limited liberal view seems to believe."

"I'll bet you a night of beers that you shave within a month."

"Deal," Charlie said.

They shook on it. Every week they met at a pub between Charlie's east side one-bedroom and Michael's west side studio. They shared a passion for sports, attending baseball and football games with religious devotion. Charlie's firm occasionally handed out courtside seats to basketball events, and Michael periodically benefited from the excesses of his students' wealthy families by snagging a pair of seats behind home plate to a Yankee game. It was, by all accounts, a perfect friendship, one that was strengthened by their sharply different views about everything except sports.

"Can we get back to the Fisher King?" Justine said. "Did he ever recover?"

"Never," Charlie said. "His recovery depended on the successful completion of the quest."

"Well," Ruby said. "There's your answer. Every relationship I've ever had has been a failed quest."

Charlie draped an arm around his sister's shoulder and hugged her in commiseration.

"Such cynicism," Barbara said. "Surely you've had some joyful sexual experiences?"

"Excuse me," Kaye said. "Do we really need to hear about her joyful sexual experiences? I think not."

"Me neither," George said. "Count me out."

"I'm interested," Gertie said. "Joyful or miserable, everyone loves to hear about someone else's sexual experience."

"Thank you, Grandma," Ruby said. "I can always depend on you."

Gertie was making her way back from the kitchen, having re-filled the soup tureen. She set it on the table and lifted the lid, looking around the table for an empty bowl.

"I'd have to agree with Barbara," Ruby said, "and with Grandma, of course." She blew a kiss to Gertie, who turned, caught it, and applied it to her cheek. "Everyone knows the best sex is at the beginning of a relationship."

"Maybe," Kaye said. "I also think that people can grow into each other, and the sex can become even better."

"Everything changes," Gertie said. She was hovering behind Ruby, trying to ladle another heaping serving of soup into her bowl. Ruby blocked this maneuver with her hand. "No?" Gertie yielded. "All right then, you'll take some home."

"Mom, sit down, please," Kaye said. "Everyone had enough soup. Relax."

"I'm sitting," Gertie said. "I remember when your father and I got married. We lived in a rented room. The kitchen was down the hall. Who cared? We hardly ate at all. We were so busy in bed."

"Did you have sex before you were married?" Ruby said.

"Of course," Gertie said. "And not just with your grandfather."

"Thank you, Mother," Kaye said, but she was smiling. "We all needed that bit of information."

"The first place Roger and I lived was tiny, but there was something so romantic about it," Barbara said. "We sort of had to do everything in concert. You're forced to be mindful of each other in a small space. Otherwise, you both wind up on the floor."

"That could be romantic, too," Michael said.

"Not when you're nine and a half months pregnant," Justine said. "Right, Mom?"

"Thank you, darling," Barbara said, raising her glass of wine toward Justine. "In case absolutely everyone at the table didn't know that I was pregnant when I got married, they have all the information now."

"Oh, big deal," Justine said. "No one cares, and everyone here knows you were pregnant when you got married."

"You were pregnant?" Michael said, pretending to be horrified. "I'm so ashamed." He pressed the back of his hand to his forehead and clutched at his heart with the other hand. "I'm a love child?"

"No, you're an idiot," Justine said, "but we do love you."

"I know you both think you're very funny," Daphne said. "But did you ever stop to think that maybe Mom would have had a different life if she hadn't felt forced to get married so young?"

Barbara shrugged, neither agreeing nor disagreeing. "I can't say I haven't given it thought. But I always go back to the same three things." She smiled at her children. "What have I got to complain about?"

"You could ask any of us a question like that," Kaye said. "Or yourself, for that matter. I mean, how is anyone to really know if life would have been better or worse?"

"I know," Ellen said. Everyone turned to her, chastened by the presumptuousness that had made them forget her loss. And then, like a benevolent royal, Ellen exonerated them all with a sweep of her hand. "I'm sorry. I didn't mean to make anyone uncomfortable. It's just that I've spent my whole life since I gave up my daughter wondering what it would have been like if I had run away and raised her on my own. Don't get me wrong. It would have been a hard life, but maybe not as hard as the one I've had. If I had kept my daughter, I could be sitting here with all of you and looking across the table at her."

Ruby jumped up and wrapped her arms around Ellen's neck, assuring her between kisses on her cheek that her daughter would be found. They would all help, Ruby promised. They would organize a search just like people did when someone disappeared.

"Thank you," Ellen said. "But thirty-two years is a long time. And I'm not sure she wants to be found."

"Of course she does," Kaye said.

"Really?" Ellen said. "How can you be so sure?"

"Because," Kaye said, "most adopted children need to know why they were given up. Even kids born from sperm donors are making a stand to find their fathers. It just makes sense."

"It does make sense," Ellen said. "What doesn't make sense was my obsessive guarding of my past. I should have told you all before. I'm sorry now. I was led to believe that I had done something terrible and the only way to make amends was to keep my past secret. I thought there was something honorable about my restraint. Maybe because everything else felt so shameful, I wanted to do something right, something that had dignity."

"There's nothing dignified about suffering alone," Gertie said. "You let your friends help you find that daughter."

"I will, Gertie," Ellen said. "I'll let them help me. I just don't want to hurt her any more than I have already."

"It wasn't your fault, Ellen," Kaye said.

"I know. I know. But it doesn't matter what I know; it matters what she thinks."

Barbara had already left the table after collecting the soup bowls. She was in the kitchen arranging lemon slices around the salmon when Kaye sashayed up next to her and bumped her hip against hers. Even then, Barbara, lips pursed, barely reacted.

"You're suddenly awfully quiet," Kaye said. "Are you all right?"

"I'm fine," Barbara said. "Just tired."

"Tired? Really?" Kaye tilted her head to one side and in a singsong voice said, "Looks more like somebody has something important on her mind."

"Do you have any idea how annoying it is when you do that? That whole somebody-has-something-on-her-mind thing?" Barbara said. "And that voice." She shuddered. "I'll bet your kids hate that too." She dug around in her pocket, pulled out a plastic cigarette, and clamped down, hard. "I mean, you really need to kick your repertoire up a notch."

"I thought you quit," Kaye said in her calmest voice, pointing at the plastic cigarette.

"You are so annoying," Barbara said.

"Apparently so," Kaye said. She took the plate that Barbara had finished arranging and looked into Barbara's troubled face. "Let me know when you want to talk about whatever it is that is making you so bitchy."

Before Barbara could answer, Kaye walked away. Instead of joining the others in the dining room, Barbara took it upon herself to plate the chicken. She knew her way around Kaye's kitchen as well as she knew her way around her own, maybe even better since she had moved. As she arranged the pieces of chicken, Gertie came in and wordlessly began to rummage in the cupboard for a serving dish.

"Can I help?" Barbara said.

"I need something for the spinach," Gertie said. "I can never find anything here."

"You have to think like Kaye, and then it all falls into place."

"Ah," Gertie said. "So wise."

She took a glass bowl from Barbara and began to fill it with the sautéed spinach. Unlike Kaye, Gertie made no effort to engage Barbara in conversation. They worked side by side in silence until Gertie, finished with her task, wiped her hands on a dish towel and asked if there was anything else that needed to be done.

"No," Barbara said. "I think Kaye and the girls took care of everything."

"And who takes care of you?" Gertie said. "If you don't mind my asking."

The question was so perfectly timed and delivered that Barbara was too stunned to think of a clever answer. Instead, she slumped into the closest chair and said nothing. Gertie took Barbara's chin in her hand and smiled.

"You need to take a rest," Gertie said. "You're all wound up, no?"

"Yes. I'm all wound up."

"Is there any reason you can't share some of your misery? Usually there's enough to go around."

There was no one reason. After Roger's death, Barbara had worked so hard to find some balance, to reassure her children that she was fine. They had no reason to worry about her. She was able to take care of herself. Women knew how to pretend they were fine. Keeping Delilah to herself was reflexive, another way to guarantee emotional safety and anonymity.

"I'm not big on sharing," Barbara said. She lowered her eyes, and Gertie released her chin. "I'm sort of a private gal."

"If you say so."

"Don't worry so much."

"I'll worry anyway. You might as well let me enjoy it."

"Well, then worry to your heart's content." Barbara stood. "I'm fine. Really."

"If you say so," Gertie said. "It's time you believed that the people who really love you are going to love you no matter what. And those are the only people you need."

Barbara arched her famous brow and said, "Have you met my daughter Daphne?"

Gertie said, "Well, you have a point there."

They had said everything that either of them was going to say, so they carried the platters into the dining room. Charlie was going around the table and pouring wine, red or white, and Michael was passing a basket of rolls. Several cross-conversations were going on, mostly about everyone's work. Ruby was telling Justine about a breech delivery she had assisted with. Daphne was talking to George about London. When Barbara looked up, she saw Kaye watching her. They smiled at each other, and Barbara raised her wineglass to Kaye, who responded in kind. Ellen saw them and, feeling left out, said, "What about me?" They toasted each other again, and Barbara said, "To Faith." Then everyone toasted Ellen's good fortune amid enthusiastic shouts of "Here! Here!" and *"Cin! Cin!"*

Gertie took a sip of red wine as she watched everyone. It seemed to her that Barbara and Kaye, and even Ellen, were subdued in the way that only someone who had spent a lifetime discerning the differences between subterfuge and sincerity could see. And Gertie saw. She saw that each of these women was still unable to take the steps necessary to ensure some sort of deliverance from her own secret. Gertie did not know Barbara's secret (but it was clear that she had one), and she knew none of the details of Kaye's infidelity, only that there had been one and that it had ended badly. Ellen's secret, forged from shame and habit, had finally been released. A genie set free from its bottle, even if Ellen's only wish was still far from realization.

Gertie decided that perhaps deliverance was what each of these women needed. And she also decided that without some help from her, deliverance would be slow to achieve.

"I went to see the doctor last week," Gertie said. "I've been having some pain in my chest."

Everyone stopped talking. Kaye paled. "Why didn't you tell me?" she said. "How long have you been having pain? Did you see a cardiologist?"

"Kaye," George gently warned. "Why don't we let Gertie tell us what's going on?"

"I can't believe she didn't tell me, tell us," Kaye said. "How could she do that?"

"I can hear you," Gertie said.

"George is right, honey," Barbara said. "Let her have her say."

"You okay, Grandma?" Ruby said.

"Fine," Gertie said. "I'm fine. A test or two. Next week. Nothing to worry about. A small blockage or nothing at all. But since I have everyone's attention, I want to tell you what I saw in the doctor's office."

"I suppose if you hadn't seen whatever it is you're going to tell us about, we would never have known you even went to the doctor," Kaye said. She knew she sounded huffy, but she was angry. "Right, Mother?"

"Maybe yes, maybe no," Gertie said. "May I tell you what I saw?"

"I'm listening," Kaye said.

"We're all listening," George said.

"I was sitting across from a woman," Gertie said. "She was so plain. You know how you can search a person's face for one good feature and find nothing? Usually I can find something, a nice nose, nice eyes. But this woman?" She looked around the table to make sure everyone was listening and then crisscrossed her hands. "Nothing. Absolutely nothing. I watched her as she read some pamphlet, maybe, or a book. I wasn't sure. And then I noticed that she was smiling, a peaceful smile. A smile a person could be jealous of."

"Did you talk to her?" Ruby said.

"You know me too well," Gertie said, chuckling in her self-deprecating way. "Of course I talked to her. I said, 'So what's that you're reading with such interest?' She looked up and showed me the title: *The Sinner's Guide to Confession.* She didn't look to me like she had anything to confess, but how could I say that without offending her? But she knew what I was thinking and that impressed me. 'Everyone has secrets,' she said. 'Everyone has sins to confess.' Still I wondered if having a secret automatically makes someone a sinner. I don't think so. I told her that a secret is only a secret until it's shared. And she told me it was the reason confession is good for the soul."

Kaye was the first to say something. "I have a very smart mother," she said. "Very smart and very stubborn."

"Stubborn is good," Gertie assured her. "I'm fine. I'm sorry if I upset you. I'll tell you everything later. I promise."

It was not unlike the moment just before the lights go out in the theater, the moment just before the performance begins and everyone is expectant, eager for the curtain to rise. Gertie looked at Barbara and smiled.

"Excuse me," Barbara said.

She left the table only to return in a few minutes with her leather satchel. She moved some plates and set the large bag down.

"I have something to tell you all. I intended to make my confession tonight." She smiled at Gertie. "I lost my nerve until Gertie helped me find it again. I just want to preface my confession with a brief statement. I never meant to hurt anyone or to alienate either my children or my friends." She took a deep breath and pulled out several paperbacks from her bag. "These are some books I've written." She pressed them to her chest. "They're books you are all familiar with, but they're not by Barbara Shore."

"What are you trying to tell us, Mom?" Justine said.

"I'm Delilah," Barbara said. "I write erotica under that name."

She paused, the way any performer would, inviting applause. Of course, no one applauded, but no one jeered either. Then Kaye stood up and sat down again. She looked stunned. Barbara had handed one book to Ellen, who was on her left, and one book to Justine, who was on her right. She smiled shyly at Michael and Charlie and George, and then she handed each his own copy. They began to pass the books around. Daphne took one and stared at the cover, her mouth set in a straight line. Michael looked confused, but when he leafed through a few pages, he was evidently embarrassed. Ellen said she had never heard of Delilah, and Kaye said she might be the only one in the world with that claim. Michael said girls loved Delilah, and Charlie admitted to reading sections of one at a friend's house. George, rather sheepishly, said they seemed quite different from the romance novels she usually wrote. Daphne stood up and left the room. Barbara started to say something to her, but Justine held up her hand, indicating that she would handle Daphne.

"Why didn't you ever tell us, Barb?" Ellen said.

"I don't know," Barbara said.

"Secrets just seem to have a power of their own," Ellen said. "Believe me, I know that. We feel so compelled to guard them that we forget why we thought it was necessary in the first place."

"It's more complicated than that. My own publisher doesn't know. How do you think Barbara Shore's fans would feel if they knew I wrote erotica on the side? I could lose my entire readership."

"Well, I'm impressed," Kaye said. "You must have done very well for yourself."

"Well, don't congratulate me just yet," Barbara said. "I think my duplicitousness may have a really negative impact on my career. There might even be legal trouble. I don't even want to think about the possibilities."

"Then don't," Kaye said. "At least, don't think about it today."

"I was inspired by Ellen," Barbara said. "My secret seems so inconsequential compared to what Ellen had to live with all these years." She bowed slightly in Ellen's direction. "You are a brave and powerful woman."

"Thank you, Barb," Ellen said. "I'll let you know how powerful I really am after my story writes its conclusion."

*   *   *

THEY all began to talk at once, caught up in the thrill of acting as co-conspirators to a delicious secret. After all, they were now the only ones (except for Carli Kavanagh) who knew that Barbara Shore, romance writer, was also Delilah, the creator of heroines who (according to Ruby) "fucked like men and were proud of it." They were wowed by her notoriety. It was like meeting a woman who worked in a mine or was a long-distance trucker, plus sex. Suddenly Barbara was someone to contend with, a woman of dauntless courage and, as George dryly summed up, a woman with balls. And Barbara agreed, smiling demurely, that balls were a major part of her work. They had a good laugh over this and toasted her with some aged brandy that George had been saving for a special occasion. Certainly *this* was a special occasion. Delilah's coming-out party.

They were all part of the adventure now, all vying for a front seat. Michael admitted that he was having some difficulty reconciling himself to the idea that his mother was the author of the books he saw peeking out of his students' backpacks. He finally acknowledged admiration for her imagination, as well as for her entrepreneurial skills. Daphne, who had been ushered back into the room by her sister, stoically congratulated Barbara.

"Thank you, darling. That means a lot to me." Barbara hugged Daphne. "I never meant to make you ashamed."

"As long you're not the one bending over a kitchen stool for a horny electrician, I'm okay with it," Daphne said.

As if on cue, everyone moved into the final phase of the evening, passing coats and gloves and scarves. Gertie had prepared care packages for the children, as well as for Barbara and Ellen. "Thank you," Barbara said against Gertie's cheek. "For what?" Gertie said. "It's just soup." Barbara shook her head and told Gertie that she was just too much. "I know. I know," Gertie said as she pressed a container of soup and some other leftovers into Ellen's protesting hands, urging, "You have to keep up your strength." Ellen kissed Gertie on each cheek and reminded her, "I'm not pregnant." But Gertie insisted that all mothers need strength. They told each other that everything would work out. Finally, Gertie warned each woman to hold herself together. She said, "You must. You must." They promised they would, although they weren't sure how to keep those promises. Promises. Lies. Secrets. In the end, they were all variations of the truth . . . whatever that might be.

Twenty-five

I N the weeks that followed, they all settled into the sort of in-between area where apprehensiveness hovered in a preamble to reality. Under the circumstances, this transition should have been predictable. After all, Barbara, unknown to either her children or her best friends, had been living a secret and questionable life, a life that challenged everything they believed had been true about Barbara Shore. On some level, it made their lives a sham. Barbara worked hard to keep her sense of humor when her children intermittently phoned to either harangue or lecture her in some shape or form. Daphne (whose support for Delilah was short-lived) questioned the impact of Delilah's stories on the increase in sexually transmitted diseases. Barbara listened and then said she would speak to her publisher about placing a caveat on every book jacket that urged readers to practice safe sex. In fact, Barbara said, she would suggest adding a disclaimer about Delilah's sex life. It would be very clear that under no circumstances did the author even have sex for plea-sure. After a contemplative pause, Daphne said, "Are you making fun of me?" Barbara said she would never do that. *Honestly*. After that conversation, Barbara screened her calls and did not pick up when it was Daphne. Three days into this fraud, Justine phoned.

"So you're not dead," she said.

"Nope. Disappointed?" Barbara said.

"Not yet. Screening your calls?"

"Survival, darling. Your Daphne started driving me crazy." Barbara sighed. "What about you? Are you disappointed in me?"

"Nah. I just want the money."

Barbara laughed. She heard voices in the background and wondered where Justine was calling from. The tinkling of glasses and laughter made Barbara suspect a party or a bar, but Justine had not volunteered her whereabouts. Asking would have been tantamount to prying, and even though Barbara was curious, she was careful not to compromise the delicate balance that defined relationships between parents and adult children.

"Of course not, Mom. I think it's pretty cool."

"I'm afraid my publisher doesn't share your enthusiasm. We had a very uncomfortable preliminary meeting. It seems the fans of Barbara Shore will be disgusted by my lewdness."

"Is that a quote?"

"More or less," Barbara said. "I wasn't really paying attention."

"Maybe you need to own up to this one."

"Oh?" Barbara was interested. "And what do you propose?"

"Make a statement. Tell your Barbara Shore readers that you're sorry to have disappointed them and then slip into oblivion. It worked for Garbo. Let your readers demand your return. They will, you know. Your romance groupies are very loyal."

Justine's suggestion made remarkable sense. After years of clandestine behavior, Barbara craved a more reasonable existence. No more secrets. No more enigmatic boundaries.

"Thank you, Justine. It's good advice."

"Thank you."

"Are you all right?"

"Perfect," Justine said. "That's what I phoned to tell you. I ended it with Clifford. I wanted you to know that."

"Thank you, Justine. Thank you for calling to tell me that."

"It's not because I didn't think he loved me. I just couldn't live with being the other woman to a father."

"I'm glad, honey. I know it's hard, but you won't be sorry."

"We'll see about that."

Afterward, Barbara remembered the brief period when Justine walked in her sleep. Terrified that she would fall, Barbara insisted on waking her. Confused and scared, Justine would shout, "Who are you?" and "Get me out of here!" Roger, always calmer and more pragmatic than Barbara, would simply lead Justine back to bed, holding her elbow and steering her in the right direction. Now Barbara wished for Roger's sure hand on her elbow, calmly steering her in the right direction. But she would keep that to herself. It would be her secret.

*   *   *

ELLEN lost her nerve. She spent weeks coming home from work and staring at the photographs of Faith and rereading the documents in the folder before making any calls. The task of locating an adoptee was daunting. Ellen reasoned that if Faith had wanted to find her biological mother, she would have pursued the hunt. Ultimately, this was Ellen's conclusion, one she shared with Barbara and Kaye on a frigid Sunday afternoon that was allegedly the first day of spring. Barbara and Kaye listened as Ellen went through her presentation step by step, arguing that sometimes it was best not to look under a rock. Besides, Ellen said, there were laws, and closed adoptions were hard to open. Barbara was the first to counter that Ellen's logic was complete nonsense. The poor child might have been told that her mother was dead. Ellen insisted that even if this were so, Faith, if genuinely committed, would have wanted at the very least to find out her biological mother's name. This discussion went on for the better part of an hour until Kaye finally put a stop to it. She had done her research and had come prepared. Even if it had been a closed adoption, there were ways to circumvent the law. And it was no longer about Faith; it was about Ellen.

"It's always about Faith," Ellen said. "It has to be."

"That's lovely, but it's also irrelevant," Kaye said.

"How can it be irrelevant?" Ellen said. "It doesn't matter anyway. We'll never find her."

"You could always hire a private investigator." Kaye took off her reading glasses and placed them on top of the file she had brought along. "It's always an option."

"That's it?" Barbara said. "That's the best you have?"

"I'm working backward. Just listen, please."

"I'm still listening," Ellen said.

"It's not going to be easy, and it could take months, maybe years," Kaye said, "but we have to start." She saw Ellen's doubtful expression and smiled encouragingly. "There are online registries. Have you ever checked those?" Ellen shook her head. "I thought not. Faith is an adult now, Ellen. Have you ever updated your information on the adoption registry? No? Well. What if she did go to look for you? Did you give permission to have any information about yourself released if she did come to look for you? I thought not. So, you see, we have a place to start."

"Impressive work," Barbara said. "But if Faith went looking for Ellen and she wasn't on file, wouldn't they have contacted her for consent?"

"Probably."

"That's my point," Ellen said. "She doesn't want to be found, and she never tried to find me."

"Not necessarily. She could have gone to the registry, seen that you never updated your file, and assumed the same thing about you. She could have reasoned that *you* never wanted to be found."

Ellen looked exhausted. Dark circles under her eyes made her skin appear almost yellowish, and she was too thin. Since her father's funeral, she had spoken to Hugh only twice. Their conversations had been brief and awkward. He had phoned both times, urging her to come back for another visit and fumbling for words when the offer was met with uncomfortable silence. Lorelei called once, and Ellen had struggled to be cheerful, insisting that she would make good on her promise to have her for a visit. "Just give me a little time," she told Lorelei. "I'm in a bit of a funk." Lorelei, sweet girl that she was, blew kisses into the phone and eased Ellen's conscience.

Kaye picked up her glasses and put them back on. "I want to show you something." She shuffled some papers. "Here it is. Wait, no, that's not it." Scanning the printed page and simultaneously nodding whenever she came across a point that was pertinent to Ellen, Kaye was flushed with excitement. Happily, she had settled back into her routines, but she thought about Frank every day, remembering how his need to hold her so close had prompted her to confess that she often felt like a cherished stuffed animal. "Is that a bad thing?" Frank had asked. Of course it wasn't. Every morning in the shower, she thought of how he had run his hands over her body. She remembered how their mouths slid against each other under the water, and how he held the back of her head as she lowered herself to pleasure him. She remembered him when she rode on the subway and in the grocery store when she pushed a cart. She had dyed her hair blond since then, returned to yoga classes, and developed an affection for bright red lipstick. They were good changes, ones she welcomed as much as her memories of Frank.

She never talked about him anymore, but ruminating on the past was her private indulgence, her new secret life.

"Aha," she said. "Here. Take a look at this." Kaye handed Ellen papers held together with a clip. "Did anyone ever tell you that your rights were violated? Did you know that there was a period after you signed Faith away that you could have reclaimed her under state law? Were any of your legal rights explained? No? I thought not. Well, it's not like you're going to sue anyone, but I thought it would help to know that you're not alone. None of the girls of our generation were advised. They didn't receive psychological counseling or legal advice. They were never told to read the surrender documents or asked if they understood the conditions of the agreement. The circumstances were appalling. Some girls never even saw their babies. I was shocked when I read all this. It's shameful. I'm sorry, Ellen. I never knew about any of this. I remember there was a girl in our neighborhood. Cheryl. She disappeared for a few months. Her mother let everyone know *she* was expecting another child. When Cheryl returned, she had a new little sister. I was too young to realize the truth, but I remember everyone whispering about it."

"At least her parents supported her," Barbara said.

"Yes, at least," Ellen said. She poured herself another cup of coffee. "Anyone?"

"When was the last time you ate?" Kaye said.

Ellen shrugged. "Yesterday?"

"Yesterday?" Barbara opened the fridge. "There's nothing in here." She opened a container of leftover Chinese food, sniffed it, and drew back before she tossed it in the trash. "I'm going to the grocery for you. This is ridiculous. You need to eat."

"Wait," Kaye said, "before you go. There is something Ellen can do." She pushed a blank pad and pen toward Ellen. "You have to write down everything you can remember about that time. The name of the maternity home, the priest's name, the lawyer who handled the adoption. Anything and everything you can think of."

"What for?" Ellen said.

"What for?" Kaye said, hands on her hips. "So we can find Faith, my friend."

Ellen brushed away her tears with the back of her hand and reached for the pen and pad. Barbara wrote out a grocery list and left to fill it while Kaye went through the kitchen cabinets and the vegetable bin and found enough ingredients to make a fairly decent tuna fish salad that Ellen wolfed down with crackers and a cup of steaming green tea. Kaye emptied and reloaded the dishwasher, wiped down the counters, sorted newspapers and bottles for the recycle bin, and prodded Ellen's memory for details. By the time Barbara returned with several bags of groceries, there was enough information to move forward.

"I remember the priest standing behind the attorney mouthing 'No' when he asked me if anyone had coerced me into signing the documents," Ellen said. She picked up a cracker crumb with a moistened index finger and curled her legs beneath her. "That was delicious, Kaye. Thank you. I guess I was starving." She took another sip of tea, closing her eyes in pleasure. "My mother told me that if I was unreasonable, they would have to pay the hospital costs as well as the lawyer's fee. I knew my parents didn't have that kind of money, and I was scared."

"Do you remember the lawyer's name?" Kaye asked.

"I don't think I ever knew it."

"What about the maternity home?" Barbara asked. "Where was it?"

"It was in Albany. It was a Florence Crittenton home. They're all over the United States. I believe it was run by evangelicals. They were good people, but they saw all of us as 'unfortunate girls' who needed rescuing. It was fairly grim."

"It sounds grim," Kaye said. "You poor thing." Her words were so heartfelt that Ellen might as well have been a terrified sixteen-year-old wearing maternity hand-me-downs, looking for comfort and finally receiving it. "I can't imagine what you went through."

"It was a time of shame and fear," Ellen said. "The home gave us a place to hide out until we delivered. I was still in high school, so I attended classes. I remember the faces of all the girls. Some were as young as thirteen or fourteen. There were some older girls, college age, but they didn't go to class. They worked."

Barbara refilled Ellen's teacup and poured a cup for herself and for Kaye. They had moved into the living room, where Ellen claimed the couch and Barbara and Kaye sat opposite her on matching chairs.

"Tell us more," Kaye said. "Tell us everything." She smiled encouragingly, and Barbara reached over to pat Ellen's knee in a show of support. "Tell us everything you remember. Give me the pad. I'll take notes. You talk."

"We had a very strict schedule. We woke early, had breakfast, went to school, and did chores. I remember the television in the lounge was on all day long. Quiz shows and soap operas were the most popular. There really wasn't much to do. We talked to each other, but we never talked about what would happen after our babies were born. There were no last names, and we didn't know anything about each other. If we did talk, it was to ask each other if we hoped for a boy or a girl. We named our babies even though we knew their names would be changed once they were adopted. It was all so sad." She wrapped her arms around her knees and rocked herself. "I mean, think about it, all those pregnant girls in one place. I remember taking long walks, but always by myself. Friendships were discouraged. Secrecy was the norm. Once our babies were born, it was as if the birth had never happened. You just never get over that kind of grief."

"How could you?" Kaye said. "There's this huge disgraceful secret that you're expected to hide for the rest of your life. No wonder you never told anyone."

As Ellen recounted some of the details of the weeks she spent in the maternity home, Barbara pored over the information Kaye had cobbled together in a short time. There were testimonies from birth mothers who described experiences almost identical to Ellen's. The girls were dropped off, typically in their sixth or seventh month, and left to negotiate the final months of pregnancy in isolation. Many of the girls described how they were forbidden to see their newborns. Some were even coerced into signing surrender papers before they gave birth, an illegal if not an immoral procedure. And some of the girls were so heavily drugged when they went into labor that they could not even remember signing surrender papers. Other girls were refused any painkillers even if their labor was progressing slowly or with difficulty. Story after story was filled with immeasurable loss. Barbara could only think about Michael's birth. Even though everyone knew why Roger and Barbara had married so suddenly, Michael's birth had been joyful. Both sets of grandparents had been able to put aside their disappointments and celebrate his birth. The only fights that ensued were over whose turn it was to babysit for him. He was so loved, so cherished. She could not imagine how lonely Ellen must have felt. And then to have to give up your baby because you had no other choice. Suddenly, Barbara missed her own mother. Oh, she had been devastated to learn of Barbara's pregnancy. Quite enraged, in fact, at her stupidity. She flung words at Barbara, calling her careless and irresponsible, lacking in any common sense. But she was there for Barbara from start to finish, showering each new baby with fresh love. When Barbara's father learned she was pregnant, he quietly told her that every child was a gift, and hers would be no exception.

". . . best interest of the child," Ellen was saying. "That's what they told all of us."

"That's so cruel," Barbara said. She had a headache from all the information. Her mouth was dry. She got up and took a bottle of water from the fridge. "Anyone?" She shook the bottle at them and took out two more. "It's warm in here, isn't it? Apartments. They're always overheated. I'll never get used to it. Our house was always cold. Roger and I argued about the temperature all the time. Stupid stuff." She handed a bottle of water to each of them and took a long swig from hers. "Just stupid stuff. I was cold, and he was hot. 'Put on a damned sweater,' he used to say." Barbara laughed. "Now look at me. I'm dying of heat."

And then she started to cry. Momentarily stunned, Ellen and Kaye quickly recovered and jumped up to comfort her, stroking her arms and easing her into a chair. She kept saying that it was all so sad, the maternity clothes that were left behind for the next girl, and the babies who didn't get to go home with their mothers. And Roger dying just like that and leaving her to handle everything on her own. She could handle it all. She was more than competent, but she was just overwhelmed with this Delilah mess, and now with Ellen's daughter.

"It wasn't all tragic," Ellen said. "I learned how to knit at the maternity home." She laughed and hugged Barbara. "I'm sorry about Roger. You must miss him. And I love you for caring so much about me, but you've both inspired me. I know it's a long shot. Sealed records and probably more disappointment. Still, maybe I can find her. Maybe I can have a chance to tell her that I never wanted to give her up. I think I'd like her to know that."

"And she should know that," Barbara said. "She should know how much you've grieved for her."

"I was so excited when I held her for the first time. I couldn't believe that everyone wasn't just as thrilled. I wasn't prepared for the depression. No one told me what to expect. I would stand by the nursery whenever they took her away from me, day or night, and I would cry. Finally the nurses told me to stop visiting her. They said I was upsetting the other girls."

"Oh, Ellen," Kaye said. "That's so horrible. You were just a baby yourself. How could your mother have allowed it?"

"Allowed it?" Ellen said. "She masterminded the plot. She never wrote to me or called me the whole time I was there. My father came to see me a few times, but he was embarrassed about my belly. He kept his eyes averted the whole time. Poor guy. He brought me some oranges and a few bags of Pepperidge Farm cookies. I said, 'What's the matter, Dad? Mom too busy to bake?' It was mean, but I felt mean. He said, 'You know your mother, Ellie. She'll never get over this.' I wanted to go out for a bit, but I knew he didn't want to be seen in public with me, not even in a strange city. He came to tell me that after 'it' was over and I came home, there would be no discussion about what had happened. 'Don't you even mention it,' he said. 'Your mother told everyone in town that you went to help out for a bit with your Aunt Bessie while she was recovering from chemo.' I told him that it was a lot of crap, and I wasn't going to be part of any more lies. But I was, and I still am."

"It's not your fault," Barbara said. "No matter what you think, it's not your fault."

"When I came home, no one said anything. My father picked me up, and we drove the whole way from Albany in silence. Hugh came along for the ride. I sat in the back, watching the milk stream out of my breasts. I wouldn't take the pills they gave us to make the milk stop. I threw them away. Hugh told me I looked pretty good. He said, 'A little diet and some exercise, and you'll be back to your old self in no time at all.' He winked at me. I remember that."

"Did you ever try to contact Faith's father?" Kaye said. "Sam, right? That was his name?"

"No, I never did. I knew that my parents had sent the lawyer to see him. I don't know what they told him, but he signed those papers. He never even tried to call me. Maybe they scared him." Ellen drank some more water. "She was born on February 16, 1975. The doctor's name was Reuben McClintlock. I remember because it was on his jacket. He told me that as far as he was concerned I had brought shame to my whole family." She looked from Kaye to Barbara. "Did I tell you that he's dead? Sam. I ran into a friend of his who told me. Poor Sam. He had a wife and three children."

"Four children," Barbara said.

They changed the subject after that. Kaye ordered in Chinese food, and they talked about the shoe sale at Neiman's. Barbara had bought a pair of fabulous dark-red heels. They would go really well with that black suit she had bought at the end of last season. They talked about books and food. Ellen had tried a recipe for chili-roasted edamame. She was thinking about becoming a vegetarian. They stayed away from talking about children, any of them, or about husbands, any of them. The food was delivered, and they ate and drank beer. By then, it was late. Kaye called George while Barbara and Ellen cleaned up. It had been a full day. As Barbara buttoned her coat and Kaye searched in her bag for her keys, Ellen thanked them for coming and for helping her make some sense of the life she had been forced to abandon. They told her that she was worthy, that she would have been a wonderful mother, and that it had not been in Faith's best interest to give her up when she was so very wanted. They cried together one more time, and then just as Ellen was closing the door, Barbara turned and asked, "What do you think about now when you think about Faith?"

It was a big question, and the answer was so telling in its simplicity.

"I think my baby is someone else's daughter," Ellen said.

Then she shut the door gently. And Kaye and Barbara knew that Ellen was alone behind that door, preparing herself for the possibility that before long she might meet an uncannily familiar stranger who was her daughter as well.

Twenty-six

DAPHNE announced that she was moving to London. Her firm was opening an office in Kensington, and she had been asked to go. She explained how she believed the offer was providential. "I'd rather not be present for the notoriety that is sure to follow once the public learns Delilah's true identity." Barbara said she understood. It made perfect sense, she agreed. Truthfully, she was delighted that Daphne had decided to take the job. It would be good for her to be away and on her own. Justine and Michael concurred, but only for the first reason. "Did she really say it was providential?" Justine asked. "Did she actually say, 'I think it's *providential*'?" Michael was on the extension at Justine's, laughing too hard to really listen to his mother's plea that they support their sister. Barbara warned them both that their sister needed them now, but they couldn't stop laughing long enough to listen. Barbara just hung up. She loved her children, but she was busy with a new Delilah book. This one was about a piano teacher who made extra cash as a dominatrix. Since Barbara had come out as Delilah, she found that there was a vast resource of untapped material she had ignored. For the first time, she explored sexual fetishes and determined that she might have discovered the ultimate deep, dark secret. Some people just liked to be spanked, and others liked to provide the service. More important, Barbara Shore, the romance writer, did not seem to be in great jeopardy. In fact, her editor was working on a spectacular public reveal that would be beneficial to Barbara Shore as well as to Delilah. Frank Fiske, however, was a bit put off with everyone. He had even phoned her to voice his dissatisfaction, in a tone Barbara found offensive enough to warrant pulling out the Clementine card and his unwarranted and hurtful betrayal of Kaye's love.

"He backed off," Barbara said. "He even apologized."

It was a Wednesday morning. Kaye didn't have patients until late afternoon, so she had called Barbara and told her to stop by for a coffee. Kaye was rinsing out a cup, gazing out the kitchen window. It had snowed, just a coating, but enough to make the world seem deceptively pristine. She shook the water off the cup, poured herself more, and said, "Coffee?" Barbara held her cup out, and Kaye refilled it. "Did I mention that I had lunch with him?"

"No, you didn't mention that. It must've conveniently slipped your mind." Barbara added milk to her cup, stirred, and added just a bit more. "When was that? And why didn't you tell me?"

"A week ago." She leaned against the counter and smiled. "I was happy to see him. And I didn't tell you because I knew you would try to talk me out of it."

"Did you sleep with him?"

Kaye stood abruptly and adjusted her clothes as if she had been actually caught in a compromising position.

"Well?" Barbara said. "Did you? Sleep with him?"

"No," Kaye said, "but I wanted to. I always want to sleep with him. It's as if I'm possessed." She looked worried. Her brow was furrowed, making her eyes look oddly close together. "Does that count? I mean that I wanted to. Is that considered emotional infidelity?"

Barbara shook her head. "It doesn't count. Not technically, anyway. I mean, I want to sleep with every firefighter I see. Am I culpable for my rich fantasy life?"

"I don't know."

Barbara searched her pocket for a plastic cigarette, found it, and drew on it several times before taking it out of her mouth and rolling it, back and forth between her thumb and forefinger. "Too bad you can't get a plastic Frank," she said. "It might take the edge off."

"Too bad, indeed."

"So what are you going to do? Will you see him again?"

A car horn honked several times. Two short blasts and then one long one. The girl next door seemed to have a slew of boyfriends who were always vying for her attentions. They came and went in a noisy stream at all hours of the day and night. Kaye had wanted to say something to the girl's parents, but George had reminded her of what it had been like on the block when their kids were in high school. He was always so conciliatory. It had grated on her nerves for the longest time, but now she found it soothing, a relief from her own heightened response to even the most ordinary events. George always knew how to do the right thing as long it was about a situation that stayed within the lines. He loved coloring books, and Kaye hated them. It was as simple as that.

"No," she said. "I don't think I will." She spilled out the rest of her coffee and placed her cup in the dishwasher. "I think it's best if I don't see Frank again." She walked behind Barbara's chair, bent over and wrapped her arms around her neck, and hugged her. "I'm sad, Barb. For the rest of my life, I will be missing that man. I'm ashamed to admit it, but I will."

"Don't be ashamed." Even though they were alone, Barbara lowered her voice to a whisper as she stroked Kaye's arms. "We do the best we can. We all do. I think we live our whole lives imagining that we're different from everyone. But we aren't, are we?"

Kaye shook her head. The phone rang. It was Ellen calling, very excited. Kaye (purposely repeating everything Ellen said so that Barbara would know what was going on) listened as Ellen explained that Alice, evidently coached by Janet, had phoned with unprecedented information: Faith's married name and address. Would they come immediately? Yes, of course they would. Immediately. Yes. Yes. Yes. The answer was yes to everything.

* * *

THE girls in the home for unwed mothers were allowed one call a week from family. This came to mind when Ellen heard her mother's voice on the phone. Alice had never phoned. Occasionally, at Hugh Sr.'s insistence, Alice would agree to say hello. Ellen always pictured her father talking to her and simultaneously beckoning Alice to take the phone and say something, anything. Ellen's conversations with Alice were invariably filled with awkward pauses and empty silences that were relieved only when Hugh reclaimed the phone, making some random joke before he hurriedly said good-bye, promising to visit soon. This time it was Janet insisting that Alice talk to Ellen. She had clutched the phone and listened to every word her mother gasped out. Alice never said she was sorry, but she did tell Ellen that Joy Anne Brown was now married with two children of her own. And, to Ellen's astonishment, Joy Anne lived in Manhattan. No, Alice didn't know where, but Joy Anne's husband was a dentist, Dr. Warren. No, she didn't know his first name. Joy Anne had kept her own name anyway. Another one with fancy ideas of her own. Her adoptive parents were snowbirds, dividing their time between Connecticut and

Florida. No, she didn't have a number for either of them. Alice was breathing harder now, and she ended the conversation by wishing Ellen good luck—they were the warmest words Alice had offered in years, maybe ever. Janet took the phone then and told Ellen that she should forgive her mother. She was old and very sick, and who knew when she would be taken from this world? Ellen thanked Janet for everything. Really, Ellen insisted. She was forever indebted to her for intervening on her behalf. That was the best she could do.

"I think you were very generous," Kaye said. "Very generous indeed." Barbara agreed. After all, forgiveness was highly overrated. "Why should you forgive that crone?" she said.

They were huddled around the computer, searching for a Joy Anne Brown in Manhattan.

"I don't want to be like the count in Dante's *Divine Comedy.*" Ellen said. She saw their blank looks and quickly explained. "After he was betrayed by the archbishop, he was arrested with his sons and grandsons. They were all sealed into a tower to be starved to death. During his pilgrimage through hell, Dante found the count and the archbishop frozen together in one hole." She paused to heighten the dramatic impact. "The count was so consumed with hatred that he died gnawing on the archbishop's skull, unable to satisfy an eternal hunger for vengeance." Ellen grimaced. "It's a horrible story."

"I'm moved to tears," Barbara said evenly without the slightest hint of emotion. "Vengeance is very cathartic. I could think of a number of skulls I wouldn't mind chewing on."

"I don't know," Ellen said. "Hatred takes a lot of energy. I should be able to forgive her. After all, she is my mother."

"I think you're right, Ellen," Kaye said. "But a mother should behave like a mother. Forget about her. We have important work to do. Gnaw on your mother's skull later on if you have to. You have two grandchildren! What could be more important than that? And they're right here in Manhattan."

Not a single Joy Anne Brown was listed in the White Pages. There were over three hundred Browns in New York, but only one Dr. Warren listed in Manhattan in the Yellow Pages. Ellen printed the page with his name and address and said, "Can we talk about something else now? Anything else." She was on the verge of tears and fanned herself with a trembling hand. "Sorry. Nerves, I guess."

"Sorry?" Kaye said. "For what? You have every reason to be overwrought. It almost seems too easy, I guess." She caught Barbara's eye. "But let's talk about that another time. Did Barbara tell you the news about Daphne?"

Barbara jumped in and told Ellen about Daphne's move to London, agreeing that it sounded like a good plan. Then Kaye confided that she had met Frank for lunch.

"I thought that ship had sailed," Ellen said. "Did you sleep with him?"

"Why is that always the first question?" Kaye said.

"It's a logical question," Barbara said. "What would you ask about? The shrimp salad?"

"Maybe," Kaye said, sulking. "Maybe I would."

"You probably would," Barbara conceded. "Was he wearing his sarong?"

"That's just what I meant before," Kaye said. "Is that really, really necessary? It's such a silly question."

Barbara shrugged. "What do you want from me? Middle-aged, balding white men should not wear sarongs. It's a fact. Look it up."

Ellen laughed and suggested that they reconvene later in the week. She had already decided that she would write to her daughter's husband, and she wanted to get to work on that letter. As soon as she had closed the door behind them, she began a first draft, offering a succinct background history and providing her contact numbers. She concluded by stating that she would do nothing to impose herself on their lives, apologizing for any discomfort her letter might provoke. *It is a search I must pursue, and I hope you will forgive me if I have opened doors Joy Anne wished to keep closed. If I do not hear from you or from her, I will understand. I wish you and your family well.*

After several revisions and agonizing over the possibility that Dr. Warren might not know that his wife had been adopted at birth (a notion she then dispelled as nonsense), Ellen printed a copy and addressed the envelope. First thing in the morning, Ellen took the letter to the post office. She sent it certified, return receipt requested, and released it to the clerk, who was entirely indifferent to Ellen's nervous questions.

As soon as she returned home, Ellen set about cleaning and cooking with a vengeance. She scoured the bathroom, straightened the hall closet, did two loads of laundry, and prepared a pile of clothes to take to the dry cleaner. She cooked a pot of vegetable soup and made a chicken stew, separating both into individual containers and dating and labeling them before storing them in the freezer for future use. She felt a great need to set everything right. Later, Kaye told her that it sounded like she was nesting. "Ah," Ellen said. "Nesting. I didn't think of that." Pleased that she had been given another chance, Ellen got to work on organizing her wallet, filing old receipts and discarding miscellaneous business cards until the day was gone.

By the week's end, Ellen had heard nothing from Dr. Warren. She was bereft. It was pointless. Faith would never be found. She should have known better. She had no right to claim her secret child. Joy Anne had a life; she had parents and a husband and children. There was no reason for her to bring a stranger into her fold, and it was wrong of Ellen to assume otherwise. Barbara and Kaye held fast while this went on for days. Then Ellen's futility turned to rage against the Browns, her baby Faith's adoptive parents. The Browns were just as culpable as Ellen's parents.

"Adoption," Ellen said. "It was more like an abduction than an adoption."

They were in a bar near Ellen's apartment. Kaye and Barbara had given in just to get Ellen out of the house. The bar was the only place she would agree to go. She held up her glass to the bartender, signaling that she wanted a refill.

"And is that your second or your third drink?" Kaye said. "I seem to have lost count."

"It's my none-of-your-business drink," Ellen said.

"Definitely her third," Barbara said, turning to Kaye.

"Sorry," Ellen said. "I'm fine. Don't worry. Lately, I just hate being alone. I come here occasionally. I don't always drink." She saw them exchange a look. "Seriously. I don't. Lately, I just can't stand being in that big apartment by myself." She munched on a handful of peanuts and took one small sip of bourbon before pushing the glass aside and asking the bartender for a seltzer with a twist of lime. Seeing Kaye and Barbara's relieved expressions, Ellen laughed. "You two are something. You really don't have to be so worried." She split a nut with her front teeth and then lightly rubbed her palms on her pants, a noticeably uncharacteristic move for someone as fastidious as Ellen. "Did I tell you that Bill phoned? He wanted to see me."

"And?" Kaye said.

"And nothing. I just knew I would sleep with him if I saw him, and that was too depressing."

"You really would have?" Barbara said.

"Sure. I haven't had sex in months, and I guess I still love him."

"How could you still love him?" Barbara said. "And what about self-respect?"

"What about it?" Ellen said.

And then her cell phone rang as though it were an exclamation point at the end of her sentence. Her cell phone ring was pealing church bells. A sound Ellen found hopeful.

"Hello?" Ellen said. "Yes, speaking. Oh, I see. Yes, of course. I understand. Tomorrow? That would be fine. Of course. No, not at all." She gripped the edge of the bar with one hand. "I'm very grateful to you for calling. Yes, yes, of course. We'll talk tomorrow. I understand. I know the restaurant. One o'clock? Perfect. Me? I'm five-six. Blond streaks. I have a red coat. I'll wear it. Tomorrow, then. I look forward to it. Thank you. Thank you."

Ellen clutched her cell phone to her chest and then took a long swallow from her previously abandoned glass of bourbon and said, "That was Dr. Warren. He's married to Joy Anne Brown, and I'm meeting him tomorrow for lunch."

"This is so exciting," Kaye said, clapping her hands. "I'm so thrilled for you."

Barbara hugged Ellen as she finished the last of her bourbon. Taking a deep breath, Ellen took out her compact from her purse, and quickly dabbed at her nose and chin. It was as though she had reemerged, worn out, though now radiant with expectation.

* * *

HE spotted her first. As promised, Ellen wore her red coat. The restaurant was bustling with the lunch crowd, and Ellen stood quietly in the pandemonium and waited to be found. She smiled at a man walking toward her and though he smiled back, he walked past her. This caused her to momentarily lose her composure, so that when Nate Warren came at her from behind and touched her elbow, Ellen jumped and gasped.

"Ellen?" He was tall, dark, and handsome in the way of movie stars from a lost era. "I'm Nate Warren."

They shook hands, and he led her to a table in the corner. He must have arrived early because there was already a glass of wine on the table.

"I was having a drink," Nate said. He smiled again. "May I get something for you?"

"No, thank you." She felt oddly compelled to make a good impression, but a glass of wine would have been wonderful. "Maybe, just a glass of white wine."

"Chardonnay?"

"Perfect, thank you."

"So," Nate said after he caught the waiter's attention and placed the order for Ellen's wine. "Tell me what happened."

Ellen had rehearsed this scene a thousand times. She kept the details simple. She was not blameful, either about her own family or about Joy's adoptive parents. She explained that she had been young and afraid. Her parents had insisted on the adoption. The arrangements had been made without either her opinion or her approval. It was the way it was done in those days. More or less, once the baby was born, it was as if the birth had never happened. Ellen told Nate how sorry she was, how each day she mourned the loss of her daughter, and how much she hoped that Joy Anne's life had been good.

"She's had a good life," Nate said reassuringly. He broke a breadstick in half and bit into one piece, returning the other half to the breadbasket. Using one hand as a brush, he swept crumbs into the palm of his other hand and made a small pile of them, looked up, and asked, "So, what did you name her?"

If Ellen was surprised (which she was), she pretended not to be. "Faith," she said, shrugging apologetically. "I was very young."

"Well, it's a good name." He smiled. "My birth mother named me Brighton. It means 'the one who is loved' in Hebrew. It's a very ambitious name for a fourteen-year-old girl."

"You were adopted too?" Ellen said. "Was that a coincidence?"

"I actually met Joy in a support group. We were college students."

"Where?" Ellen tried not to seem overly curious, though every bit of information was a revelation of a life she had missed sharing. "If you don't mind my asking."

"The University of Cincinnati. And I don't mind you asking at all."

The waiter interrupted and took their orders. Nate ordered a hamburger, explaining that he ate meat only when he was out, since Joy kept a strict vegetarian kitchen. Ellen, in deference to her daughter's beliefs, ordered a grilled vegetable and cheese sandwich. Already Ellen was modifying her behavior. It was silly, of course, but she couldn't help herself. So much new information at one time. She wanted to ask what Faith had majored in. What kind of student had she been? Did she like to read? Was she artistic? How old were their children? What did Faith do? Instead, Ellen smiled gratefully and thanked Nate for indulging her. But she kept her questions to herself and waited for him to make another offering.

"You should know," he said, "that most adoptees just want to hear that they weren't given up because they were unloved or unwanted. No matter how often they are reassured by their adoptive parents, it's never the same as hearing it from your birth mother."

"And you believe Joy needs to hear that from me." Ellen's eyes welled with gratitude, and she rummaged in her purse for a tissue. Nate handed her a starched white handkerchief, and she took it, admiring its crisp whiteness. "How nice. So few people use handkerchiefs these days."

"Joy is a bit of an environmentalist nut. I'm just grateful she lets us use toilet paper."

University of Cincinnati, vegetarian, environmentalist.

"Well, I'm very glad about the toilet paper as well," Ellen said, laughing. "Joy sounds very principled."

"Bulldogged might be a better description." He ran his hand through his dark hair. "I haven't told Joy anything, not about the letter or about meeting you. I wanted to be sure that you were sincere. Joy has been through a lot."

"I'm sure she has."

"In many ways, Joy was a textbook case of an adopted child. She was angry at everything, acting out against her parents and suffering from a sense of rootlessness. By the time we met as juniors, she had already moved six times. I fell in love with her immediately. She's very beautiful." He paused, took a sip of water, and smiled. "She looks like you, Ellen."

Pleased, Ellen flushed and inclined her head in appreciation. She so wanted to see a picture of her daughter, but it seemed impertinent to ask for anything. Folding her hands on the table, she breathed slowly, hoping to still her hammering heart, and waited. Just waited.

"Are you married?" Nate asked.

"Separated, but soon to be divorced. I was married for sixteen years. We tried to have children, but it just never happened. I tried everything. He left me for another woman, a younger woman. It's so cliché that I am embarrassed to admit to it."

"I'm so sorry. I shouldn't have asked."

"No matter," Ellen said. "Asking doesn't change anything. It happened. It happens to many people. It wasn't the definitive event in my life." They both waited, knowing what she would say next. "Giving up Faith, I mean Joy, however, was. I have been irrevocably altered by the loss."

"I believe you."

"Thank you."

They talked easily. He told her about his practice; she told him about her business. They discussed politics (she was thrilled to learn that Joy was a liberal Democrat and an activist). Nate was Jewish. Joy had converted to Judaism. Ellen asked very few questions, hoping to be rewarded for her restraint. She was, especially since her delight in each piece of information was so evident. Nate was forthcoming about his family. The girls, Amelia and Maude, were three and six. Amelia loved music and gum. Maude loved animals and anything purple. Joy was a weaver. She also made batik, using the painted fabric to create unusual clothes, jackets mostly.

"The girls wear a lot of the clothes Joy makes," he said. "A few local galleries take her work on commission. She's very talented."

"I'm glad." The waiter set her plate down in front of her. "I'm really hungry. I was too excited to eat anything this morning."

Nate was already fixing his hamburger. He looked up and nodded in understanding. He had been nervous as well.

"I kept asking myself, how much can you really tell about a person from a first meeting?" he said.

"I actually think you can tell a lot about someone," Ellen said. "I can tell that you're a kind and loving husband and father. I can also see that you are a very good dentist."

"And how can you tell that?"

"I can't really," Ellen said. "I just made that up to win you over."

"You've already won me over, Ellen." He wiped his mouth and his hands on the napkin. "I brought some pictures of Joy and the girls. Would you like to see them?" He laughed at her unbridled enthusiasm, and said, "Foolish question, I guess." He reached down for a slim leather briefcase and rested it on his knees. Ellen reached for the folder with both hands. There were pictures of Joy and the girls, and a picture of Joy in what appeared to be her studio. There was also one family portrait, a girl on each lap. Amelia, the three-year-old, was on Joy's lap, staring directly at the camera and looking far too serious for someone her age. And Maude, smiling ebulliently, was on Nate's lap, reaching across to seemingly contain her younger sister with one well-placed finger on her arm. Joy's face was both familiar and strange, like someone Ellen was sure she knew, but couldn't place. Joy's hair, straight light brown with blond streaks, was cut to flatter her narrow face. Her cheekbones were more pronounced than Ellen's, but they shared the identical nose, a small, yet interesting presence in an otherwise classically pretty face. Joy was gazing down at her daughters, showing off eyelashes that resembled peacock feathers. Ellen looked more closely. The effect was glamorous and sexy, and apparently Ellen was not the only one who thought so. Nate's head was turned toward his wife, and he was smiling broadly. Ellen looked at each picture very carefully, commenting on everything: the girls' expressions, their coloring, their clothes, Joy's evident complacence in their presence, and Nate's pride in his family. It was no surprise, however, that Ellen could not resist inquiring about Joy's eyelashes.

"Joy's weakness," Nate said. "She never leaves the house without putting on her falsies." He shrugged apologetically. "That's what I call them. It's been that way since the day I met her. It's the most bewildering affectation, almost an obsession. That woman loves false eyelashes." When he noticed Ellen crying, he seemed genuinely alarmed. "What is it? Are you all right? Did I say something to upset you?" He reached across the table for her hand and looked even more concerned when she began laughing, almost uncontrollably.

"I'm sorry," she said, dabbing at her eyes again. "You must think I'm insane." She leaned over as far as she could and closed her eyes. "See? They're falsies, as you like to call them. Mink, actually, but don't tell Joy. I put myself on a waiting list when I read about them. I never told anyone. In fact, I never leave the house without *my* falsies, mink or otherwise. I even ordered a pair for Joy in a preliminary burst of optimism."

Nate had been nodding throughout her explanation. It was almost unbelievable, even though there were so many similar stories. Mothers and daughters who had never met, but who hung the exact same obscure wallpaper in their bathrooms; siblings separated at birth who finally met only to discover they had given their own children, even their own pets, the same names. It was unbelievable in a way that made perfect sense. Nate confided that Joy had longed for the mink lashes, but even though the claim was that they had been harvested by gently brushing live animals and no cruelty was involved (only absurdity, according to her telling), she just couldn't allow herself to purchase them, settling instead for the synthetic peacock pair and several others in the most outrageous colors imaginable. She had falsies in hot pink, and in turquoise and orange; she even had a pair in gold for formal wear. Ellen said she was delighted and jealous as well.

"They're for you," Nate said, pointing at the envelope of pictures, making the ultimate offering. "I want you to keep them." The tips of his ears turned bright red, and Ellen wondered if Joy found this response equally sweet. She must have. Ellen was certain. "I wasn't sure if I would leave them with you, but I'm sure now."

"Thank you, Nate." She lowered her voice and said, "Please don't tell Joy about the mink lashes."

Nate laughed and reached over to pat her hand. "She would be touched that you thought of her, but I won't say anything if you don't want me to." He took his hand away and studied her expression before continuing. "I think it's important that you know that everything I told you before about Joy, about her rootlessness and her fear of abandonment, none of those feelings is the result of the way she was raised. Adoptees tend to romanticize their histories, more so when they don't have the facts. That's just the way it is. Joy's parents are decent people, and they raised her with a lot of love. They just could never understand what she was feeling."

"And now?"

"They would feel threatened if they knew you had found Joy, but that's not your problem. Personally, Ellen, I'm thrilled. Joy needs this. She needs to talk to you. Crazy as it seems, she needs to know you've suffered because of her."

"I'll be happy to oblige," Ellen said. "Truly happy."

Over coffee and a piece of plum cake that they shared amiably, they agreed that Nate would sit down with Joy that evening and tell her about Ellen, promising once again not to mention the mink lashes. In turn, Ellen would wait for Joy's call, something Ellen had begun doing since the day she said good-bye.

*   *   *

THE first time they spoke, Ellen sat crouched on the kitchen floor, hugging her knees with one hand and resting her cheek on top, trying not to cry. She struggled to stay focused and to frame her words carefully. They were cautious with each other. "What should I call you?" Joy said. Ellen quickly answered, "Ellen, of course. You have a mother." Joy seemed to relax after that. The next time they spoke, Ellen told Joy about her family in Connecticut, trying to be upbeat and positive rather than overly critical. Instead of maligning them, Ellen concentrated on her brother Hugh, Joy's uncle, and her many cousins, especially Lorelei. "You'd like her," Ellen said. "But would she like me?" Joy countered. They laughed easily together, and it was a turning point. Ellen described Kaye and Barbara, and explained how her friendship with them sustained her, especially after Bill left her. "I'm so sorry, Ellen," Joy said. "You seem like such a nice person." Tears sprang to Ellen's eyes, and she said, "Thanks, sweetie." It slipped out, heartfelt, but possibly premature. Ellen cursed herself for her presumptuousness, reminding herself of her promise to let Joy be the guide. When she was ready, she would welcome Ellen into her world. Then, balance regained,

Joy said shyly, "Nate told me you love false eyelashes. That's wild, isn't it? That we both love falsies." Ellen agreed it was wild indeed. Joy rewarded her by telling her about the girls, how much fun they were, how interested they were in everything, absolutely everything, especially that little Maude. Ellen kept her questions simple. Did Amelia have any favorite books? Did Maude go to a play group? What about the museums? Did they love the Met? Had Amelia ever been to a ballet?

"I'd love to take her to the ballet some day," Ellen said. "I used to fantasize about taking you."

Silence. Yet another blunder for which Ellen cursed herself.

After that, they didn't speak for a few days. Ellen was miserable. She had pushed too hard, asked for too much. Barbara stroked Ellen's hair while she sobbed into Kaye's lap. They told her it was a process. Everything would be fine. They urged her to be patient. Joy called the next day. "I think it's time we met, don't you?" Ellen nodded into the phone and, when she was able to finally speak, said, "Oh, yes. That would be just wonderful. Why don't you come for brunch next Sunday with Nate and the girls?" Too much enthusiasm? Had she been too effusive? Their conversations always left Ellen exhausted, but exuberant.

Without warning, Joy said, "Tell me about my father." Ellen was taken off guard, though it was a perfectly reasonable question, one she had been expecting. "Sam?" Ellen said as if Joy knew him. "He was a college student at the University of Connecticut." She didn't want to tell Joy that beyond that there wasn't much to share. Ellen had a long forgotten image of herself drunk, half-naked and vomiting into a toilet bowl while Sam placed a cool cloth on the back of her neck. He tried to comfort her while she heaved and cried because she felt so sick. Never once did she even imagine that their awkward sexual encounter would leave her pregnant. She had been inflamed by Sam's kisses, eager to lose her virginity, and innocent enough to believe that he was more capable than she. But Ellen skipped that part and calmly said that a mutual friend had just recently told her Sam had married and had children (yes, half siblings to her!). Sadly, he had passed away only a few years ago. Yes, it was too bad. Ellen was certain he would have been so delighted to find his daughter. He too would have wanted her to know how much he had missed her.

Quieted by this, Joy said she had a surprise for Ellen, a present that she would bring on Sunday. "Really?" Ellen said. And Ellen, although she already suspected it was a pair of peacock feather eyelashes, pretended to have no idea what the present might be. Joy, in a girlish voice that was new to Ellen (yet reminiscent of the voice she had heard in her dreams), said it was a secret and would have to wait until Sunday. Ellen saw Joy as a little girl, her hand cupping Ellen's ear in that proprietary way children have when they want to, when they must share a secret. Ellen closed her eyes and savored the image, the delicious urgency of it all.

Twenty-seven

WHEN the phone rang in the middle of the night, Kaye reached for it, already praying that neither of her children was hurt. Her prayers were answered, but it was Gertie, apologizing for waking her.

"I called an ambulance. I think I'm having a heart attack," she said. "At first, I thought it was indigestion, but I was sweating and nauseated. Just yesterday I got an e-mail from my friend Belle with all the warning signs of a heart attack—"

"Mom, slow down. Are you sure?" Kaye said. "Are you sure the article didn't just put ideas in your head?"

The stony silence at the other end was enough of an answer. Gertie had once worked with pneumonia for two weeks before collapsing in the very kitchen she was now calling from. She refused to have a phone in her bedroom, insisting that one phone per household was plenty. If Gertie thought she was having a heart attack, she was sure.

"I'm on the way," Kaye said. She was reaching for clothes, trying to stay calm. "I'm getting dressed. How do you feel now?"

"A little dizzy, but I'm okay. I'm sorry I woke you, but I knew you would be angry if I didn't. You have your father's temper."

"Oh, Mom." Kaye started to cry. She was terrible in these situations. "Please don't say that. I love you."

"Why are you crying? I'm not dead yet."

Kaye started to bawl, and so George, who was up and pulling on his pants, took the phone from her. He was good in emergencies, always calm and always thorough. He asked Gertie if she had any aspirin in the house. Yes, she had a bottle of Bayer. He told her to take one. They would leave within ten minutes and would call from the car. If the ambulance arrived before they did, they would meet her in the emergency room at Columbia Presbyterian.

"Stay on the phone with me," Gertie said in a very low voice. "I'm afraid."

Later, George would say that this more than anything else had stunned him. He had never even known that Gertie was capable of fear. She was always so intrepid, once even fending off a mugger with a trail of expletives and a warning that she hoped his poor mother was dead so that she would never find out that her son had attacked an old lady for a few dollars. He, the mugger, had gone skulking off, with nothing to show for his efforts but his injured pride.

"I'm going to call you right back from the cell phone," he said. "Just hang up, and I'll call you immediately."

"Thank you," Gertie said. "Don't tell Kaye I'm afraid. You know how she gets."

"I do," George agreed, simultaneously giving Kaye a thumbs-up and smiling. "Hang up now, Gertie."

"I'm hanging up," she said.

Kaye was already dialing from her cell phone as George hung up. She was fully dressed and stepping into a pair of flats.

"Mom?" Kaye said. "We're almost walking out the door. We

should be there in twenty minutes. Why don't you turn on the television?"

"I don't care much for television," Gertie said. "I have the radio on."

"That's good, Mom."

"Stop talking to me like I'm a child."

"Sorry, sorry. I don't mean to."

"Did you take my living will?"

Kaye's hands shook as she nodded. "I have everything ready in my office, Mom. All the papers are in an envelope. I'll get everything as we leave."

"I hear an ambulance siren," Gertie said. "Maybe it's for me."

"Maybe," Kaye said. "We'll be there soon. I'm going to give the phone to George while I get the papers."

She hurried down to her office and took the file that contained copies of her mother's health insurance card and a list of her medications, as well as her health care proxy form and her living will. George was waiting by the door, talking to Gertie. Immediately he handed the phone back to Kaye and held her coat as she slipped into it. Gertie was calm and talking about Belle's husband, who just had a heart attack last week. Kaye listened as she followed George out the front door, stepping out with her right foot first. Gertie had always made Kaye do that the morning of an exam, or the day she was going for her first job interview. Kaye stepped out right foot first both times she left home to deliver her children.

"They're here," Gertie said. "I have to answer the door."

"I stepped out with my right foot, Mom," Kaye said.

"You're a good girl, Kaye. Don't be afraid. My yoga teacher told us that everything is temporary."

"Yoga?"

"I'm going to let them in now," Gertie said. "I'm walking to the door."

"When did you start taking yoga?" Kaye said.

Next, she heard strange voices. Gertie had let the paramedics in. She was answering questions. Someone laughed. Kaye relaxed a little. Gertie must have made a joke. As George turned onto the highway, Kaye kept the phone pressed to her ear, listening for the muffled signs of life.

*   *   *

BY the time Kaye and George reached the hospital, Gertie had been stabilized and was waiting to be admitted. The attending physician, Dr. Gomez, a young woman not much older than Ruby, explained that it seemed likely that Gertie had indeed had a heart attack, though not a very severe one. They would need to administer several tests to determine the extent of the damage before even discussing treatment options. Gertie was asleep, snoring gently while Dr. Gomez explained all this to Kaye and George.

"We are often a bit more conservative with someone her age. The procedures tend to be invasive and since her body is more fragile, she is at a higher risk for complications."

"So you do nothing?" Kaye said.

"Not *nothing*," Dr. Gomez said. "We'll probably take her to the cardiac catheterization laboratory to evaluate the status of her heart and arteries. If there is any serious blockage, we might consider stents or even an angioplasty. Right now, I'm waiting for a call from her internist. It depends on the general condition of her health. We may even be able to treat her with medications."

George had questions that Dr. Gomez answered thoughtfully and thoroughly. In the middle of this, Dr. Weinstein, Gertie's internist, phoned and Dr. Gomez excused herself.

"She's going to be fine," George told Kaye. "She's in great shape, and she's a fighter."

"She's eighty-three," Kaye said. "She's old."

"Not that old. Give her a chance."

He put his arm around her shoulder, and she rested her head against him. She was so glad he was there. So grateful to let him take over. They agreed to call the kids in the morning. There was no immediate emergency. Gertie opened her eyes, but she fell right back asleep. By the time she was admitted to a semiprivate room, it was five o'clock. Reluctantly, Kaye agreed to leave. Gertie needed to sleep. The nurse assured them that Gertie was in good hands. Kaye took the number at the nurses' station and went back in one more time to kiss her mother. She looked lost in the bed. Kaye smoothed her cheek with the back of her hand and bent low to kiss her.

"I'll be back in a few hours," Kaye said. "Are you comfortable?"

With apparent effort, Gertie opened her eyes, smiled indulgently, and said, "I make a living."

* * *

THE good news was that the heart attack was minor enough to be considered a warning. Gertie was sent home with detailed instructions about diet, daily exercise, and medication. Though only days had passed, Kaye thought her mother had noticeably aged. She was quieter, more passive. George told Kaye it was in her head. He said that Gertie was tired, that's all. But it was Gertie's eager willingness to stay with them after she was released that worried Kaye. George had some business out of town, so Ruby came to be with Gertie, freeing Kaye to have an early dinner with Ellen and Barbara.

"It's sort of weird to think of my mother as old," Kaye said. "She seems so different."

"She went through a traumatic event," Barbara said. "Don't you see that in your business every day?"

"Of course," Kaye said. "But have you ever known me to use the word *meek* to describe my mother?"

"Kaye," Ellen said very gently. "We all love Gertie, but she is old."

"She is old," Kaye agreed. "She is old, and I hate it."

"She's going to bounce back." Barbara said. "Trust me." She squeezed Kaye's hand across the table. "Oh, and speaking of trust, I have some exciting news." She looked around to see if anyone was listening and whispered. "I'm going to be on the radio. Delilah is coming out."

"Really?" Kaye said. "When? What station?"

"NPR," Barbara said. "I'm really excited."

"That's so great," Kaye said. "After all these years, your secret identity will finally be revealed. Are you nervous?"

"Of course."

"Has it been scheduled?" Ellen said.

"Next month, I think." Barbara took a sip of wine. "My people are talking to their people."

"Your life will change," Kaye said.

"Again?" Barbara said. They all laughed. "I'm due for a change. It's been a few weeks."

"I think you'll be terrific," Ellen said. "Do the kids know?"

"Justine and Michael know."

"And?

"Well, Justine seems okay with it, though it's sometimes hard to read her. She's so private with her feelings. Michael is a little stunned. He likes to think of himself as open-minded, but in some ways it must be like finding out that your mother is a porn star or something equivalent."

"He'll get used to it when you buy him a new car or help with a down payment on an apartment," Kaye said. "They all adapt after that."

Barbara laughed and agreed. "Daphne doesn't know about the interview," she said. "I don't think she ever listens to NPR anyway.

Besides, she probably thinks NPR is a shoe outlet. And Justine will be fine. She's the most adaptable. Anyway, we have really important news to discuss."

The impending reunion with Joy was three days away. Everyone had been so preoccupied with Gertie's hospitalization that there had been no chance to catch up on plans for the forthcoming brunch.

"Tell us what's going on," Barbara said. "Is everything all set?"

"I guess so," Ellen said. "They're coming on Sunday. This Sunday. Can you imagine that I'm going to meet my daughter this Sunday?"

"I'm so happy for you," Kaye said.

"Everyone is happy for you," Barbara said. "And excited."

Kaye checked her watch. "I have to get back soon and see how Ruby is doing."

"I'm sure Ruby is doing fine," Ellen said. "She's a midwife, for goodness' sake."

"Unfortunately, Gertie is not having a baby," Kaye said.

"No," Barbara said. "But our little Ellen is. A great big thirty-two-year-old baby."

"My *baby*," Ellen said, close to tears. "I wouldn't know her if I passed her on the street."

"You'll know her," Kaye said. "And it'll seem as if time hasn't passed at all."

"Nonsense," Barbara said, as she signaled for the check. "Everyone notices that time has passed. All you have to do is look in the mirror."

"I think we've all had enough reality for one day," Kaye said.

"One day?" Ellen said. "I've had enough reality for the rest of my life."

*   *   *

AFTER her first meeting with Nate, Ellen had gone home and written down everything she could remember. Joy was a weaver. She was also skilled at batik. She was an environmentalist, a liberal Democrat, and a vegetarian. She had converted to Judaism and was studying for her bat mitzvah. Maude was six. She loved animals and anything purple. Amelia was three, and she loved music, notably opera, and gum, all sour flavors. Maude went to a small private progressive school. Joy didn't believe in overscheduling children, but Maude studied piano and took an art class at the Metropolitan Museum on Saturday mornings. Four days a week, Amelia attended a nursery program at their synagogue. They had three cats: Vladimir, Violetta, and Vicki. Vladimir was also a girl, but they didn't know that when they named him, so they stuck with Vlad. In deference to Joy's vegetarian kitchen, Nate ate meat only when he was out. They liked to take the girls to the zoo in the winter. They often went to Tanglewood in the summer, so the girls could move around while they listened to classical music.

Ellen was exhausted from going over the list. She shopped for small presents for the girls. Nothing extravagant, just little offerings. She bought a stamp set of all different animals for Maude and a purple ink pad. The ink was washable, but then Ellen worried that maybe Joy was a stickler about messiness. After much deliberation, Ellen decided it was fine, and she added a notebook bound in purple cloth. For Amelia, Ellen settled on a music box that played "Nessun Dorma" from the opera *Turandot*. The music box was a sturdy piece that could survive a three-year-old's inquisitive hands. Joy's acorn necklace was waiting, but Ellen thought it would be premature to give it to her the first time they met. *Joy*. Ellen had started to think about her only as Joy, forcing herself to forget that she had first been named Faith. Still, Ellen worried that she would accidentally call her Faith and ruin everything.

"Why would that ruin everything?" Kaye said, trying hard to

be patient. Ellen had been calling several times a day, and night, perseverating over minutiae with alarming intensity. Kaye lodged the phone between her neck and ear, guaranteeing that she would be in pain later that night. She was cutting an apple into slices for her mother, who had just recently discovered television and was glued to a rerun of *Law & Order.* "Joy is a young woman, a mother, a wife, and an artist. She is a well-rounded, intelligent, and talented person. She will be relieved to meet you and to see that you are all those things as well."

"Thank you," Ellen said. "Thank you." She paused, took a breath. "Do you think I can serve fish?"

"Ellen, you can serve anything you want."

"I bought lox, and I made two broccoli and mushroom quiches. And I'm going to make a green salad. Should I make something else?"

"I have to go," Kaye said, "I have to wipe the drool from the chin of my suddenly helpless mother."

"Is she that bad?" Ellen said.

"I don't know. Don't worry about it. Concentrate on your daughter and her family."

"Give her time, Kaye. I know you think Gertie is invincible, but no one is."

"I know. I really, really know. I just hate it."

"Can I do something for you?" Ellen said. "Anything?"

"Yes," Kaye said. "You can relax."

Tomorrow was almost here. The house was spotless. The pillows on the couch had been plumped. There were irises on the coffee table and tulips in the kitchen. Fancy guest soaps and towels were in the bathroom—real towels, not the paper ones she usually used for company, but cloth towels. Joy would have disapproved of paper. Ellen had even bought environmentally friendly toilet paper and paper towels. The children's gift-wrapped presents were ready. In the morning, she would pick up fresh bagels and rolls and muffins. Everything had been ordered. All the fruit was ready to be combined into a fruit salad that she would drizzle with vanilla yogurt and honey. The mesclun salad mix was washed, wrapped in paper toweling and bagged, just waiting to be dressed. The dining room table was set. At the last moment, just before she was ready to turn out the lights and get a few hours of sleep, Ellen thought about Bill. A deep wave of sadness caught her by surprise. It would have been something to have him by her side, greeting Nate and hugging Joy. Bill was a master in such circumstances. He would have charmed the two little girls with a few silly magic tricks. It would have been quite a morning. Ellen reached for the phone, just to tell him, just to let him know that she was going to meet her daughter at last. But she stopped herself. He had lost all his rights to share her happiness, she reminded herself.

When she had been shopping for gifts for Maude and Amelia, Ellen had come across a blow ball pipe. She hadn't seen one since she had been a little girl herself. The improved revival of the old classic plastic toy was made of wood now and came with two foam balls. The store had been empty when Ellen came in, and the salesclerk, an intense young man, saw her examining the blow ball pipe and was eager to explain Bernoulli's principle. He told her that as air was forced around the ball, it had to move faster in order to "catch up" on the other side. He went on, elaborating on how the "decrease in air pressure around the ball keeps the ball in place," and how "the force is strong enough to resist other forces acting on the ball, even one as subtle as a finger tap." He said that if the flow of air was strong enough, it could even overcome gravity. "Watch," the young man said, turning the base of the pipe a good twenty degrees. He blew into the pipe and demonstrated. The ball remained suspended in the air flow even though it was not directly above it. Ellen had been transfixed. She bought several blow ball pipes, though she had no intention of parting with them. Now she thought that she might send one to Bill. She could see him, examining the toy, wondering why she had sent it. Maybe, just maybe, he would understand her intent and see that she was just like the ball, spinning madly, yet staying afloat—somehow, defying all logic.

*   *   *

ELEVEN o'clock came and went. By eleven forty-five, Ellen was wiping perspiration from her upper lip. She had checked and re-checked the platters of food, decided to cut the bagels and cover the basket with a cloth, but postponed dressing the salad or mixing the fruit. She spoke to both Kaye and Barbara, who separately assured her that Joy would be there. "She's just coming across town," Ellen moaned. "How much traffic can there be?" Her palms were damp, and she felt ill with anticipation. Her cell phone rang while she was on the phone with Kaye. "Answer it," Kaye said. "I'll wait." It was Joy. She was downstairs. She was alone. No, the girls and Nate would join them in an hour, but she had thought it would be better if they saw each other alone first. It might be too much for the girls if she became too emotional. She was sorry she was late, but she was nervous. She had been waiting in the lobby all this time, fending off questions from the doorman. She was coming up now. No, Ellen didn't have to come down to get her. Joy laughed, and she sounded more relaxed. "I'm scared," she said. Ellen said, "I'm terrified." They told each other it would be all right.

"She's on her way up," Ellen said. "She'll be here any minute."

"Oh, Ellen," Kaye said. She was crying. "Oh, Ellen, this is so incredible."

The doorbell rang.

"I have to go," Ellen said.

It would always be miraculous to Ellen how one sweet moment could offer a reprieve from loneliness and suddenly illuminate a life. She opened the door and looked into Joy's eyes. They were the same color as Ellen's, and they were framed by the peacock lashes that she recognized from the photograph.

"I love your eyelashes," Ellen said.

It was so not what she had planned on saying that she couldn't think of anything else to say.

"They're not mine," Joy said.

And then, she was equally speechless.

"That went well," Ellen finally said, laughing. She opened the door wide and said, "Come in. I'm sorry. Please. Come in."

Joy nodded and walked in. She was wearing a red coat, not un-like Ellen's own winter coat.

"May I take your coat?" Ellen said.

Joy was holding a bouquet of something exotic that she seemed reluctant to part with.

"You can set that down over there," Ellen said, pointing to the small sideboard where she usually left her keys and purse. "Or you can hold it. I'll get a vase for them in a moment."

"No," Joy said. "It's fine. Okay. Here, you can take it." She handed the bouquet over and took off her coat, revealing a brown pleated skirt and a pale blue sweater. Her fine hair was held back with a black velvet bow, but a few strands had escaped, and she brushed them out of her face. She looked around the pristine apartment, frowned just slightly, and said, "Do you want me to take off my shoes?"

"Heavens, why would I want you to do that?" Ellen said, setting the bouquet on the sideboard and taking Joy's coat.

"My moth . . ." Joy looked horrified and clasped her hand to her mouth. "I'm so sorry. It's like that old joke. Tell someone not to think of a pink elephant, and that's all she'll think about. I was downstairs for an hour, concentrating on what *not* to say." She took a deep breath. "And what I want to say is that I am so, so happy to finally meet you." She held out her hand. "I've been looking forward to this moment for as long as I can remember."

Ellen took her hand. Joy was small-boned, like Ellen, and her fingers were long and thin, like Ellen's. Joy was wearing a narrow gold wedding band and no other jewelry except a watch and a pair of silver earrings, tiny clusters of grapes, or so they looked. Joy put out her other hand, and Ellen took that one too. They held hands, shyly at first, and then moved with more confidence toward each other and into an embrace. Joy was a good four inches taller, bringing Ellen's nose even with Joy's neck, allowing her to inhale her lemony scent. Ellen wanted to say something memorable, something that Joy could retell when she spoke to others of this day, but nothing came to mind. Ellen had questions and more questions, but she kept them to herself. *Did you feel my love every day? Do you know how sorry I am? Have you felt how much I missed you? Have you been loved? Have you been happy? Will you forgive me?* Instead, Ellen wrapped her arms around Joy and concentrated on not squeezing her too hard. They held each other like that for a minute or so, silent, awkward, full of need and uncertainty. It was Joy who pulled back first and, taking Ellen's hands again, said, "You're so young. I never expected you to be so young."

"I was sixteen when you were born," Ellen said.

"I know. That's amazing. You must have been so scared."

"Not as scared as I am now."

Joy nodded. "Let's go sit," she said. "I'm suddenly exhausted." She dropped Ellen's hands. "I'm pregnant." She touched her belly. "It's sort of a surprise. I haven't told anyone yet. Not *anyone*. I mean, Nate knows, of course, but not *anyone* else." She said this meaningfully. "I think I'm about two months along. I haven't even been to the doctor yet."

"How wonderful for you and Nate," Ellen said, quietly pleased to have been made privy to this secret. "And the girls will be thrilled, I'm sure."

"Well, we'll see about that."

Ellen ushered Joy into the living room. "Please sit down. Thank you so much for the flowers. They're so unusual. And would you like something to drink? I want to get those flowers in some water."

"I'd like some water too, please." She made herself comfortable on the couch. "I think those odd ones are called antorium, and there are some lilies mixed in as well." Joy frowned again. "But you already have so many beautiful flowers."

"But nothing orange, and orange is one of my favorite colors."

"Mine too!" Joy said. "That's so weird." Then she shrugged and giggled. "Or maybe not."

"Or maybe not," Ellen agreed. "Let me put these in a vase and get you some water. I left some photo albums there for you to look at."

When she returned, Joy was absorbed in the photos and barely looked up when Ellen set the vase on the table and sat down beside her, holding the glass.

"Tell me who everyone is," Joy said, reaching for the water. She had kicked off her shoes and curled her legs beneath her. She was wearing dark tights that, with her pleated skirt, made her look like a schoolgirl. Her face was flushed, and she patted the space next to her, inviting Ellen to come closer. It was all strangely seductive, like a first date, unfamiliar and full of promise. Ellen inched closer and adjusted the photo album so that half of it was resting in her lap. "Who is this?" Joy said, pointing at Owen. "He looks so angry."

"He is," Ellen said. "He was born angry, I think."

And so they proceeded through the photographs, piecing together a history that Joy could comprehend. It was a slow and cautious ascent, and they gradually found their common ground, the loss they had each felt in spite of how much others loved them.

They cried together, and even though Joy said she understood what had happened, Ellen knew it would take much more to convince her that she had never wanted to give her up.

"I just can't imagine it." Joy said. She looked down at her flat belly. "I just can't imagine giving my baby away."

"It is inconceivable," Ellen agreed quietly. "It's still inconceivable to me."

They were intermittently restrained and then intensely passionate, hugging each other and promising that they could and would make up for lost time. But there was no way to do that. They could only move forward, create something new.

Joy phoned Nate and said it was fine to come over whenever he was ready. Ellen opened the door. He was holding Amelia, who stared curiously at Ellen. Maude, less bold than her younger sister, was wound around her father's leg, pressing her face into his trousers. Nate kissed Ellen on the cheek and introduced the girls. Joy was behind Ellen, smiling, letting her girls know everything was fine.

The girls were hungry, so they went directly into the dining room. Ellen made coffee, and Joy helped the girls pick out bagels. Maude sat on Nate's lap and hid her face any time Ellen looked her way. They passed plates and chatted about politics and movies. Ellen had prepared hot chocolate with candied violets for the girls and (after asking Joy's permission) served it in beautiful china cups that she had bought just for them. "Whenever you come over," Ellen said, "these will be your special cups." Maude wanted more candied violets, and she eased herself off Nate's lap to follow Ellen to the kitchen. It was their first time alone, and Ellen was careful to follow Maude's lead. Maude examined the dish of candied violets and asked if she could bring them to the table. "Of course," Ellen said. "Ab-so-lute-ly." Maude clasped both hands to her mouth and laughed. "I love to bake," Maude said. "Really? Maybe one weekend, if Mommy says it's all right," Ellen said, "you can come over, and we can make cookies." Maude considered this. "With violets?" And again, Ellen said, "Ab-so-lute-ly!" This time she added a little wiggle as she said it, and Maude imitated her. They returned to the table, equally triumphant. Joy smiled at them. Ellen (with Joy's permission) gave the girls their gifts. Amelia climbed onto Ellen's lap to watch as Ellen showed her how to wind the music box. A look of delight crossed her face, and she made herself more comfortable on Ellen's lap. As Ellen had predicted, Joy had brought her a pair of peacock eyelashes. They went into the bathroom together, and Joy watched as Ellen applied them. In spite of herself, Ellen confided that she had ordered two pairs of genuine mink lashes, one for each of them. Joy was thrilled. "But don't tell Nate," she said. "He thinks I'm above reproach, but who is?" Ellen promised. Maude and Amelia crowded into the bathroom, exclaiming over the lashes and touching them with the tips of their fingers.

When it was time to go, they all stood at the door for another twenty minutes, talking and hugging. Finally, Nate said he would take the girls and get the car, so Joy and Ellen could have a few minutes alone. Ellen knelt down to say good-bye to the girls, holding out her hand for a handshake. Amelia, at Joy's suggestion, hugged Ellen, but Maude was a little more cautious. She took Ellen's hand and hung her head. "It was wonderful to meet you," Ellen said. Maude nodded, but wrapped herself around her father's legs again, clearly overwhelmed. When they left, Ellen said, "I know just how she feels." Joy said, "Me too." They said good-bye again and thanked each other for a wonderful day. "I'll call you," Joy promised. And Ellen said, "Thank you." Joy patted her purse, making them accomplices to the mink lashes she had stored there for safekeeping.

As soon as Joy left, Ellen called Kaye and then Barbara. She told them everything, describing in detail how Joy had looked, what she'd said, how the girls looked. Yes, it had all been glorious. Better than she could have imagined. She felt lucky, truly blessed. Then, late that night, a little past eleven, the phone rang.

"Ellen?" Joy said, slightly breathless with anticipation. "I didn't wake you, did I?"

"No, not all. Is everything all right?"

"Yes, everything's fine. I wanted to thank you for today."

"I should thank you for sharing your family with me," Ellen said.

"They're your family now too," Joy said.

"Thank you, Joy," Ellen said simply. Anything more would have been too much.

"Ellen, there's just one thing I have to ask you."

"Go ahead."

"Did you love him very much? My father. Were you madly in love with him?"

It might have just as easily been Maude or Amelia asking if there really was a Tooth Fairy. There was that much hope in Joy's voice. And Ellen believed in hope; it had sustained her all these years.

"Very much," Ellen said. "We were very much in love, Joy."

Later, Ellen told herself (and Kaye and Barbara confirmed it) that she had made the right decision. Kaye insisted that some things were just best left unsaid. And Barbara echoed this, adding that some things were best not said at all.

Readers Guide

1. Why do you think this book is titled *The Sinner's Guide to Confession*? Who are the sinners in this story? Do they find redemption through confession?

2. Why does Ellen keep her past from her friends? Do you think she is right to hide her past?

3. How does writing as Delilah help Barbara to live a more fulfilling life? What does she gain from her secret writing? Do you think she is ashamed to write so unabashedly about sex? Why or why not?

4. Discuss Kaye's affair with Frank. What attracts her to Frank to begin with? Do you empathize with her situation or do you think she should have divorced her husband?

5. Why does Ellen take such joy in tutoring Marisol? What does Marisol represent to Ellen? When Marisol leaves, what does Ellen lose?

6. Ellen has always kept her past and her family hidden from Barbara and Kaye. So why does she ask them to come to her father's funeral with her? What does she gain by telling them the truth?

7. What is the role of marriage in this novel? Did any of the women in the novel have happy marriages? Do you think they love their husbands?

8. Why do you think Bill turns up at Ellen's father's funeral? Do you think they have any chance of reconciliation? In Ellen's place, do you think you would be able to forgive Bill?

9. How is Gertie a pivotal figure throughout the novel? How does she care for her family? What does she represent for Kaye? How do Kaye, Barbara, and Ellen compare as mothers to their children?

10. Why do you think Justine ends her affair? Why does Kaye? What toll does Kaye's affair take on her family?

11. When Kaye goes to Frank to end the affair, she lies and tells him that she was going to accept his proposal. Why does she tell this lie? What purpose does it serve? In what other ways do characters in this novel lie to save face?

12. Discuss the adoption of Ellen's daughter. Do you think Ellen was too passive when her daughter was being taken away? Was there really anything she could have done? Why do you think she waits so long to begin searching for her daughter?

13. Do you think Ellen, Barbara, and Kaye are strong women? Why or why not?